Harper's Donelson

A Novel of Grant's First Campaign

Sean K. Gabhann

Harper's Donelson by Sean K. Gabhann

Cover Design Sean K. Gabhann and Livia Reasoner
Cover Grant at Donelson Painting Chicago History Museum, ICHi-62709. Paul Philippoteaux, Artist
(Rifle) The Horse Soldier Antiques Store Item 633-01 1/2
Sundown Press
www.sundownpress.com

ISBN-13: 978-1517117511
ISBN-10: 1517117518

This book is dedicated to the Daimon Writers: Helekaye, Sarah, and Faith, without whom it would not exist.

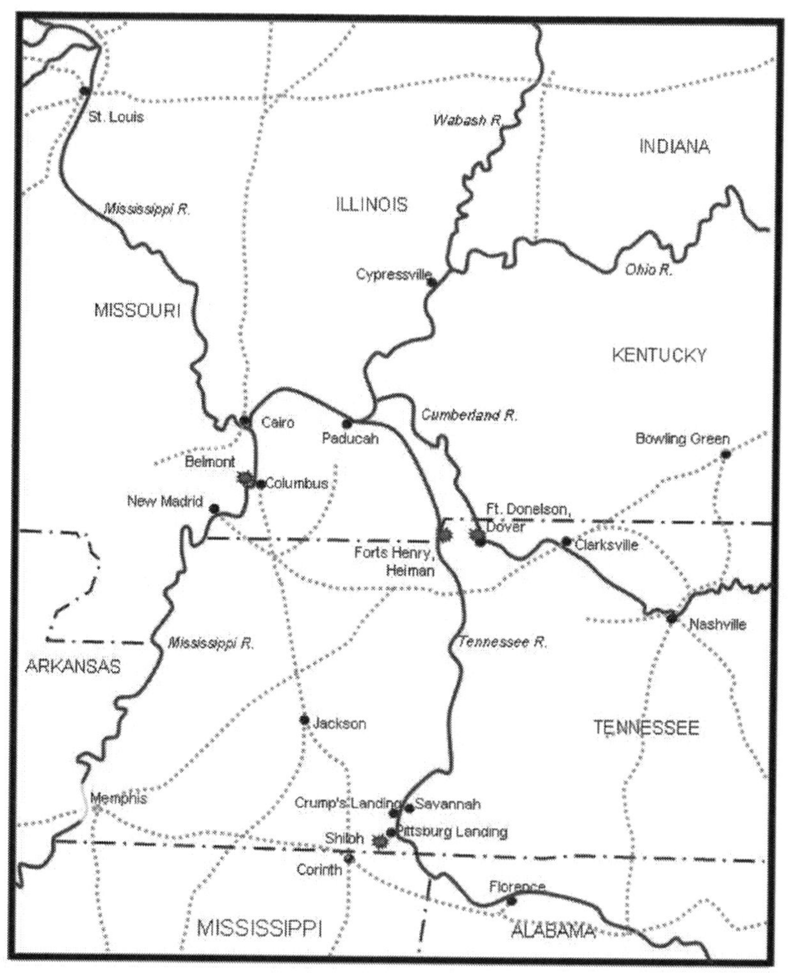

Grant's Winter Campaign 1862
(Map prepared by Sean K. Gabhann)

List of Characters:

Lieutenant James Harper—Adjutant, 1st Iowa Mounted Infantry
Corporal Gustav Magnusson—Fourth Corporal, Lead Skirmisher, Company B
Katherine (Katie) Malloy —Saloon girl, *Lafitte's Hideout*

Brigadier General Ulysses S. Grant— Commander, District of Cairo
Brigadier General John McClernand—Commander, First Division
Brigadier General Charles Smith—Commander, Second Division
Brigadier General Lew Wallace—Commander, Third Division

Colonel Jacob Lauman—Brigade Commander, Second Division
Colonel Morgan Smith—Brigade Commander, Second Division
Colonel John Thayer—Brigade Commander, Third Division
Colonel Charles Cruft—Brigade Commander, Third Division

Lieutenant Colonel Wesley Monroe—Commander, 1st Iowa Mounted Rifles
Major Asbury Porter—Executive Officer, 1st Iowa Mounted Rifles
Captain Brice McKinsey—Commanding Officer, B Company
Lieutenant William Pierson—Commanding Officer, C Company (acting)
Private Benjamin Bailey—Soldier, Company B
Private Johnny Cooke—Soldier, Company B
Private Joseph Davis—Soldier, Company B

Franklin Bosley—Co-Owner, *Lafitte's Hideout*, whoremonger
Loreena Bosley—Co-Owner, *Lafitte's Hideout*, manager
Eleanor St. Croix—Co-Owner, *Lafitte's Hideout*, saloon girl

Ferdinand Hummel—Gunsmith, Paducah
Harriett Wells—Nurse, Paducah

John Edmondson—Sheriff, Nashville
Jonathan Morris—Deputy Sheriff, Nashville
Julius Shepperton—Deputy Sheriff, Nashville

Captain Anderson Bell, CSA—Commanding Officer, Bell's Partisans
Captain Francois Dupree, CSA—Adjutant, 8th Texas Cavalry Regiment

PART 1
BELMONT, MISSOURI

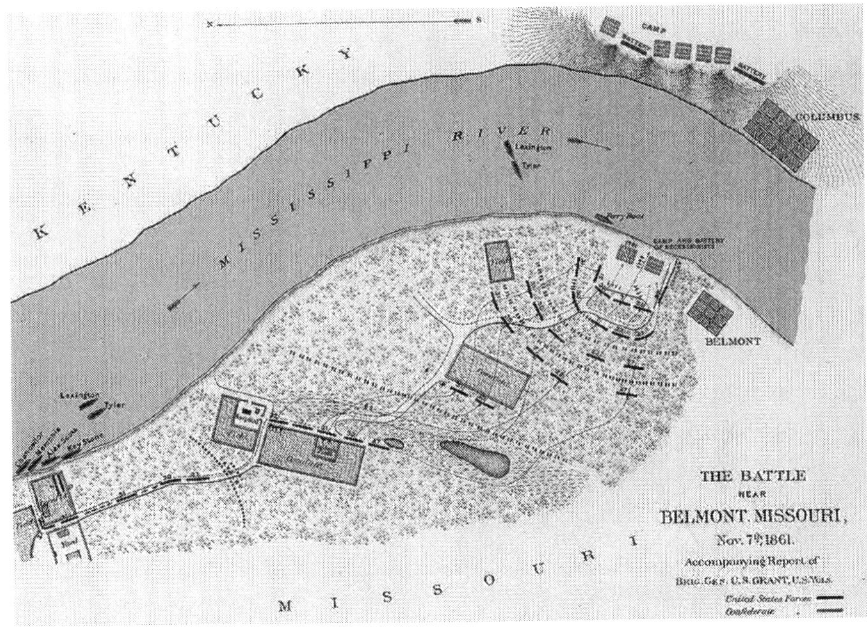

Battle of Belmont

November 7, 1861

The low-slanting rays of the later afternoon sun cast the riverbank into shadow. From the upper-deck promenade of *Chancellor*, Lieutenant James Harper watched the commander of Company B emerge from the mass of men and horses on the foredeck. The rotund captain took one step at a time up to the upper deck while his soldiers completed their re-embarkation. His company had been the rear guard for the Iowa infantry and was the last of the Federal soldiers to return.

"Well Harper, looks like we didn't need your help at all." Standing at the top of the ladder, Captain Brice McKinsey brushed his clothes smooth from the day's riding and combat.

"Our boys did well, Captain." Harper refused to use the honorific 'sir' when addressing McKinsey. Formerly the First Lieutenant of the disbanded Company K, Harper now served as the battalion adjutant–a desk job more suited to an accountant than to a man who had spent eight years as a United States marshal in the territories beyond the Missouri River.

"Not really sure why you're here, Harper."

Harper did not respond and McKinsey brushed past him to the door into the staterooms. Harper saw no need to remind McKinsey that he was here because it had been his idea to convert the First Iowa from a foot infantry regiment to a mounted infantry regiment. The expedition to Belmont was the first battle in which the unit would operate in its new configuration. Harper had written his own orders to accompany the first two companies from the battalion to receive their horses – tamed mustangs donated by Harper's brother from the ranch near Sergeant's Bluff.

"Mister Harper, you'd better come look at this." Sergeant Joshua

Featherstone called from amidships. Where Featherstone pointed, a lone galloper emerged from the forest and raced down the narrow road which sliced through fields of tall dry cornstalks. A ragged musket volley from the wood behind the rider caused the brown leaves nearby to twitch, but he kept coming, the tail of his blue overcoat flapping over the rump of his chestnut roan.

Harper chuckled at the irony of war, at how this one rider now making a frantic dash to escape the Secessionist Army, would arrive at the landing seconds after the final boat had departed. Alone, the man would need the best of luck if he wanted to avoid capture. Hopefully, he was not from the First Iowa.

God help ya, ya poor bastard.

Chancellor, the last boat of the Federal expedition, backed into the Mississippi. The other transports, *Alexander Scott, Memphis, and Key Stone*, waited in mid-stream with the rest of Grant's Brigade, while the escorts, *Lexington* and *Tyler,* fired blindly into the woods and tall corn to harass the advancing Rebels.

"It's General Grant!" The captain of the *Chancellor* snapped his telescope shut. He used a megaphone when he yelled from the pilot house down to the foredeck. "Run out gangplank! Now!"

General Grant was not just some poor dumb soul to be left behind. He needed to be got aboard safely. Harper looked for McKinsey or his lieutenants but saw none of them. Here was the opportunity he hoped would come when he joined the expedition.

From his vantage point above the riverbank, Harper could see a Rebel column trampling the dried cornstalks between Grant and the landing, angling to intercept the road. In minutes, they would cut Grant's escape route.

Again, he looked around the promenade but saw only crowds of enlisted men from the Seventh Iowa Infantry. None of McKinsey's officers were in sight. Besides the riverboat captain, Harper was the only officer aboard the *Chancellor* with a clear view of the drama ashore. Grant might be captured or shot in the time it would take to find McKinsey and mount a rescue party. Time for Harper to take the lead.

"I'm goin' to help him." Harper pointed aft where most of the Seventh Iowa crowded. "Get some of those men up here to cover us."

Featherstone smiled when he saluted, always ready for action. “Yes, sir.” He faced the nearby idlers on the promenade and yelled for them to open fire on the Rebel column in the cornfield. After seeing each of those men loading their muskets, Featherstone moved to the aft ladder.

Harper had no direct authority over any of the soldiers aboard the *Chancellor,* but he trusted his former sergeant to carry out the orders. He ran to the ladder to the foredeck as the *Chancellor* nudged onto the muddy riverbank. There seventy of McKinsey’s men and horses intermingled with a few infantrymen. Harper called for those nearest the ladder to join Sergeant Featherstone.

After half a dozen men climbed the ladder, Harper slid down and pushed his way through the press of men and horses to Santee, his own horse. Her white-gray coat and black mane made it easy to find her in the living mass. He untied her from the boat’s railing and led her forward, pushing his way to where deck hands worked to lower the gangway. Once he mounted, the men jammed together in the foredeck would be able to see him. Harper mounted Santee. Visible now to all of the men on the foredeck, he yelled to the nearest non-commissioned officer he saw. “Get a dozen men and follow me.”

Without waiting for a response, he turned in the saddle and spurred Santee over the gangplank. Not knowing if anyone followed, he urged the horse up the bluff along the river bank, looked around to find the road he thought General Grant would use, and galloped away.

On the level road, he let Santee choose her way under slackened reins, while he unhooked the cover of his holster. He pulled out his Army revolver, looping a custom-made lanyard around his right wrist.

Where the hell is Grant?

He passed a group of Federal medical orderlies and severely-wounded soldiers gathered in the yard of the farmer whose corn was being trampled by the contesting armies. Now, with the *Chancellor* back at the landing, these men might avoid capture if they could get aboard. Harper pulled up to the fence of the farmer’s yard.

“Get down to the landin’,” Harper told a soldier standing in the yard. “We’ll cover ya.” But when Harper looked behind him, no troops had followed. “God-damn it!” he shouted to no one in particular. But the curse had the effect of getting the doctor and orderlies moving faster.

Disgusted with his own men, reacting without thought, Harper turned back to where he last saw Grant. Pistol ready, he kicked Santee to a full gallop.

From Santee's back, he could see over the corn while he tried without success to determine where the Rebel column would intercept the road. Nor could he see General Grant.

Is Grant still on the road?

After covering a hundred yards, he saw a reddish-brown hide of a dead horse lying motionless in the center of the lane. He slowed to a cautious trot for the next fifty yards or so, looking for the general.

A shadow crouched in the corn near the fallen horse. It was Grant, wearing a blue private's overcoat with general's epaulets sewn to the shoulders. Shots from the field to Harper's left drove him to put spurs to Santee, and she leaped ahead. Musket balls whizzed past, but the poorly-aimed firing was high and behind him.

Shooting resumed from the forest ahead, but the height and density of the dried corn plants should hide himself and Santee from most of that fire. Harper stretched his left hand down to grab Grant's arm. Santee stopped alongside Grant, turning so her body shielded the general from the enemy in the forest. Grant hoisted himself onto her back behind Harper, using the stirrup for purchase.

"Ready!" Grant yelled and Harper urged Santee back onto the road.

Shooting from the forest intensified when the riders raced toward the landing. It cheered Harper to see many small puffs of gun smoke coming from the upper deck of the *Chancellor* and from the upper decks of the other three transports farther out in the river. If the men on the boats engaged the first Rebel formation ahead, that might give him enough covering fire.

The Rebel column burst from the cornfield and filed across the road three hundred yards in front of them. This regiment formed a double line facing the river boats, blocking Harper and Grant from the safety of the *Chancellor*. He would have to ride through the cornfields to get around them.

"Damn!" Harper yelled as he pulled Santee to a stop. He turned to see the regiment behind him leave the cover of the forest and march toward them. Harper and Grant would be within musket range of these graycoats in seconds.

A lieutenant in the rear of the Rebel line blocking the road looked in their direction and started pulling men to face the riders.

He had no choice. Harper would have to bowl his way though the lines of soldiers before the Rebel officer could add more men to those already facing him and Grant.

Harper wrapped the reins around his left wrist and transferred the pistol to the same hand. He reached across his chest with his free hand and drew his sword. Not a proper cavalry sabre, but the standard-issue infantry officers' sword. It would have to do.

"Ya ready, General?" Harper called to Grant.

"What are you going to do?"

"I'm goin' to ride right through those bastards and get ya back to the boats. It would take too long to go around them."

Grant looked at the men in the road and shook his head. He grunted and drew his own revolver from under his overcoat. "Ready."

Most of the Rebels blocking their path faced the landing, their two ranks stretching across the road and into the fields on either side. Twenty or so men lined up in the road, with a half-dozen of them facing Harper, loading their muskets. Their officer stood to Harper's right, with his own pistol drawn.

Puffs of rifle smoke from the road beyond the gray line caught Harper's attention. Several men in blue uniforms fired from prone positions. Others fired on the Rebels from the cover on each side of the road. Harper would have to ride through the Rebel line to reach them.

"Hold on!" Harper bent low over Santee's neck and put heels to the horse. Grant bent over, his left hand around Harper's waist grasping the belt buckle, his head next to Harper's right hip.

"Go girl," Harper told Santee. From years of experience in the territories, the horse knew what Harper expected. She started straight at the Rebel line. At fifty yards, she broke into a full gallop.

Grant shot at the officer, but missed. The Rebel lieutenant raised his pistol. On the other side of Santee, one of the soldiers aimed his musket but Harper fired first, breaking the man's concentration.

Grant's second shot hit the Rebel officer, but not before that officer fired. The Rebel officer's shot zipped through the hair of Santee's dark mane, leaving a bloody trail across the crown of the horse's neck.

Many of the Rebels in the road were down, while others crawled to the corn fields, grasping their wounds. Santee ran for one of the gaps in the line. Harper's focus narrowed to the five feet on either side of the gap.

At fifteen yards, Harper shot at another man who had raised his loaded musket. The man fell backward. Two soldiers directly in front of Santee raised their muskets while Harper's original target drew a bead and fired, too hasty. Harper shot one of the men in front, at the same time he felt the ball from the man's musket burn a slice across the top of his thigh. Harper aimed his sword at the other man, point down, hand held high, the way he remembered the Regular dragoons charge in Mexico. It was enough. This man flinched when he fired and the ball went wide.

Grant fired at the officer again, striking him cleanly in the middle of his chest and knocking him backward. Two men next to the officer raised their muskets. One of them toppled forward, struck in the back by the Federal skirmishers.

Five yards from the gray line, Harper saw the fear in the man directly in front of Santee and the hatred in the faces of the men around the fallen officer. Grim determination showed on the face of the remaining Rebel with his musket raised. Harper waved the sword toward the man in hope of distracting his aim; but the man was beyond Harper's reach and retained his composure.

The man took slow and deliberate aim and fired at point-blank range just as Santee bowled into the line of Rebels. The ball hit Harper's holster and shattered on the insignia plate. Fragments peppered Harper's right buttock, burrowing into the muscle with an instantaneous burning. He kept slashing his sword at the Rebels around him.

Santee pushed past two unloaded soldiers, knocking one to the ground while the other dodged away.

"Yahh!" Harper slashed his sword across the running man's face, cutting through his cheek and into his mouth. Now, in the midst of the

Rebel formation, he felt Santee choose her footing with care as she passed a fallen man. Harper swung his sword in frantic wide arcs and searched for more targets for his pistol. He fired into the back of a man in the front rank who blocked the way. Grant fired at another Rebel somewhere to the right.

They were through the Rebel unit. Heart pounding and hands shaking, Harper spurred Santee toward the Federal skirmishers fifty yards away. The bluecoats fired faster at the Rebels and Harper realized with satisfaction that they used breech-loading rifles, the signature weapon of the Mounted Rifles. The weapon Harper's father had bought when the First Iowa Volunteer Infantry Regiment reorganized into the First Iowa Volunteer Mounted Infantry Battalion.

They closed the distance to safety while several Rebel musket balls zipped past with the characteristic buzz of a fast-moving, pollen-laden bumble bee. Ahead, one of the Iowa men lay still in the road while a pool of blood spread around him. Santee leapt over the dead man and into a cloud of gunsmoke hovering over the skirmish line.

Twenty yards past the Iowa skirmishers, Harper felt Santee falter an instant before she stumbled. Grant must have felt it, too, because he slid down from the horse's rump as she went down. Harper pulled his feet from the stirrups and brought them forward at the same time he let the reins unravel from his wrist. The horse went to her knees. When Santee dropped to the left, Harper fell to the right. Both he and Grant reduced the impact of their falls by rolling away from the Santee's flaying hooves.

Five Federal skirmishers ran from the cornfields to cover the two officers. Grant got to his feet first and pulled Harper up. Harper stood with difficulty while the burning pain from his wounds finally registered. He looked for Santee and saw blood stains in her gray coat from a single wound in her rump.

Musket balls buzzed nearby or thudded into the dirt road around them, forcing them to crouch-run, Harper limping, until they reached the relative safety in the cover of the cornfield. Harper knelt down to assess his own wounds. He could still function.

Santee lay in the road for a few seconds, breathing heavily. Harper waited and watched the horse, his companion for eight years on the trail of outlaws, his last contact with home.

She has to be all right.

Santee had been Harper's horse for most of his years he had spent as a marshal in the Nebraska-Dakota territory. Pulled from a herd of mustangs bought by his brother from the Sioux, she was a gift from his sister-in-law. Harper had tamed her on his brother's ranch on the Iowa side of the Missouri.

During his years as a marshal, Harper had spent more time with this horse than with any human being. She knew his moods and his methods and in Harper's mind the horse was an extension of his own body whenever he rode her.

He watched while she lay there. Her breathing could be heard over the din of shooting. Harper waited while seconds ticked away. Was she suffering? He couldn't tell. Tears blurred his vision when he realized she might not get up. Reluctantly, he looked at the cylinder of his pistol for at least one loaded chamber, but the water in his eyes blurred his view.

"Come on, girl. Stand up." Grant had seen Harper's distress, and with a hand on Harper's shoulder, called to Santee. "There you go."

Harper looked back at his horse. Santee shuddered through her chest, rolled her feet under herself, and stood up. She walked over to where Harper and Grant hid among the corn stalks and Harper expelled the breath he had been holding.

He pulled her into the cornfield out of sight of the Rebel musketmen while he examined her injuries. Santee limped and bled from wounds in her rump and neck; scraped skin showed angry red on her knees. Harper stroked her face while the horse twitched her ears and pawed at the ground – their signal from the old days that she was ready to run.

Satisfied that Santee could reach the *Chancellor*, Harper looked around, trying to orient himself to the situation. The Rebel regiment had abandoned the road, the soldiers having moved into the fields on either side. Eight of their men lay dead in the road.

Three Iowa riflemen still fired from the road. Others, perhaps ten or so, fired from the cornfields on either side. More Federal soldiers fired from the riverboats, aiming not at the Rebel force in front of the skirmish line, but beyond Harper's left at some new threat Harper could not see.

"You need to get your men back to the boats," Grant told Harper. The commanding general bled from pin-prick wounds to his cheeks, nose and chin.

"You first, General." Harper pointed to Grant's face and reached for a handkerchief in his pocket. "You're bleedin'."

Grant ran his gloved hand across his chin. He laughed when he saw the blood there. "That was one hell of a ride, Lieutenant." He waved away Harper's handkerchief. "I'll manage." He looked toward the *Chancellor*. "Looks like I've got a hike yet to go."

Harper looked at Grant, then at the distance back to the *Chancellor*. "Take Santee, General. She'll get ya back."

"I can't leave you here without a horse."

Harper took hold of the bridle and stroked Santee's nose. "I'll get one from my men." He pointed to the dead man in a blue uniform lying in the road. "It looks like there'll be at least one spare."

"What's your name, Lieutenant?"

"James Harper, sir. First Iowa Volunteers." Harper pulled his own Sharps rifle from its saddle holster and took a canvas haversack containing boxes of paper cartridges from a saddlebag. Harper moved in front of Santee and pulled the strap of the haversack over his head and across his shoulders.

"Come see me when you get aboard, Harper."

"Yes, sir."

****

Harper ran back to the skirmish line. He had to pull these men back quickly. If the Iowans faced a full regiment, there could be as many as eight hundred men opposite them.

Firing had ended by the time he reached the skirmish line. The silence bothered Harper more than the shooting. When the Rebs fired, Harper knew where they were. In this sudden quiet, they could be doing anything. Because of the thickness of the cover, Harper could not tell if the Rebs were falling back, holding position, or moving to surround his men.

When he looked right and left along the cornrows, he could see about a dozen Federals in the group. Fortunately, the rapid firing of the breechloaders must have surprised the Rebels and stopped them in their tracks. However, the surprise wouldn't last long. Harper guessed he had only minutes before they realized how few men made up the Federal line.

"Who's in charge of you men?" he asked the private crouching next to him.

"Corporal Crawford is, sir." The man pointed to a soldier across the road with two sky-blue chevrons on the sleeves of his dark-blue tunic.

Crawford gave a small wave from the edge of the cornfield to acknowledge Harper. Harper put his finger to his lips in a sign for silence. If the Rebs overheard that a corporal commanded the detachment, they would know how small it was.

Using hand gestures, Harper signaled for the group to move back to the landing.

Crawford nodded to acknowledge the order and signaled the men on his side while Harper relayed the message to the men on the others. Crawford moved into the road to give the order to the men on the ground and to check on the dead man.

"Get his rifle and ammo," Harper whispered.

The men in the road stood up while Harper retrieved his own sword. A volley sounded from the Rebels hidden in the cornfield, kicking up dust plumes around them. The Federals in the road scattered into the cornfields and the Rebels stopped firing. Crawford ran to Harper.

"Let's go, Corporal," Harper ordered. "Stay in the cornfield." Harper waited while Crawford watched the men on the far right of his line start to withdraw, clustering together as they did so.

"Where are your horses?" Harper asked.

"Didn't bring them, Mister Harper. Wasn't time to sort them out on the boat."

"I see." Harper recalled the mob of men and horses on the deck of the Chancellor. Someone, probably one of McKinsey's sergeants, had taken the initiative to send the men on foot rather than wait to sort out their horses. A good decision at the time; however, without horses, the withdrawal would turn into a foot race. "All right, keep moving."

Crawford looked down the line of men on the left and acknowledged a hand signal. Harper turned and saw a short, thin soldier signaling, "Come to me."

"Private Bailey, sir." Crawford sprinted down the row between corn stalks until he reached Bailey. Harper followed. A wounded soldier lay on the ground, clutching his bloody left shin.

"Private Monroe's hit, Corporal," Bailey said.

The wounded man had his lower lip clamped tightly between his teeth, fighting the urge to scream out with the pain of his wound. Still, a whimpering sound like that of a wounded dog, slipped out.

"How bad is he?" Harper asked.

Bailey glanced between Crawford and Harper before he answered. "He's hit in the shin, sir. I think his leg's broken."

Harper tried to look for the Rebel line through the tall, dried corn stalks. No soldiers appeared through the four or five rows which were the limit of his vision. Wind rustled the leaves nearby, or it could be the Rebels. The regiment the Federals on the riverboats had targeted would be somewhere off to his left and rear by now. If those Rebs had continued in that direction, Harper estimated they would already be between the Iowa skirmishers and the *Chancellor*. But they, too, were impossible to see through the cornfield.

"Can he walk?" Harper asked.

"I don't think so, sir."

Musket fire from the riverboats continued to target the Rebels who might cut them off from the *Chancellor*. Harper heard the Rebels in this regiment returning fire, and he saw gunsmoke rising from the cornfield, still to his left and rear. If those Rebels stayed in place, the skirmishers' path back to the *Chancellor* would come very close to the end of this regiment's line – assuming they did not extend farther to the left, in the meantime.

The Rebels in front of him would attack soon. The regiment coming from the woods would definitely get the first group moving. Harper looked down at Monroe who watched his friends wrap bandages over the bloody leg of his sky-blue trousers. In that moment of silence, Monroe looked up at Harper and smiled at Harper through the pain visible on his face.

Harper needed to make a decision about Monroe. He needed to move these men away from here soon, or they might all be killed or captured. Having to carry a wounded man would not only slow them down, but would also require at least two men – men who would not be able to use their weapons if they ran into trouble. Harper looked away from Monroe's trusting face.

"Take his rifle. The Rebs will get him to a doctor." Harper could not risk all their lives for the sake of one.

All of the soldiers stared at Harper.

"Get movin'," Harper ordered.

No one did. Instead, they looked at Corporal Crawford.

"I'll carry him." A large blond-haired man at the end of the line called out.

"Leave him, I said."

None of the men moved.

"No, sir." The large soldier came to where Monroe lay. "I ain't gonna to do that." He looked at Harper and shook his head. "Hold this, Ben." The soldier handed over his rifle and lifted Monroe onto his shoulder as gently as if he were lifting a lost lamb. "Ready, Corporal Crawford."

"Get moving, Magnusson," Crawford ordered.

With Monroe across his shoulders, Magnusson angled across the field toward the road and the landing. Cornstalks in his way seemed to bow low when the powerful man pushed through them. Bailey followed, carrying their three rifles. The two remaining men on this side of the road back-stepped while they covered the retreating group.

Crawford turned to Harper and pursed his lips. "I'll take it from here, Lieutenant." He ran back to watch his men on both sides of the road retreat, keeping level with those screening Magnusson.

He followed the retreating line of Federals. If they survived this, he would have to do something about Crawford's disobedience. He had made the logical choice, and he could not tolerate either Crawford's or Magnusson's actions if he were to wield any authority within the battalion.

After a hundred yards with no reaction from the Rebels, Crawford's men stopped back-stepping and began to trot to the landing with Magnusson setting the pace. Harper fell behind, limping, using his rifle as a walking stick to relieve the stress on his wounded leg.

With battle-fever gone, Harper fought the physical pain from the wounds and the angry embarrassment of being ignored by men whom he sought to command. He did not dare to call out for their help when they ran ahead to the safety of the boat. They might not come.

Firing increased from the *Chancellor* while the skirmishers ran for the landing. Several of the Federal shooters shifted their target to the regiment which had blocked the road. Harper tried to find the Rebels he thought were approaching from the side, but could see nothing through the rows of dried cornstalks. No one aboard *Chancellor* fired at that group any more. It must mean that the side group of Rebels had stopped advancing–or that he had imagined the threat.

Harper reached the riverbank last and waited while soldiers ran from the *Chancellor* to help Magnusson and the others lower Monroe down the slope. The rest of the skirmishers descended the bank in the closing, purple twilight while the men on the second deck of the *Chancellor* continued to fire over their heads at targets in the cornfields. After the men from the skirmish detail were aboard, Harper slid down the slope with his rifle tight against his chest, leaving a trail of blood in the dust.

Grant waited at the bottom of the bluff, cigar stub poking from his smiling lips. "Glad you made it, Harper." He lifted Harper's arm over his own shoulder to help him board. Deck hands crossed the gangway, and Grant let them carry Harper aboard. Grant was the last man to board the *Chancellor*.

Harper found Santee on the foredeck hitched to a railing while the *Chancellor* backed away from the riverbank. While he examined the wound in Santee's rump, the excited talk on the foredeck slowly died away. When Harper looked up to see what was happening, the nearest men turned away. Those farther away broke eye contact. The story of the Monroe boy had spread like a prairie fire.

PART 2
PADUCAH, KENTUCKY

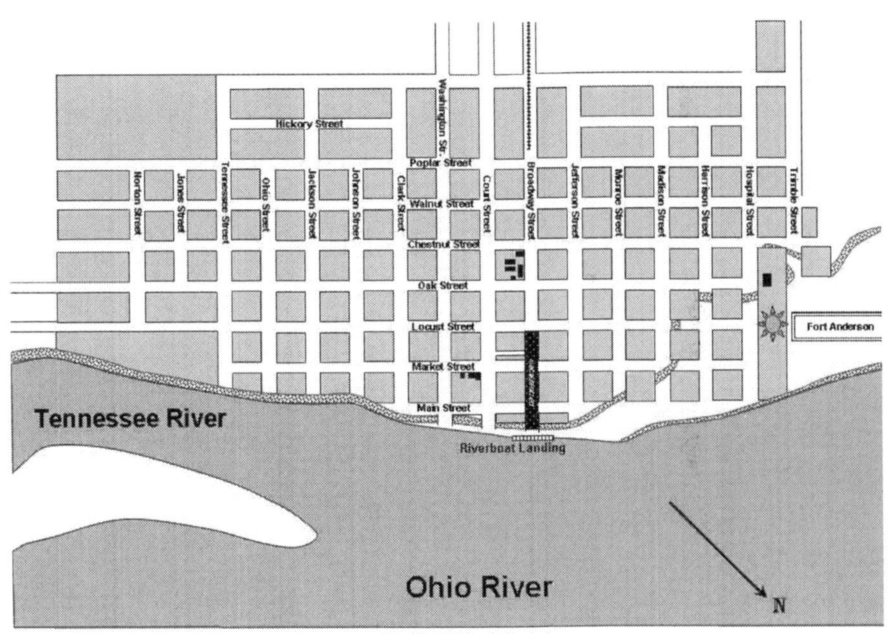

Paducah, Kentucky
1862

(Map prepared by Sean K. Gabhann))

Monday, January 20th, 1862

Jamie Harper sensed movement in the room even though he was not yet fully awake. Feeling no immediate threat, he let himself drop back to a deeper level of sleep, the way he learned to do during years in the Sioux Territory. When the girl climbed into the bed, she slid her naked leg over his thigh until her knee rested on his belly; she nestled her cold foot between his knees.

"Ready for another go, mister?"

Harper didn't open his eyes yet. He could smell the girl's woman-scent mixed with her perfume from the night before as her body warmed from its brief exposure to the January cold. She shivered when a gust of wind from the river penetrated the window frames and poked under a corner of the thick, warm quilt covering them.

She squeezed tight against him. He could feel the strong muscles of her arms, shoulders, and legs, now half on top of him. His body responded inevitably to her movement, and Harper was now wide awake, trying to recall where he was.

Paducah. He was in Paducah, Kentucky. Six weeks had passed since he had left Saint Louis to convalesce from his wounds at Belmont. His orders required him to report today. However, the First Iowa could wait an hour or so. The day had not yet begun.

He had paid twenty dollars to have the girl, the one they called Baby Red, for all night—and that included her soft, warm bed as well as her companionship. He had heard that in the legitimate hotels in Paducah, the guests slept three to a bed with two or more on the floor.

Harper savored the feel of the girl's body against his, even though her hip and leg pressed down on the scars from his most recent wounds.

After he reported to the battalion, he knew it would be a long time before he would find a woman's comforts again.

Through the girl's curtains, he could see the night beginning to yield to morning twilight–if there were any roosters left in town, they probably would start crowing shortly. That made the time about a half-past six.

The light in the room shifted from black to fuzzy gray, and Harper took in details of his surroundings, another habit from the trail. The growing light first revealed the white linen trim the girl used to give the room the comfortable feel of a home and not entirely a place of business. Cut lavender branches, now dried, stood in a vase on the dressing table, struggling to mask the residual smell of cigar smoke and stale whiskey from the saloon below.

She had replaced the blankets, which still covered a few of the other second-story windows in the building, with red and white flower-printed calico draperies. They gave the room some color and allowed for privacy when closed. The blankets now served as rugs in what he guessed was a failed attempt to combat the drafts and noise coming through the floorboards.

"Well, come on, mister. Are you ready for me, yet?" She straddled Harper's hips, grinding down on them, but careful to keep the warm quilt draped around herself and her customer. Harper flexed and felt a twinge of pain in his rear from where a Rebel musket ball had peppered the muscle weeks earlier.

"I ain't never seen a man with them color eyes, sort of gray in the middle but with a brown circle around the edges. What country are you from?"

"My father was half-Irish, half-Spanish. My mother had green eyes." He smiled at her. "Like yours."

Although the girl stood only half a head shorter than Harper's six feet, and taller than most women, Harper guessed her age at fifteen or so. But he really didn't want to know. She was older than his own daughter would have been, and that was good enough.

Now, she hovered over Harper smiling wickedly and pinning his shoulders with her hands, her red hair hanging past his ears, mingling with his own shaggy, honey-colored hair.

Harper knew from the night before that red was her natural hair color; besides, the girl seemed too new at the trade to color her hair. The anticipation in her eyes and the movement of her hips gave the lie to the proprietor's promise of her virginity last night. He suspected virginity would return tonight if any new customers came into the saloon.

Sadly for Harper, his thirty-year-old body insisted only on using the chamber pot. As she moved against him, he battled with the decision to stay in the bed or to climb into the cold morning. Soon, biology decided for him, and he gently rolled the girl to the side.

"Excuse me." Harper slid out from under the quilt cover, slowly adjusting to the chill in the room. The fire in the stove radiated heat onto his naked body, but he quickly lost the warmth as he walked behind the dressing screen to use the chamber pot, stepping over her crinoline collapsed on the floor. As he stood there adding to the bowl, he looked through the window and guessed he had about fifteen minutes before full sunup.

When he finished, a slight scent of residue perfume wafted past from the party dress and frilly petticoats hung carefully over the dressing screen. The smell inevitably led to arousal as he recalled the events of the previous night.

But before returning to the bed, he looked for his own belongings and saw the pile of dark uniform clothes outlined on the chair in front of the white muslin the girl used to skirt the small dressing table. His pack still lay next to the chair.

The girl held the quilt up, tent-style, as he hopped across the cold floor and fell back into bed. She softly lowered the quilt over him as he gave her a kiss on the top of her head. She reached between Harper's legs with her now-warm hand to get him ready, then rolled back on top of him.

****

Later, he dressed in the new uniform from St. Louis and gathered up the few belongings he used last night and this morning, surveying them all to make sure none had disappeared while he slept. He worked everything into his pack. The leather pouch lay loose on top of the rest of the contents – the special leather pouch. Inside were the only two things he had left from his life before he became a marshal, besides Santee.

Crochet trimmed the frames of two images set nearby his pouch, one showing a man and a woman, each with the stern, time-worn faces of people who worked in the sun to earn a hard living. The second showed the same woman seated with a younger version of the girl in a gingham dress standing tall beside her. The pictures and three dolls on a shelf above were the only indication of the girl's past life, before the war started.

He shifted the pouch carefully along the sidewall so it wouldn't be crushed. He knew the girl watched him. He took five dollars from his billfold.

There was no telling how much of his twenty dollars Bosley would give her. Staying here cost Harper a week's pay, but damn it, he would be comfortable on his final night of leave, so he left his last greenback, a fiver, under the image of the girl and the woman.

"What's your name, mister?" She sat up in the bed to watch when he shifted the daguerreotype. When he set it in place again, she pulled the quilt tight around her.

He thought for a moment.

"Lieutenant Andrew C. Ray, ma'am, Twelfth Illinois Volunteers." Poor Private Ray had died from bloody flux in Missouri the previous July, and Harper had seen the flag of the Twelfth Illinois camped along the river the day before. He made it a rule never to give a hooker his real name.

Harper picked up his official issue, Hardee-style, black felt hat with the bugle badge in front identifying him as an infantry officer. He saw the numeral 1 above the bugle for First Iowa with a blank space above it where the company letter should go. He fingered the space and wondered what he had yet to do before the the colonel would assign him to a company.

"Illinois, hunh. So am I!" She smoothed some wrinkles in the quilt. "I'm from near Cypressville, close by Shawneetown on the river."

"Which river is that, the Mississip' or the Ohi-ah?"

"My ma once told me we lived near the Ohi-ah River, but I know that Ohi-ah's a state, not a river."

Not the smartest of women, but she was pretty enough that he did not object to having a conversation. "Well, I'm from up in Chicago. Have you ever heard of that?"

"Of course I heard of Chicago." She pointed to the dressing screen. "Hand me them drawers hangin' on the screen."

Harper took the pantaloons from the pile of clothes draped over the dressing screen, without letting the party dress or petticoats fall to the floor. He handed them to the girl who struggled to put them on while staying within the warmth of the quilt.

"Y'all don't talk like someone from Chicago." The quilt fell from her shoulders revealing her small, girlish breasts, not more than large bumps on her chest. "When y'all comin' back, Mister Ray?" the girl asked.

Of course, she wanted him to return. He had been a good customer for her. "Can't really say, ya know? It depends on when the colonel lets me go." Harper's gaze shifted from her breasts to the etched muscles in her arms, shoulders, and chest. Those were the muscles of someone who had spent most of her life working on a farm.

"I like y'all, so's you won't keep me waiting too long, will you?"

Prostitutes always seemed to like Harper. Besides the extra money for his stay, she probably enjoyed having to entertain only one man last night. "It may take a while for me to save another twenty dollars." He lied. After he reported for duty, his position would require that he not be seen consorting with prostitutes or frequenting saloons, especially ones shared with enlisted men.

"That ain't true. Y'all bein' an officer and everythin'." She pulled the quilt back around her shoulders with a shiver. "Officers come into the saloon whenever they want."

"What did you do in Cypressville?"

"We worked our farm, jes' like everybody else. But after my ma died, my pa took to the bottle, so I did all of the work myself." That would explain the muscles. Harper found something attractive about a woman with muscles. He felt the strength in those arms and legs last night. The Sioux women were strong that way.

"Why don't ya go back to Cypressville and wait for me there?"

The girl's face clouded over and he knew he went too far.

"You know I cain't do that, mister! Mr. Bosley bought me fair and square from my pa. They'll both beat me if I run away." Her eyes filled with tears.

Things on the farm must have been desparate for a father to sell his daughter, especially a white woman. The father must have known how Bosley intended to employ the girl. Harper could guess the only way she would get away from this house was if someone bought up her bills to Bosley, and Bosley was not about to let that happen with his youngest and prettiest attraction.

The tears triggered Harper's sympathy for the girl's hopeless situation before he could catch himself. An image of Magda working in a saloon pushed into his brain, and he had to shake his head to force it away. Damn women and their damn tears.

"What's your name, girl? Your real name, not the one Bosley gave ya."

"Katie. Katie Malloy."

"How long ya been workin' here?"

"A few weeks. Since before Christmas time."

He needed to change the subject.

"Stop crying. At least ya have it pretty good here right now, eh?" What did she think crying would help? There was nothing Harper could do to change things, even if he cared what happened to her. She obviously had not yet realized she would work for Franklin Bosley for a long time.

"I suppose you're right, mister." She used the sheet to dry her eyes. "Miss Loreena and Miss Eleanor take good care of us girls. And they says we're helping Mister Lincoln win the war by bein' nice to the soldiers."

That was a clever way to make her feel like less of a whore.

Harper was ready to leave. "Well, good luck to ya, Katie Malloy."

"And to y'all, Lieutenant Ray. Be careful in the war."

With the war nearby, the girl-whore was a damn sight better off here than on some pig-farm in down-state Illinois. She'd probably have more money in a month than Harper could make in all of next year. And if it meant she must lay back and spread her legs once or twice a night, well, that's what the money was for.

He put on his overcoat and picked his hat up from the bed. Hefting the pack onto his right shoulder, he left without looking back at the girl.

****

"Mornin', Lieutenant." Sergeant Joshua Featherstone greeted Harper when he came down the stairs into the saloon. "I thought I'd show ya the way, eh, since ya ain't never been to Paducah before."

Featherstone had been Harper's First Sergeant in the old Company K, but the regiment reorganized after their initial, ninety-day enlistment. After the reorganization, Companies K and F merged into Company B while the regiment shrunk in size to a five-company battalion. Featherstone now served as Fourth Sergeant in Company B.

Harper smiled when he saw Featherstone waiting. The soldier was returning from Christmas leave, and both came from the western counties of Iowa. The forty-two-year-old Featherstone owned a tannery and stable at Fort Dodge that his brother-in-law now managed.

When Harper reached the bottom of the stairs, Featherstone lifted his pack from a chair and slung it over a single shoulder, revealing hands permanently stained by tannin. "Ready?"

The sergeant had accompanied Harper for most of the trip back to the army. Harper spent his Christmas recovering at his brother's ranch near Sergeant's Bluff. The two soldiers had discovered each other on the train to Dubuque and traveled together since.

Harper had come to trust Featherstone during the time they served together in Company K. Harper was the company's first lieutenant, elected based on his reputation as a United States marshal, and Featherstone became the company's First Sergeant based on his role in the Fort Dodge militia. They had fought together through three campaigns in Missouri before Harper received his injuries at Belmont.

Now, they addressed each other with the familiarity of men who had faced mortal danger together and come out alive. Rank still defined the differences in their responsibilities, but Harper held an unspoken, unabashed respect for Featherstone that he felt certain was mutual. Being two of the few remaining westerners in the battalion strengthened their bond.

"Looks like Grant's gettin' ready for somethin', eh?" Featherstone commented as they stepped through the door.

"I hope so." Harper shuddered in the sudden cold. "The army's been here three months already."

Lafitte's Hideout fronted on Market Street and connected to Bosley's other enterprise *The French Pelican,* a dining room which fronted on Court Street. One block above the landing, both establishments were an easy walk for the river men and their passengers when they tied up at the Paducah landing.

By good fortune for Bosley, the Union army established a number of camps south and west of the town. Soldiers needed to pass directly in front of the restaurant and the saloon behind it when they moved their supplies, which arrived every day. The location brought a steady flow of customers all day long.

The night chill left frozen little peaks of mud in Market Street, but Harper and Featherstone walked on the duck boards bordering the building. The air smelled of wood smoke from hundreds of fireplaces being revived against the morning chill.

"How was your night?" Featherstone asked Harper, with an insinuating smile.

"Probably better than yours."

"Ya smell like it. That girl's perfume is all over you."

At the corner, a sign nailed to the corner of the *Pelican* announced they were crossing Court Street. Featherstone led Harper into the morning market, past open stalls in the center of the street where vendors operated their booths. Paducah's main market stretched for most of the city block, with a brick building in the center and porticos extending nearly the entire block to protect the open stalls.

"Jealous?" Harper forced his legs to match the sergeant's pace, testing the strength of the muscles around his most recent wounds. Even at forty or so, Featherstone used the brisk walk of a man with important business. In spite of the sergeant's shorter stride, Harper felt pain in his left thigh and right buttock and struggled to keep the pace.

"I'm a married man." Featherstone reminded Harper. "And I appreciate ya lettin' me use your stateroom on the boat last night. I saw one of the hotels this mornin'–more like a pigsty for humans."

They passed the *European Hotel* on its narrow lot and Harper saw for himself an example of the over-crowded accommodations in the city. He congratulated himself on his choice of arrangements for the previous night. At the three-story brick mercantile on the corner, the pair turned away from the landing and up Broadway Street. Here, the mud and gravel streets yielded to a macadamized road surface, and there was no need for wooden sidewalks.

The slanting rays of the morning sun threw the shadows of buildings and naked trees completely across the street but failed to deliver any warmth where the men walked. Their breath formed clouds of condensation in the still air. These dispersed when the men walked through them.

"Jes' three blocks more." Featherstone slowed his pace and Harper could keep up.

Harper stopped when they crossed Oak Street to look at the fort Grant's army had built at the northern end of town. The strength of it surprised him.

"That ditch weren't there last month," Featherstone remarked.

On the landward side, facing the town, a ditch fronted an earthen palisade. From his time in the Mexican war, Harper guessed the spoil from the ditch probably formed the elevated firing platforms for the cannon now nosing through embrasures atop the palisade. They watched while soldiers opened the two doors of the main gate onto Oak Street.

"Guess Grant means to stay, eh." Harper hitched his pack higher on his shoulder.

"That's just the headquarters for the garrison. The real defenses for the city are outside of town, but we're not part of that. They figure our boys'll be part of the new division when the fightin' starts."

"Did anyone say when that will be?"

"Most think it'll be next month. Folks here-abouts say the freezin' and mud ends sometime in February. Most expect we'll be movin' out once that happens."

They continued walking on Broadway, watching townspeople scurry to ensure the quartermasters and the provost guards protected the private warehouses. Paducah had become a depot and most of the warehouses in the city appeared to have been commandeered by Grant's Army.

"Think there'll be trouble when we get back?" Featherstone broke the silence..

"We'll have to see."

"Those Company F fellows took it kinda hard that ya wanted to leave the Monroe boy behind."

"I know. I had a lot of time the last couple of months to think about that day. Maybe it would have been a mistake to leave him there if we weren't going to be surrounded." Harper knew he had made a mistake at Belmont, but he would not admit that to Featherstone or anyone else.

" 'Cept we were almost cut off from the landing, and I needed to get as many as I could back to the boats." A pain shot into Harper's spine from the nearly-healed wound in his thigh. "I'd probably do the same thing again, if I needed to." That battle was in the past, and whatever was to come, his actions at Belmont couldn't be changed. He would deal with the repercussions when they came.

"I understand why ya did it, but you'd best not be talkin' that way when we get back." Featherstone stepped around a mud puddle. "Things are gonna be hard enough for ya."

"A-yeah. 'Spect so."

They traveled a few steps before Featherstone broke into Harper's thoughts.

"They say the new commander wanted to make the boy his aide, ya know. Make him a lieutenant," Featherstone added. "It turns out Private Monroe was Colonel Monroe's son. The boy never told us."

"Yeah, I heard that too." Fate seemed to hate Harper.

Their path took them in front of two warehouses where loaded wagons waited for workers to unload them into the buildings. Inside the first warehouse, they could see cases of hardtack stacked nearly to the rafters.

"Now, I wish I coulda sent some of the old Company K boys to you, instead. Wouldn't have been such a fuss, then."

"Maybe. Maybe not." The men from Company K might have done what he ordered, but leaving a friend behind might have been too much even for them.

At the second warehouse, civilians and soldiers moved spare saddles, bridles, and other tack inside, stacking them alongside fifty-pound bags of feed grain piled ten bags high.

"Company F boys don't really know ya."

"I know. They only wanted to protect one of their own." Harper led the way around the wagon being unloaded.

"Well, we're all Company B men since re-enlistin' last August, so we'll have to learn to get along, eh."

In spite of his friendship with Featherstone, Harper wanted to change the subject. "Looks like the local folks don't seem to mind so much having Federal troops here."

He would learn the consequences of his actions at Belmont in due time.

"It ain't right, though, ya know?"

"What ain't?"

Featherstone stopped and faced Harper. "It ain't right that you ain't in command of one of the companies. Ya need to do somethin' about it."

Harper knew better than to discuss the politics of the officers, especially with an enlisted man, even a trusted friend. "Well, I've tried already but Major Porter wants me on the staff, and adjutant was the only position left."

"We've got a bunch of dandies runnin' Company B. We'd be a hell of a lot better off if you was the company commander. Them lieutenants don't listen to the sergeants, only to what Cap'n McKinsey says. It's harder'n hell just to keep from kickin' 'em in their fancy-pants butts sometimes."

McKinsey held his commission by virtue of his political influence in Iowa City rather than by any ability to lead a company in a real battle. In answer to the president's call for ninety-day troops, the governor of Iowa organized the First Iowa Volunteer Infantry Regiment by mustering the militia companies of the cities in eastern Iowa. The militia company from Iowa City formed the cadre for Company B, but since the removals of hostile Indians across the Missouri River, the eastern militia companies served mostly ceremonial functions. Membership had become a system of political patronage, especially among the officers.

At fifty-four years of age, McKinsey had held the captaincy of the Iowa City militia since Millard Fillmore was president, and he was well past the age when anyone would have expected him to lead his company to war. Fifteen years before, he may have been a dashing officer of dragoons. Now, that officer lay hidden under a hundred pounds of middle-aged fat. Harper believed that the man should be sent home. Instead, McKinsey retained command and drilled his men according to the school of 1843.

Harper walked again. Featherstone followed. Harper would not speak ill of any officer with any enlisted man, even Captain McKinsey. No matter what he believed, personally.

"I'm doin' what I have to do, sergeant. Doin' what I'm told."

They continued on the sidewalk a few more steps.

Harper had been in Iowa City on business at the first call for volunteers. He had no strong feelings about slavery but it certainly was not a good enough reason to destroy the Union. The enthusiasm of the day for forcing the rebellious states to return to the fold had captured his imagination and swept him into the recruitment office in the state capital.

"Once campaignin' starts, there might be some openin's." Featherstone spoke what they both knew.

"Maybe." Harper paused.

After enlisting, Harper sent a letter of resignation to the Federal judge at Yankton and made his way from Iowa City to the mustering of the regiment in Burlington. By the time he arrived, all of the billets in the first seven companies were filled by militiamen. The mustering officer organized Company K to receive the overflow of volunteers, Companies H and I being reserved for militiamen who had not yet arrived. Once his fellow enlistees learned that Harper had served as a deputy federal marshal in the Nebraska/Dakota territory for eight years, they elected him as the company's first lieutenant.

Harper chuckled. "You got anyone in mind you'd particularly like to see get killed?"

"Ya know it ain't like that." Featherstone bounded across another muddy puddle; Harper went around. "It's just that things happen in a battle and sometimes we need more officers–like for special assignments."

"If that happens, I'm probably in the best place get a special assignment." Harper stopped at the next corner to look down the blocks to his left and right. "It depends on what the new commanding officer wants to do."

"Yeah. I suppose so, but we need ya in a company. You're too good to be a pencil-pusher." Featherstone pointed to three large structures in the middle of the block on the left, their raw wood not yet turned gray. "Our boys built them stables. Good thing we got boys who know barn raisin'. Our enlisted men stay in the lofts above the horses."

To their right, the blue flag of a new regiment scarcely rippled in the slight breeze. The horses for the new arrivals stood corralled in the open center of this city block, their rumps pointed into the chill wind. Soldiers there tended bonfires in some of the corrals while construction continued on new stables.

They made their way across Chestnut Street to where the regimental flag of the First Iowa stood at the main entry to a white, two-story brick building. Above the doorway, the name *Saint Mary's Academy* appeared, engraved into the stone lintel.

Featherstone followed Harper into through the door. "Good luck, Mister Harper."

Harper returned the salute of the guards as he and Featherstone entered the former school. For better or for worse, he was back in the army.

Tuesday, Janury 21st, 1862

"Good. You're back," Major Asbury Porter, the battalion's executive officer called to Harper from the parade ground.

Harper smiled from the doorway at the rear of the former school as his friend approached. "Got back yesterday, Major. Just now finished checkin' in." He saluted before he took the offered handshake.

Porter, in his fifties and a surveyor in civilian life, stood straight, as tall as Harper. He had Harper's wiry build, a man who had spent much of his life in the saddle. Porter kept his pre-war civilian office in Council Bluffs but, like Harper, his work had taken him into the Nebraska-Dakota territory much of the time and the two men shared an understanding and a respect for each others' abilities.

Porter grinned at Harper. "Well. I'm certainly glad to have our adjutant back, eh. Your Corporal Powell has loaded up my desk every morning with all nature of reports, anything that needs an officer's signature, and I'm glad you're back now to deal with it. I didn't join the army to sign reports, I can tell ya."

Harper scowled at this reminder of the dull work waiting for him. "Powell had everything under control." He searched Porter's eyes. "Didn't he?"

"True. But I still hated having to spend most of *my* morning going through *your* paperwork. That's why we need our adjutant around here and not at the *soirees* in St. Louis."

The smile reached Porter's brown eyes when he said this and let Harper know that Porter spoke in jest. Harper chuckled at the thought that he could have spent his leave dancing in Saint Louis while his wounds healed instead of in a bed with thick pillows under his buttocks, on a ranch at the edge of civilization in Sergeant's Bluff.

"This way." Porter pointed to the rear of a white two-story frame building which housed the battalion's junior officers. It lay directly across The Commons from the new stables and fronted on Chestnut Street.

"How are your wounds?" Porter asked.

"Better. Still a little tender, though." The question brought his attention to the dull throbbing at the wound sites, exacerbated by the January cold. His sister-in-law had managed to dig out most of the bits of musket ball, but Harper suffered in the cold weather.

Harper wanted to get a small lunch before he took Santee on a run. "So, adjutant's still my job, Major?"

"What's that? Oh, the paperwork. Right ya are, Jamie. And welcome to it."

They passed the tall flagpole in the center of The Commons flying thc battalion's thirty-five star national flag. White-painted rocks poked through trampled snow to mark the boundary of an exclusion area around the flagpole.

"Look, Major. I know that job is important, but when are ya going' to find some clerk to do it? I need to get moved into a company." Harper stopped and turned to look Porter straight in the eyes. "I think I'd do a hell of a lot better job for the battalion gettin' the men to kill Rebs and not shoveling papers."

Porter's eyes hardened around the edges. "Keepin' the battalion's fixed headquarters *is* important in a battle. Ya know that. We need to keep the communications moving with the brigade, and to make sure orders get recorded and sent out to the companies quickly."

"A clerk could do it. It's not where I want to be in a battle."

"Ya know all of the companies have their full allowance of officers already, except Company C."

Harper halted in his tracks. "Because all those officers know someone."

Porter stared at him in silence. They both knew it was true. The only way to get a commission in a former militia company was to be approved by the mayor of the city which offered up the original militia. Even Porter held his commission because he knew someone on the governor's staff. The only reasons Harper was still around after the reorganization were because Porter wanted him, and because of the rifles and horses which his family donated. It was ridiculous that, after all the experiences he had had and all of wilderness skills he had learned in the past eight years, the best job he could find in the entire United States Army was to be a records clerk. It made no sense.

"Besides, you're the only officer in this outfit other than me with brains enough to make the staff work the way it should. That Catholic college did right by ya."

Porter looked around to see if anyone else was in ear-shot. The Commons was nearly empty except for a pair of sentries at the rear of the former school and some soldiers crossing the open area, huddled against the morning cold. Even so, Porter led him around the corner of the officers' building. He lowered his voice. "You've got bigger problems."

This brought Harper up short. Porter had not yet mentioned anything about the consequences of Harper's actions during his last battle. "What would those be?"

"Your biggest problem is that Colonel Monroe does not want you here. His first day here, he ordered me to prepare discharge papers for you for misconduct at the battle at Belmont."

"Discharge? Misconduct? What the hell for? Rescuing General Grant?" Harper could feel the blood rush boiling hot into his face while his heart twisted in is chest. He took a deep breath to collect himself. Porter was a friend. Maybe there was more to the story. "So, what did you do? Am I being discharged?"

"No. That argument's over. I reminded him that your commission comes from the governor, just like mine. He would need to have the discharge approved by the governor's office and it might mean a formal inquiry. He backed down."

"Damn right he did. I can imagine what would happen if there was a formal inquiry."

"It helps that Governor Kirkwood won the election. I don't suppose the colonel wanted to face Kirkwood after having spent all summer and autumn campaigning for the Democrats."

Harper chuckled. "Maybe Colonel Monroe isn't entirely stupid."

"Even so, you'll have to be very cautious around him. He still wants me to find a different officer to be adjutant. I told him I would review all of the likely candidates."

Harper dropped his pack and leaned his shoulder against the wall. He wondered how he could be effective as the adjutant if the man he was supposed to support hated him. His thoughts progressed to another issue. "You said there were other problems?"

Porter nodded. "Yes. First, I think you should not expect to be promoted as long as Colonel Monroe is in command. Either that, or you'll have to find a way to get into his good graces."

"How do I do that, Major?"

"For now, just do the job you've been assigned as best you can. With the campaign about to start, there might be more opportunity for you to show your value to the battalion. In fact, I have an assignment in mind for you for you that might be a way to start."

So Harper would have to behave himself until Monroe deemed him capable enough to be given a useful position. That meant he would be stuck in the adjutant's position. How would Monroe decide that Harper was an asset to the battalion–by how well he pushed papers? Indefinitely? "You said there were *issues*...more than one. What else is there?"

Porter looked at the ground. "It's difficult to say this, particularly since I know for a fact that it ain't true."

"What is it?"

"Well, you know how rumors spread around the camp."

"Yeah."

Porter looked into Harper's eyes. "Well, Jamie, it seems that the enlisted men don't trust you because of what happened at Belmont."

"That doesn't surprise me."

"Uh-huh. The problem is that none want you to be one of their officers. Sergeant Major Compton relayed the message from the sergeants in each company. None of them want to work under you – except, I expect, Sergeant Featherstone. He wasn't here when all of this talk was goin' on. Some of the others from your old Company K still support you, but there aren't many of them left and they're all scattered throughout the different companies, so they're drowned out by the others."

This didn't surprise Harper, based on how McKinsey's men treated him during the return trip from Belmont. During his convalescence, he had thought about ways to get past the mistrust he knew the men would feel toward him. But those plans depended on him remaining in the battalion and getting into the fight when the battalion began operations.

"What about the officers? Do they trust me?"

"Can't say for sure. No one has objected out loud to your staying in the battalion as the adjutant. I haven't asked any of them if they'd object to assigning you to their companies."

Harper was stuck. He had no way forward to take a command if he stayed with the First Iowa. He might resign his commission with this battalion and try his luck in one of the new regiments. But to do that, he would need some influence in the governor's office, and Porter was the only person he knew who had such a connection. His new colonel would want to see a letter of recommendation from his prior commander. If Porter was correct, Monroe would never sign such a letter.

He might resign and go home to raise his own regiment of men from Woodbury County. That would take a lot of money, which Harper did not have. He couldn't expect more help from his family after they had donated so much to convert the First Iowa to mounted infantry at his insistence. It would also require him to obtain commissions from the governor for himself and the other officers in his regiment. Again, he would need political influence at a level where he had none. If he resigned, his only real option was to return to Yankton as a deputy marshal and watch from a distance while his countrymen fought to save or destroy his country.

"Damn." Porter was right. Harper's only option was to stay and do the best he could under the circumstances. "So that's it, then. Stay here, push paperwork like a demon, and wait until something happens to change things."

Porter reached across the gap between them and put his hand on Harper's shoulder.

"And while I'm doin' all that, hope that Monroe doesn't come up with a way to force me to resign or to send me home."

"I won't let that happen."

"Shit." Harper stood away from the wall and picked up his pack.

"I need you to stay here to help me run things." Porter looked around again. When he spoke, it came out barely more than a whisper. "And I want ya close by, just in case."

Harper thought about that for a minute. Gossip had started when it was announced that Porter would not take permanent command of the battalion in favor of a new man, another politician. No one would say it out loud, but many believed Lieutenant Colonel Wesley Monroe held command solely by virtue of working for the political campaign of the regiment's former executive officer. William Merritt successfully installed his own man as commander of the reorganized First Iowa Volunteer Battalion before he lost the election for governor the previous November.

"Did ya know Grant now has two whole divisions? Ten thousand men, with more comin' in every week. We're part of the Second Division."

Harper didn't like the progress of this conversation. He watched the smoke rising from the chimneys of the stable-*cum*-barracks. There was going to be a big battle and he wasn't going to be in it.

Porter continued. "Also, I think your trackin' experience as a lawman in the territories is going to be needed once the men learn how to use their new rifles. I expect we're goin' to get those kinds of special assignments."

"Well, I didn't join the army to push papers either, Major. Just because I was in the damn hospital, doesn't mean it was right to skip me over when ya made the company assignments. Especially in favor of some of them dandy-boys. That all happened before we knew about Colonel Monroe."

"Hell, Jamie, that's water under the bridge. Ya know as well as I do men were dyin' from that fever last August, and you was terrible sick. And, ain't your father providing our rifles and your brother providing our mustangs? That was your doing, wasn't it? You need to be on the staff to work with them officially. Anyway, *I* need ya on the staff."

"Maybe I should command the whole battalion, Major. That'd make it easier to work with my pa and brother, too."

"Maybe you will, one day."

Harper paused to take a deep breath and look around the Commons. There was a second part of Porter's statement about being on the staff. "What do you mean, you need me on the staff?"

Porter looked around The Commons once again, before turning his back to the open area and whispering. "Colonel Monroe insists that we are going to stay as mounted infantry, movin' around by horse but fightin' dismounted, in a massed line, the same way the regiments did in the last war."

"What does he think is the purpose of us havin' the rifles? Doesn't he know how bad the casualties will be?"

Porter stopped and looked around again to ensure no one could hear them. "He wasn't with us in Missouri. He didn't see the killin'." Porter lowered his voice even further. "He's still learnin' and he's only been here for six weeks. He's readin' Hardee's manual, but he seems more interested in the political news from Des Moines."

"*Hardee* didn't write about a rifle that could kill someone at half-a-mile."

"That, too." Porter nodded. "I showed him in the book where it talks about the need for skirmishers in front of the firin' line, and so I got him to agree that we need to train some of the men as designated skirmishers."

"Only some?" Harper asked. "Hell. *All* of them need to know how to skirmish."

"For now." Porter paused, thinking about what he had to say next. "I have a favor to ask of you."

It made sense that Harper should be on the immediate staff if his role in the next battle, and that of Major Porter, would be to ensure Monroe did not make any fatal mistakes. If Porter didn't trust Monroe's abilities, what did he think Harper could do about it, a lieutenant against a lieutenant colonel? Porter must have a plan. "Go ahead."

"Tomorrow afternoon, I want ya to take twenty men from each company and teach them how to operate on their own. We'll call it skirmisher training but what I truly want ya to do is train them to be scouts and sharpshooters, as well as skirmishers."

Harper smiled and nodded in agreement. This assignment came closer to what he thought the battalion should become. Maybe he could eventually train the entire battalion. Based on his conversation with General Grant following the Belmont battle, he knew this would make the unit more useful to the army.

Again, Porter looked to see that no one was nearby. “If ya can, try to teach them some of the spyin’ tricks ya learned chasin’ outlaws in Indian country.”

It was an assignment Harper had to take. He was the only person in the battalion who could accomplish what Porter wanted. It also meant he would not have to deal with Monroe or the battalion’s paperwork for two weeks. “I’ll do it.”

Harper had a day to put together the schedule and to figure out how to teach secrets which had taken him eight years and the help of Sioux warriors to learn. He’d get an outline done tonight and work the details as he went along.

“Jamie, if the colonel learns we’re goin’ beyond basic skirmish training, ya know he’ll stop it. He’s a by-the-book man.”

“I understand.”

“So ya won’t have any written orders for the extra training.”

“Oh.” It took Harper a few seconds to understand the implication. He would bear full responsibility if anything went wrong. He looked past Porter and the rows of buildings to the large exercise yard where patches of dirty snow still lay on dead yellow grass. Harper trusted Porter to protect him as well as possible but Harper would bear the final punishment for exceeding orders. “Well, it needs to be done, doesn’t it?” He looked down and shook his head before looking back at Porter. “I’ll make it work.”

Porter smiled back. “I thought ya’d say that.”

They turned back to the door of the junior officers’ quarters. The first scent of food cooking for the mid-day meal floated from the nearby buildings.

“I guess I better get to work.” Harper stopped and faced Porter. “But dammit, one day I’m goin’ to have a company of my own. Ya know I can do it! If I can’t do it here, then I’ll join a different regiment.”

“You could always try that, Jamie.” Porter’s face lost its kindness. “In the meantime, ya have five companies to train up in three weeks.

Rumor has it the army is headin' south sometime in February." He paused. "So, I'll talk with ya later. I'd like to see your ideas for the skirmisher trainin' tonight. We'll show them to Colonel Monroe in the morning."

"Yes, sir."

Porter put his hand on Harper's shoulder. "Don't worry, Jamie. You'll get your chance."

****

At suppertime, Harper made his way from his office where he had worked on the training plans all afternoon. He crossed the parade ground to the junior officers' quarters in the fading afternoon light. The smell of beef stew surrounded the building but, for Harper, supper would be the test of how the incident at Belmont affected his relationships with his closest peers in the battalion, since this was the time when most of the junior officers gathered. When he opened the door, complaints rose from the eight men seated at the table of the mess.

"Close the door, damn it!"

"You're causin' a draft!"

"It's freezin'!"

A short, dark-haired man with blue eyes rose from his place at the table and grinned at Harper. Lieutenant Theodor Guelich served as the battalion's quartermaster, a post he held since the original unit of ninety-day men mustered into service. "You're back. It's good to see ya." Guelich offered Harper his hand. His welcome seemed sincere.

"Hi ya, Theo." Harper liked Guelich. Unlike Harper, Guelich contented himself to serve in the rear areas, moving supplies for the battalion forward from army depots. Together they oversaw an effective battalion staff, with Harper in charge of the affairs of the men and Guelich in charge of the materiel support. Harper smiled as he shook his friend's hand, holding his hat with the other. Conversation at the table ended while the other men listened.

"How are your legs? Recovered yet from gettin' shot?" Guelich asked.

"Doin' fine. Still hurts a little to sit down, though."

The dining area occupied the refectory of a former nunnery, part of the Saint Mary's School complex. Two arched entries on either side of the central fireplace led into the front parlor, while a narrow staircase wound around the chimney to the second floor. At the opposite end of the refectory were two doors, one leading to the kitchen and the other leading to a small butler's pantry.

"Might inconvenient gettin' shot in the ass." Lieutenant Bill Pierson called from the table, starting a round of laughter. Pierson still held temporary command of Company C due to the death of their captain at Wilson's Creek the previous August. No one understood why he had not yet been confirmed in the position.

"A-yeah, but at least it missed the important parts around front." Harper locked eyes with Pierson. He would use Pierson as his barometer of the feelings of the officers other than Guelich. "They're still workin' fine." He smiled directly at Pierson. "Ask your sister."

This brought another round of laughter, which broke the tension. Pierson hesitated for a minute before joining in. "I know Bea wouldn't have you, Harper. You're much too ugly for her taste. And you smell like a mule."

"Maybe so." Harper smiled at his former friend, and Pierson's wide return smile was confirmation that their friendship held. "Some ladies like that in a man." He winked at Pierson, who kept his grin and nodded his head. Command of Company C was the only vacant captaincy in the battalion. Harper hoped he might be promoted to the position, but Pierson held the advantage.

All of the lieutenants were in their late twenties to early thirties, much older than the lieutenants in the newer regiments. All had listened to the exchange between Harper and Pierson and appeared to appreciate the good-natured jibes. The exceptions were Harvey Goodrell and Andrew Jackson Reynolds, the lieutenants in McKinsey's company. These were the officers who had missed their opportunity at Belmont when General Grant needed help.

"Did ya get to see your family while ya were gone?" Guelich asked.

"Yeah, sure did." Harper smiled, because he knew Guelich's next question.

"So, are they going to keep helping us with the horses and rifles?"

"Uh-huh. They both signed supply contracts at army headquarters in Saint Louis while I was there."

"That should do fine," Guelich said. "Maybe now *the officers,*" he took a broad look at the men still seated, "will stop complaining about the quality of the horseflesh we get from the army, eh."

One of the Company D officers said, "Maybe someday, Theo – when the war's over!" More laughter followed. Goodrell and Reynolds kept silent while they glared at Harper.

Harper turned to climb the staircase to his room so he could wash.

"Hey, Harper, you didn't *leave anyone behind* in Iowa did ya?" Goodrell's voice caused Harper to freeze with a foot on the first step. So, there would be trouble…at least, with these two.

Harper faced Goodrell. The room went silent.

Harper let the silence drag a few moments before he crossed to the table and stood opposite Goodrell and Reynolds, still in their seats. Reynolds glanced at Goodrell and back at Harper.

Finally, Harper spoke. "Of course not, Goodrell. I'd never do such a thing unless the situation demanded it." He smiled back with a confident grin which he knew did not hide his aggression. "I did run into two officers from Iowa City, though." Iowa City was the home town for the original Company B, including Goodrell and Reymolds.

After a moment, Reynolds took the bait. "Oh, yeah? What were their names, maybe we know them."

Harper glanced at Reynolds before returning his stare to Goodrell. "I never found out. *They hid in their cabins* the whole trip down from Des Moines to Cairo. No one ever saw them on deck – *where the action was.*"

The blood rose in Goodrell's face. Harper broke eye contact and faced the other officers in the room. "Lord only knows what they are doing in there all day *by themselves.*"

No one laughed. Goodrell stood up but remained in his place. "You bastard."

Harper laughed and turned back to the staircase. While Harper climbed to the second floor, he heard Goodrell's response. "We'll settle this later, Harper." A pause. "Meanwhile, I know how busy ya are. Ya need to get your ass back to tallying the numbers of how many new cases of clap came in today."

The top of the stairs opened into a short hallway which started at the door to the former chapel, above the parlor, then led down the center of the building to the doors of four nun's cells. The house was just large enough to accommodate the junior officers of the battalion, with the first lieutenants sharing each of the four cells, two to a room, and the second lieutenants assigned to the former chapel.

Goodrell's words pursued him until Harper found his billet at the end of the hallway. Guelich's belongings lay scattered over one side of the room, but Harper saw his friend carefully avoided any incursions onto the other side. At least Guelich still seemed to appreciate having Harper in the battalion. It was difficult to know about the others. Since most came from upper-middle class families, they would be skilled at showing one face and believing another. At least, they were professional about it. Certainly, Goodrell and Reynolds could be counted as enemies.

He stripped to the waist before using the nearby pitcher and bowl to wash his face, chest, and hands. He took a moment to look through the room's single window across The Commons below, trying to clear his head of the day's events and organizing his thoughts for the training plan he had yet to finish. Then he pulled his undershirt back on, followed by a clean shirt.

When he returned to the refectory, he sat in silence thinking about the training plan while the other officers talked and finished their meals. But the cover page of a newspaper left lying on the table interrupted his thoughts. *The Statesman* contained several stories about how poorly the Republicans ran the war; in particular, how Governor Kirkwood and his cronies profiteered from the sacrifice of the Iowa volunteers. Not surprising, for the state's Democratic party newspaper.

Harper opened the paper and scanned the headlines. On page two, he found a short article about the battalion. It announced that Wesley Monroe of Cedar Rapids now commanded the battalion at Paducah, relieving Major Porter of temporary command following the departure of the prominent Cedar Rapids banker and Democratic candidate for governor, William Merritt. It seemed odd to Harper that he could not find any reports about the other units from Iowa, even though he had heard an entire brigade was on its way to Grant's army.

When the orderly set a plate of stew in front of him, Harper put the paper aside and tried to steer the conversation toward Monroe. Rumors around the mess held that the new commander was a *somebody* in the Democratic Party in Des Moines. The man did not serve in Mexico, even though, at forty-one, he was the right age to join one of the volunteer units. The officers had learned that Monroe came from New York to Iowa in the late 1850s to work for the former commander of the First Iowa Volunteers.

With dinner finished, Harper returned to the adjutant's office to prepare for his meeting with Monroe the next day.

Wednesday, January 22nd, 1862

The madam of *Lafitte's Hideout* sat at her desk in the office with the ledger open in front of her. She worn a plain gray dress buttoned to the neck with white ruffles at the collar and at the end of the long sleeves. A line of pewter buttons running up the center of the bodice was the only decoration. "Foah, five, six dollahs," Loreena Bosley counted out the coins, "and fifty-five cents."

"Thank you, ma'am." Katie smiled as she folded the bills into her small purse, followed by the coins.

"Y'all are doing *ve'y* well, Katie." Loreena's soft, southern accent drew Katie to the older woman. Loreena folded her hands over the ledger book on the desk. "How're y'all gettin' along with everyone? Are you happy heah?"

Katie couldn't help but notice how the lines of the bones and veins in Loreena's hands showed through her pale skin. Loreena was thinner and paler than any of the people Katie knew. She was not sure how healthy Loreena was, but the boss's wife showed no lack of energy.

"Yes, ma'am. Everyone is so nice and I love dressing up each night to entertain the soldiers." Katie thought for a moment. "I never seen clothes this nice before. Even my ma's Sunday dress weren't so nice as the day dresses we wear here. And she only had the one."

"No one is bein' mean to y'all are they?" Loreena tucked a lock of jet-black hair into the braid along the left side of her head. A matching braid ran along the right side, with the two braids meeting in a bun at the back.

"Sometimes a soldier will say somethin' mean; but when that happens, I just go and sit at another table." Katie couldn't help but stare. She could almost see through the other woman's skin. "I cain't understand why those boys need to say such awful things," Katie continued. "My pa never, ever talked like that to me, even after he took to the bottle and I couldn't keep up with the chores by myself."

"All of the soldia-boys seem to like it when you sit with them." Loreena Bosley stopped talking and looked into Katie's face. "We're not workin' you too hard, are we? You look tired."

"To tell the truth, ma'am, sometimes havin' three soldiers up to my room on a night makes it hard. If I have to take a fourth soldier, I need to go to sleep after that. And the quick ones don't spend much money, either. It's the easiest when I can keep one man for the entire night."

"You mean like on Sunday night with the tall lieutenant?"

"Yes, ma'am. He was so nice." Katie felt her heart twitch at the memory. "He even talked with me afterwards."

Loreena paused to look Katie up and down. "You keep cleaning yourself the way that I showed y'all afta' each time with a man?"

"Yes, ma'am." Actually, Katie did not do that after every time, but she did it at least once a night before she went to sleep, and that seemed good enough.

"Good. We don't want to have any accidents." Loreena Bosley smiled. "Y'all be needin' anythin', sweetie?"

"No, ma'am."

"We'll see if we can't get you more customers for the full night from now on." Loreena fiddled with the pins in the bun of hair at the back of her head while turning to look at the bright, clear weather through the office window. "Enjoy your day off."

Katie smiled at the mistress. "Thank you, ma'am." She gave a quick curtsey with the full skirt of her undecorated sky-blue day dress and stepped into the hallway connecting *Lafitte's Hideout* with *The French Pelican.*

Back in the saloon, she had to pass the bar where Noah Kirchner inventoried the bottles of liquor in the morning light. "Mornin', Katie."

Katie gave the balding man a bright and genuine smile in return. She liked Noah because he always treated her politely, and the shotgun that he kept behind the bar kept the rowdy men in check.

Three men worked in the main part of the saloon, cleaning the tables and chairs, repairing any damage they found.

"Marnin', Baby Red," one of the workers called to her as Katie crossed the room to the stairway. She ignored Virgil McGurn and she hated the nickname that Bosley gave her when she first arrived at *Lafitte's Hideout*. Toby, a negro, and Thomas, a mulatto, looked up from their work to watch her. Katie shivered when McGurn leered at her with a hungry smile, before she hurried up the stairs.

Katie always felt uncomfortable around Virgil. When she first came to Paducah in November, Mister Bosley locked her into The Box, a secret cell dug into the wall of the cellar under his office. He explained that he needed to teach her how to do her new job. The cell had no light; only a dusty bed with no mattress, pillow, or sheets; and a bucket for wastes. Virgil and Mister Bosley were her daily visitors in those days, bringing her food and asking if she was ready to be nice so she could leave. But one time, Virgil had pushed her down onto the bed and pulled her drawers away. Loreena must have heard her shouts because she came into the cell while Virgil was unbuckling his trousers.

"We don't want her forced, you drunken Irish pig." Loreena had hit him in the back with a large stick and chased him away. "When she's ready, we'll give her to William to open her up, not some bastard of an Irishman."

The next day, Katie had agreed to go with William, and the Bosleys let her out of the box. After five days with William, they made her promise to do her new job with the soldiers and not to run away. Loreena Bosley let Katie know she had no place to run anyway, because no one would want her now that she had lost her innocence. She knew they were right, no one would take in a saloon-girl.

The Bosleys gave her a nice room for herself upstairs, but the memory of the dark, dank cell gave her chills every time she saw Virgil McGurn.

"Katie, there you are!" she heard her friend call her when she reached the top of the stairs. Eleanor St. Croix stood smiling from the doorway to her room, next to Katie's. "*'Ave* you been paid yet, *chéri*?"

Eleanor's shoulder-length, walnut-colored hair was uncombed and her hazel eyes still showed signs of sleep, although it was an hour before mid-day.

"Yes." Katie smiled in anticipation of what Eleanor would say next.

"*Bon*. Then let us go shopping this aft-*air* noon!" The lady's slight French accent captivated Katie when it mixed with her deep southern draw. Eleanor's smile illuminated her dark complexion. The older woman was half-a-head shorter than Katie, and her face had a mature, but stunning, attraction even in the morning light. Katie believed Eleanor was the most beautiful woman she had ever seen. "I would love that."

"Wonderful. We'll go aft-*aire* dinn-*aire*."

Katie giggled at Eleanor's French-laced words.

****

"I'll bet they're making a good profit anyway, Mister Harper, aren't they?" Lieutenant Colonel Wesley Monroe did not look up from a newer edition of *The Statesman* than the one Harper had read the night before. Monroe, a distant relative of the former president, sat at the big desk in the administrator's office of St. Mary's School, now the office complex for the First Iowa Mounted Rifles and the several Regular Army companies of cavalry in Grant's army.

Standing in front of Monroe's desk, Harper finished the report on the contracts the Army awarded his father and brother. Porter stood next to Harper. Both waited to be invited to sit in any of the several chairs spread in front of the colonel's desk.

"Damn printer misspelled '*Wesley*'." He folded the newspaper and set it to the side of his desk. "Did you see the article, Porter? We made the newspapers. That'll serve us when we get back home, eh?" Monroe words came out with the speed typical of his native New York.

"Yes, sir." Porter's reply was a noncommittal monotone.

Harper spoke up, a touch of pique in his voice. "They made fair deals with the Quartermaster General in Saint Louis, Colonel. General Halleck's staff seemed satisfied. Plus, my brother Thomas will add thirty telescopic sights to the contract for free." No man would label Harper or his family as war-profiteers.

"Halleck's staff." Monroe huffed. "They would, wouldn't they? What do they care about the cost of these things? They only want to keep the generals happy so they can gain more influence for themselves. Not sure we'll use the telescopic sights. Aren't they too tender to use in the field?"

Monroe appeared of average height and build, although it was difficult to tell while the colonel stayed seated. He wore his uniform jacket opened at the front, revealing a white shirt underneath.

"Not if ya know what you're doin'–Colonel. I'll teach them how." Harper stared at Monroe until the seated man looked away. "It takes some skill, but most of our country boys should be able to do it. They're used to caring for their weapons in the field." Harper waited but saw no reaction to his reference about Monroe's New York City background. Perhaps the reference was too obtuse.

Monroe's most distinguishing feature was prolific sideboards of thick, black hair. Unlike Harper and Porter, who were clean-shaven, Monroe's facial hair extended from in front of the ears, down, across his cheeks and connected to a full moustache, leaving the center of his chin and his neck clear. The side-whiskers extended several inches below his cheeks.

Major Porter gave Harper a cautionary glance before he addressed Monroe. "I agree, Colonel. Having some sharpshooters in the battalion gives us a unique ability. I'm sure General Grant and General Smith could make good use of them. It'll be different than it was during the Mexican War."

Monroe picked up the Orders for the Day. "Umm…"

"The men still don't have anything to fight with when they're mounted." Harper extended his open hands toward Monroe. "I've never tried to kill a man from horseback with a bayonet, Colonel, but I can't imagine it's easy. Pistols would be better for all of the men."

Monroe dropped the orders in front of him. "Listen, Harper, we're supposed to be mounted infantry. *That's* what General Grant wants." Monroe cast an irritated glance at Porter before he continued. "Porter and I have already discussed it. We fight from the firing line, the same as foot infantry. The horses get us there faster than a foot battalion, but we aren't going to do any cavalry fighting, so the men won't need pistols. Nor will they need sabers. The officers will continue to carry their personal swords, *infantry* swords, and pistols, but that's all."

Monroe was wrong. Harper had some idea about what Grant truly wanted from the battalion, having discussed it with the general on the boat returning from the battle at Belmont. "I know, sir, but don't ya think …"

"I've already given you my answer." Monroe picked up the plan for the skirmisher training. "Now, leave it be and tell me about your plans. I understand you will lead the training yourself?"

"Yes, sir." The man didn't understand what the battalion was headed into.

Even now, Monroe did not invite them to sit, although several chairs sat close at hand in front of Monroe's desk or lined the walls of the office.

Harper explained his plans to take the designated skirmishers out to a farm somewhere south of town for the next two weeks. He explained the exercises he intended to run to develop the men in marksmanship, teamwork, maneuver, and how to protect themselves against their counterparts in the Rebel army. He did not divulge his plan to take the hundred men on a long march for the final week of the training when he would teach them what he could about scouting and reconnaissance, reading sign in the field, how to survive without shelter, how to see without being seen; and, if time permitted, teach them how to use the rifles for sharpshooting–the ability to hit selected individual targets at extreme ranges.

"Did you review these plans, Porter?" Monroe asked.

"Yes, sir. I've ordered Sergeant Major Compton to go as Mister Harper's assistant. Each company will provide a corporal to supervise their men."

Monroe remained silent while he looked through the plans.

"Sir, I would like to take Sergeant Featherstone, Company B, with me, as well," Harper asked. "Featherstone was my first sergeant in the old Company K. He knows what I expect from the men."

"Does Captain McKinsey approve?" Monroe asked Porter not Harper.

Harper fought to keep the irritation off his face. Nothing needed thinking about. Monroe should just sign the damned orders. "Yes, sir." In fact, Porter had to order McKinsey to allow Featherstone to participate.

"All right then." Monroe signed the orders. "But Sergeant Major Compton stays here. I have better things for him to do."

Because he neglected to read the orders, Monroe did not appear to notice the paragraph buried in the text which authorized Harper to lead any additional training he thought necessary if time allowed. Porter came up with the scheme to add the paragraph as an attempt to protect Harper in the event he was able to conduct the extra training Porter wanted for the men. Harper's judgment would be needed to decide when the training went beyond the intent of the orders.

"Thank ya, Colonel." Major Porter collected the papers and handed them to Harper. "We'll muster the men after noon meal today. You'll leave before nightfall, Jamie."

"Yes, sir." Harper saluted and turned to leave.

"You didn't ask, Harper, but my son made it back to Des Moines, alive. He's still recovering from his wounds; will be for a long time. He lost the bottom of his left leg, including his foot. "

Harper turned back to face the colonel. It would have been more politic if he had remembered to ask after the Monroe boy, but Harper's mind was too distracted by his own situation in the battalion and the preparations for the training session. "I'm glad to hear he survived, sir. He was a brave man. Ya have my sympathy."

It was the decent thing to say, though Harper knew Monroe was better off than many of the parents of First Iowa men whose sons wouldn't be coming home at all. So many men had already died or been injured for almost no progress. Too many more were destined for that path before the war ended. A person had to harden his personal feelings for each one of them, lest it affect his performance. The Rebs would get what they deserved for causing so much mysery.

"It's nice you feel that way, considering you're the reason he got shot."

"Me, sir?" Harper had expected the topic and braced for whatever Monroe would say.

"You're the one who ordered those men ashore after they were safe aboard the boats at Belmont, aren't you?" Monroe's stare was cold and unwavering.

Harper would not be intimidated by this *politician*. "Yes, sir. We needed to save General Grant before the Rebs cut him off from the landing."

"None of the other officers who were there saw that. I'm not so convinced Grant needed saving. What would he be doing so far in front of his own lines?"

"Grant doesn't fear the enemy, sir. He had gone forward to confirm that the last regiment knew of the retreat. He did, Colonel. You can ask his staff." Harper paused to think. "Captain McKinsey was asleep in his stateroom at the time. All of his officers had gone to their cabins. None were on deck."

"Are you accusing Captain McKinsey of misbehavior?" Monroe's right eyebrow arched. Harper stood motionless, not meeting the colonel's eye. Monroe continued. "What I *do* know is my son got shot because of a joyride you led, and then you wanted to leave him behind to get captured."

"I thought we would be surrounded." Harper locked his eyes on the wall behind Monroe, trying to avoid escalating the argument. "I felt the loss of one man would be better than the loss of all of them." Harper paused, frustration rising. He had rehearsed his next statement and recited it slowly rather than allow his anger to take control at Monroe's lack of understanding. "I did not know he was your son–Colonel." He watched for Monroe's reaction.

Monroe's face flushed but he kept his composure. "But you *weren't* being surrounded, were you? Thank God, that big fellow Magnusson brought him back, in spite of your orders."

"Yes, sir."

Monroe sat back in his chair. The sides of his jacket opened wider, exposing the soft, bulging belly under the white blouse. "Otherwise, Abel might be dead now instead of safe at home with his family." He paused. "You weren't even supposed to go on the expedition, were you, Lieutenant?"

"I suppose not, sir." Harper's gaze returned to the wall behind Monroe. He did not need to justify his actions to this politician who had avoided reporting to his command for three winter months. He watched while a line of ants crawled up the rear wall, the way he had in the court at Yankton whenever lawyers asked him stupid questions about his methods. "I thought someone from the battalion staff should go to act a *liaison* to General Grant's staff."

"Of course you did."

"I concurred with Mister Harper's recommendation, Colonel. I wanted an assessment of how our men performed from someone outside of the two companies involved." Porter's statement caused Harper's chin to notch a bit higher.

Monroe continued to stare at Harper for a few moments. Harper stood in silence. The tension between the men grew in the quite of the room. Harper understood that Monroe waited like a cat, ready to pounce on any excuse he would offer. Harper refused to enter the trap. Meanwhile, the line of ants extended up the wall through a crack in the ceiling and into the attic.

Porter cleared his throat after a few moments.

Monroe eased back into his chair when Harper said nothing. Either he could not think of a response, or chose to put the argument aside for now. "I've promoted Magnusson for bravery. I still haven't decided what to do about you, Mister Harper. For now, we need an adjutant and Major Porter tells me there is no one better in the command. So, you'll stay until I can find someone I find more suitable."

Harper hesitated, about to respond when he saw Major Porter from the corner of his eye surreptitiously shaking his head. "Yes, sir."

"Good day, Lieutenant Harper." Monroe turned to address Porter. "Now, Porter, let's talk about who should command Company C. Have we heard from the mayor at Davenport, yet? Do we know who he wants?"

Harper saluted and left the office. He knew Porter was correct: he would have to struggle just to stay in the Army.

****

After the mid-day dinner, Katie waited at the office door while Eleanor collected her own weekly pay. Katie watched Loreena show Eleanor the accounts book as she had done with Katie. Together, Eleanor and Loreena calculated the total income. Where Katie made two cents for each drink sold and one dollar for each upstairs session, Eleanor's allotment was five cents for the saloon drinks and two dollars for each encounter. Katie guessed that the difference must be due to Eleanor's experience. Katie wondered what she had to do to get as large a share.

"Business has been *ve'y* good, Ellie. We're doin' quite well."

"*Tres Bien*, Lolo. P*aire*haps I can stop working now and become the madam, *non*?" Eleanor winked at Katie. There was a mischievous twinkle in her eyes.

It was an old joke between Loreena and Eleanor. Loreena answered in her sweetest voice, "But Ellie dear, y'all's the *main* reason why the offic-*ah*s come and spend so much money," Loreena said with an over-exaggerated smile. Then harsher, "Besides, we already have a madam – me. That *was* our deal, wasn't it, sweetie?"

"*Mais oui, madam.*" Eleanor executed a mock curtsey with perfect ballroom grace.

Loreena and Eleanor laughed together.

"Here's the money for my share of the food," Eleanor dropped out of her French accent while she counted out seven dollars, one for each day of the past week. When not using French, Eleanor's accent became that of the deep South, similar to Loreena's.

Katie watched and wondered why Eleanor didn't pay any money for debts to the Bosleys. Besides her food, Katie was repaying loans for the money spent to get started in the business. In addition to the one hundred-fifty dollars paid her father, Katie owed the couple for all of the clothes and accessories she needed to look appropriate in the saloon, plus various smaller items she needed or wanted since she began working. Katie owed the Bosleys over three hundred dollars in the beginning. After eight weeks, the debt was reduced to two hundred and ninety-three dollars.

"Ready, *chéri*?" Eleanor asked Katie after she settled accounts with Loreena.

Katie watched while Eleanor counted out a few of the bills and tucked them with the loose change into the lady's purse hanging from her wrist. The remaining bills went into a pocket hidden somewhere in Eleanor's undergarments, accessible through an opening at the top of the pocket in her skirt.

"Cain't keep *all* of the eggs in one basket, can we?" Eleanor said to

Katie.

"Y'all goin' out?" Loreena asked.

"Yes," Eleanor answered. "I intend to show young Katie how to spend some of her hard-earned money."

"Sometimes earnin' the money ain't that hard," Katie said, blushing. "Especially if the soldier stays all night."

"I know, dear." Loreena smiled. "That's the beauty of our profession. Sometimes, you can do what comes naturally."

Eleanor nodded.

Katie wondered if the two older women truly believed having three or four men each night was ever 'natural'–at least for human beings.

"And we're helping with the war by keepin' the soldiers from becomin' lonely." Eleanor winked at Loreena.

"That's important," Loreena said. "And it helps us to understand what's happening in the war." She looked at Eleanor who returned a sly smile.

"That's right," Eleanor said. "The soldiers at the fort know just about everythin' General Grant's army is plannin'." She laughed. "We could start a newspaper with what we learn from pillow-talk."

Loreena gave a laugh as well, but it didn't seem sincere to Katie, and it was followed by a look of caution to Eleanor.

"I'll send Thomas to go with y'all," Loreena continued. "Proper ladies shouldn't go out on the street without an escort."

"Of course. *Merci*, Lolo."

****

Harper returned to work. He must get the morning muster report out to brigade headquarters as well as the battalion's requirements for boat space in the coming campaign. These he must finish before departing on the training assignment. While he climbed the wooden steps leading directly from The Commons to his office, he greeted the two guards standing their post bundled in overcoats with scarves covering their faces.

When he stepped into the former classroom he shared with his assistant, Harper hung his overcoat on one of the pegs in the wall next to the door. He appreciated the respite which the windows provided from the smell of horse dung hanging over the entire stable area. Instead, the office smelled of the smoky creosote from the small pot-bellied stove.

He picked up the morning reports from Corporal Powell's desk. Four-hundred-and-ten men present for duty this morning. Counting twenty still on leave for Christmas, and a further dozen still in the hospital but expected to return in time, that made four-hundred-and-forty-two available to leave when General Grant's order came. Leaving out the bummers from each company who would be scavenging or working with the quartermasters, the battalion would still have at least eighty men per company out of an allowance of one hundred.

There would be enough horseflesh for all of them, thanks to being able to stable the horses during the winter months, with probably five or ten spare horses. The quartermaster would need space for his thirty mules, plus the five battalion wagons. Corporal Powell had completed the tallies and Harper signed the reports.

When Harper handed the battalion returns back to Corporal Powell, he followed the corporal's glance to the corner of the room opposite the coat pegs. There, an elderly gentleman with a mid-length gray beard sat quietly on the only spare chair. The visitor wore an out-dated black suit. A recent cleaning and pressing had failed to hide the wear in the elbows and knees. The man fiddled with a worn, black, broad-rimmed farmer's hat.

Something about the way the man carried himself said *religion* and Harper didn't need a Bible-thumper around right now. He suspected if he asked, at least half of the men of the battalion would show signs of having spent the previous night trying to empty the town of Paducah of all of its liquor. Maybe there was a way to pass him off to the chaplain.

Corporal Powell introduced the visitor. "Lieutenant, this is Mister Magnusson. He is from back home in Salem. He is asking after his son."

"Hello, sir, welcome to Kentucky." Harper gave a slight bow to the seated man. "May I ask the name of your son?" A formality. There was only one man named Magnusson in the battalion, and Harper knew him well enough from the Belmont incident.

The elder Magnusson's voice carried a strong Scandinavian accent.

"I am lookink for Gustav Magnusson, we tought he vould come home last fall but we haff not yet seen him."

"Yes, sir. I understand. Can I ask ya to wait here for just a few moments while I finish with this morning's muster?"

Without waiting for an answer, Harper turned back to Powell.

"Sir, Mr. Magnusson has a letter from the governor." Powell arched his eyebrows to show Harper that this was a matter which demanded his careful attention.

That bothered Harper. Didn't the governor have anything better to do than interfere with the operations of a single battalion? He brought his full attention to the older man. No doubt, Monroe would want this man treated well, even though he was more of a nuisance.

Magnusson gave Harper a purposeful smile while he produced two letters and handed them to Harper. Harper set the letters on his desk without reading them while he warmed his hands over the stove set between his desk and Corporal Powell's. After he sat down, he glanced at the papers. Thankfully, the bottle of red-eye sometimes displayed on his desk had disappeared during Harper's leave, perhaps hidden by Powell in one of the desk drawers, or donated to Powell's messmates.

"How may I help ya, Mr. Magnusson?"

Magnusson moved his chair to face Harper across the desk.

"I haff here a discharge for my Gustaf tat General Fremont und Governor Kirkvood signed." Magnusson pointed to the letters. "Tey tell me in Saint Louis–Colonel Merritt take discharge in August, before the regiment muster out of service."

Magnusson continued in his Scandinavian accent. "Ve haff vaited for Gustaf to come home. Ve see no sign of him. My family and ta congregation, ve haff prayed for his safe return since he leaf in May. But now, many people in Salem, tey say he has been kilt or lost and tat maybe the Army hides tat from us." Magnusson looked straight at Harper, frustration and anger clear on his face.

Harper stared back, unblinking. He knew where Gustav Magnusson was. He saw the corporal earlier this morning when Harper visited Santee. The younger Magnusson had moved away to avoid speaking with Harper. Harper understood the young man's hostility. He had lived through the same feelings when he lost a friend during the war in

Mexico.

The elder Magnusson continued, "Some of the men who come home in August tought he join new regiment in St. Louis. Tey suggest ve contact 'Tenant Colonel Monroe to help search for him." He watched Harper's reactions intently.

Harper guessed that Old Man Magnusson knew how to read people. Harper would need to control his expressions and body movements. Elder Magnusson was in the right place but Harper felt certain Monroe wanted to keep Gustav Magnusson in the Rifles because Monroe thought Magnusson would serve as an example for all of the men. They weren't going to give him up.

Breaking eye contact with Magnusson, Harper addressed his assistant, "Corporal Powell?"

"Yes, sir."

"Do ya recall receiving a discharge order for a Private Gustav Magnusson?"

"Yah, I do, sir." Powell picked up a journal book from his desk and opened it to an earlier page. "We delivered it to him the day after the original First Iowa Volunteers returned from Wilson's Creek." He pointed to the book. "But he wanted to stay for the following week so he could muster out with all of the other ninety-day men. Gustav told me he worried that he would look a coward if he left before his discharge date."

Harper faced Magnusson to watch his reaction to this news.

"My son is no covard! Why say you tis? We are Quakers. We don't believe in varr as solution for problems! Can you not understand tat?"

"Sir, I know your son is not a coward." Harper interrupted Magnusson, trying to calm the older man. If Quakers didn't fight for religious reasons, then Gustav Magnusson was no longer a Quaker. "I saw him fight alongside me and he saved a man's life at Belmont. Corporal Powell was only reporting Gustav's own reaction to the discharge."

Powell continued, "Sir, I know for certain that your son mustered out of the service in Saint Louis on August Twentieth, Eighteen Sixty-One with the rest of the ninty-day men. I can show ya the entry in the unit diary with his signature. And I attended the ceremony myself."

"Do we have any men in the unit named Gustav Magnusson?" Harper already knew the answer. The younger Magnusson had re-enlisted as Gus Manson.

"No sir."

"I am sorry Mr. Magnusson but Gustav Magnusson is not with the battalion."

"Tat is very puzzlink." Magnusson sat back in his chair, the anger in his expression draining to hopelessness. "Now, I am quite confuse." The old man looked around the office, as if he could find his son on one of the shelves or under the stove. His focus returned to Harper. "I don't know vat more I can do to find him." It was a plea for help.

Harper feigned an attempt to comfort the man, but he also needed to get Magnusson out of his office before anything happened to reveal the lie. "Why don't ya go to a hotel in town and have a good lie down for a while? That'll give ya some time to think about what to do next; meanwhile, I can send men to ask among the other Iowa regiments in Paducah."

Harper stood to help the elder Magnusson from his chair.

"Tank you, Lieutenant, for your help. I know you are quite busy preparink to bring The Lord's justice against those tat vould enslave others."

Harper stiffened. Magnusson was an Abolitionist. The Southerners had seceded when no more compromises were possible over abolition. Harper fought to preserve the Union because of the trouble caused by the damned Abolitionists, while the Confederates fought to tear it apart because Abolitionist politics had made compromise impossible. All over a bunch of darkies whose born fate was to be slaves.

Besides, based on Harper's experiences in Mexico, the notion a war could be a just or holy thing could be believed only by those who sat at home and never saw what a round of canister did to a formation of infantry. Harper doubted God, if He existed at all, cared who won. Adoph Magnusson seemed perfectly happy to send other families' men and boys off to fight for his cause, as long as his own people stayed safe at home. Disappointing this old man had now become a pleasure.

"Let me find someone to escort ya into town." He stood and came around his desk to help the old man stand. "Corporal Powell, would ya assign someone from the guard detail to go with Mr. Magnusson?"

Powell raised his eyebrows.

"What is the matter with you?"

"Sorry, sir. A little too much toasting to the Union in the corporal's mess last night."

"Well, if you've recovered, find an escort for Mr. Magnusson."

"Right away, sir. I'll get someone who is off duty." Powell closed the record book in front of him and quickly left the office.

Harper waited while Mister Magnusson buttoned his overcoat and put on his gloves, then stepped into the chill light of the January morning. He saw no sign of Powell. But two guards stood sentry outside of the adjutant's office, still bundled in their winter coats.

"Corporal, accompany this gentleman into town. Take him to Mrs. Heath's." The wives of several of the officers in the battalion could keep Mr. Magnusson company, hopefully until the order came to begin the campaign. Harper would ensure he included Corporal Magnusson's name on the list of designated skirmishers leaving for training that afternoon.

Harper watched, satisfied with his lie, while the elder Magnusson and his escort walked out of camp. Corporal Powell came running up, hauling a disheveled private with him.

"Well, with luck, that's the last we hear about Gustav Magnusson." Harper smiled.

"I doubt it, sir."

Harper gave Powell a quizzical look. "Why do ya say that?"

"That's Corporal Manson with Mr. Magnusson."

"Oh, shit."

****

A half-hour later, Katie and Eleanor stood in the saloon waiting for Thomas. Each wore their day dress from dinner, with a plain cloak thrown over their shoulders, a pearl-gray woolen one for Katie and a fleece-lined buckskin for Eleanor. Woolen scarves covered each of their shoulders under the cloaks.

When Thomas arrived, Eleanor led the way through the rear door into the fenced yard. The afternoon sun bathed their cloaks in warmth, but the late-January cold bit their cheeks and noses. Katie followed Eleanor's example when she raised the scarf from her shoulders, across the crown of her bonnet, and tied it under her chin.

Katie's flaming red hair hung down her back and fluttered in the slight breeze. Eleanor contained her long hair with a bonnet in a style more appropriate to a woman of her age. After they stepped through the side gate of the yard onto Court Street, they merged into the crowd of townswomen who were making their way between the marketplace and the riverboat landing.

They walked on the newly-laid gravel in the street with Thomas remaining two paces behind, playing the role of both servant and protector. They went one block toward the waterfront, crossing Main Street to stand on the bluff above the landing. Below them, three riverboats docked at the town wharf while others sat beached with their bows on the mud bank and tied side-by-side. Crews on all the boats displayed goods from up-and-down the river on their foredecks and the adjacent landing. Front Street, along the waterfront, was a midway made of duck boards. Some vendors from the city sold local items from canvas booths across the way from the riverboats.

Katie stopped at the top of the causeway and asked, "What river is this?"

"This one is the Ohi-ah." Eleanor pointed to the river flowing below the bluffs. "That one is the beginnin' of the Tennessee." She pointed to the right where the rivers came together with one branch curving from the east and another flowing up from the south.

"Ain't it funny how they name the rivers after the states?" Katie said. "Even when they ain't nowhere near those states."

"I think it works the oth*aire* way 'round, chéri." Eleanor slipped into her French accent, reserved for when she was in public. "First they name the riv-*aire*, then they name the state, aft-*aire* people have settled the land nearby."

"Still, it's strange that they use the same name. Ain't there enough names to go 'round?"

Eleanor laughed softly. "I think that maybe you might be too logical to be one of the politicians who decide these things, Katie." Eleanor stood back, watching while Katie traced the flow of the Ohio

River to where it disappeared around a headland to the east.

"I think Shawneetown and Cypressville are that way." Eleanor pointed to the eastern horizon. Katie frowned. "Although, why you would ev-*aire* want to go back, *chéri*, I cannot understand. Didn't you tell me that you lived on a *porc* farm–where they raise pigs?"

Katie *had* been thinking about her hometown and wondering what her father was doing at that moment. Was he tending to Mama's grave? What did he do with the money that he got from Mister Bosley? Would the farm be in terrible condition now that he was alone? Katie felt her throat tighten at her thoughts of home. A bitter taste at the back of her throat swelled into seminal tears. "We raised some corn too, least while Mama was still alive." Defiance tinged her words.

"Let's go see what the boatmen have brought us today," Eleanor said as she took Katie's arm and pointed her toward the causeway, away from thoughts of Shawneetown and Cyressville.

Katie was grateful to have Eleanor as her friend. They were like big and little sisters. Eleanor always knew the right thing to do and to say. It was Eleanor, along with Loreena, who taught Katie how to treat the soldiers when they came to her room and how to enjoy what they did there. Eleanor was right; life was better here in the city than it ever was on the farm, even if she was a saloon-girl. And she was old enough to leave home, anyway.

"Are you from nearby, Eleanor?" Katie asked as they descended the causeway.

"No, *chéri*. I was working in Memphis when the war started. Before that, I was in boarding school in New Orleans. My people are called French Creole. Have you ev-*aire* heard of them?"

"No."

"They came from France over seventy years ago and settled in Louisiana. We were Frenchmen until Napoleon sold our land to the *les Americains*."

"Why'd you leave home?"

"Loreena and I ran away from the boarding school. We found jobs on a paddle-wheel riverboat that was going north. That was in forty-nine. We thought we could go all the way to California and find gold. Loreena's *frère* came with us. He was sweet *pour moi* back then. 'Is name is *Alexandre*."

Once down the causeway, they stepped into the crowds at the riverside market. Bundled in their winter cloaks and scarfs, only a few of the townspeople appeared to recognize the pair, in spite of Katie's very noticable hair and Thomas's looming presence. A few of the men smiled and tipped their hats as they walked past. Other men who recognized them turned away.

"Memphis is where the *capitaine* threw us off of the boat. One of the passengers accused Loreena of stealing jewelry." She smiled back at one of her regular customers who nodded in passing. "When our money ran out, Loreena and I were taken in by one of the madams. *Alexandre* found work on the railroad and moved to Clarksville. He's married. I think he is in the army by now."

They stepped aboard a number of the riverboats, looking at jewelry and other luxury goods, but they did not see anything they liked. Each time Katie saw a brooch or a set of earrings that interested her, Eleanor shook her head, as if to say 'Don't waste your money on that.'

"But you came here from Memphis?"

Eleanor picked up her story as they walked between riverboats. "Loreena and I were not simple saloon-girls. We worked in a high-class house where the men had to make reservations ahead of time. Often, they would pay us just to be a companion for visiting businessmen or to attend important parties. We made much more money doing that than the girls workin' every night in the saloons. We were *courtesans*."

They left the last of the riverboats, still not having bought anything.

Katie asked, "I hear Memphis is a bunch bigger than Paducah. Why'd you leave there?"

"Well, Loreena *marier* four years ago and came to Paducah to be with her husband. I missed her. When the Yankees came to Paducah last fall, Loreena and Franklin came for a visit and asked if I would lend them money. They needed to buy a large building for a saloon so they could entertain the soldiers and add a restaurant separate from the saloon." Eleanor acknowledged a large well-dressed woman with a broad smile, along with the woman's entourage of hovering ladies and servants. The *grande dame* turned her head until she passed Eleanor and Katie, acting as if a horrible smell filled the air. Eleanor laughed.

"Who was that?" Katie whispered. "She didn't seem to like you very much."

"*That* is one of the richest women in Paducah, *chéri*. She and her husband own a *'otel* on Madison Street, the 'good' side of town. Plus, they own a large farm south of town. It's more of a plantation."

"Why's she so mean?"

"Her husband is one of my regul-*aire* and best customers, and she knows it." Both women laughed.

"I guess there are some things that proper women cain't manage." Katie took hold of Eleanor's elbow. "I know you're close to Loreena. I seen her come to your room at night when Mister Bosley is not in town."

"We shared a room when we were in school," Eleanor explained. "It gives us a chance to act again like *juenes filles*. Loreena added the second 'e' to her name so that our names would be anagrams of each oth-*aire*."

Katie guessed that an anagram must be something special you did in a boarding school.

"Afternoon, Miss Katie." A young soldier tipped his kepi with a smile.

"Good afternoon, Jacob," Katie answered with a friendly smile.

The soldier turned to walk alongside the two women until Thomas took him by the shoulder and pushed him away. The soldier was about to object, but since Thomas towered over him by a full head and was four inches wider at the shoulders, the soldier just stopped, smiling hopefully at Katie.

"You come see me soon, all right, Jacob?" Katie said.

"I sure will, ma'am." Jacob continued on his original course, but standing a bit prouder. Katie and Eleanor continued to make their way toward the causeway with Thomas following.

"Nicely, done *chéri*. Don't become too friendly with the custom-*aires* but give them just enough to keep coming back."

Katie was surprised. Her smile for the young soldier was genuine. If Thomas hadn't been here, she would have enjoyed the soldier's company. After a few minutes of trying to understand what Eleanor meant, Katie picked up the thread of their previous conversation. "So did you lend them the money to git started?"

"Bett-*aire*, I told them I wanted to be *associee* – a part-*naire* – and they agreed. Things have been working very nicely since then."

Katie thought about how Eleanor was a partner in the business, not just a worker. She had heard the girls in the saloon talk about it before, but never understood what they meant until now. "So is that why your share of the money is larger than mine?"

"Partly," Eleanor answered. "I'm paid for working, just like you are, but I take a fifth part of the profits from the business, too.

"Also, Katie, have you noticed that I can choose my custom-*aires*?"

"I noticed you always seem to be with the officers." Katie asked, "Is that part of being a *quart-of-sand*?"

"*Courtesan, chéri*. It's French." They stopped at a booth belonging to the town gunsmith. The booth attendant, a boy about Katie's age, rose from his stool at the back of the booth while Eleanor studied the two pocket-pistols on display. Katie stood beside Eleanor, watching while the older woman frowned at the weapons.

"I'm sorry, ma'am," the attendant said. "We jes' cain't git good civilian firearms since the war started. I don't think the manufacturers make them anymore.

"Umm..." Eleanor shifted to her most coquettish French, "*Alors. Merci, mon brave...Lancelot, oui?*"

"Yes, ma'am, I'm Lancelot...maybe I can send y'all a message later if we git any better ones."

"*Ah, bon, Lancelot. Merci.*" Eleanor flashed a seductive smile at the young man, causing him to blush. Katie also smiled at him as they turned to go, leaving Lancelot standing there red-faced and grinning stupidly, with words caught in his throat. Katie giggled.

Eleanor picked up their conversation. "Being with the rich custom-*aires* needs social skills that most of you girls would need to learn. You must be more of a *confidante* and a companion; you don't simply jump into bed for a quick *bumpetty-bump*. That's how you make them spend more money, and sometimes they buy things for you–special things." They were at the end of the midway. "The men like to talk about things they are not able to discuss in their regul-*aire* life. You need to be able to listen and to carry on the conversation, even if you don't like what they are talking about or don't understand it. If you can learn to read well, or play a musical instrument, you might be able to be a *courtesan*. I'd be pleased to teach you."

Katie considered that prospect. Maybe she *could* become like Eleanor.

"Are you 'appy with us, Katie?"

"Oh, yes." She thought a moment. "I was scared when Mister Bosley first brung me here. But after I learned how to git out from The Box, things got better. The house sure is a lot nicer than the farm I grew up on." Katie went on, "Besides, I have girl friends like I never had in Cypressville. The ladies are so nice, and I suppose it ain't like bein' a real whore." It was a word Katie had learned only since coming to Paducah.

"Why do you say that, *chéri*?"

"Well, we have a real home at Mister Bosley's, with our own rooms and all. And we are helping Mister Lincoln win the war, ain't we?"

"I suppose that's one way to look at it." Eleanor chuckled. "Mostly, it's really the only way for women like us to have enough money to live properly."

"What do you mean when you say 'women like us'?"

"I mean, women who cannot count on their families to keep them."

Katie nodded, looking at the duckboards while she thought about what Eleanor said. Her own family fell apart. Mama died and Papa sent her away. She wondered if Papa ever regretted selling her to Mister Bosley.

She forced herself to think about nicer things. "I had an officer last week!" she blurted out loud enough to attract the attention of the people nearby. "A lieutenant. He stayed all night."

Those women who heard Katie turned and moved to avoid the pair. Some of the men shook their heads, while a few others snickered. Katie heard 'Baby Red' being whispered somewhere in the nearby crowd.

Eleanor blushed then regained her composure. With a broad smile toward the bystanders and speaking loud enough to be heard by all, she said, "Come along, Catherine, let us to home. Lieutenant Jones's visit ends today, and there is nothing here that a prop-*aire* lady would *want* to wear."

She took Katie's arm and quickly climbed the causeway, heads down so their bonnets hid their faces.

"What'd I say?" Katie whispered.

"The good people of this town, especially the womenfolk, don't want to be reminded there are women living well while working in our profession, *chéri*. They tolerate it because of the money the Bosleys spend and the bribes, but we cannot be too forward outside of the saloon."

Smiling men tipped their hats as the ladies passed.

Saturday, February 1st, 1862

"Battalion ready for inspection, sir." Major Porter barked loud enough that the report could be heard by all four hundred and thirty-seven men of the battalion on parade in a farmer's pasture.

"Very well," Lieutenant Colonel Monroe replied.

From his position in the second rank of Company B, Corporal Magnusson found if he shifted slightly he could see past the men and horses of his company's first rank and commanders to watch the battalion commander and his staff as they moved about.

Magnusson watched Monroe hand the reins of his horse to an orderly and step forward to where the big-wig general waited. With the general, there were a colonel who was supposed to be the senior man from Iowa in Grant's army, the general's aide, and a major whom no one recognized.

"First Iowa Mounted Rifles, ready for inspection." Monroe saluted the one-star general.

One week earlier, the First Iowa Mounted Rifles moved out of the town and set up a tent camp on a farm five miles southwest from Paducah. Now, at the start of February, the entire battalion trained to operate under field conditions while it formed a part of the intelligence screen behind which General Grant built his force.

The battalion's principal staff officers, Major Porter, Lieutenant Harper, and Lieutenant Guelich, stood in a triangle in front of the first row of troops. Harper was the son-of-a-bitch who was going to leave Billy Monroe to the Rebels back in November, Magnusson thought. God help us if he ever he gets to command.

Magnusson chuckled at how easily he had come to use swear words since joining the Army. Not the language that he would be using if he followed his father's wishes and became a recorded minister in the Meeting at Salem, Iowa.

A bright morning sun lit the parade ground, warming the dark blue jackets of the battalion in spite of the slight breeze blowing along the line of companies. The national flag displayed its bright colors in contrast to the dark-blue field of the of the battalion's flag.

The battalion arrayed in two double rows of companies: Companies A, B, and C in front and Companies D and E in the second row. Each man led his assigned horse. The enlisted men of the various staff sections, with their own horses, the pack mules, and the battalion wagons formed behind Company C, led by the quartermaster sergeant.

The wives of the battalion, those who had made the trip from Iowa and "wives-of-convenience" from the local area, watched the proceedings from the rows of tents which marked the battalion's bivouac, along with assorted negroes who had attached themselves to the battalion. These were persons who exchanged personal labor and services for protection, food and shelter.

Magnusson checked himself again. Like all of the enlisted men, he held his Sharps rifle at the "Order Arms" position, rifle butt on the ground, barrel aligned with the seam of his trousers, and his right hand holding the weapon at the stacking swivel. In his left hand, he held the reins to his horse, elbow bent with his hand close to the bridle, encouraging the horse to hold its head high.

He looked down the line of his men. "Hand higher, Cooke." He wanted the posture of his men perfectly aligned to each other so someone looking from the side might see only a single person and that meant that Private Cooke needed to lock his elbow at a square angle and not allow his hand to droop. Ben Bailey, Magnusson's skirmishing partner at the far left end of the line, had it right.

"Yes, Corporal," came the reply.

Magnusson knew the rumor that Colonel Monroe called this inspection so he could show off the unit to the new division commander, General Charles Smith. Magnusson and all of the trained skirmishers had returned the previous night from living rough out in the open. After ten days outdoors, he'd be lucky if none of his men came down with anything. But, now they were part of a division, and General Smith was the division commander.

General Smith replied, "Very well," and returned the salute. "Carry on."

Magnusson wondered how many men were in a division if there were eighty men in a company. He watched Monroe escort Smith to the first rank of soldiers in Company A on his right. He took the opportunity to check his own men a final time.

As the fourth corporal in the company, Magnusson stood alongside the third corporal in the center of the back row of the company. In combat, he would be expected to pull the dead and wounded men out of the firing line and push the remaining men toward the center to fill the gaps. The corporals also kept those who lost their nerve from running away. So, in the ceremonial formation he and the third corporal stood near the center of the second rank while the first and second corporals anchored the ends.

When the inspection party reached Company B, Magnusson watched closely from the rear rank letting only his eyes leave the straight-ahead pose of the rest of his head and body. The general stopped briefly in front of each man in the front rank, looking at them from head-to-toe with the seasoned eye one might expect of the former commandant-of-cadets at West Point. He took in each soldier's vital equipment quickly: first a look into each soldier's eyes, then a quick scan of his hat, moving quickly to the operating mechanism of their rifle, then an examination of the horse tack and furniture, finally, a look at the eyes and legs of each horse.

Magnusson noted that Smith spent more time inspecting men in the second rank than the first, as if he knew the trick of putting the best-looking men in the front rank. His men were ready, though.

When Smith came to Magnusson, he followed the routine of the inspection. "You're a tall fellow, aren't you, Corporal?"

"I guess so, sir." Magnusson held his eyes straight forward, the way the Regulars did. He was a whole hand taller than the general.

Smith looked at Magnusson's eyes and hair. "Swede?"

"No, sir, Iowan—and proud of it." Magnusson locked his eyes

straight ahead on the battalion's blue flag with the territorial eagle flying in the center.

The remark caused General Smith and Captain McKinsey, standing next to Smith, to chuckle. Monroe, standing next to McKinsey, looked annoyed.

"My grandfather came over from Sweden, but I was born and raised in Salem, Iowa, sir."

Magnusson took the opportunity to examine General Smith without moving his eyes from their locked position. Under the wide-brimmed Hardee-style hat, Smith wore a neat moustache reaching to his jawbones on either side, but no beard. He wore the standard uniform with a long dark-blue coat and gold buttons, opened at the top. Oddly, though, General Smith wore his collar high, in the old-fashioned way, with a thin tie around his neck. Magnusson wondered if the general actually wore the tie into battle.

"Magnusson earned those stripes because of his bravery during the battle at Belmont," Monroe said.

"Well, good for you, Corporal. This division needs men like you."

"Thank you, sir."

Smith moved to the next soldier in line, which placed Captain McKinsey in front of Magnusson. McKinsey stood shorter than General Smith, the crown of his hat even with Magnusson's chin. Gray hair punctuated McKinsey's full, close-cropped beard.

The general moved to the next soldier in line, bringing Monroe in front of Magnusson. The battalion commander smiled at Magnusson, then directed his attention to Smith's remarks about Private Cooke. Smith continued down the line in the same manner. When he reached the end of the rank, Magnusson could hear Smith compliment McKinsey on the appearance of the company and on the ability of the sergeants and corporals to have the men prepared.

General Smith was savvy enough to know who did the real work in the army. It hadn't been easy. They had just spent most of the past week sleeping on the ground, while the bastard Harper led them all over this part of Kentucky trying to teach the boys to scout. After he nearly got everyone killed, it didn't make much sense to Magnusson that Harper would be teaching them how to scout out the Rebs.

Skirmishing was supposed to be about running out between the front lines and taking pot-shots at any officers they could see, not going spying all over the countryside by themselves.

A gust of wind blew down the ranks and Magnusson filled his lungs with clean, fresh air. At least everything didn't smell like horse-shit out here.

Magnusson heard, more than saw, General Smith repeat the inspection for each of the other companies. He allowed his mind to wander.

They had ridden all the way to the Mississippi and back, only to return in time to learn about this inspection. Fortunately, Mrs. Featherstone organized the ladies to help do the washing and mending. The horses looked good, as if they actually enjoyed the chance to run. Magnusson wondered who had the smart idea to use tamed mustangs instead of the regular army stock. He imagined himself as a wild horse and decided he'd be happy, too, finally getting to run after spending all winter in a stable.

Of all of Magnusson's men, Ben Bailey seemed to take to scouting better than most. Ben would make a good scout because he was so short and skinny. He could sneak up on anyone.

In a way, Magnusson felt as good as he imagined the horses felt. Colonel Monroe and Major Porter convinced his pa to let him stay in the army after Harper led the old man straight to him. How stupid could the man be?

But now, he could use his real name. And he actually enjoyed being outdoors again instead of stuck in the winter barracks with men going sick every day. Now, it looked like they'd soon be on their way to fight the Rebels. Not a minute too soon. He knew what the congregation back home would think of that, but he didn't care. He was in the Army, and that meant he was here to fight.

Smith's inspection of the staff sections passed more quickly than that of the companies. When finished, the general directed Monroe to have the men gather around in a large circle for news of the upcoming campaign.

The general stood tall and straight on a pair of hardtack ration crates so he could see and be seen by every man in the battalion. "Men of the First Iowa." His voice carried across the crowd of six hundred or so people, soldiers and wives, gathered around the make-shift podium.

"Shortly, we will be marching on the Confederate forts upriver." He paused and looked across the circle of officers and men around him. "Our goal is to take those forts and then continue on to Nashville. We will open up the Cumberland River with our gunboats, and that'll force the Rebels out of Kentucky!"

Magnusson and the other men of the battalion cheered.

"Capturing Nashville will also give us a good staging area for driving deeper into central Tennessee and beyond into Mississippi and Alabama. And, it provides a place for those Tennesseans who remain loyal to the government to join us."

Magnusson wondered what the hell a *staging area* was.

"You men form part of the cadre of veterans in this army and I am looking forward to having you in my command. I am going to assign you to Colonel Lauman's brigade so you can fight alongside other Iowans.

"I know you have trained hard out here in the cold for the past few weeks. And I know that being a mounted infantry force, you give me a tool unique in the army. I am still considering how best to employ that special capability."

Magnusson's thoughts ran through the training of the past ten days under Harper. He tried to picture the general riding alongside them to learn how to use the battalion.

"But, rest assured. You will have plenty of opportunity to get at the Rebs! I want you to whip the hell out of those boys if that's what it takes to show them the error of their ways!" Smith's voice had been rising during his speech and now became a shout.

Magnusson heard the general use a swear word and his attention returned to the speech. Officers, especially generals, weren't supposed to swear.

"Those traitorous bastards won't stand for a fair fight. They're just as likely to try to slink away once our army gets moving, so we are going to be moving fast. We can corral them all and get this war over with."

The Rebs in Missouri hadn't slunk away. Magnusson remembered that battle. They had been nearly sick with hatred.

"Also, know this…" Smith paused, waiting until the men gave him their full attention. "Your actions in this campaign will play a significant role in shortening the war and restoring the Union." He stopped to look across the crowd. "So, let's have three cheers for the First Iowa Mounted Rifles!"

The soldiers and their wives responded, "Hip, hip, hurrah! Hip, hip, hurrah! Hip, hip, hurrah!"

"And three cheers for General Ulysses S. Grant!"

"Hip, hip, hurrah!"

"And lastly, for the sacred Union! May God always protect her!"

"Hip, hip, hurrah!" Many of the Kentuckian wives-of-convenience stayed silent for these cheers, especially the last. Magnusson suspected they might have relatives in the Secessionist armies.

The general climbed down from the hardtack boxes and walked among the soldiers for another fifteen minutes, meeting those he could and answering their questions. Promptly at eleven-thirty, the general's aide brought his horse from behind the command tent and the general mounted. When he was ready, he faced the men as he sat on the horse.

"Take your last looks at Kentucky, boys. We are on our way to Tennessee!"

The crowd gave one final cheer as the general turned and rode away toward Paducah. Colonel Lauman and the unknown major stayed behind.

Monroe mounted the hardtack boxes. "Company commanders, have your men stand-down for the rest of the day, except those men on duty." He waited while the five company commanders acknowledged the order. "Keep your men in camp. No Saturday leave is authorized."

While the company officers passed the orders throughout their companies, Monroe led the two visitors into his personal tent and invited Porter and Harper to join the group.

****

"Well, Colonel, what did you think of our boys? They look ready to go, don't they?" Lieutenant Colonel Monroe ushered Colonel Lauman into the commander's tent.

Harper held the tent flap open for Porter and for the major from Smith's staff so he could get a better look at the major.

"They look fine, Monroe. Thank you for inviting me to the inspection."

Chairs and stools surrounded Monroe's work table in the front room of the tent. Monroe offered the chair behind the work table to Lauman while he took the other full chair and left the stools to Porter, Harper, and the unidentified major.

Behind Lauman, a canvas screen carried along a rope, separating the tent into two rooms. It stretched tightly between the side walls of the tent and tied shut at both ends. The rear room of the tent was Monroe's personal area and off-limits to everyone except the commander's orderly.

"This is Major Rawlins." Lauman used his open hand to introduce the stranger. "He is a personal aide to General Grant and he's accompanying me to try to learn something about how to use mounted infantry in a battle."

Rawlins stood and shook hands with the three officers of the First Iowa. Harper saw how Rawlins carried himself upright and shook hands as if he was attending a formal ball. His hair was neatly combed back from his forehead and he was clean-shaven. Although he appeared to be the same age as Harper, Rawlins's face was smooth and pale, showing none of the effects of a life outdoors.

"Please, tell the general how pleased we are to be under his command," Monroe told Rawlins. "We're all looking forward to testing the idea of mounted infantry, the way the general wants."

How would he know what General Grant expected from mounted infantry? Maybe he had met with Grant while Harper was out training the skirmishers. Last night, Porter told him that Monroe did not join the encampment until two days before the inspection, thus missing the worst of the weather.

"Major Rawlins will be here a while longer, so if you have any ideas for him, you can discuss those afterward." Lauman paused, looking to see that he had the attention of the other officers before he spoke next. "First Iowa is assigned to my brigade for this campaign."

Monroe nodded. Harper had wondered how mounted infantry might fit into a brigade of foot infantry ever since General Smith made the announcement.

Lauman looked slowly at each officer before he revealed the message which caused him to visit the First Iowa. In a soft voice, he said, "The campaign begins tomorrow, Sunday."

Here's a surprise.

Harper, like most of the officers and men, suspected they would march in February, but believed Grant would wait until late in the month when the weather warmed and the roads might be drier. If they hit the Rebs this early in the season, they might catch them before the Rebs finished digging in, but they would have to rely on the rivers for supplies. A good plan – if it worked.

There was a knock on the post holding up the door of the tent. The five company commanders filed in, all of them still in their parade uniforms. With no more seats available, they lined the side walls of the tent, and Harper surrendered his stool to Captain Brice McKinsey, the oldest of the battalion's captains.

"Grant's plan is to move McClernand's First Division by riverboat from Cairo, up the Tennessee to go against Fort Henry. But, he only has enough boats to carry one division at a time, so after they unload McClernand, the boats will come back down-river to load the Second Division in Paducah." Lauman paused, appearing to collect his thoughts. "The problem is, there is not enough room on the transports to carry this battalion if we take your horses."

Harper felt the last words hang in the air. Without their horses, all of their special training was a waste. There was silence in the tent while the officers stared at Lauman until a scuffling noise outside the tent indicated someone had run away. The news would be all over the camp in a few minutes.

"So, Colonel, are you saying we have to leave our horses behind and become regular foot soldiers?" Monroe turned to Porter looking for support.

"Would it be a problem if we stayed in Paducah, and followed along in the next available transport to go up-river?" Porter asked.

"We could do that, but you would get separated from the brigade and there's no telling how long it would take for the next transport to be available." Lauman looked at the company officers. "You might end up becoming train guards instead, or reassigned to the local garrison."

The officers lining the walls of the tent shuffled their feet and grumbled to each other. Harper heard some of their mutterings: "Train guards?" "All of this work with the horses to become a garrison?"

"What if we marched overland with the horses and met the army at the landing point?" Captain McKinsey asked Lauman. "It isn't very far upriver, is it?"

Rawlins shook his head. "You'd be cut off from supplies. The roads are too muddy still to allow wagon traffic."

Harper tried to come up with other alternatives. He wondered how far it was to Fort Henry and if an overland march was possible without the wagons. Using only horses and mules, they might arrive at the same time as the rest of the division.

"Mister Rawlins may have a solution, if your men are ready to march." Lauman faced Rawlins.

Everyone turned to the major.

"Well," Rawlins began. "It turns out that the Rebs have begun a new fort across the river from Fort Henry, on the Kentucky side. They're calling it Fort Heiman. Now, the land on the Kentucky side of the river is higher than on the Tennessee side, so if we attack Henry without first controlling Heiman, we would have trouble from Rebs firing across the river and down into our flank." Rawlins used his hands to show the effect of firing from higher to lower ground. "We need to take both forts if we want to open up the river."

The company officers nodded in understanding. Monroe, Porter, and Harper watched Rawlins's expressions closely, waiting for him to get to the battalion's assignment.

"Since we don't have enough riverboats, anyway, we're going to send mounted troops overland to attack Fort Heiman from the landward side." Rawlins continued. "If we move quickly, we can take it before the Rebs finish building it."

"How do you plan to do that, if there aren't enough riverboats?" Monroe asked.

Harper already knew the answer.

"General Grant wants to keep the Regular Army cavalry companies with McClernand, so that leaves about a thousand Illinois cavalry for the expedition. Last night, we decided to add your battalion, so they have some infantry support when they attack the fort. Your mustangs should allow you to keep up with the cavalry on the muddy roads."

There it is. Exactly the right assignment for the battalion.

Porter and Harper smiled at each other. Monroe sat silent, thinking. The company commanders voiced their approval.

"Good."

"Damn right."

"Yah, finally."

"When do we need to be ready, Major?" Monroe asked.

Harper pulled a notepad from his jacket and began writing.

"You'll report to Colonel Dickey of the Fourth Illinois. We need the force in place at Heiman by Thursday, the sixth of February. It's sixty miles from Paducah, so because of the condition of the roads, Colonel Dickey plans to leave tomorrow, Sunday. He'll meet you south of town at eight o'clock, where the Plank Road crosses over Island Creek."

Harper could not write fast enough. He looked up at Rawlins, about to ask him to repeat the instructions.

"Where the Plank Road crosses Island Creek, eight o'clock." Rawlins repeated. Harper gave a nod of appreciation when he caught up.

"What do we think the Rebs will do when we attack their forts?" Monroe looked concerned.

"It depends on how far along Fort Heiman is." Rawlins glanced at Monroe. "We don't think they'll have time to move any cannon into Heiman if we move now."

"Let them bring the cannons," Captain George Streeper said. Streeper commanded Company E and, at twenty-six, was the youngest of the company commanders. "More for us to capture." Streeper looked to the man next to him, Lieutenant Pierson. In response, Pierson elbowed Streeper in the ribs.

"Maybe we'll let Company E lead the frontal assault against emplaced cannons." Porter cast a skeptical glance at the captain. "Ya wouldn't want to miss the chance for *posthumous* glory, would ya

George?"

Streeper started to agree to lead the charge, but the word 'posthumous' must have sunk in. "No, sir." He lowered his gaze to the ground.

Maybe a frontal assault wouldn't be needed. Harper could conceive how an attack would succeed if it was led by a thick line of skirmishers–if they were well led. Led by himself.

"Once we control Heiman, Henry can't be defended because then we'll be the ones firin' down into Henry from the Kentucky side." Again, Rawlins demonstrated the difference in elevation with his hands.

"What about a field army?" Porter asked. "Do ya know if we'll run into any Rebs during the march to Heiman."

Lauman drew three imaginary lines parallel on the top of the desk. Harper recognized them as the three rivers in west Kentucky.

"As far as we know, all of the Rebs in this area are tied up in their forts, not only here along the Tennessee and the Cumberland," he pointed to the two imaginary lines to his right, "but they have quite a few posts along the Mississippi." He opened his hand as if to push all of the imaginary Confederates in western Kentucky up to the line representing the Mississippi. "The only mobile troops we know of are farther east, in central Kentucky." Lauman looked at Monroe. "So the issue is: can you be ready to march by tomorrow morning?"

Porter sat up straight on the stool. "Of course we can, eh."

"We'll do the best we can by that time," Monroe corrected. Ever the politician.

Harper knew the battalion could be ready by tomorrow – if the battalion's leaders did their job. He did the math in his head of exactly what the battalion needed to do to arrive at the rendezvous point in twenty hours. *Four days to move sixty miles on horseback, so issue six day's rations. The mustangs should be able to make that pace, even if there's mud. Use the mules to carry fodder, so we don't have to stop for grazing. We should be able to get there in good time, unless we run into the Rebs. The men can carry their own extra ammo in their saddle bags. Let the wives follow later with the quartermaster's wagons.* Harper nodded to Porter, letting the major know he had the details under control.

"I thought that would be your answer." Lauman sat back in the chair and smiled. After a moment, he stood to indicate the session was over. The other men stood, as well. "Major Rawlins, thank you for making the trip down here. Is there anything else you'd like to see?"

"Yes, Colonel. If you don't mind, I'd like to take a look around the camp for a while."

"I think Lieutenant Harper would be happy to show you around," Porter replied. "Jamie?"

"Actually, Major," Lauman interrupted. "There are some additional matters I need to discuss with you and Colonel Monroe and particularly with Lieutenant James Harper. Perhaps there is another officer who can accompany Major Rawlins?"

What's this about?

****

Magnusson made his way to the shelter he shared with Corporal Crawford ever since his promotion. The tent was one of a cluster centered by the tent Sergeant Featherstone shared with his wife. Sarah Featherstone liked having "her boys" around her, and provided some of the best cooking and housekeeping to be found in the camp. Negro women helped her tend to almost three dozen enlisted men of all ranks. But none of the wives-of-convenience camped near Sarah Featherstone. "I won't have them," was one of her favorite sayings. Sarah also served as the wives' representative to the commanding officer, working closely with Porter and Harper on matters affecting camp life.

"When d'ya think we'll be leavin', Gus?" Ben Bailey came alongside Magnusson. Bailey was nearly a foot shorter than Magnusson. He and Magnusson became friends in the old regiment after they learned they shared Salem as their hometown.

"Who knows? One officer says 'Get ready' but we don't move for days. Another one says 'We ain't goin' anywhere', and an hour later we get orders to march in thirty minutes. It's hard to know who ya can believe."

Bailey and Magnusson were a skirmish team, paired off during the training of the prior weeks. They worked well together.

"But this time they ain't letting no one have leave."

"Don't matter to me. I'm tired from all of the ridin' we done for the past two weeks." Magnusson stopped and looked at the men following him, mostly the Company B skirmishers under his command.

"No leave. Ya hear that?" Magnusson looked around to make sure his men paid attention. "Tend to your horses and get your gear cleaned. Get some rest. It looks like we might be gettin' ready to move."

"But, Corporal," Private John Cooke said, "I promised the ladies at *Lafitte's* that I'd be back as soon as the training was over."

"That's your problem, Cooke. But, I don't think the *ladies* will miss ya for one day." Magnusson and Bailey had never been to *Lafitte's Hideout* and only had a vague notion of what went on there from the stories that the men told. Neither was married, and both had yet to lose their innocence with respect to women. "If you have that much energy, then I'm sure Missus Featherstone could find some work for you helpin' the darkies."

Bailey and some of the others nearby chuckled. Cooke's appetite for the ladies at *Lafitte's* was becoming a legend in the battalion.

Cooke pouted for a moment. "I'll find something to keep busy."

"Good, just don't leave the camp or you'll be peeling potatoes until Independence Day." Magnusson looked to Cooke's skirmish partner. "You too, Davis, if either one of ya gets caught where you shouldn't be."

Private Joseph Davis, at six-feet-four inches as tall as Magnusson and built just as heavily, laughed. "Don't worry, Corporal. I'm too tired to be much use to those gals."

Magnusson scanned his men. "I'm going to sleep all afternoon. If anyone has a problem, keep it to yourselves until tonight." He turned to Bailey. "Ben, I'll see ya at supper."

"Okay, Gus."

****

Harper looked at the colonel. Lauman's face revealed nothing.

Porter seemed surprised as well. "Of course, Colonel. Captain Streeper, would ya show Major Rawlins the camp."

"Is that the same Harper who was at Belmont?" Rawlins asked

"Yes, Major. This is Lieutenant James Harper." Monroe indicated Harper from among the crowd of battalion officers.

"Well, sir, I want to shake your hand for what you did to rescue the general." Rawlins took Harper's hand. "It was First Iowa boys who came off the boats to protect the general, wasn't it?"

"Yeah. It was." Harper looked at Porter and nodded with a grin.

Rawlins turned back to Monroe. "General Grant is not a very demonstrative man, Colonel, but I know he's grateful to your men, and especially Lieutenant Harper, here, for coming back to help him."

"We lost two men on that little galavant," Monroe said.

Rawlins ignored Monroe's reproach and looked back at Harper. "I heard you were shot up yourself, Harper. Are you healthy?"

"Good enough, Major. I got back two weeks ago."

"Well, I'm glad to make your acquaintance. I'll let the general know you've recovered. He'll want to know." Turning back the Monroe. "The way General Grant tells the story, you've got a hell of a fighter here, Colonel." He walked toward the door of the tent. "Now, how about that look around, Captain?"

Monroe frowned at Harper while Rawlins and the company commanders left the tent. Harper smiled back at Monroe and his chin rose a fraction of an inch. Monroe couldn't ignore this proof of the rescue and its value. With Grant's praise, now maybe Monroe would ease up on him. After all, the man only seemed motivated by the approval of senior officers. Harper's attention returned to Lauman.

Monroe asked, "So we'll operate with Illinois men and not your Iowa brigade?" Monroe's voice revealed his disappointment and confirmed Harper's opinion of his motives.

"You will reattach after we rendezvous at Fort Heiman. This is a better assignment for your unit, Colonel."

"Of course, sir. I hope the folks in Iowa won't forget about us."

Lauman paused and stared at the battalion commander. "Don't worry, Monroe." Lauman's reply sounded cold and flat. "There'll be plenty of opportunities to make reputations in this campaign."

Lauman began. "Lieutenant Harper, you're that deputy marshal fellow from the Dakotas, aren't you?"

"Yeah, Colonel." Harper wondered how Lauman would know that.

Perhaps he had read some of the exaggerated stories various Iowa newspapermen had published over the years.

"Well, son, that is probably the only thing saving your hide; that, and the episode with General Grant."

Harper stared at Lauman. The self-satisfaction he felt from Rawlins's praise quickly evaporated. His suspicion rose.

Monroe looked at Porter who shrugged his shoulders and shook his head.

"Do you recall a certain Mister Adolf Magnusson who came to see you?" Lauman asked.

Harper could not recall the name immediately. After two weeks of training exercises in the January cold, anything which happened earlier was a blur.

Monroe, however, appeared to remember the man very well. "Mr. Magnusson came to see us in Paducah." He looked at Harper, trying to help him recall. "He was looking for his son."

"The old Quaker?" Harper tried to recall the churchman's visit.

Colonel Lauman nodded. "It turns out that after his visit to Paducah, Mister Magnusson wrote a letter to Governor Kirkwood describing how the officers lied to him when he came to visit the First Iowa Rifles. Apparently, he was upset somethin' terrible, and he mentioned you by name, Lieutenant Harper, as the person responsible for hiding his son from him."

"But, sir," Porter spoke up. "Corporal Magnusson reenlisted on his own accord and he's a full-grown man. We explained all of that to Mr. Magnusson, with his son there." Porter looked to Monroe to confirm his version of the story. Monroe nodded slowly, but didn't say anything, his gaze shifting between Porter and Lauman. Porter continued. "Corporal Magnusson wants to be here. He refused to go home with his father."

That's what this is about? Some goddamn preacher didn't like the fact his son had grown up and joined the army, and he wanted to blame someone.

"Well, Magnusson the Elder must have been extremely upset with all of you." Lauman looked at each officer. "Because he had the letter signed by all of the Quaker elders within a hundred miles of Salem, reporting how badly managed this unit is, and in particular, what a criminal and a drunk the adjutant is, one Lieutenant James Harper." As he ended this statement he turned in his chair to look directly at Harper.

"What's that supposed to mean?" After all of the problems he had with Monroe and the men of the battalion, this was too much. His muscles tightened as suspicion transformed to high anger. Harper stood up, fists on hips, leaning over the camp desk. "The goddamn Bible-thumper came into my office trying to get his little boy to slink back home with him." Harper took a breath. "Magnusson's a damned good soldier, Colonel, and he doesn't want to go back to that bunch of pious, hypocrictical, Abolitionist bastards. Hell, Magnusson's the one who carried the colonel's son back to the boats at Belmont."

When Harper stopped to take a second breath, Porter pulled him backward and stood between Harper and Lauman. Monroe stood to help Porter. Lauman shifted his feet to stand during Harper's outburst, but sat back when he saw Porter and Monroe would control Harper.

"Stand by the door, Mister Harper," Monroe ordered, his voice rising. "Get yourself under control."

Harper stared at Lauman, his teeth and fists clenched. But Lauman did not react and the calm face gave Harper time to understand how out-of-line his action was. Harper did as he was told, shaking the tent when he slapped the tent pole at the doorway.

Lauman watched Harper for a moment longer before continuing. "Off the record, my feelings are close to the lieutenant's." He looked across the tent to Harper. "Perhaps not so energetic." His gaze returned to Monroe. "But you all need to understand that most of the religious folk in Iowa are pro-Abolition and voted Republican in the last two elections."

A gust of cold wind blew through the door. Harper grabbed the tent flap and tied it to the post next to him.

"After he read Magnusson's letter, the governor made some inquiries about the First Iowa Mounted Rifles and you can imagine his reaction to learn the battalion commander was a Democrat from the staff of the man he defeated in the last election."

Monroe reacted as if Lauman's words struck him physically. He dropped into his chair.

"I reckon he sees the opportunity to gain some political capital with the church-goin' folks, and at the same time, give out some patronage by replacing you, Monroe, with someone he owes."

Now, it was Monroe's turn to receive bad news. The battalion commander let out a sigh. He looked down at the straw floor with his hands clasped together, drew a second deep breath and appeared to recover. He looked back at Lauman with the expression of a person waiting to hear of the death of a family member. "I've only been here two months. We haven't had time to show what we can do."

Harper went stone cold, his anger flared into hatred for Adolph Magnusson. He refused to believe that, because of some pathetic old man, now both he and Monroe might be dismissed from the army. Being in the army was supposed to be about fighting, not cow-towing to pasty-faced Abolitionist preachers.

"Now, I also reckon…" Lauman paused to look at each of the three officers, "…that it isn't the smartest thing in the world to remove a unit's CO on the night before a major campaign begins. General Smith agrees with me. So, we've asked Grant to endorse a letter back to the governor expressing our desire for you to remain in place, for now. By the time the letter reaches Iowa, we'll all be in Tennessee."

Monroe exhaled an explosion of air. He stood up and began pacing in the small space between his chair and the canvas divider.

"As for you, Lieutenant Harper, the governor has directed me to take whatever discipline measures I feel appropriate to this case."

Harper felt helpless to do or say anything. His mind raced to find something which would let him escape the blame. Nothing came to him. But, if Monroe was to stay, maybe his own punishment would also be less severe. He stepped closer.

"Lieutenant, you are under arrest until such time as you shall write a letter of apology to Mister Magnusson, explaining your reason for *unintentionally* misleading him. You understand: *unintentionally*? You will report to Major Porter each day until the letter is written. And you will show it to the major when you have it ready to send." Lauman smiled at the little conspiracy he had created.

This was no punishment. Harper reported to Porter every day already. All he had to do was write one goddamn letter. If it meant he would stay in the Army, it would be one of the sweetest damn letters ever written.

Harper relaxed and smiled back at the colonel. "Yes, sir. Thank you, sir."

"Major Porter, you will report to me personally when the conditions of Mr. Harper's arrest are completed."

"Yes, sir." Porter had a grin on his face.

"Good, good." Lauman stood up. "Now, I've heard the First Iowa runs a wet camp in spite of General Grant's standing orders. Is that true?" He rubbed his hands together and looked at each of them.

Monroe looked surprised. Porter and Harper fidgeted before looking at one another, expecting the other to answer.

"Well, sir, that would be against regulations, wouldn't it?" Harper said after several moments of uncomfortable silence.

Colonel Lauman nodded. "Yah, Lieutenant. It certainly would." Lauman relaxed into his native accent.

"But as it happens, we did just yesterday *capture* a bottle or two of fine Kentucky bourbon liquor from a south-bound Reb-sympathizer. We let him go, but we, uhh, *confiscated* all of the *contraband* in his wagon." Harper rejoined the group around the camp desk. "We planned to turn it over to the provosts the next time we see them. Would the colonel care to, uhh, inspect it?"

"Sounds like an excellent idea, Lieutenant." Lauman kept a straight face.

"Mitchell," Monroe called to his orderly. "Bring in cups for our visitor and for the three of us."

Harper left to collect the *contraband.*

After the supplies were ready on the camp table, Harper poured the bourbon into the four cups, filling each halfway.

"Gentlemen," Lauman held up his cup. "To the Union!"

"The Union." The three Iowa officers clinked their cups with Lauman and took a sip of the bourbon.

"And to victory at Fort Heiman."

"To victory."

PART 3
FORT DONELSON

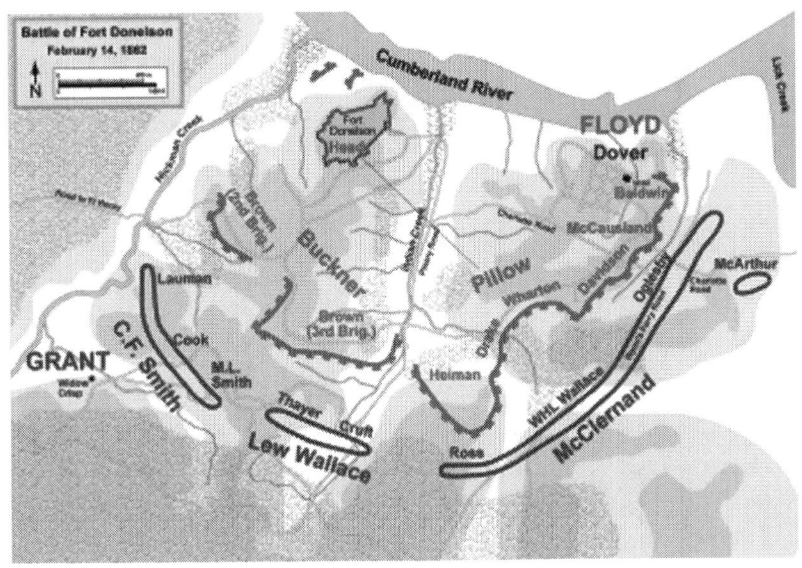

Battle of Fort Donelson
Positions and Order of Battle on February 14th, 1862
Map by Hal Jespersen, www.posix.com/CW

Wednesday, February 12th, 1862

Grant surprised the Confederates by starting the campaign in early February. On February 6th, 1862, Flag-Officer Andrew Foote's river flotilla landed McClernand's Division on the Tennessee River, five miles below Fort Henry. The mounted column, including the First Iowa, took possession of unfinished Fort Heiman the same morning. They found the place deserted, except for a few slaves left behind by the Rebel engineers. The remainder of Smith's Division arrived at Heiman later that afternoon.

General Lloyd Tilghman, CSA, consolidated the single brigade under his command at Fort Henry to oppose McClernand. Finding the fort untenable due to rising water in the river, he ordered the fort's commander, Captain Jesse Taylor, to fight a delaying action while the remainder of his brigader retreated overland to Fort Donelson. Tilghman remained at Fort Henry and became a prisoner when the fort surrendered to the U.S. Navy on the afternoon of February 6th.

On February 7th, Second Division crossed the Tennessee River and occupied the former Rebel barracks at Fort Henry. The Second Division's march to Donelson began six days later. The First Iowa Mounted Rifles resupplied for six days and headed east through the forest with the rest of Smith's Division.

****

"Ya reckon we'll get to fight this time, Jamie?" Captain William Pierson asked.

Harper shifted his attention from examining the bare trees alongside the road, looking for any sign of new buds, to the man riding next to him. "I don't know, Will. Maybe the Navy will do the job for us again." Harper rode among the officers of Company C while the First Iowa Mounted Rifles led Colonel Lauman's brigade across the neck of land between the Tennessee and the Cumberland Rivers. Every man in the army knew Donelson was their next objective. If it remained in Rebel hands, the Federal army could not defend Fort Henry.

"That'd make things easier for us, I suppose." Pierson let his horse plod onward, finding its own way. "Still, we have to get these boys into some sort of action. They're all eager to try out their new rifles and they're gettin' tired of shootin' at squirrels or pine cones." Monroe had promoted Pierson to permanent command of Company C while the battalion waited in the barracks at Fort Henry.

"I expect it won't be too long now before that happens." Harper tried to look through the naked trees alongside the road to see deeper into the forest. "I think Grant is plannin' to take Nashville once Donelson falls. All of the supplies for the Rebel armies in Kentucky cross over the river at Nashville. Take it and they'll have to move farther east, away from the large cities or fall back across the river."

The battalion now traveled through a forest of mixed hardwoods and evergreens, over muddy roads made slippery from five days of cold rain and snow.

"Let's see if I can't learn somethin'." Harper pulled out of column and let Santee trot forward to join Major Porter who rode with the brigade staff. Porter nodded in greeting when Harper joined the column of staff officers.

After a few minutes, someone called from behind him. "You're Jamie Harper, ain't ya? From near Sergeant's Bluff?"

Harper looked around to see who had spoken. A number of men stared at him waiting for an answer. "Yeah, I am." He looked at each of the riders to see which one responded.

"Ya probably don't remember me, but I used to work on your brother's ranch." It was a young lieutenant riding alongside the man behind Harper.

"I don't think… sorry, but it's been ten years since I worked on Johnny's ranch. Ya don't seem old enough…"

"Oh, no. You'd left the ranch by then," the younger man

interrupted. "No. I only saw ya when ya would come back for visits. I started workin' there around 'fifty-five. Even so, I was just fourteen. I didn't do much back then 'cept feed the horses and muck out the stables."

The officers from Lauman's staff within earshot chuckled. "That's still a good job for ya *now*, eh, Jed."

Jed blushed. "It got better." His horse slipped in the mud and he recovered control with the easy grace of long experience. Once the horse calmed, he continued his story. "Mister Harper, Mister Johnny Harper that is, let me start breaking the horses in a year or so, plus ridin' on round-ups."

Harper nodded. He vaguely recalled a skinny teen-aged stable hand with blond hair, who always smelled like what he cleaned from the stables.

The lieutenant went on. "But Mister Jamie, here, was famous around Woodbury County. He used to be a lawman in the Nebraska Territory. They say he would go off into the Indian lands by himself for weeks, or sometimes months. A couple of times, Mister Harper got a letter from the judge in Yankton sayin' Mister Jamie was away too long and the judge feared he wasn't comin' back. Missus Harper, Johnny's wife, would always say, 'Oh don't worry. He'll be back in his own good time.' The Harpers buy mustangs from the Sioux, ya see, and if he was really hurt, they would've sent word."

"Well, it's a pleasure to meet someone from the ranch," Harper reached behind him and offered the lieutenant his hand.

"I'm Jedediah Stumpf from Sergeant's Bluff." The lieutenant shook Harper's hand.

Since all of the men on Colonel Lauman's staff were from Iowa, Harper suspected most of them knew some of the stories about a crazy man who went into Sioux country by himself to catch outlaws. They all stared at Harper.

"I heard ya never brought a live man back to the judge." This came from one of the captains ahead of Harper.

Harper gave the officer a long, hard stare to let the speaker know he wasn't fond of that particular rumor. He raised an eyebrow to signal an unspoken challenge to the captain. "Them ain't the facts."

"Whoa! Hold on, friend. I don't mean nothin' by it–it's just what some people say."

Because of rumors like that, Harper usually avoided spending much time around townsfolk. When he was in Yankton waiting for a new arrest warrant, he stayed to himself, taking his meals with the local sheriff and his family.

"No offense taken." Harper relaxed his hostile pose. "Besides, the only outlaws I killed were the ones who weren't willing to go back *peace-able*."

He smiled at his own joke; nearly all of the outlaws he went after didn't want to go back *peace-able*. Only a very desperate white man would flee into the Sioux territory to avoid the white-man's law.

A few of the officers in the group chuckled and nodded. Most of them understood Harper had played a major role in making northwest Iowa safer from bandits and from Indian raids. The exaggerated newspaper stories had much to do with his fame but they reported about a man Harper could not recognize.

"So, how did you get along with the Indians, Harper?" It was Lieutenant Colonel Heath, Lauman's chief-of-staff.

"Quite well, thanks to my brother." Harper turned to face the major. "Johnny was already friends with the Yanktons and the Poncas along the Missouri. He has a trading business with them to buy any wild horses they can round up. Santee, here, is one of those horses." Harper patted his horse on her gray neck near the scar creasing her mane. "Besides, once the Indians learned I was there to catch renegade whites on their land, they often as not would send some braves with me to help."

"So you used red men to kill whites? Not sure how I feel about that."

"Hunt them." Harper paused to see that Heath noted the correction. Satisfied, he went on. "Easiest way to get the job done. Besides, the folks those outlaws killed or robbed didn't seem too upset about how I went about it. Those I caught weren't much better than rabid dogs, anyway."

They rode along in silence for a while, with the officers around him avoiding eye-contact.

"Looks like another squall headed this way," Stumpf called out.

Harper could see the dark mass of air over his left shoulder as the latest snow shower made its way toward the column. He looked to make sure the oilcloth still covered the firing mechanism on his rifle. Next, he checked the cover flaps on his saddle holster and the holster at his hip to make sure his Colts were protected. Only after securing his personal weapons did he lift the slicker from his horse's neck and put his wide-brimmed hat on the pommel of his saddle.

He pulled the slicker over his head, spreading it around him so it covered his entire uniform down to his boots and spread over the saddlebags and rolled blankets behind him. Once everything was in place, he put his hat back on. With luck, the snow would pass quickly.

The shower arrived within ten minutes and passed over in even fewer. Snowflakes which fell on the exposed mud of the road melted immediately, adding their moisture to the puddles in the road. The brigade kept moving over a road where rivulets of melted snow now ran, increasing the depth of the mud. The mounted men of the First Iowa moved along without difficulty, their wild-born horses plodding through without tiring.

Shortly afterward, however, word came up the line-of-march that the foot soldiers following behind were struggling to keep up because the mud stuck to their boots with each step, making the next step harder to take. Harper could see the effect even within his own battalion. The mud became worse for the men farther back in the column, since each horse made depressions which filled with water. This softened the clay in the road even deeper for the horses following. Hundreds of men marching behind the First Iowa must be churning the road's surface into a knee-deep porridge.

According to General Smith's orders for the march, he expected the division to cover the six miles between Fort Henry and Fort Donelson in less than half a day, but because of the condition of the roads, Lauman's Brigade covered less than half the distance in the allotted time.

Lauman called a halt to the column and allowed the men to break ranks for the midday meal. The men of the First Iowa simply led their horses off of the road and dismounted. The foot soldiers farther down the column climbed the short step up out of the road and dropped down onto spots where the leaf litter showed through the snow under the trees. Harper watched them scrape the mud from their boots, after which they ate various cold foods taken from their packs. Lauman sent a captain from his staff to determine the condition of the five foot regiments and Harper followed in order to check with each of the companies of the First Iowa.

When he returned, Harper tied Santee to a tree next to Porter's horse. He took a feedbag from his saddle and strapped it to the bridle before he walked around the horse, checking her condition. He rubbed the scar in her rump from a second bullet taken during the battle at Belmont. The scar added an accent mark to the unique brand which his brother had devised for the First Iowa horses, the standard letters 'U S' surrounded by an outline of the state of Iowa.

After attending to his horse, Harper opened the saddlebag holding his personal belongings and retrieved a flannel cloth. As he did so, the leather pouch fell out, landing upside down in the snow. Harper snatched it up and pushed it between the buttons of his jacket.

He opened the sack holding his own rations for the next six days and took out a quarter of a cooked chicken, placing it into the flannel. He lifted the canteen from the pommel on his saddle and walked over to where Porter sat with Lauman's staff officers, selecting a spot behind the group and slightly to the side, since Porter was already in conversation with several officers.

Harper set his food onto the ground, laying the flannel with the food inside on top of the canteen to keep it out of the snow. He took off his slicker, shook the wetness from it, and spread it wet-side-down over the snow.

The conversation with Lieutenant Stumpf triggered the memories. As he sat eating the chicken, he fingered the pouch under his jacket. Inside was a lock of chestnut-colored hair tied with a purple ribbon from his wife. It was all he had left of her. He took it on the day he said good-bye and the folks from Johnny's place laid her to rest in the cemetery which served the ranch. With it was a second lock of hair, a little lighter shade of chestnut with scorch marks still on it. Little Magda died during the same attack.

He was at Johnny's ranch that day helping to train the latest batch of mustangs from the Indian Territory. They saw the column of smoke shortly before sundown as they were leaving the corral. Harper jumped on a horse and galloped bareback across the prairie, while his brother and the others followed as quickly as they could.

When he crested the hill separating his soddy from Johnny's ranch, he could see smoke spilling from the door and windows. In the distance, four cowboys rode westward. He galloped on until he reached the front door to his home but when he opened it, a fireball flared through the opening, knocking him to the ground and burning his face.

Johnny grabbed him when he tried to go inside the second time. Taller than Johnny, Harper broke away and rushed into the house. At first, he didn't see Emily. There was a flash of hope that she had escaped. But then he saw her lying on their bed, still in death. The scorching air seared his throat. Something hit him from behind and knocked him to the floor.

The rest was a blur. Two of Johnny's men had pulled him from under a flaming beam. Others formed a bucket brigade between the well and the house to knock down the flames.

Before the flames were out, two of the braver men went inside. Coughing from the burns in his throat, Harper grabbed the shirt of one of the men and followed. They found Emily's burnt body on the bed in a puddle of incinerated blood at her throat. What was left of her clothes were ripped and thrown around the hut. Baby Magda lay dead against the wall with her skull smashed.

Harper's career as a lawman began the following week. The family learned later the four attackers had killed several citizens in Cedar Rapids while trying to rob the bank. They had fled north along the Missouri until they came to Harper's soddy.

It took Harper a season of searching, but with the help of the Yanktons he eventually found the men. The renegades made the mistake of camping in their territory without permission from the tribe. With the help of some of the younger Yanktons, Harper tracked the outlaws to a cave in a secluded draw. Harper watched while the braves take revenge on the men. None survived to go to trial.

Rabid dogs.

"Mount up!" Word came down the length of the column. Harper carefully placed the pouch into the inside breast pocket of his jacket. He mounted and took his place in the column, throwing the unfinished chicken into the woods.

****

It was Wednesday. Katie hated Wednesdays.

Grant's army had left Paducah and now they fought the Southerners somewhere up the Tennessee River. Behind them, other Federal soldiers called "quartermasters" remained to operate the supply depot at Fort Anderson. The quartermasters were very different from the soldiers who had gone on campaign. They reminded her of the county bosses back in Cypressville. Katie despised them. Each one seemed to have a plan to get rich during the war. Major Evilface commanded the quartermasters, and that made him a valued customer of the Bosleys.

Katie and the other girls had assigned that nickname to Major Eagleton, a veteran of the Indian wars. The scarf hid a hideous burn covering almost half of his face. The major told a tale of torture by the Apache in the New Mexico Territory before the war. There was no reason to disbelieve this tale, except most people thought it odd how the major escaped while being protected by a squaw who fell in love with the white man. The story gave Major Eagleton a second derogatory name: Captain Smith, of Pocahontas fame.

The foul weather beyond the saloon window matched Katie's mood. On each of the last two Wednesdays, Eagleton chose Katie to be his companion. The major normally arrived promptly at six o'clock–half an hour away. Tonight, Katie would escape Evilface by being upstairs with a customer when he arrived. Tonight, Evilface would have to choose from among the other girls.

Katie surveyed the barroom from the staircase, below the cloud of cigar smoke which usually hovered near the ceiling. Fewer soldiers than normal stood at the bar and several unoccupied tables signaled that tonight would be a slow night. The cold rain outside probably had kept most of the soldiers in their warm barracks. She examined the faces of the soldiers below, trying to decide which table to visit for her first customer of the night. The timing had to be right if she were to avoid

Evilface: too soon and the customer would be finished while the major waited below; too late, and Loreena would force her to entertain the scar-faced man. She targeted a table and skipped down the stairs.

"Hello, Miss Katie. We're glad you joined us." A soldier whose name she should remember but couldn't stood while she took her seat. He wore three red chevrons on both sleeves. The four other soldiers stayed seated but did smile at her. One point for manners for the standing soldier–Orville! That was his name, Orville, from the Illinois artillery. "Good evenin' Orville. So nice to see you again." If she must work tonight, Katie chose to spend her time with Orville and his friends. This artillery sergeant was a man she would welcome to her bed in place of Evilface. The smell of burnt gunpowder which usually surrounded the artillery men made her insides go tingley.

Orville gave her a broad grin, which showed his clean, even teeth.

The artillerymen were the nicest of the soldiers. They seemed smarter than most of the infantry soldiers and not as arrogant as the men in the cavalry. Katie glanced at the door before she asked, "So, what're we talkin' about tonight?"

The private across the table from Katie took a puff from his clay pipe and blew a smoke ring from his whiskered face toward the ceiling. "We was just talkin' about how we could catch up with the captain and the rest of the battery."

"Oh? What happened? Why did they leave y'all behind?" While she feigned interest in the man's answer, Katie tried to find Loreena but couldn't. Maybe Major Eagleton wasn't coming tonight. Normally when he planned to come, Loreena would walk among the tables watching each girl and making them uneasy by doing so. Katie wasn't the only girl in the saloon who knew tonight's potential for pain. She returned her attention to the table.

"...the lame horses aboard one of the boats takin' supplies upriver." The man across the table from her ended his explanation.

"And how do you plan to do that?" Katie saw Loreena leave her office and speak with the bartender.

"Quartermaster says we'll need to wait our turn, same's everybody else."

Katie felt more comfortable around these men than she did with the swindlers-in-uniform whom the army had left behind. These artillery men were ready to fight. If the quartermaster men talked about the fighting, it was to make grand pronouncements about how *they* would make the South howl when the army moved into Rebel lands. Presumably, they would do so while being protected by the real soldiers.

Loreena finished her conversation with the bartender and walked out among the tables. Katie watched several of the girls glance at Loreena before they darted their eyes away to avoid eye-contact.

"Buy a lady a drink, Orville." The drink signaled to the sergeant he would be her customer, but not right away. Orville came to *Lafitte's* often enough to understand. He stood and went to the bar.

"So, what're all y'all's doin' while you wait?"

Orville returned from the bar with Katie's lady's drink, water mixed with root beer for color and a tiny amount of whiskey for scent, along with four mugs of beer. "Here we are." Orville set the mugs on the table for his friends. The soldiers made a rule among themselves: if one of them planned to disappear upstairs, he would leave a round of drinks if he wanted them to wait for him to come down. He shoved the mugs of beer across to his friends and sat next to Katie.

Loreena walked among the tables, trying to place at least one saloon-girl at every table. There never were enough women available to accommodate all of the customers, even on a cold, rainy night like tonight.

"Shall we go up now, Miss Katie?"

"Not yet." Katie saw her new roommate, Julia, walk to the staircase. She and Julia had created an arrangement where each agreed to stay downstairs while the other entertained upstairs. "Let's set and talk for a few minutes."

Please don't be too long, Julia. Evilface will be here soon.

Orville followed Katie's glance to Julia and frowned. He looked too much like a sad puppy, so Katie took his hand in hers.

****

Smith's Division arrived in the vicinity of Fort Donelson and found its place on the left of the Federal lines. Harper watched Lauman and

Lieutenant Colonel Monroe discuss their orders several yards ahead while he and Porter waited with Colonel Lauman's staff. Lauman pointed to the top of the ridge in front of them. Monroe saluted and Harper heard him say, "Yes, sir."

Monroe rode back and relayed his orders. "Porter, we are to screen the arrival of the rest of the brigade. Establish a picket line at the top of this hill." He pointed to the top of the ridge. "See to it."

Harper looked but could not see the top of the ridge through the leafless trees crowding the road.

"Jamie," Porter said. "Pass the order to the company commanders. I'll ride ahead to see the lay of the land."

Harper saluted and rode to obey Porter's instructions. Porter was out of view through the leafless trees by the time Harper finished.

Harper followed the last company to the top of the ridge where he joined Monroe and Porter behind the center company. He could see that most of the battalion's men were still mounted and formed in a loose line abreast but below the actual crest of the ridge. The company commanders each led a foot patrol to a position where they could see over the crest. Once satisfied, they posted dismounted pickets in the selected positions. These men would detect any approaching threat to the marching column behind them without revealing the actual strength of the battalion to the enemy.

Harper looked back down at the road where the dark column of Federal infantry stretched to the west beyond his view. The road from Fort Henry ran past a large farmstead before it ended where it intersected a better road paralleling the ridge. Except for the farm, an open forest of bare trees covered the countryside in every direction. Below him, staff officers led the foot regiments to their assigned camp areas. Each regiment arrived, and the men in its column flowed across the snow-covered ground looking for the best places to set their campsites. Harper turned and stood in his stirrups, trying to see the Rebel works over the top of the ridge.

"Mister Harper," Porter ordered. "Take ten men from each company. Report to the brigade adjutant to stake out an area for the battalion's camp tonight. I'm looking at that area across the creek in front of those farm buildings." Porter's desired area lay across the road from the ridge, alongside a small creek visible in the snow and free of ice.

"I see it, Major." Harper had hoped to catch a glimpse of the Rebel fort, but it appeared that the brigade would advance no farther today. Disappointed, he collected the designated men from each company and made his way down the ridge.

After the final regiment in the brigade column arrived, Lauman called the regimental commanders together. The setting sun peeked under the clouds, lighting up the slope where First Iowa still stood guard. With Porter in command of the men on the ridge, Harper accompanied Monroe to the meeting.

"Tomorrow morning, gentlemen, we will close up on the enemy's trenches just beyond the ridge." Lauman pointed uphill to the line of the First Iowa. "In the meantime, I want you to establish a picket line on top of the ridge for tonight and relieve Monroe's people."

The commanders of four of Lauman's foot regiments acknowledged the orders.

Lauman continued. "Colonel Burke, your sharpershooters will disperse along the front lines wherever they can be of the most use."

The commander of the Fourteen Missouri acknowledged the order.

"Monroe, I see that your men have already staked out their camp in front of Widow Crisp's. Once your battalion is relieved by the infantry, you'll form the flank guard. Stretch your outpost line until you come to Hickman Creek, about a quarter-mile in that direction." Lauman pointed north to an area beyond the end of the ridge. Any questions?" He scanned all of the assembled officers. "Good. By the way, Monroe. Keep your men away from Missus Crisp's farm. Grant's headquarters is in there."

****

Julia's customer had come down without Julia, his business upstairs complete. To the anxious Katie, it seemed they had overstayed their allotted thirty minutes. Now, she had to wait while Julia cleaned herself and returned to find another custormer. Evilface would be here any minute unless he decided not to battle the storm outside. As if in reply, a gust of wind rattled the the plateglass window and pelted it with a surge of raindrops. Katie saw that as a sign. The storm outside might soon break into the saloon—and that storm's name was Evilface.

"Come on, Orville." Katie stood and held out her hand for the sergeant. Orville's arched eyebrows let her know she had surpised him. Probably, he knew about the arrangement between the roommates and had also been waiting for Julia to return. It did not matter. Tonight, Katie would take him up early and if Julia did not like it, Katie would apologize later. She needed to leave the barroom as soon as she could.

"Are you sure, Katie?" While he stood up, Orville glanced to the balcony above and back at Katie.

"Now, Orville. Let's go."

"Whoa-ho." The corporal across the table from Orville spoke up. "She's ready to ride, sergeant. Best catch some of that while it's still hot."

Katie reached across the table and rewarded the loud-mouth corporal with a slap across his face.

"You see, boys? She jes' can't control herself." The corporal smiled back at Katie while he rubbed the red spot on his cheek.

The heat of a blush rose in Katie's face. She grabbed Oville's hand and led him across the floor and up the stairs, ignoring the hoots and whistles behind her. At the top of the staircase, she waited to let Orville catch up.

Julia stepped from their room and arched her eyebrows when she passed Katie. She smiled when she saw Orville. "Evening, Orville. Is Corporal Eddie here tonight?"

"Yes, ma'am. He's waitin' for you."

"Nasty man," Katie said.

Julia glanced at Katie, then turned to Orville. "Thank you, sir." She performed a short curtsy to Orville. Her scent lingered after she made her way down the stairs.

Katie put her arm into the crook of Orville's elbow and led him to her bedroom. Eddie's salacious words would not spoil her time with Orville. A cold gust of wind and rain reached to the balcony. It drew Katie's attention to the front door of the saloon where Major Eagleton stepped through, his overcoat and hat dripping rain water, his scarf pulled high enough to cover his disfigurement. Katie hid her face in

Orville's sleeve.

Back in her room, Katie had several options for how she could entertain a customer. The escape from Major Eagleton buoyed her spirits, and she decided to make this encounter with Orville a special one.

****

As the day ended, the wind shifted from the southwest to the north, bringing a steady drizzle and speeding the arrival of colorless twilight. The men of the First Iowa walked their horses down from the ridge covered by their slickers, dark silhouettes among the trees moving over the stark white snow covering the ground. With the sun now gone, the temperature dropped below freezing, turning the drizzle to sleet.

While his men dismounted to find whatever comfort they could, Captain Brice McKinsey approached Harper. Slightly shorter than Harper, McKinsey walked with a limp from a Mexican fusilier's bayonet. Harper noticed that his limp was now much more pronounced than in the past. The effects of campaigning might be beginning to show on the fifty-four-year-old. McKinsey's boots made a crunching sound as they broke through a crust of frozen sleet lying on top of the snow.

"Looks like a cold night, eh, Mister Harper?"

"Yeah, probably so." Harper was busy and did not stop to talk with McKinsey. He needed to find a sheltered place to establish the battalion headquarters, out of the weather so Corporal Powell could write the daily reports and orders.

"I think it's a bit colder than last night, eh?"

"Might be." Harper hadn't decided yet whether to move Powell into one of the farm out-buildings in spite of Lauman's warning.

"What about the men?" McKinsey asked. He put both his hands on his hips and leaned forward.

"What about them?" Harper said, distracted by his thoughts, not looking at McKinsey.

"How do they stay warm?"

Harper knew how to survive in this cold. He had spent enough freezing nights in the territory. Only now did it occur to Harper that most of the men in the battalion did not know this basic survival skill. The men who had participated in his field training knew. Perhaps they would show the others.

"Orders are for no campfires where the Rebs might see them," Harper said. He looked uphill, but the dark trees and the overcast obscured the view. He could not see how far they were below the crest of the ridge. If they were deep enough in the valley, they might be able to light fires. "We don't know the lay of the Rebel lines yet, so no campfires. They'll have to wrap themselves up and huddle together. The skirmishers will know what to do."

"That won't be taken well," McKinsey replied.

Harper turned to look into McKinsey in the eye. "They'll survive." He paused. "Staying in the open will make the men tougher. It'll make them better soldiers." He knew it sounded stupid as soon as the words left his mouth but he wasn't going to take orders from McKinsey.

McKinsey pointed to a barn up the slope from the creek. "I was thinkin' that, if we picket the horses outside, then there's probably enough room for all of the men in the battalion to fit into that barn yonder. That way we'll all be under shelter, eh?"

Harper resented McKinsey and McKinsey's opinion. Harper resented the fact that McKinsey, too old, too fat, and too lame to be on an active campaign, still led one of the five companies—while Harper remained on the battalion staff doing paperwork. Harper resented McKinsey's feigned politeness and the way he spoke. Harper resented the fact that the suggestion was a reasonable one, which *he* should have already made to Major Porter. Above all, Harper resented being instructed by McKinsey.

"That'll put the men too far away to support our front line, and on the wrong side of the creek." Harper pointed to the picquets leaving the camp to establish the flank guard.

McKinsey's face revealed his surprise at Harper's answer. "That barn is less than a half mile from the ridge, eh. The men could be in the front lines in minutes."

Harper hurried to reinforce his argument. "Besides, Grant's staff has taken over that farm for the army's headquarters. They don't want us there." He wouldn't let McKinsey tell him what to do.

"One of these days, Jamie, ya gonna to have to learn about taking better care of the men, don't cha know?" McKinsey's voice was loud enough that several by-standers turned to watch. McKinsey poked a finger in Harper's direction. "Keepin' 'em healthy is part of our responsibility, too; not just pushing them into the battle line, eh?"

"Well, I know that already now, don't I?" Harper said. He cast a furtive glance at the spectators.

"Do ya, Harper? Sometimes, I wonder."

Harper fought to control his rising anger. "I'll see what I can do, Captain."

Harper needed to bring the argument under control before it became camp gossip. His reputation still had not recovered from the episode with the Monroe boy, and he did not need to add to it by appearing to expect the men to remain outdoors during the night when there was a shelter nearby.

McKinsey bobbed his finger in Harper's face. "Do that–*Lieutenant*." McKinsey's emphasis sounded like an insult to Harper, reminding him that the adjutant really held no authority to make decisions about anything in the battalion. "Where the hell is Porter, eh? Let's see how he feels about this."

****

Most soldiers could only afford a half-an-hour of her time, including Orville. Loreena would knock five minutes before the time was up. That gave Katie plenty of time for what she called The Full Treatment. Katie knew Orville would be gentle with her and he had good hands that would excite her body if she gave him enough time. So, Orville would get The Full Treatment.

Katie kicked out of her slippers and turned to face Orville. She let him unfasten the hooks on the front of her gown while she unbuttoned his uniform jacket and the white shirt underneath. She let him help pull her shoulders and arms through the sleeves of the gown. After the top of the gown fell backward over the skirt, she flipped his suspenders from his shoulders and the trousers dropped around his ankles. She reached between the legs of his long underwear and rubbed. Orville was ready, and Katie giggled. Orville wrapped her up in his arms and pulled her close with her hand still below. She gave those parts a squeeze before she pushed back and away. "Just a minute."

Katie ducked behind the dressing screen and removed her gown and petticoat. These, she carefully draped over the top of the dressing screen. She removed her gown for every customer because she didn't want some clumsy drunk soldier ruining it. She took the bottle of horse liniment on the floor and dripped a few drops onto her hand, then rubbed the greasy liquid onto her woman's parts. Normally, she wouldn't need it for Orville, but tonight she would be busier than usual, so it was best to be sure.

"Do I need to wash you, Orvillle? Have you been with anyone else since the last time?"

"No, Katie. I've been in the camp every night since then. I swear."

"Good." It meant they could get right down to business and Katie wanted her business with Orville to start as soon as possible.

When she walked from behind the screen in her chemise, pantaloons and stockings, she saw Orville standing in his underwear, with his boots and outer garments lying across the chair in front of the dressing table. She came up close to him and let him pull her against him again and kiss her on the lips. This was a privilege she gave only to her best customers. She felt his strength rise against her lower belly. "You're ready, aren't you, Orville."

"I suppose so."

"Well, come here, then." She reached low and grabbed the bulge. Using it like a handle, she pulled him to the bed and pulled back the blanket and top sheet with her free hand. She released Orville and lay back on the bed in expectation.

This was the time when Orville earned the right to be one of Katie's preferred customers. He sat on the bed next to her and placed his hands on the sides of Katie's chest, level with her breasts. Instead of working them to the front, he used the strength in his hands to knead the muscles in her back. Katie closed her eyes and relaxed to the feeling of being in the grip of a strong man.

"Mmm..." Katie allowed herself a cat-sound to encourage Orville to keep going.

Orville worked his fingers lower on her back and stopped at the top of her pantaloons. Only now did he work to the front of her belly. He slipped them under her chemise. While his fingers held her in the back, his used his thumbs to rub her belly, slowly working his way upward. The hem of the chemise worked its way upward, pushed by Orville's wrists. When he reached her breasts, she sat up and pulled it over her head. This exposure was another item she reserved for only her best customers. Most of her other customers were not interested in these parts of her body anyway, while most of the ones who spent time with them handled her too roughly.

Katie purred again while his thumbs teased her. Orville bent over her and took one breast in his mouth while he shifted his hand on the other one so he could use all of his fingers. This was the first part of Orville's routine that Katie anticipated, the combination of pleasure on one side and pain on the other where Orville pinched at the tenderest parts of her breast. She gasped for breath. She could smell the sulfurous odor of burnt gunpowder coming from his hair and her woman's parts warmed for more attention.

Orville moved his free hand lower, onto her stomach and under the hem of the pantaloons. Katie pushed the top of the clothing down until it reach just above her knees, giving the man easy access. This was her third concession to Orville's tenderness. She let him use his hand to help get her ready in the place where she did not allow most customers to touch.

The heat rose in her chest and face. She wrapped her arms around Orville's shoulders and pulled him down harder onto to her. The wetness began to flow, covering Orville's fingers. Katie moaned, not a pretend moan, but a deep, release of tension. She rolled her hips forward pushing into his hand. He pushed back. Her heart pounded. She covered his lower hand with hers and pushed while all her muscles harden and the explosion filled her. She gasped for breath.

After a moment, she relaxed her grip on his shoulders and Orville sat up, smiling. He watched her take deep breaths. When the heat drained from her face, Katie curled into a ball to pull her pantaloons off and threw them onto the floor. Orville opened the front of his underwear and climbed onto the bed. She helped guide him to her woman's place, unafraid of any pain from the coupling. Katie used both hands on Orville's backside to encourage him. She felt the heat rising again from her belly to her shoulders and face. She breathed the gunpowder scent deep through her nose. Her insides turned to liquid and the second explosion claimed her body. She felt Orville's culmination, and squeezed his buttocks until it ended. He drove into her several times before he was spent, and collapsed on top of her.

They breathed in time with each other for a few moments before Orville rolled onto his side next to her. After she caught her breath, she rolled into him and he wrapped her under his arm. Katie's body sagged in place. With a sense of well-being, she looked at Orville's face and laughed. "See what y'all done to me? I cain't control myself." She threw her top leg across his hip because she knew he wasn't finished.

Through a part in the curtains, Katie saw that the rain had turned to snow.

****

In West Tennessee, a freezing mix of rain, sleet, and snow fell during the first night of the siege, depositing three inches of ice and snow, and depriving most of the Federal army of sleep as they lay exposed along the front lines. Some died from the exposure, especially among those who had thrown away their blankets and overcoats during the march from Fort Henry. The rest were torpid when the sun reclaimed the sky.

Thursday, February 13th, 1862

Harper rode with the command group at the center of the battalion. The companies advanced in two lines with Company C ahead of the formation in open order. The men held their rifles loaded and ready. While the rest of the brigade crested the ridge, most of the men in First Iowa advanced over snow-covered, but relatively level, ground along Hickman Creek.

As expected, orders had come at sunup to advance closer to the Rebel fortifications. By mid-morning, Lauman had formed the brigade with the two veteran regiments in the front line and the two junior ones behind. The First Iowa now protected the left flank, covering the three-hundred yard gap between the infantrymen and the creek.

When they rounded the end of the ridge, Harper could finally see the outline of the Rebel works as a scar across the face of the ridge less than half-a-mile in front of him. Such a thin line on the ridge, but Harper knew it would become more formidable when they came closer.

On the upper slopes of both ridges, the trees were more scattered than in the camp areas. In the middle of winter, the trees offered very little cover to Lauman's advancing lines. The tree cover increased at the bottom of the ridge and he assumed that this thicker band of trees marked the trace of some watercourse at the foot of the Rebel-held ridge. But today, a flooded marshland covered most of the area between the ridges, disguising the true course of the stream

The battalion advanced in silence with the sun in their eyes, except for the occasional order from a sergeant or corporal to "Maintain your line, there."

To Harper's right, the foot infantry descended the ridge without incident. In front of Harper's battalion, the flooded ground spread wide until it emptied into Hickman Creek on the unit's left flank. Looking through the stunted trees in the wetland, Harper could still discern the outline of the Rebel fortifications part-way up the next ridge, but the trees obscured any detail. Harper estimated the range to the fortifications at about a quarter-of-a-mile.

B-Boom!

A single Rebel artillery battery opened fire on Lauman's formed lines of infantry, but their shots were wildly off-target, and they stopped firing after the first line of infantry reached the cover of the band of trees at the bottom of the ridge.

"Halt," Monroe ordered. The five captains repeated the order and the lines of horsemen stopped at the edge of the marshy ground. Harper could see that the stunted trees extended all the way to the foot of the Rebel ridge.

Monroe looked across the marsh, then back at the officers in his battalion. Harper realized that, on this exceptionally cold day, Monroe would send someone into the marsh to test its passability. The water temperature had to be close to freezing, judging by the tendrils of frost jutting from clumps of dead grass poking through the water's surface.

As far as Harper could tell, the marsh didn't need to be scouted. The stunted trees were enough evidence to indicate that it reached all the way to the Rebel hill. Trees that grew around a marsh cannot grow very tall. After a certain size, they'd fall over because of the loose soil around their roots. Still, someone was going to get cold and wet for no good reason and Harper had a pretty good notion of who that was going to be.

Monroe's gaze settled on Harper. "Mister Harper, take two men and determine how far this wetland extends across, and how deep it is."

Bastard.

Of course, Monroe would send his least-liked officer to scout it out. Harper looked at Porter hoping to gain his support, then back at Monroe. "Colonel, that marsh ain't passable to anyone on foot without gettin' themselves soaked. Ya see that it's wet all the way across, so it probably has a muddy bottom this close to the larger creek."

Monroe stared back at Harper, listening without expression.

"And do ya see how high the water comes on those oak and elm trees?" Harper pointed. "Their wide bottoms are covered and the water is all the way up to the straight part of trunk. That means the water is at least two feet deep at the edges, and goin' all the way up to maybe eight to ten feet in the middle by the looks of how close the water is to the first branches."

"Did you hear my orders, Lieutenant?" Monroe asked.

"Of, course, Colonel, but…" Harper looked back at Porter.

Porter shook his head. "Best git goin', Jamie. We need to know for certain."

Harper did not want to believe that these two men would actually order him into the freezing water on a day like this. Especially to prove what he already knew. He looked up into the sky and exhaled slowly to avoid letting his anger take control.

"I'm waiting, Lieutenant."

Harper lowered his gaze until it fell on Monroe. "Yes, sir."

Monroe nodded. "Then get started."

"Yes, sir. On my way."

Harper walked Santee over to newly-promoted Captain Pierson and requested the two men. Pierson assigned them from his trained skirmishers and Harper directed each man to transfer their saddle bags to companions. Harper gave his overcoat, his rifle and telescopic sight, and his two saddle pistols to Pierson's messenger.

Under the eyes of the entire battalion, the patrol led their horses into the marsh. Sensibly, the animals hesitated at the edge of the cold water and the riders had to use their spurs to drive them forward. Once wet, they let the horses find their own footing. When the water became chest-deep, the horses naturally formed into a column behind Santee.

Harper had to clear his head of thoughts about Monroe's incompetence and concentrate on the job at hand. He knew he was exposed to the Rebels above him. The patrol was an easy target, all bunched together and slowed by the water.

B-Boom!

No sooner had he thought it, than he heard the Rebel cannons above him fire, and the first cannonballs flew overhead, raising geysers of water but not causing any injury. Harper and his escorts bent over the necks of their horses. The Rebel gunners must have set their fuses too long. Before the artillery could adjust, Harper and his men were in the cover of the thickest trees.

The water remained chest-high to the horses for the next few paces. It rose over Harper's legs until it reached his thighs. At a point where an open track separated the naked trees, Santee suddenly found no footing and had to swim. The water rose over her shoulders and across her back. Harper drew his pistol before the water reached the holster at his hip, holding it clear of the rising water. Santee tried to swim back to the solid ground but Harper tightened his grip on the reins and used his spurs to compel her to swim forward. The two troopers had similar difficulties but, since they were less able to control their horses while keeping their rifles ready, their horses carried them back to where they found solid footing.

Santee found footing again under bare trees on the opposite side of the open track and Harper stopped to assess his situation. The world had gone silent around him, except for the slow swirls of water around Santee. The cold in his legs changed to pain from toe to hip. He was wet across the front of his chest and from the waist down. He knew he had to end this patrol in the February chill before he and Santee lost too much body heat. He rubbed Santee's neck to comfort her.

Looking back, he assumed that he and his escort were now on opposite sides of the bed of the stream where it lay in dryer weather. On both sides of the clear track, the horses stood in chest-deep water.

"Stay there and give me cover."

The two soldiers acknowledged the order and separated. After each found the protection of a tree, they drew bead on the portion of the Rebel works immediately in front of Harper but held their fire.

Harper resumed his scout across the marsh. The cover provided by the trees through their intertwined branches gave way to a more open area and the water became shallower. Before Harper reached the end of the marsh, he came under scattered firing from the Rebel trenches. The two men of his escort fired up and this alerted the men of battalion. The subsequent volley, though ragged, comforted Harper when he saw the bullets impacting against the earthen fortifications on the ridge above him.

The effort to keep Santee moving forward distracted Harper from the musket balls continuing to plop into the water around him. Now, he could see the end of the marsh. The ground fifty yards ahead was covered in undisturbed snow and its slope here confirmed that the Rebel ridge began at the end of the marsh.

With musket balls zipping past into the water around him, he guided Santee back the way they had come. Miniature geysers caused by the musket balls hurried him along. Harper had seen what he needed to know.

I'm out here on a fool's errand. Gettin' shot at. Ordered by a fool. So that fool can show off for other god-damned politicians. Monroe's a jackass who ought to be back home pushing, no, pulling a peddler's cart.

The shooting stopped when Harper found cover under the thicker trees near the center of the marsh. He gathered up the two escorts and returned to the battalion commander with Pierson's messenger following.

A messenger appeared from the direction of the infantry regiments. "Colonel Monroe, sir. Colonel Lauman sends his respects. He orders that your battalion halt on line with the infantry. When you are ready, he asks that ya send scouts forward to the edge of the marsh to map out the Rebel fortifications. He asks for your assessment if the works in front of ya can be assaulted successfully."

Harper felt Santee shaking in the cold air. Or was it him? Or both of them? Water dripped from all parts of Santee's thick winter coat creating droplet-sized holes in the snow. The water on Harper's chest soaked through to his underwear, while that in his trousers collected in his boots before overflowing from the tops and making larger holes in the snow among those from Santee.

"Very well." Monroe signed the messenger's receipt and the man galloped back to the brigade commander. Monroe turned his attention to Harper. "What did you learn, Mister Harper?"

In her shivering, Santee urinated in the snow.

Harper gripped the pommel of his saddle to keep his hands from shaking. "Sir, the wetland goes all the way to the foot of the Reb's ridge. Most of it is chest-high to a horse, so shoulder-deep for a man.

But there's a thirty-foot section where it would be over a man's head. Once across, it's a fairly steep climb. About a hundred-and-fifty yards, I say. We'd be in the open going up the ridge to the trench line."

"In the open with wet powder." Porter watched Harper's legs shavering in the saddle.

"Humpt!! That doesn't sound like it would be feasible to attack, either on foot or on horse, does it, Porter?"

One-by-one Harper took his saddle pistols, rifle, and scope from Pierson's messenger and with hands still shaking, returned each to their separate holsters.

"Jamie, did ya scout far enough ahead to draw fire? We heard shooting."

"Y-Yes, sir. They were able to shoot at m-me while I was still in the wat-t-t-ter. It would be a tr-trick for our men to get across and k-keep their weapons and ca-cartidges d-dry."

Porter interrupted the report. "There would be no way for the infantry to use their muzzle-loaders until they reach the slope, assuming they can keep their ammunition dry while they were crossing the marsh."

"Well, that settles it then, right Porter?"

Harper took his overcoat from Pierson's messenger and draped it across Santee's neck, then positioned his saddle bags across the horse's rump. He could tie them off later. He found his gloves in a pocket of the overcoat and pulled them over his shaking hands. The pain had left Harper's legs, replaced by numbness.

"One last thing, sir," Porter answered Monroe. "Jamie, did ya see how well their fortifications were manned? Are they watching this end of the line?"

Harper dismissed Pierson's messenger. He answered Porter while pulling himself into the overcoat, "Y-Y-Yes, s-s-sir. They s-seemed to have enough m-m-men up there to st-t-top whatever we could throw at them."

Porter continued. "Jamie, I know you're cold but think carefully: Is there room between them and the creek to work around them?"

Harper's teeth chattered, now. "I d-doubt it, sir. F-F-From what I saw, anyone m-m-m-moving along the cr-cr-creek would take f- fire in the flank from them on the ridge and s-s-still be in waist-deep wa-wa-water."

"In that case, Colonel, I agree. I don't think an attack across this marsh would accomplish anything."

"Very well then, Major. Have someone draft up a sketch map of this area showing the Rebel works, the ridge and the marsh. I'll sign it. Mister Harper can deliver it."

"W-W-With your permission, C-C-Colonel, I'd l-l-like to take Santee for a run to h-h-help her warm up before she gets sick." Under the overcoat, Harper fought his own shivering. He bit his teeth together to gain control over his chattering jaw.

Monroe looked at Santee. Her shaking was clear to anyone. "Go ahead, but be back in thirty minutes to carry the report to Colonel Lauman.

"Y-Y-Yes, sir.

****

The brigade's advance was the major event of the first day of the siege for Smith's division. The battle on this front settled into a sniping exchange between the Federal skirmishers among the scattered trees and the Rebels in their works. From time-to-time, Federal officers allowed groups of men to return to the rear to the warmth of their campfires. At mid-afternoon, they heard firing coming from the right side of the Federal line, but no orders came for Lauman's men to advance. Later in the afternoon, the second line of Lauman's regiments went into the front line in order to extend the line and cover the portion vacated when another of Smith's brigades moved to support McClernand's division.

First Iowa established a dismounted skirmish line on the brigade's flank and supported by a single company, while most of the men returned to the camp area. Harper spent the remainder of the day with Santee and Corporal Powell close to a campfire which Powell kept at a high blaze.

Friday, February 14th, 1862

“Major Porter,” Harper called as he made his way back into camp in the pre-dawn light. He carried his personal Sharps rifle with one of the long-ranged telescopes mounted.

Like most of the men, Porter appeared to have slept poorly in the cold night. Now, he stood next to his own and Monroe’s orderlies tending a small campfire under the cold gray sky.

“Here, Mister Harper.”

Harper picked his way through mounds of new-fallen snow hiding sleeping soldiers still cocooned in overcoats and slickers.

“Morning, Major.” Harper pointed to the top of the ridge. “I’ve been up to the skirmish line to take a look around. It looks like the snow is about done for today.”

“Uh-hunh,” Porter replied with a frown. He looked into the depths of the cup of steaming coffee he held in his hands.

Harper stepped closer until he was in the major’s line-of-sight from the coffee mug. “I think we might be able to move a few of our men to where they can fire at the Rebel lines. It looks to me like they’re in range of our rifles, only a couple of hundred yards.”

“So, ya think our boys can hit something at two hundred yards?” Porter blew on the hot liquid and swirled the cup.

“At that range, easily. Hell, they can reach all the way up onto the hill behind the Reb trenches. Most of the trained skirmishers are that good. The rest are close. If nothing else, it’ll force the Rebs to keep their heads down during daylight and make their lives miserable. Maybe we could even pick off some their sharpshooters.”

“I’ll suggest it to the colonel when he wakes up.”

“I’m awake.” A dark bundle on the opposite side of the campfire stirred. Monroe threw back his slicker, scattering snow into the morning air. "Do you really believe that?" Monroe stood up, shaking ice crystals from his slicker, before wrapping it around his overcoat.

"Yes, sir." Harper turned to face Monroe. "Maybe not hit every shot, but they sure can get close enough to worry those boys. I trained them for this; they'd know what to do, even if the range was eight hundred yards."

"Well, here's something to make the First Iowa stand out, eh Porter?" Monroe stomped his feet in the snow. "What do you think?"

Porter stared at Harper a moment, then blew on his coffee again. He looked to the top of the ridge as if he could see the friendly lines on the opposite side. "Should be able to do it. We can use just the skirmishers. Not sure what the range of the Reb rifles is, though."

"The officers from the Second Iowa said the Rebs have smoothbores, mostly," Harper said. "So far, they haven't hit any of our men.

The prospect of even this limited action now seemed to energize Porter. "We could assign a company to each of the foot regiments; spread our men across the entire front. If it works, it'll keep the Rebs pinned down all day; none of them will be able to move during daylight."

"And it will give our men the chance to use what they've learned," Harper added. To emphasize their unique weapons, Harper raised his rifle across his chest and cradled it in his crossed arms. He was ready to lead the men whom he had trained.

"All right, I'm convinced." Monroe addressed Porter. "Give me a few minutes, then you and I will go see Colonel Lauman."

****

"Lieutenant Harper said we should let the corporals take charge of the trained skirmishers," Captain McKinsey told Magnusson. "So, I'll leave it to ya, Corporal."

"Yes, sir," Magnusson answered. He had practiced positioning the men often enough during the two-week scout ride with Lieutenant Harper last month. Now, the officers expected him to do it for real–in a real battle; commanding the lives of other men. He couldn't imagine his father or the church ever giving this much responsibility to a nineteen-year-old.

At least, Harper wasn't in command this time. He'd been doing staff work since the campaign started so he could not get anyone else hurt.

Several men from Company B stood watching and listening nearby. The rest of the company spread across the ground behind the Seventh Iowa, looking for dry places to get comfortable.

Magnusson addressed his tiny command; nineteen expectant faces stared back at him. "Pair-off. Bailey, you're with me." He waited until the men formed into ten teams. "They want us to go up to the skirmish line and take positions. Remember what ya learned: One man stays loaded at all times; stay back from the tree line so the Reb sharpshooters can't find ya; pick your targets; check the range on your sight; aim careful; squeeze the trigger–don't tug on it; aim low." He looked into the distance. "Did I forget anything?"

A pile of snow cascaded through the branches of a pine tree, causing snow on the lower branches to shake loose and blow across the group. Some of the men checked their rifles.

"Don't think so, Corporal," Harvey Gettings replied. At twenty-four, Gettings was the oldest of the Company B trained skirmishers and Magnusson relied on the older man's judgment to help lead the men. By answering, Gettings signaled that Magnusson had it right. Although the oldest of the Company B skirmishers, Gettings had no desire to be in command,

"So," Magnusson continued. "We're going to operate with the skirmishers from the Seventh Iowa. They want us to force the Rebels to stay in their trenches. Ya can let the guys from the Seventh shoot at targets inside the trenches. Our job is to shoot any Rebs who are trying to move around behind their trenches and especially anyone trying to move up from the fort." He pointed to his left. "Four teams will go with Gettings, the others will come with me." Magnusson examined the nineteen faces. Everyone looked eager, ready to start. "I'll take the first shot when everyone's ready. That way, we won't give away what we're doing until we can put a mass of fire on 'em at the start."

He looked at the men a last time. "Ready? Follow me." Magnusson led the way forward while the men followed in silence, trained specialists ready to begin their deadly business. The lieutenant from Seventh Iowa who commanded the skirmish line returned Magnusson's salute. The Seventh's skirmishers already in position stared when Magnusson and his men arrived.

About fifty men from the Seventh operated in groups of three or four in an open line which extended along the forward edge of the open wood, where the wood met the cleared fire zone in front of rebel trench line. In most cases, one man watched the Rebel works from a hidden position, while the others in the group waited farther back in the woods.

It appeared to Magnusson that the battle of the skirmishers stood at a stalemate, with most of the Northerners trying to avoid becoming a target for the Rebels, while the Rebels endeavored to do the same and stayed hidden behind the logs and dirt of their fortifications. To his left, a musket popped in the Rebels trenches and two shots returned from the Second Iowa's skirmishers.

When Magnusson looked at the Rebel trenches two hundred yards across the cleared field, he understood why there was so little shooting between the two lines. He could not detect any men in the trenches.

The Rebels had placed logs along the top of the piled earth to provide protection for their men. Another row of logs stood above the first, elevated enough so a man could fire through the gap between the two rows of logs. The lower row would protect a firer below the shoulders, while the upper row would protect him from the eyes up. Magnusson realized it would require an above-average Federal marksman to place a round between the two rows of logs if a shooter appeared.

But no shooters appeared in the Rebel trenches. To do so would make them a target for a dozen muskets, in spite of the dirt and logs. Magnusson reappraised the deployment of the Seventh's skirmishers. The way they stayed hidden, it would require a Rebel sniper to watch the wooded area for a long time to detect a target; during that time, the observer would be vulnerable to fire from the unseen Federals.

One of the Seventh's men on Magnusson's left fired his musket.

"Did ya git him, Clem?" one of the man's team asked.

"Naw. Don't think so. Gave him a lesson in keeping his head down, though." Clem reloaded his musket.

What surprised Magnusson about the Rebel works was the number of men who moved or sat in the open on the hillside behind the trenches. Perhaps three or four dozen men sat or lay on the snow-covered ground enjoying the warmth of the sun on what had become a clear, sunny day. Almost as if the war in the trenches had become a Sunday picnic.

"I suppose those men behind the trenches are why we were sent here," Magnusson told his men.

"That's exactly right, Corporal." It was the lieutenant in charge of the Seventh's skirmish line. "Some Lieutenant Harper came by this morning and told us First Iowa could clear those men from the hill. Force 'em to stay in their trenches all day."

"Yes, sir." *So all of this was Harper's idea. Maybe he doesn't have enough staff work to do to stay out of our business.*

"Well, can ya? The muskets my men carry won't reach up there." He looked to a group of his own men. "We can put some rounds partway up the hill, but not with any kind of accuracy."

At least Harper had found something for them to do that was better than riding a picquet line behind that frozen swamp. "I 'spect that won't be a problem for us, Lieutenant." Magnusson looked back across the lines. The Confederates made perfect targets silhouetted against the snow on the hillside. "Maybe four or five hundred yards, ya figure?" He paused to think about the skill of his own men. "We should be able to take care of 'em."

"Then you'd best get started, Corporal."

"Yes, sir." Magnusson forgot to salute the officer before he walked over to his men. "Harv, take your five teams to the left. The rest of ya, come with me." He led his teams to the right, looking for good hides that the men from Seventh Iowa didn't already occupy and which offered usable views of the Rebel lines.

His men found spots faster than he could. He allocated the teams until he reached the end of the Seventh Iowa's line. Cooke and Davis would operate from this end of the line. Looking beyond the flank through the scattered trees, he saw Eddy Straub from Company C deploying his own men among the Indiana regiment.

With Bailey following, Magnusson made his way back to the

middle of the line. As he passed each team, he watched them prepare their positions: dragging deadfall logs, rocks, or whatever else they could find to disguise the position. Magnusson made sure his men were back far enough from the edge of the wood to make them too hard for any snipers to find.

Returning to the center of the line, he found a likely spot where he could not only watch the Rebel works, but also observe the performance of his own men. "Now, Ben." Magnusson addressed Bailey. "Let's see what ya can do to get this position ready. I'm thinking we should use the notch in this tree for a rifle rest."

Bailey had found a depression near the tree where they would take turns reloading. He went about the business of converting it into a hide by cutting half-a-dozen tree branches and piling them in front of the depression. Dead leaves from the forest floor created a mound when Bailey piled them over a frame made of the branches. Lastly, he threw snow over the leaves, trying to make the hide less conspicuous against the scattered snow covering the nearby ground.

Meanwhile, Magnusson looked down the line of skirmishers waiting for each team to signal they were ready.

The lieutenant from the Seventh came back and asked, "So what is so special about the First Iowa's skirmishers that my men can't do?"

"Well, sir. I reckon it's these Sharps rifles." Magnusson handed his weapon to the lieutenant. "They got a reach that's better than the muskets your men have."

"Really? So, how far can they shoot?"

"Supposedly, they'll go to a thousand yards. I ain't never tried to fire one that far, though."

"How far have ya gone?"

"Just over five hundred yards. After that, the targets get too small for me. A man won't be no bigger than the half the height of the front sight."

"Well, Corporal, I'll be watching to see how well ya do." He handed Magnusson's rifle back.

"With your permission, sir. I need to get my men ready." Magnusson could see Captain McKinsey approaching. He saluted to the lieutenant, hoping that would end the conversation.

"Of course, Corporal. Carry on."

Magnusson held his hand in the air, the signal the teams who were ready would repeat. Gettings waved his readiness from the far left team. Davis signaled their readiness on the right.

His team was the last, and just in time.

"Ready, Magnusson?" McKinsey asked.

"Yes, sir. Ready."

McKinsey looked down the line at the teams from his company. "Good work, Corporal. Proceed."

"Yes, sir."

Magnusson looked beyond the open ground and past the line of Rebel works. He stepped up to his firing position behind the chosen tree, aimed quickly and fired, not intending to hit a target as much as to give the signal for his men to start firing. Nine other shots rang out, the distinctive *crack* of the Sharps resonating over the *bang* of the Seventh's muskets.

None of the shots fired by his teams found their mark. The Confederates relaxing behind the trenches did not appear to notice the bullet impacts in the snow and the mud around them.

"That's not what I expected, Corporal," McKinsey said.

"They'll get better, sir."

The second man from each team now fired and they, too, missed their marks.

"Well, I certainly hope so, after all the folderol about these damn rifles."

The first shooters fired their second shots when they finished reloading. Magnusson watched to see how many of his men adjusted their aim. Of nine shots, two scored hits on the men lounging behind the Rebel lines. *That* got the Rebels moving. Some helped their injured men farther up the hill. Others pointed at the Federal skirmish line, while others gathered up their gear and moved higher. Still, none showed any sign of urgency. They must have thought these were wild shots.

"Bailey, stay here. Fire whenever ya have a clear shot."

"Yes, Corporal."

Magnusson walked in front of his own team's hide. He wanted to see if the woods concealed his men as well as he thought they would. He was able to locate the positions of his men under the clouds of smoke rising into the naked tree branches. But most of the men fired from positions with at least partial cover. Having chosen hides far enough back from the edge of the wood, they were probably better protected than the men from the Seventh, as long as they stayed careful. Some of his men had removed their overcoats to provide a dry place to sit when it was not their turn to fire. Magnusson returned to his own hide, where Bailey fired as fast as he could reload.

"Take your time, Ben. Aim your shots better. You're gettin' too excited. Squeeze the trigger."

"Easy for you to say, Gus. Why don't you try it?"

Magnusson chuckled. "In a minute."

A group of a dozen Rebels drew Magnusson's attention as they marched and slipped up the hill through the snow to the Confederate rear. They stopped to look back when the first distinctive reports from the Sharps rifles sounded but continued on their way when the initial shots had no effect. Magnusson brought his rifle to the ready, quickly aimed and fired.

One of the twelve toppled backward. Gettings fired next–a second Confederate buckled at the knee. Two soldiers moved to help the first casualty who lay still, surrounded by reddening snow.

Magnusson looked at his teams to the left and right. Now, they had the range and the wood roared with the discharges from their rifles.

McKinsey watched through his binoculars. Magnusson had never worked this close to the company commander, and was a little nervous. But his men were doing well, and their looks of determination showed they were concentrating on the bloody business.

A Rebel with two blue stripes on his gray coat knelt down to talk with the screaming man holding his knee. The remaining Rebels in the column looked on, or pointed to the Federal lines and yelled to each other. Magnusson felt a twinge of sympathy for these men who were the unlucky targets of the new weapon that the First Iowa had brought to the battle.

All of Magnusson's skirmishers concentrated on this group. Magnusson watched two more Confederates fall. Their corporal yelled and waved at the survivors. He directed them uphill toward the Rebel rear while he tried to pull the knee-injury toward the trenches. Puffs of smoke appeared from several points along the Rebel line but Magnusson could hear the musketballs buzz high over the heads of the sharpshooters.

A man at the rear of the group running uphill fell face-first into the snow, propelled by the impact of a Sharps' .52 caliber round. The leading man fell over. The man next to him tumbled sideways, falling face-up in the bright morning sunlight; not moving. The four survivors turned back to the Rebel works. Three more fell before they took two steps in the new direction.

The last man began zigzagging as he ran. Fountains of snow popped all around him but none hit. He dropped his own rifle so he could run faster. He twisted right, ran five steps through the ankle-deep snow, and twisted left. He fell heavily in his next dodge to the right, puffs of snow erupting around him. But he scrambled to his feet still healthy, having slipped in the snow. Five feet from the Rebel trench, he dove for the outstretched arms of the men from his own regiment and they pulled him to safety.

Firing ceased all along the line when the man disappeared. Cheering started, both sides amazed at the man's escape. Magnusson's men and the skirmishers from the Seventh Iowa held their fire, allowing the Rebel corporal to carry his injured man into the trenches. Gunsmoke from the Sharps drifted over the Federal lines, confined by the branches of the pine trees.

The pause in the firing continued for a dozen heatbeats after the two Rebs disappeared from view. The remaining Rebels on the hill behind their trenches found safety during this break by climbing to the top of the hill or returning to the trenches. Perhaps a dozen more men lay where they fell, scars in the smooth complexion of the snow on the hillside.

"Very impressive, Corporal." McKinsey lowered his binoculars. The lieutenant from the Seventh stared at the hill behind the Rebel works.

"Yes, sir." Magnusson turned to examine the hill where minutes before dozens of Rebels had been relaxing. Now, the only movement was three men from the marching group who rolled on the ground in pain.

My men did that. It was too easy. It happened so fast.

He stared at his Sharps, surprised at its lethal ability. The air around Magnusson smelled of burnt sulfer. Maybe Harper was right. This rifle made the First Iowa special, but the sulfer smell made Magnusson think of the Lord of Evil.

"What's wrong, Gus?" Bailey pulled his rifle back from the notch in the tree.

"Nothin', Ben. Just thinkin'."

In time, Gettings yelled across the lines, "Yo, Johnny Reb. Bes' be keepin' your heads down from now on. We're gonna start up again." And so they did.

****

Satisfied with the performance of the trained skirmishers, Harper walked back up the ridge and saw Lauman and Monroe watching the skirmishers operate across the marshy valley.

"Ho-ho, that's got them worried," Lauman told Monroe.

"Yes, sir." Monroe nodded and smiled, ignoring Harper. "It surely does."

"You've trained them well, Monroe."

"You're very kind, Colonel."

Harper shook his head in disgust when he passed Monroe. *He* had trained them. Now someone else got to command them and the damn politician who hated the whole idea in the first place takes the credit. He tried to catch Monroe's eye, but his commanding officer ignored him as he went past.

Harper continued up the ridge toward the rear area, moving through the scattered trees. He was still carrying his Sharps and had the telescopic sight mounted. Nearing the crest, he came to a large stone outcrop which created a break in the tree cover and permitted a clear view of the ridges on the opposite side of the valley. A number of officers stood on the outcrop, using binoculars to assess the Confederate positions. General Smith, the division commander, saw Harper and signaled him to join the group. "You're from the unit with the Sharps rifles, aren't you, Lieutenant?"

"Yes, sir. James Harper, First Iowa Rifles." Harper stepped up to the general and saluted.

Smith returned the salute. "I recognized that rifle you're carrying. Was that your boys who shot up the Rebel squad down there?" Smith pointed to the spot where the Company B skirmishers destroyed the squad marching up the hill.

Harper looked across the valley. He needed to shield his eyes against the glare of the sun on the snow lying on the ground. The dead men still lay where they fell alongside the road. "Yes , sir. It was."

"Well, give your people my compliments. That was some excellent marksmanship."

Harper smiled. "Thank you, general. The extra training I gave some of them seems to have worked." Since the division commander had seen what First Iowa could do, maybe Smith would have some better ideas about how to use the battalion.

The general looked down at Harper from his position atop the outcrop. "Stay with us for a few minutes, Harper."

Harper nodded, "Yes, sir." Harper joined two staff officers standing farther back on the rock. Behind them, aides held the horses for the group far enough back in the trees to avoid becoming a target for the Reb artillery. Harper used the telescopic sight on his rifle to examine the Rebel works in detail for the first time since the siege began. The staff officers stepped back and stared at him.

"Don't worry. I'm jes' lookin' them over."

Across the marshy valley, the Rebel trenches cut across the slope of the hill opposite at about the same elevation as Harper, a brown scar in the snow. At several points along the line, cannon barrels poked from small earthen bastions built tall enough to protect the gunners from musket and cannon fire. Along the length of their lines, the defenders had leveled the woods in front to provide an open field-of-fire. The tree stumps were cut to three or four inches inches above the ground, so they wouldn't provide cover for an attacking force. Any attack would have to climb the hill through the open killing ground.

Smith spoke to the colonel standing next to him. "You see the way their trenches run along the side of the hill? They form sort of an angle just there." Smith pointed to a notch in the ridge opposite where a rivulet flowed in the creek separating the armies. "And then come toward us for a couple hundred yards before running off to the east."

"Yes, sir," the colonel replied.

Harper looked to the portion of the line holding General Smith's attention. The enemy hill formed an inverted 'Y'. Lauman's brigade faced Rebels on the left arm but the Rebel trenches extended onto the right arm as well.

"If we send Lauman forward, he'll have to deal not only with the Rebs to his front but also with flanking fire from that part of their lines." The colonel nodded, as did the staff officers standing near Harper.

"So, if Grant wants us to mount an assault, we'll have to have Cook's brigade keep that side occupied."

Smith's inspection shifted to the road leading from the trenches back to Fort Donelson. "Once we get past their trenches, there's room beyond them to emplace our siege guns so they'll be close enough to have some effect against the main fort." Smith lowered his binoculars. "It seems that the Rebels did their job very well. They've built the glacis higher before finishing the actual fort. I can't see any tanglefoot, but if we wait too long I'm sure there will be some."

Using his binoculars, Harper scanned the ridge opposite, starting at the Rebel trenches then upward until he could see Fort Donelson proper on a hill, three-quarters of a mile beyond. There was a clear change in the melt pattern of the snow on this, the western face. Along the bottom sections, straw-colored dead grass poked through the snow. It insulated the ground from the sun's heat, causing the snow to melt more slowly. Higher up, the snow lay thinner on the hill, with naked earth showing through in some places; here the darker color of new-turned earth would have absorbed more sunlight, causing the snow to melt sooner.

"Do you think Grant will be that patient?" the colonel with Smith asked.

"I would be surprised," Smith said, continuing to watch Fort Donelson. "General Grant is of the opinion that clearing the Rebels from Kentucky and Tennessee as quickly as possible will disrupt their recruiting efforts and keep the rebellion contained in these parts. I tend to agree with him. Once past Donelson, we can take Nashville and install a loyal governor."

But Harper could see, any assault against the fort would have to climb fifty or sixty feet of glacis before reaching the earthen walls at the top, all the while receiving canister and musket fire from above. A direct attack on this face of the fort would be a bloodbath.

"Mister Harper," Smith called.

"Here, sir." Harper hurried to Smith's side.

"We're discussing how to keep the Rebs in those trenches." Smith pointed to the right leg of the inverted 'Y'. "Do you think your five companies could force the Rebs on our right to keep their heads down?"

"Yes, sir. We can do that."

"You might want to consult with your commanding officer, Harper," the colonel commented.

"I know what our men can do, Colonel," Harper said. "I trained them." He looked at the Confederate positions. "We can reach them from this ridge. Firin' from here will let us fire over the heads of our own troops."

"Hell, Harper, it's nearly a quarter-of-a-mile from here."

"Yes, Colonel." Harper looked across the valley. "A little more, I think."

Smith stared at Harper without expression and without saying anything.

Harper continued. "Most of the men would fire from lower down, so they're closer." He pointed to the trees lower on the ridge. "I'd put the best marksmen up here with me and use our long-ranged scopes. As long as the attack comes before the trees come into bud, before spring, obviously. It'll get harder when the trees leaf out."

"It's hard to believe you could be very effective, Harper."

Harper looked at the colonel with an annoyed frown. "Shall I show ya, Colonel?"

"How are you going to do that?"

"Watch." If he had to demonstrate what the Rifles could do to every senior officer in the army, he would. "I'll need a minute and a set of binoculars." Holding his rifle with one hand, he pulled the straps of the satchel with his extra ammunition over his head; he set them on the ground. He rested his personal Sharps on the satchel, being careful that the firing mechanism stayed clear of the snow. Last, he placed his overcoat, sword belt, and holster belt into a separate pile and patted them into place. Picking up the elements of the first pile, he made his way onto the leading edge of the rocky outcrop.

Harper looked for a suitable spot where he could lie down on the sun-dried boulder and rest the barrel of his rifle. The range would be extreme, but Harper had made similar shots before. Besides making the demonstration to General Smith, Harper wanted to challenge himself and to prove to himself that he still had the skills from his days in the Nebraska-Dakota Territory, or find out if office work had made him stale.

The fact that men would die or be maimed so Harper could prove his point did not trouble him. They were soldiers in the enemy's army. Was it fair that he could kill them by surprise at very little risk to himself? He didn't care. This wasn't a tennis competition.

He found a spot ten yards past a telescope being used by a signal corps lieutenant and two privates; they stopped to watch Harper. From this position, Harper could see the forward-most line of Federal troops operating on the hill opposite, marked by the gun smoke from their weapons. They were over a hundred yards from the Rebel trenches. He would have to set up his shots so his height advantage would result in the bullets passing over the heads of the friendly troops.

Smith and his staff moved up to stand behind Harper. One of the staff officers handed Harper the requested binoculars.

Harper knelt down and scanned the Rebel positions, looking for suitable targets. He soon found a group sheltering among a copse of oaks a hundred yards behind the trenches and hidden from view of the Federal front line. No such obstructions impeded Harper's line-of-sight from the outcrop.

"General, along the line of my rifle there are some Rebels sitting down to lunch. Focus on that group."

Harper stretched out on the rock and went through his mental checklist. The sun-heated rock offered welcome warmth through his dark-blue uniform. The Hardee hat shaded his eyes. He created a rest for the barrel of his rifle by stacking several stones together and covering them with his overcoat. He loaded his first round–pushing against the bottom of oversized paper cartridge with his thumb so that no air gaps showed in the chamber. He set five more rounds on the boulder within easy reach, along with his box of percussion caps. After he confirmed that the settings on the mount of his telescopic sight were those he knew aligned the scope to the barrel, he dialed in the estimated range on the rear sight, six-hundred-fifty yards.

Harper used the binoculars to re-acquire his targets and by aligning the binoculars on top of the telescopic sight, he could capture their images in its smaller field-of-view. He set the sight picture on the center of the back of the nearest man and estimated the offset needed for the crosswind. He slowly pulled back on the first trigger until it clicked into place. This would take up most of the force needed to fire the weapon; it also gave the second trigger a hair's weight trigger pull. He exhaled slowly, caught his breath; locked the rifle on the off-set target; tapped the second trigger.

Crack!

The distinctive discharge of the Sharps exploded across the outcrop. The muzzle of the rifle rose up several inches from the recoil only to drop back into position while a wind-devil blew the gun smoke back along the rifle, covering Harper's face with sulfurous residue.

The smoke obscured his view for a moment but blew away in time for Harper to see a fountain of snow rise in the lower right quadrant of the gun sight. He had over-estimated the effect of the cross-wind and underestimated the range. The group of soldiers did not appear to notice the near-miss.

With practiced skilled, Harper reloaded and re-capped the rifle while keeping his eye at the gun sight. Without adjusting the range setting, he aimed the second shot closer to the target and raised it to the man's head.

Crack!

When the smoke cleared, the man still sat in his previous position without moving. Harper could not see where the shot fell.

Damn!

Two misses. That never happened in the old days.

What is Smith going to think?

Harper reloaded and replaced the firing cap automatically, all the time watching his target. He exhaled, began his pull on the first trigger, caught his breath, and stopped. Through the sight he saw a dark circle spread across the back of the man's jacket. He watched as the discoloration spread to the bottom seam of the jacket and drops fell beside the ground-cloth, staining the snow bright red. Harper looked over the telescopic sight for the next target.

The man's companions raced to retrieve their weapons and scampered to shelter behind the trees. But they misunderstood the direction of the bullet that hit their friend. They watched below them on the hill, toward the Federal front line, placing the oaks between themselves and the Federals on the hill below them. Harper still had a clear view to several of them from the outcrop and watched with cold efficiency to see which man would be next. He selected his next target kneeling behind a tree close by the first man. Harper set the first trigger, aimed, adjusted using the same offset as the last round, exhaled, held it, tapped the second trigger.

Crack!

The man dropped his musket and grabbed his shoulder, falling over at the same time. Harper reloaded and re-capped without thought while he watched the man roll on the ground in pain. The remaining men in the group now stared at the hillside where Harper lay. Some pointed at the cloud of gunsmoke from his last shot as it drifted away to Harper's left.

He aimed at the man in the group who appeared to be doing the most talking, captured him in the telescopic sight, set the first trigger, offset from the target, exhaled, held it, tapped.

Crack!

The man fell to the ground with a hole in his chest.

Like a machine, Harper looked for his next target. He saw a man with graying hair and beard aligning his musket in the crook of an oak. The Rebel kept most of his body hidden by the tree, exposing only enough of his face and hands to hold his musket. Harper found the man's face in the telescopic sight.

Got ya, Pappy.

The muzzle of the man's musket filled the center of Harper's sight.

Using the same offset as before, Harper set the first trigger, exhaled, caught it, tapped the second trigger. His sight filled with smoke from the man's weapon at the same time the Sharps fired.

The wind blew the smoke away from both weapons at the same time. Harper saw his bullet gouge the gray trunk of the oak and spray wooden shards across *Pappy's* face. He heard a bullet splat against the outcrop a dozen feet below him, sending bits of stone flying upward. Harper's mind registered that *Pappy* must have been an experienced shot to come so close. Through his telescopic sight Harper watched *Pappy* drop his musket and roll behind the tree clutching his face.

The remaining Confederates in the group fired at the outcrop, causing Smith and his staff to back away from the skyline. Exuberant because he retained his skills, Harper reloaded, scooped up the box of primers, closed the lid, pushed it into his trousers pocket. He stood and climbed to the closest part of the outcrop to the Rebels while bullets continued to impact the rock and zip overhead. When he was sure he stood in silhouette against the sky, he raised his Sharps over his head and let out a Sioux war-whoop to taunt the Rebels.

"Aye-yai-yai-yai-yai." Any resentment over not commanding the trained skirmishers fell away in the flush of his personal victory over the Rebels. Smith and his staff applauded and shook his hand when Harper walked off of the outcrop.

****

When Harper arrived at camp, he greeted Corporal Powell with a laugh. "Isn't it a great, bright, sunny day, Corporal?"

"If ya say so, sir."

Harper approved the morning reports. With Powell watching, He extracted the round from his rifle and used a leather patch and the cleaning pick to clear residue from the breech and barrel. He checked the condition of the telescopic sight before returning the rifle and the sight to their separate saddle-holsters, along with the satchel full of ammunition and the box of primer caps.

"Done some shootin', sir?"

"Yes, I have, Corporal. And so have the trained skirmishers." He rubbed his hands over the campfire. "This war could be over soon, ya know. If they let us at the Rebels with all of our men."

"That'd be nice, sir. Maybe home in time for plantin', do ya think?"

"Oh, yes, Corporal. Definitely." They laughed together. They'd heard that particular story repeated too many times in the past year.

Too excited to sit still, Harper sought out Santee and groomed her as a way to keep his hands busy before returning to the campfire. Sensing his excitement, Santee twisted her head to watch him and pawed at the ground. "No, no, girl. We ain't going for a run today. Sorry."

When he finished brushing, Harper took the satchel with ammunition from his saddlebag and slung it over his shoulder. He arranged it across his body so it rested at his right hip, the dull white of the unbleached canvas prominent against his tunic's dark blue.

"Where're ya goin', Jamie?" It was Major Porter.

"Thought I'd go up there and see how the boys are doing, eh? See if they remember what I taught them. Maybe fire a few shots."

"I haven't seen the letter to Mr. Magnusson, yet."

"Working on it, Major." In truth, Harper had forgotten about the apology to the old Quaker.

"Well, before ya go trying to win the war by yourself, there's something else I want ya to do."

Harper frowned; the war was just over the hill. He had a taste of it and he *liked* the taste. In frustration, he took a hopeless look up the slope where he could pick out the distinctive *crack* of the Sharps rifles from the *bang* of the muskets used by both sides. Resigned to the inevitable, he turned back to Porter. "What's that, Major?"

They walked toward Porter's campsite, Harper downcast at the prospect of more paperwork with a battle less than a mile away.

"After ya wash the gunpowder from your face, I want ya to see if Grant's staff is using the big barn on that farm."

Harper knew he was caught. He rubbed his cheek with the back of his hand and stared at the black smudge.

"We might want to move the men there tonight."

McKinsey, again. God-damned McKinsey.

Saturday, February 15th, 1862

"Colonel Monroe! Colonel Monroe!"

It was half-past nine on the third day of the siege. The men of the First Iowa not needed in the siege lines went about their morning chores in the Widow Crisp's barn. The horses and mules waited outside, picketed along the downwind side of the barn in the clear morning. But the unremitting cold persisted, freezing the wheels of the wagons and artillery to the ground and depressing the spirits of the soldiers.

Harper looked up from his paperwork when the courier rode into to the barn. All activity stopped while the men watched the rider. "Over here." Harper shouted so the courier could hear him. The rider trotted over to the corner of the barn where Harper and Corporal Powell operated the adjutant's office.

Most of the men in the barn this morning worked in the staff sections, but the crowd included men from the line companies who spent the night prior along the skirmish lines sniping at the Rebel fortifications. Now, they slept in the straw wherever they could find a quiet corner or an empty horse stall.

"Mornin', sir," the courier saluted. "Urgent orders for Colonel Monroe from army headquarters!"

"I'm the battalion adjutant, you can give it to me," Harper replied. "What's in it?"

The rider pulled the sealed letter from his saddlebag. "Colonel Webster's respects, sir, and he orders the First Iowa to be ready to march in thirty minutes." He handed the letter to Harper. "You're to accompany General Grant over to McClernand's Division."

"And where might McClernand's Division be?" Harper asked.

"Over on the right, is all I know. They've been attacked and are falling back."

Harper signed the receipt for the orders and returned the courier's salute. "Let Colonel Webster know we'll be ready on time."

A change in orders might liven up what looked to become a dull day. The trained skirmishers were too successful. Now, a day after sending the men with the Sharps rifles into the skirmish line, no Rebels dared leave their trenches during daylight. Even during the night, the moonlight made them easy targets for the First's sharpshooters whenever they tried to move against the background of fallen snow.

The courier dropped the receipt into his satchel and left the barn. Clods of dirt and snow flew from the horse's hooves when he galloped back to army headquarters in Widow Crisp's farmhouse.

Harper opened the envelope and read through the orders while the men in the barn returned to their own work, speculating out loud on what the orders meant for them. As the courier said, army headquarters ordered the battalion to report to Grant's headquarters as soon as possible to escort the general. Harper noted that a copy of the orders also went to General Smith's headquarters for their information.

"Corporal Powell." The barn became silent when Harper spoke. "Send men out to notify the company commanders to get their men mounted. I'll find the colonel and Major Porter to let them know." He handed the written orders to Powell, before he turned to face the men in the barn. "Best get ready, boys. We're moving out."

"Do ya think we'll get there in time for fighting, Mister Harper?" one man asked.

"I expect that depends on how long it takes us to get there. If the Rebs are still out by the time we arrive, I'll bet *we* can to push them back, right, boys?" He looked at all of the men in the barn.

"Yes, sir!"

"We sure will!"

"We'll get the bastards."

Powell drafted copies of the orders and gave them to the company couriers to carry up to the front lines. Harper found Monroe and Porter attending Colonel Lauman's morning war council at brigade headquarters near the top of the ridge above the regimental camps. The council stood in the open air with Lauman at the top of the circle and the other officers standing or leaning against nearby trees

"General Wallace arrived last night with two new brigades," Lauman told the assembled officers. "They're on our right, filling the gap between us and McClernand."

Harper signaled to Porter who stepped away from the circle of officers. Several others in the circle looked up, but returned their attention to Lauman's briefing when Harper gave no indication of urgency. After Porter read the orders he returned to the group and handed them to Monroe.

"The Navy tried to attack the fort yesterday after they put Wallace's men ashore, but this time, they lost," Lauman told the others. "It may be that most of the gunboats were badly damaged. Some might have sunk. We don't have any of the details yet."

The Army officers present did not seem disturbed by the Navy's defeat.

"That leaves it up to the Army to take the fort," one of the regimental commanders said. "I guess the Navy can't do everything."

The others murmured their agreement. The Navy's defeat meant Donelson would have to be captured by land attack. Would Grant order an immediate assault which would probably result in heavy casualties? Or would he commence a siege requiring months to succeed and which would end inevitably in a final, bloody storming up the hill Harper saw yesterday?

Monroe interrupted the brigade commander's announcements. "Gentlemen, it appears I must leave you. My battalion is ordered to army headquarters immediately. Sounds like something is astir this morning."

"Does it say why they need an entire battalion, Colonel Monroe?" Lauman asked.

"Yes, sir. We are to accompany General Grant over to First Division. It doesn't say anything else. Sorry, sir."

Without thinking, Harper added, "The courier who brought it mentioned something about a Reb attack on the right." Monroe furrowed his brow in irritation at Harper before he watched for

Lauman's reaction. He relaxed when the brigade commander acknowledged Harper's comment.

"Strange that we haven't heard any fighting from there this morning," Lauman said. "All right, then. Off you go, Monroe. Send a report back when you find out what's happening. Godspeed."

Turning to the other officers, Lauman added "Well gentlemen, perhaps today will not be so quiet as we have been led to believe. Have your men prepare in case there's to be some action."

****

In less than an hour, the men of the battalion gathered their belongings and saddled their horses, those coming from the front lines being helped by their mess-mates. The battalion stood in mounted formation in the snow in front of Widow Crisp's commandeered home, the breath of each man and horse forming vapor clouds in the cold. Harper waited atop Santee in front of the color guard, alongside Major Porter. Santee and several other horses pawed at the ground, working their cold-stiff muscles.

Major Rawlins, Grant's personal aide, came out to talk with the battalion officers. Monroe, who had been checking the condition of the troops, trotted up to the group and signaled the company commanders to join him.

"The general is not ready to leave. He visited Flag-Officer Foote aboard the *Saint Louis* this morning and is not back yet. We've sent for him. He should be here shortly." Rawlins looked north, along the road to the riverboat landing.

"So, what's happening?" Porter asked. "There seems to be a battle over on the right, but we can't hear anything and we don't have any orders from General Smith's headquarters."

Rawlins looked up at the mounted Monroe and Porter. "It looks like the Confederates came out from their trenches at sunup and tried to overwhelm McClernand. At least two of his brigades routed. As far as we know, the entire division may have lit out by now."

Harper understood with two brigades gone, there must now be a huge hole in the ring of Federal troops surrounding Fort Donelson. If the Rebels destroyed McClernand's whole division, the entire Federal army would be in jeopardy.

"Wallace is next in line. We've convinced him to send help to McClernand." Rawlins glanced at the road again. "At first, he refused to move his men unless he had an order signed by General Grant, himself. He didn't move anyone until he heard the shooting getting closer to his own men."

Harper wondered what kind of a general would do nothing while the army was being attacked. A gust of wind from the south carried the sounds of the battle, the artillery in particular recognizable to Harper. But *whose* artillery? Harper's trained ear could also discern musketry–not the disciplined volleys of troops well under control, but the ragged sounds of a free-for-all.

"Since Grant will have to ride past Wallace's old positions, Colonel Webster wants a strong escort. We aren't exactly sure what the conditions are, and there may be gaps in Wallace's lines, as well." Rawlins looked down the road toward the river landing. "Hopefully, the general's on his way back by now."

All of the officers in the group looked to the road where Grant might appear. Porter pulled out his pocket watch and Harper looked over his shoulder at the watchface: ten forty-five.

"Gentlemen, inform your companies," Monroe ordered. The company commanders saluted and returned to wait with their soldiers.

Fifteen minutes later, half-a-dozen riders appeared on the road to the landing. "Ah, there he is," Rawlins said.

None of the riders gave the appearance of a general officer, but Harper recognized Grant in a private's overcoat as the party rode past and dismounted in front of the farmhouse. The general looked older, more haggard than he had aboard the *Chancellor* three months ago. But in his face, Harper saw a mean, determined, chiseled hardness.

Orderlies took the reins for the party's horses. Grant stopped to look at the First Iowa before he went inside the headquarters building. Rawlins followed, signaling Monroe to come with him.

"How serious do ya think this is, Major?"

"No idea, Jamie. Webster must be worried though, if he wants this large of an escort." He pulled on the reins to keep his horse in position. "I suppose we'll find out when we get over there." Another sudden gust carried more sounds of the battle.

After a few minutes, Rawlins and Monroe returned. Monroe gathered the battalion officers into a group and issued his orders. "Captain Compton, Company A will take the lead. Major Rawlins will ride with you to act as a guide."

"Yes, sir."

He turned to the other officers. "The rest of the battalion will follow behind the general. I will take the lead with Major Porter and Lieutenant Harper. The supply mules will follow in the rear. Captain Streeper, detail a couple of squads to escort the mules. Any questions?" He paused to look at each officer separately. The subordinates all shook their heads.

"All right. See to it. We will be on our way shortly."

Grant stepped out of the farmhouse and looked across the road while the officers returned to their companies. Rawlins waved to the general and mounted. He looked down at Monroe.

"I expect the general will set a pace faster than your supply mules can manage. If they cannot keep up, we'll leave you to catch up when we arrive at McClernand's." Monroe and Porter both nodded their understanding.

Rawlins rode to the head of Company A. "Column of twos," Compton ordered and the soldiers moved onto the trail, arranging themselves two abreast, the widest formation the trail would permit. Grant's command group remounted and fell into place behind Compton's company. Rawlins set a trotting gait and Company A soon disappeared southwards, into the woods.

Monroe mounted and led Porter and Harper onto the trail with the four-man color guard following. Once they passed the line of formed horsemen, Captain McKinsey shouted the order, "Column of twos," and Company B moved behind the battalion command group. The other companies joined in sequence and the battalion was on the move in the cold morning air.

With the distance to Company A opening, Monroe, Porter, and Harper attempted to bring their horses to a trot but could not establish the gait because of the condition of the trail. Where Company A rode over the night's crust of frozen mud, the rest of the column found the road choked by the soupy mess left behind. Walking was the best pace the horses could manage, in spite of the urgings of their riders.

When it became clear the rest of the battalion could not keep the pace set by Company A, Monroe left Porter and Harper to join Grant's command group.

In three-quarters of an hour the battalion covered only a half-mile. Porter and Harper lost sight of Grant's staff and Company A. Harper turned to see the companies behind him strung out as each company negotiated a trail made worse by the passage of the company ahead of it, leaving progressively wider gaps between the pairs of riders. A rider appeared ahead of them, a courier whose horse struggled in the mud.

"Whoa, what news," Porter called out, and the man pulled up when he met the command group.

"Orders for General Smith, sir. He is to extend his line to the right as far as Indian Creek. General Wallace will leave his position to support McClernand."

"Any orders for the First Iowa?"

"None written, sir. But Major Rawlins asks that you close up as best as you are able."

"Damn," Porter cursed to no one in particular. "All right, on your way." Captain McKinsey rode up while the courier galloped down the road, past the halted column of mounted men. Turning to McKinsey, Porter said, "Well, Grant won't be happy if we become too far separated."

Harper watched the rider negotiate the woods alongside the trail.

"With respect, Major," Harper said, "the road is terrible muddy. If we stick to it we ain't goin' to go any faster than we have been."

"I can *see* that." Porter looked at Harper.

Harper knew Porter needed recommendations, not statements of the obvious. "The ground is firmer on either side of the road, up in the woods. So, if we put one file on either side, we'll probably find faster going there under the trees. The leaf-fall should have kept the ground from getting too muddy."

Porter addressed McKinsey. "What do ya think, Brice?"

"That's what I figure, too, Major. Break column and let the horses pick their own way. They won't have to step in the tracks of the horse ahead. There's enough space between the trees that we should be able to ride as fast there as we would on the road normally."

"All right, Jamie, tell the other company commanders to follow McKinsey's example." Porter turned to the captain. "McKinsey, let's move out."

It was good McKinsey agreed with Harper's suggestion. This was not the time for an argument among the officers. Harper rode back along the column, staying to the side of the road and out of the mud. He passed the orders to each of the three remaining company commanders before galloping back to the head of the column.

By staying to the sides of the trail, the column reached the Wynn's Ferry Road intersection after another half-hour. Wynn's Ferry Road ran east-west, behind the right side of the Federal line. Porter turned the column east, toward the sounds of the battle.

Harper heard gunfire ahead of the column and saw hundreds of men of all ranks, scattered in groups along the road. These must be the men who ran away. Junior officers and sergeants tried to organize them, shouting orders to the men and arguing with each other. None appeared to know what to do and no senior officer seemed willing to take charge. But, Harper noticed none of the men seemed especially frightened by the Confederate attack.

Wynn's Ferry Road was one of the few improved roads in this area, wide, with good drainage. The column moved quickly, unimpeded by mud. Half-a-mile farther on, they caught up with Company A and Grant's command group. Porter and Harper dismounted and joined Monroe, standing among Grant's staff officers.

Even here, the sounds of the battle did not match the volume of the battles Harper had experienced during the war in Mexico. There were no sounds of continuous volleys or shouts and screams one might expect from a major assault. It was surprisingly calm in what should have been the rear area of a defeated division fighting for its life. An occasional boom of cannon-fire sounded from the trenches to the north, but there was nothing in this area to suggest a battle in progress except the groups of stragglers who wandered past or stopped to stare at the army commander. In front of the staff officers, General Grant led a discussion with several generals and colonels.

"This army wants a head, Grant." The voice of the tallest of the three generals carried across the snow-covered landscape. The anger in his tone matched by the rising color in the man's face. "We cannot operate by trusting only the cooperation among the division commanders." The shorter general, facing away from Harper, nodded.

Grant's own face darkened at the rebuke. He took a step toward the taller man and thrust his face to within a few inches of the officer's nose. "It seems so, General McClernand. Perhaps my division commanders are not capable of cooperating with each other?"

Grant and McClernand stood there staring at each other for a number of seconds, McClernand's long beard quivering as he stared down at Grant; but he broke eye contact and backed away a step. "Yes, sir." McClernand's response was almost inaudible to Harper, standing just a dozen feet away.

Keeping the same look of intensity, Grant turned to an officer standing next to McClernand. "Colonel Oglesby, did you say the Confederates in front of you had their knapsacks full?"

"Yes, sir. Some did. Not all."

Grant looked toward the noise of the battle. "You took prisoners?"

"Yes, sir," Oglesby responded.

"Whose division did they belong to?"

"Pillow's *and* Buckner's, General."

"Buckner's?" Grant's stare returned to Ogelsby. "Are you certain of that?"

"Absolutely, General."

Grant looked back toward the battle. Harper followed the look, trying to see what Grant saw. Half a mile to the east, four Federal regiments stood across the Wynn's Ferry Road firing at Rebels who could not be seen beyond the Federal lines. It seemed a pitifully small force to hold back the entire Reb army.

Grant stared at the smoke cloud rising from the battle. Harper had the impression Grant could see the movements of the formations under it.

"Why would men who are making an assault carry rations with them, gentlemen? It's just extra weight."

Harper had trained the skirmishers to travel light when scouting and to burden their horses with only the very minimum gear needed in a battle. In the Mexican War, the American regiments would pile their packs in the rear before forming up to fight.

Grant turned around to address the group. "They wouldn't, unless they planned on a long march." He paused as if expecting someone to answer. None did.

"It tells me, gentlemen, that the Confederates are attempting to break out; escape; *not* lift the siege."

He looked straight at McClernand. "Now, the door has been thrown wide open for them." The accusation was clear to everyone who heard it. "*That's* why they've stopped attacking. They're holding the escape route open."

Grant paused, looking again at the thin line of blue uniforms holding back the Rebel attack. "Gentlemen, the position on the right must be retaken–and as quickly as possible, before too many of them get away."

The realization came to Harper slowly. Grant's order meant the Federals would counterattack this day in spite of their defeat in a morning.

By god, Grant's a tough one.

Grant addressed McClernand. "General, it looks to me that most of your men are still fit to fight. Get your supply wagons up here. Have your men refill their cartridge-boxes and get them back into line; the enemy is trying to escape. He must not be permitted to do so."

Grant took a few steps toward the sound of the battle. "When you're ready, you will support Wallace's attack to retake the ground that was lost." He waved his arm in the direction of the battle to the east when he spoke, his forearm imitating a moving wall driving the Rebels back. "We must seal off the road to Charlotte before they can escape." The imaginary wall bounded past the immediate battle to encompass the land all the way to the Cumberland River.

"Yes, General." McClernand turned to the colonels commanding his brigades. "See to it. We'll form ranks behind General Wallace's brigades." The four officers saluted and hurried to gather up their men.

Harper understood Grant's gestures. They showed Grant's broader vision of the goals for the counterattack beyond simply halting the

Rebel advance. He looked to see the reactions of the groups of men outside of the staff circle. Those within earshot murmured and nodded in agreement.

"General Wallace." Grant spoke to the shorter general with a vandyke styled beard. "As soon as you can bring your regiments into position, you will lead the counterattack."

"Yes, sir. It will be an honor. There's one brigade in position now, and another moving up."

"Good. Then you'd best attend to them." Grant paused, looking at the thin line of blue-uniformed troops. "I'll send whatever additional help I can round up."

"Yes, sir. Thank you, Grant." Wallace smiled and saluted. "By your leave." He mounted and rode east to rejoin his division, followed by his staff.

Grant took a minute to stare after Wallace, before walking to his horse. His staff followed, as did the command group from First Iowa. "Some of our men are badly demoralized, Webster." He addressed a white-haired colonel next to him, but did so loud enough for the nearby officers to hear. "But the enemy must be more so. He attempted to force his way out, but now, his attack is faltering." He looked again to where the four regiments held back the Rebel advance, the sounds of battle reduced to sporadic musket fire or an occasional cannon.

The one who attacks first *now* will be the victorious one." Grant took out a stubby cigar, lit it. "By God, General Pillow will have to be in a hurry if he gets out ahead of me." Grant took a puff from the cigar, head bowed in thought. He took three steps, stopped short on the fourth, the worry on his face easing.

Harper watched the army commander closely. Only now did he understand the responsibility the man bore. If the Rebels get away, we'll have to fight them again and again–not only us, but the entire United States government. Grant would carry the responsibility for prolonging the war, and losing so many men for no purpose.

"Webster," Grant turned back to the colonel. "If Buckner's men are here, then Pillow must have used most of his force to mount this attack on our right." He held his right hand out, palm up, cigar clenched between two fingers. "Including Buckner's men who *were* facing our left yesterday." He repeated the gesture with his left hand. "There should be only a few men left to hold the rest of his works." He took a puff from the cigar but kept his left hand extended. "If we order General Smith to hit him hard on the left, we should be able to break into the fort." Now his left hand became a broom sweeping away the imaginary Rebels on the left.

Webster did not answer; he appeared to be considering Grant's idea. "Smith has only two brigades with him. We ordered him to send McArthur's brigade to McClernand yesterday and this morning we told him to send Morgan Smith's brigade."

"*Morgan* Smith? Is that one of the new brigades? How good is he?"

"No sir. It's Wallace's old brigade. Morgan Smith was the commander of those Missouri zouaves."

"I see. Well, I suppose that will make Wallace happy to have his old command under him." Grant smiled and blew a smoke ring into the air.

"Two brigades should be enough, I think. There can't be more than a few regiments over there." Grant turned to the rest of his staff, determination hard-set in his eyes. "We have to ride fast, gentlemen. Today's battle is just beginning."

Grant's aggressiveness surprised Harper, especially since Harper couldn't understand how Grant could be so confident that there were only a few regiments still facing Smith's division. Here it was, already into the afternoon and not only would he counterattack on the right, but he would also mount an unplanned attack on the left.

An attack on the left simultaneous with the one on the right would leave no reserves for the army, except whatever men McClernand could reorganize from his division. If Grant was right, they would carry the fort today. If Grant was wrong, the army would suffer so many casualties they would be here for months besieging the fort.

Worse was the risk both attacks would result in heavy casualties, and the Federal army would be driven away in a mob. The nation would have to rebuild Grant's army and hundreds of lives would be wasted. The newspapers would eviscerate Grant.

After Grant mounted for the ride back to the left of the line, he saw the First Iowa mounted and ready. He looked around to find Monroe.

"Colonel, I doubt we will need an escort for the rest of the day. My guess is Pillow has committed all of his army to the attack this morning. Most his army is here. I want you to report to General Wallace for duty. I think the more we can fortify his counterattack, the more aggressive he will be."

"Yes, General." Monroe saluted.

"And Monroe, remember this." Grant punctuated his words with his cigar-hand. "We need to shut the door completely against the Confederates leaving the fort. If both Wallace and Smith are successful, I think some of those people might try to escape tonight after dark."

"Yes, General. We'll do what we have to," Monroe replied.

Grant returned Monroe's salute. As he turned to leave, Grant recognized Harper. "Another hectic day, eh, Harper?"

Harper's blood was up. "Yes, sir. It sure is." Grant's plan was spectacular in its scope and audacity. He wanted to be part of it–now.

"Hopefully, we have a better outcome than we did at Belmont," Grant said.

"We will, General. They ain't expectin' us to hit them back right now." Harper grinned, honored because Grant recognized him and remembered his name. "And, this time, we've got enough men." Harper was eager to get going. But when he looked at Monroe, he saw suspicion in the man's eyes although the face remained a mask. Harper averted his eyes. Still, it surprised him that he had made such an impression on the general.

Grant rode off, back down the Wynn's Ferry Road with his staff following. Monroe, Porter, and Harper walked over to where the First Iowa waited and mounted their horses. Monroe called the company commanders to him and explained their new orders.

"Column of fours," Monroe ordered. The battalion began its shift to the new formation. Without turning to face Harper, Monroe said, "For today, Mister Harper, try to remember you are the adjutant of *this* battalion. Don't go rescuing any generals without my orders."

"Yes, sir." Harper's face flushed at the rebuke in Monroe's comment.

The column finished the doubling. Monroe continued to look straight ahead. "And try not to get anyone else killed, if you please."

Monroe raised his voice. "At the trot, forward… march!"

Anger choked any response Harper might have made as the First Iowa Mounted Rifles rode east for its first action as a full battalion.

****

Harper and Porter approached the brigade commander with Monroe. "Colonel Thayer, I've been ordered to attach to your brigade by General Wallace." Porter and Harper followed, and now sat astride their horses on either side of Monroe.

"I'm Wesley Monroe," he continued. "I have a battalion of mounted rifles ready."

Thayer commanded the four regiments Harper saw during the confrontation among the generals. For a time, Thayer's men were the only Federal forces opposing the Rebel attack. Harper recognized the flag of the First Nebraska, but the other three regiments appeared to be newly formed, based on the undamaged condition of their battle flags.

"Rifles? What kind of rifles are they?" Thayer looked up at Monroe and the formation of mounted soldiers waiting to the side of his infantry support.

"Sharps," Monroe replied. "I have four-hundred-and-twenty men in the battalion."

"Good, good." Thayer turned back and surveyed the situation in front of his troops.

Harper watched while four more of Wallace's regiments deployed behind Thayer's men. The condition of their flags signaled to Harper three of these regiments were also new, although they appeared well-drilled. These must be some of the men from Lincoln's call last summer for three-year volunteers. If so, this was their first battle.

Thayer had his men deployed astride the Wynn's Ferry Road, facing east. Looking past the lines of Federal infantry, Harper could see the road as dark stripe in the snow where it descended into a shallow valley and disappeared into a forest at the bottom. The forest continued up the opposite slope to the top of that ridge. The escape route which concerned General Grant must lie beyond the ridge occupied by the Rebels.

"I'm going to put you over on the right flank. Do you see those

Rebs over there?" Thayer pointed south to the far left of the Confederate line. Harper could see a thick skirmish line cresting the ridge opposite and advancing on foot into the valley, their men visible as they moved from tree to tree across the snow. There were no Federal troops opposing them.

"Well, I think those fellows are actually cavalrymen fighting on foot, and I ain't got no one to put against them. If they decide to use their horses, they'll be behind us quick as spit and I'll have to pull back." Thayer gave Monroe a sly grin. "I want you to block their way, keep them from getting behind me. We just might be able to surprise those folks, especially since your boys have them long-range rifles."

"Yes." Monroe looked at the advancing Rebels, apparently assessing his assignment. "Indeed. So, we'll be out there by ourselves without support?"

"That's the best I can do for you right now. We need to stop them now."

The group of Federal officers presented a wonderful target for the Confederate sharpshooters in the heavy timber. Several bullets zipped past Harper and Porter or thudded into the ground nearby while Monroe and Thayer talked. Harper held himself steady and silent in imitation of Porter. He knew if he showed any concern about the bullets passing nearby, the story would be all over the battalion by tomorrow. And he couldn't set a precedent for the enlisted men when they came under fire. Even Monroe remained stoic in spite of the passing bullets.

At least he's not a coward.

****

The First Iowa rode along the ridge and the remaining companies dismounted, extending the Federal front line. The officers and men removed their overcoats and tied them to their saddles. The men counted off horseholders and one man in five led the horses down the reverse slope of the ridge, away from the line-of-fire of the advancing Rebels. At Porter's recommendation, Monroe sent Company B to occupy the face of a hill farther to the right which dominated the flank of the Union line. Monroe ordered the remaining four companies into line formation along the top of the ridge. When the formation was complete, Harper joined Porter behind the color guard. The battalion was in position in time to watch the mob of Rebels opposite them reach the bottom of the valley.

"Captains, advance your skirmishers and engage the enemy!" Monroe watched the trained skirmishers deploy.

One thing soon became clear to Harper, as well as everyone else in the battalion. The advancing Rebels in this sector outnumbered them by at least three-to-one, probably more. Harper looked back to Thayer's position.

I wonder how long we need to hold them back.

From this angle, Harper could see that the heavy timber in front of Thayer's men extended up and over the crown of the opposite ridge. But the Rebels opposing the First Iowa extended the Rebel line southward beyond the wood. These Rebs operated in the same area of scattered trees as the First Iowa. The lightly-scattered timber gave some cover to individual skirmishers, but in mid-February the naked trees did not conceal the First Iowa in their massed formation.

Harper guessed the range to the leading Confederates at four hundred yards, well within the effective range of the Sharps rifles, but probably not within the range of most of the Confederate weapons. "Come on, boys. Open fire." In his concern, he spoke his thoughts aloud.

"What was that, Jamie?" Porter asked.

"Major, if we don't open fire on them soon, we'll lose the range advantage the rifles give us." Harper looked down at the advancing Rebels. "We can slow them down if we force them to take cover."

Crack; crack; crack... The first shots from the Sharps sounded, rising in volume when the rest of the Iowa skirmishers where ready. Harper watched with satisfaction as the teams operated independently, each team firing whenever a target presented itself in the valley below. They worked in pairs, exactly the way he taught them. One man would keep a rifle loaded and ready to fire at anything which might attack the team. The other man sought out a distant target, took deliberate aim, and fired. The first man maintained a defensive posture, looking for likely targets. Once the original shooter reloaded, the team reversed roles.

Monroe took a position in front of the color guard, between the skirmishers and the main body of the formation.

The Confederates presented ideal targets to the Federals firing down into the valley, but the Confederate carbines were not as effective at this range and they fired up-slope, making it more difficult to find a target. Nor could they match the First Iowa's rate-of-fire with their muzzle-loading weapons. The Iowans might have dominated the fire fight if the entire battalion could operate in open order. Nevertheless, their skirmish line forced the Confederates in front to remain under cover despite their far greater numbers. Muzzle-flashes and rising gunsmoke denoted when the men below fired at the Iowa skirmishers. Fortunately, Harper could not see any effect against his skirmishers from the enemy fire.

Crack! Crack! Crack!

To the right, McKinsey's company opened fire on several hundred Confederates trying to move around the right flank of the First Iowa's formation. The shooting forced those Rebs to take cover.

Harper turned to see if any Rebel skirmishers attempted to move around the left. For now, these rebs chose to remain in place, maintaining a continuous line with their countrymen fighting against Thayer. All-in-all, it seemed to Harper that First Iowa could hold back the Rebels on this flank the way Thayer ordered them to do. They might even be able to attack if all of their rifles could be brought to bear.

How much longer would they need to hold out? The trained skirmishers had enough ammunition for perhaps an hour, but they could be replenished from the men in formation. And the supply mules were near-to-hand. Harper looked down the slope behind him to confirm the mules were with the horseholders. "I guess we can hold on like this for the rest of the day, Major."

"I'm not so confident, Jamie. We don't have a reserve, and there's no one behind us if they break through." Porter looked at the top of the ridge across the valley. "We have to see what the Reb commanders come up with next."

Harper followed Porter's sightline. On the ridge opposite their position, stood a dozen Rebel officers and men, including several flag bearers, silhouetted against the blue, eastern sky.

Without explanation, Monroe rode to a position in advance of the formed line. "Prepare to advance!" He waved his sword over his head to motion the men down the slope to their front.

"What the hell is he doing, Major?"

Porter looked as surprised as Harper.

"Company, ready position," the company commanders ordered, and the men in formation brought their rifles to the ready position: gunstock against the right hip, muzzle lowered in the direction of the enemy.

Porter tried to push his horse through the line of soldiers.

"Forward…" Monroe yelled.

Harper followed Porter working his way through the two ranks of soldiers.

"Forward…" four company commanders repeated.

Porter slapped his horse on the rump; it was the only visible indication he gave there was something seriously wrong. But following behind, Harper saw how hard Porter used his spurs on the horse to push past the soldiers.

"March!" Monroe brought his sword down, pointed into the valley.

"March!" The companies moved forward, down the hill.

Caught in the mass of moving men, Porter let them carry him forward until he reached Monroe. Harper bought Santee to a halt to let the waves of men on foot flow past him. Once the way was clear, Harper joined Porter and Monroe, hoping that Porter had been successful at convincing Monroe to halt the advance.

"Colonel," Porter asked. "Do ya *really* think that's wise? We have better shots at them from up here on this hill than we will if we drop down into the valley."

"Need to move closer to them so we can hit them better." Monroe watched the battalion's advance.

"If we do that, Colonel, we'll lose the advantage the rifles give us. Men will be killed who don't need to be." Harper saw the Rebel skirmishers on the left moving forward to get on their flank. "Sir."

Monroe hesitated.

"Christ-Jesus!"

The officers turned to see the national color-bearer yell and clutch his chest. As he fell to his knees, he looked at Monroe. To Harper, the man's face seemed to distort into a question: *Why?* A color-sergeant took the injured man's flagstaff, while two others pulled the bleeding soldier behind the line.

"Back in ranks there," yelled Sergeant-Major Compton. The two helpers returned to their places while Compton tried to stop the bleeding and to make the wounded man comfortable.

Harper stared at the pair until the color bearer died. It was a wasted death.

Harper and Porter turned back to the colonel.

"All of these boys can hit pretty well from this distance." Harper spoke as calmly as his anger over the loss of the color-bearer allowed. "I taught them all to hit targets at four hundred yards and more, Colonel. Ya saw them do it yesterday, sir."

"The Rebs will have to get to about two-hundred yards to have a chance to hit us up here." Porter added. "But we'll lose that advantage if we march down to them." Porter swung his hand in an arc covering the entire Confederate force opposite them. "There's a hell of a lot more of them than there are of us, Colonel. Let them get in close and we'll be shot to pieces."

Monroe looked at Harper, brow furrowed and his mouth twisted in irritation. The Iowa troops halted when they reached their own skirmish line. Firing stopped all along the Iowa line, while the battalion watched the three officers conferring. The Rebs on the left could now fire into the battalion's flank.

Need a decision quick, Colonel, before this all goes to hell.

"Colonel, those Rebs are moving around behind us." Harper pointed to the swarm of Rebels on the left, his tone a plea for the colonel to halt the advance.

"Let me handle this, Colonel," Porter said.

Harper could almost smell Porter's concern. He looked at the formation, where behind each company three or four men lay on the ground, some not moving, others crying for help.

A Rebel bullet ripped into Monroe's left glove at the high cuff and spun away into the distance. It wrenched Monroe's hand across his saddle. It also prompted a response from the man. Monroe finally nodded his assent.

Porter spun his horse to yell to the company commanders. "Move your men forward to get them into better cover." Porter's order surprised Harper until he realized Porter was helping Monroe save face. It was part of the deputy commander's job. It might be something worth trying himself to get along better with Monroe. There was very little difference between the cover at the top of the ridge and the cover twenty yards down the slope. Some of the men hesitated to move.

"Do it!" Porter yelled. "And commence firing!"

The officers and sergeants moved the men forward as ordered. The skirmish line resumed its fire, but the Confederates had taken advantage when the Iowa men stopped firing. They now were closer and able to fire effectively with more of their weapons. Some of them rushed to the lower slope of the ridge the Iowans occupied, making them far more difficult targets. Bullets landed in the ground around Monroe's and Harper's horses or flew past overhead. A color-sergeant lost his hat and fell to his knees, bleeding from his scalp.

"Time to become less of a target, I think, Harper." Monroe dismounted and handed Harper the reins to his horse. "Give this to Private Mitchell to hold for me. Dismissed, Lieutenant."

Although surprised at the dismissal, Harper made his way to the rear with the colonel's horse, his mind rushing with a mix of embarrassment, bitterness and anger. When Harper was beyond the danger from the Confederates' fire, Private Mitchell rode up. "Take this." He threw the reins at the soldier.

Porter climbed back to where Harper waited and looked back at the fire-fight going on below them.

"God-damn, Major. We could drive them completely over the next ridge if we used the entire battalion in open order."

So far, the soldiers in the First Iowa's formed line had not opened fire, although several more were hit.

"Those boys wouldn't be getting shot for no reason. Times have changed, Major. If he thinks we can use the formations they did in the Mexican War, then Monroe is the dumbest man out here today. Hell, it's the same damn formation Napoleon used fifty years ago–and we know what the British did to him."

"I don't like it either, Harper."

Harper noticed when Porter used his last name instead of his first. It was a clear signal of Porter's irritation.

"But we, Harper, are not in command. *He* is. And as long as he is, we both need to support his decisions. Otherwise, this battalion will fall apart."

Harper stared at Porter. It was the first time he ever saw the major's face so flushed.

"Do you understand me, Lieutenant?"

"Yes, sir." Harper tried to look contrite, but wasn't sure he convinced Porter.

"That kind of talk has no place in this battalion; either out here in the field, or in the barracks. Understood?"

Harper remained silent. He broke eye contact and looked down at his saddle. Of course, Porter was right. There could be no disrespect shown by the officers toward the commander. He smothered the anger he felt toward Monroe. Harper would concentrate on his own role in the battalion's battle.

Porter turned his back to Harper when he guided his horse to face the battalion. "They're doing well, Jamie. The training you organized must have worked. Look at them." Porter surveyed the Iowa soldiers.

Harper guided Santee alongside Porter and watched the skirmishers operate. What he saw cheered him after the rebuke from Porter.

Each team continued to work the way he trained them. Harper looked for casualties among the skirmishers, but saw none. The skirmisher battle was at a stalemate, although occasionally, a bullet would find one of the men standing patiently in the formed line. A thin cloud of gunsmoke rolled over the ridge in front of the First Iowa.

Harper watched George Streeper shift his skirmishers to protect against the Rebels trying to work their way around the left. Streeper stepped the end of his line backward so his company formed an angle bent back from the battalion's main line. With the skirmishers out of the way, all of Streeper's men fired at the flankers, hitting perhaps a dozen and forcing the rest to fall prone in the snow.

"Very good, George." Porter watched Streeper pin down the flank attack. "That'll hold them."

Harper wasn't listening; instead, he retrieved his own rifle and telescopic sight from their saddle holsters. He fit the scope to the rifle and dismounted. If Monroe wasn't going to let him fight, he would do it on his own. He looked up at Porter. "Watch this."

He lay on his stomach. Chill water from the melting snow seeped through his woolen trousers and jacket. Propping the rifle in his left hand with his elbow planted on the ground, he aimed at the group of officers standing on the ridge opposite them.

"About eight hundred yards," Porter guessed as he stayed mounted to watch through his binoculars.

"A little more, I think," Harper answered as he adjusted the rear sight. Set the first trigger, aim, a slow exhale, stop, check his aim, a gentle tap on the second trigger.

Crack!

The loud discharge surprised Monroe's horse. It reared up, and Mitchell struggled to bring him under control.

Porter called the shot through his binoculars. "Looks like ya got one of the guidons. Nice shot. Why don't ya try for the officer in the front? Looks like an ornery old coot."

Harper repositioned the rifle after the recoil and reloaded. He knew it broke the unwritten code of war for officers to snipe at each other across the battlefield, but if Monroe wouldn't let him into the battle, he would do what little he could by himself. Besides, Porter told him to do it. He scanned the far ridge through the scope, trying to find the man Porter saw. The battalion's firefight continued, but Harper's world narrowed to the personal challenge he set for himself.

A messenger rode up to the two officers. "Captain McKinsey's respects, sir."

"Yes, what is it?" Porter returned the salute.

"The captain asks that Colonel Monroe join him on the hill yonder." The messenger pointed to the hill where Company B was posted.

"Why is that?"

"He thinks the Rebs might be retreating."

Porter pointed to Monroe. "The colonel is over there, on foot."

The messenger rode off.

"Jamie, let's go." He turned to Mitchell. "Get the colonel's horse ready."

Harper took one last look at the officer on the opposite hill and squeezed off a hasty final shot usuing the first trigger only. He took his eyes from the target when he stood up. Since the man stayed upright, he assumed the shot went wide.

Harper mounted and followed Porter to where Lieutenant Colonel Monroe directed the battalion. After hearing the messenger's report, Monroe issued orders. "Harper, come with me. Major Porter, take command here until I return."

Monroe and Harper followed the messenger to where Captain McKinsey watched the Confederates through his binoculars.

"Afternoon, Colonel," McKinsey greeted the battalion commander. He pointed across the valley to the ridge in front of Thayer's brigade. "D'ya see the wood on top of the ridge?" McKinsey pointed to the large wood sheltering the Confederate main force. "Well, if ya move the glass along their ridge, then just where the wood ends, ya can see where a road comes out the back and goes down the other side, eh."

Monroe and Harper both dismounted. Monroe took his telescope from his saddlebag and extended it to look where McKinsey pointed. He steadied the telescope against a tree to scan along the top of the ridge. He paused to let his eye adjust to the image and watched for over a full minute.

"Harper, take a look at this and tell me what you see."

Harper took the telescope and repeated the process Monroe used to find the image he wanted. In the small circle of the lens, he could see movement. He concentrated his focus there and slowly the picture of gray-and brown-jacketed men moving away from him became clear. Next, he observed the muskets the men carried, and as the men moved away, they appeared to become shorter, as if they were marching down the far side of the ridge.

"Sir, what I see is a column of Reb infantry marching away from the battlefield." Harper could think of no logical reason why the Rebels would retreat.

Monroe asked McKinsey. "How long have you been watching them?"

"Nearly fifteen minutes now. Only infantry, no wagons."

Harper nodded. There were multiple reasons why wagons would be moving away from the battlefield; but infantry moving away would mean only two possibilities: they were retreating, but that seemed unlikely if Grant was right and they wanted to keep an escape route open; or, they were pulling back to attempt a different approach.

Harper lowered the telescope. "They could be trying to maneuver around Thayer, sir. But I don't think that's likely. There's no room for them to Thayer's left, and it'll be dark before they can move around us."

Monroe and Harper looked left to Thayer's men. This line lay slightly forward of the First Iowa, still firing at the Rebs in the heavy timber. Thayer was too low to see the Confederates withdraw.

"Mister Harper, ride over to Colonel Thayer. Give him my respects and report to him what we've seen here."

"Yes, sir." Harper saluted and mounted Santee. He galloped away. This was a time when Monroe *needed* an officer to carry the message. If Wallace could mount his attack when some of the Rebels were marching away, he could catch them at a disadvantage and maybe destroy a good part of their army. At least, he would spoil their plans to shift the attack.

But, while he rode along the crest of the ridge, he saw that the Confederates across the valley from First Iowa did not retreat. He also saw the men in the four formed companies now lying on the snowy ground to avoid the Rebel fire coming out of the valley. *Good for Porter–doing the smart thing while Monroe was away.*

The ground felt soft under the high sun, making unsure footing for Santee. Harper let the horse choose its way. The mustang came from the wild and could cover the ground faster without being guided. Once the horse understood the direction to take, man and horse fairly flew over the ground, throwing clods of mud and snow in their wake.

Harper found Thayer with a small group of staff officers. The man stood in his stirrups trying to see over the heads of his men, but making himself an ideal target at the same time.

He's lucky some sharpshooter hasn't gotten him, yet.

"Sir, Lieutenant Harper, First Iowa with a message from Colonel

Monroe."

Thayer sat back in his saddle. "Yes, Harper, what is it?"

Harper reported what he, McKinsey, and Monroe saw. Santee's shoulders twitched at being brought to a sudden stop.

"You say you can see it? I surely can't."

"Yes, sir. From that hill over there." Harper pointed to the hill where he left Monroe. "I just came from there and saw them with my own eyes."

"Well, then, if what you say is true, it is certainly welcome news." He turned to a staff officer. "Lieutenant Sloan, my respects to General Wallace. Tell him it appears the Rebs may be pulling back in front of my brigade. Harper, you ride with him and tell the general exactly what you saw."

"Yes, sir," Harper and Sloan replied at the same time.

****

General Wallace was with Cruft's Brigade, deployed in two lines next to the untested units supporting Thayer. "What news?" Wallace asked.

Harper waited for Thayer's messenger to report; Santee pawed at the ground.

"How does Colonel Thayer know they're pulling back, Lieutenant?"

"This officer, sir." Sloan pointed to Harper who stroked Santee's neck to calm her.

"Sir, Lieutenant Harper, First Iowa Rifles." Harper saluted.

Wallace returned Harper's salute. "So how do *you* know, Mister Harper?"

Harper repeated his report.

While Wallace considered this news, General McClernand rode up to the group with his staff following behind.

"I have two regiments ready for you, Wallace. They're coming up now."

The sounds of a new battle starting somewhere in the distance caused each man in the group to look to the northwest.

"That'll be Grant getting Smith's Division going against their right," McClernand told the group. "Old John Floyd will have quite enough to do for the rest of this day."

"In that case, we need to attack, now!" Wallace pounded his fist into his hand.

Harper suddenly realized how much time had been lost since Grant left. There were only a few hours before sundown. Grant had expected Wallace's attack to precede Smith's. If Wallace didn't attack soon, the Rebels might be able to move enough of their men back into the trenches facing Smith and defeat both attacks.

A fresh brigade of two regiments arrived on the Wynn's Ferry Road, both dressed in *zouave*-style uniforms. The lead regiment wore blue jackets with red trousers and kepis. This unit marched under a green regimental flag indicting its men were of Irish descent. The second regiment wore black jackets and trousers with lighter blue facings showing across their chests and in their kepis.

Harper had seen this type of uniform before. Like many of the veterans, he thought they were overdressed and maybe even a bit gaudy. By adopting uniforms patterned after elite units of Louis Napoleon's army, the men in these regiments declared themselves to be braver than most and able to use *zouave* tactics. Harper never saw a unit operate using *zouave* tactics, so he reserved his judgment. The brigade commander, wearing the blue and red uniform of the lead regiment, rode over to the group of officers.

"Good day, General Wallace, General McClernand." It was a cheerful Colonel Morgan Smith who had marched all the way from the left flank. "We've been sent to reinforce First Division."

"McClernand, if you'll order the *zouave* brigade to report to me, I will attempt to recover the lost ground, according to General Grant's orders." Wallace sat back in his saddle waiting for a response. "This is my old brigade. I know what they are capable of."

McClernand's pursed lips revealed the chagrin he must have felt at having someone else recover the position his troops had lost. "Very well, Wallace. I wish you luck." Grant's orders were specific. Wallace would lead the counterattack.

Wallace smiled as he saluted McClernand and joined Smith's *zouaves*. Harper rode with Wallace's staff, curious to watch the general put the attack together. The brigade raised a cheer for their former commander.

Wallace told Smith, "These are the boys to lead the attack."

"We'll get the job done, General."

"I want you to use the special tactics we practiced, Colonel."

"Yes, sir."

Harper delayed his return to the First Iowa so he could see what *zouave* tactics involved. Would they be any better than the tactics he taught the trained skirmishers?

The new brigade deployed between Thayer's men and the untested regiments, with Cruft's brigade to their right. Colonel Leonard Ross arrived with two re-formed regiments from McClernand's Division. Wallace arrayed them on Smith's left, supporting them with three Illinois regiments from the untested units. Including the First Iowa, there were thirteen regiments ready for the counterattack. Thayer's embattled men would provide support.

Wallace turned to Harper, "Lieutenant, be so kind as to ride back to your command and inform them of my intentions to attack in ten minutes. I expect your battalion to cover the right flank as we go. Got it?"

Harper hesitated. He wanted to ask Wallace's staff about the 'special tactics'. Wallace stared at him waiting for a response.

"Yes, General." Harper saluted and wheeled Santee to ride along the ridge crest back to the First Iowa. He found Monroe returned to the four formed companies with only the skirmishers engaged.

"What news, Harper?" Monroe stood behind the lines of prone soldiers waiting with Porter.

Harper delivered Wallace's orders for the First Iowa to cover the flank of the main attack.

The three officers watched as Smith's regiments stepped into the attack. They heard Thayer's men give a cheer when they opened ranks to allow the wave of *zouaves* to pass through their ranks. The men of Cruft's and Ross's brigades stepped off, ten paces behind the zouaves in the center.

"Stand up!" Monroe gave the order. The four captains repeated it. When Wallace's force came abreast of the First Iowa, Monroe ordered,

"Forward...March!"

Still curious about the 'special tactics', Harper watched the progress of the *zouaves* while he rode beside Porter behind the Iowa line. Wallace's lead regiments descended the slope in a wedge formation, aimed straight for the wood at the bottom of the valley. Two waves of blue, three-quarters of a mile wide, marched over the white snow in the bright afternoon sun. Harper chest swelled at the sight–a magnificent display of power, especially when a sudden breeze spread the twelve pairs of battle flags over the heads of the attacking regiments.

White puffs of gunsmoke blossomed all along the Confederate line, from the heavy timber and from points all along the ridge. Smith's two regiments broke ranks when the advance neared the valley floor–each man picking his way forward individually over the broken ground leading up to the wood.

Harper found it difficult to turn his attention away from Smith's individual soldiers and how they operated. When the firing was intense, they would fall prone becoming smaller targets. They would crawl along the ground from cover to cover. And when the Confederate fire allowed it, they would stand and run. None stopped to fire. These were not the tactics he taught the skirmishers.

Smith's attack appeared to be hundreds of blue and gray ants swarming toward the wood. Denied a target of troops lined up in a mass, the Confederate fire did not seem to cause many casualties.

Increases in the roar of close-by musketry snapped Harper's attention back to his own battalion. The Confederates in front of the First Iowa increased their fire when the battalion moved forward. Iowa skirmishers sought cover, bringing the advance to a halt. The Rebels were able to use more of their weapons effectively and the disadvantage in numbers began to tell against the battalion. Dispersed among the rocks and trees, the Confederates were difficult to see, while the men of the First Iowa suffered because they stood massed together.

With the situation a stalemate in front of his own unit, Harper pulled up when the leading *zouaves* came within pistol shot of the Rebels in the wood. The two *zouave* regimental commanders waited until most of the men caught up. After a pause of a minute or so, each regiment stood and quickly delivered what must have been a devastating volley into the wood, followed by a headlong charge with bayonets fixed. When they charged into the Confederate position, Harper heard them let loose a maniacal scream over the noise of the muskets and rifles around him.

Now, he understood the purpose for having held fire during the approach. The smoke from the *zouaves'* own volley helped obscure the charge. With their bayonets fixed, the men would take too long to reload while exposed to enemy fire, so no man dared to stop charging. It would be a do-or-die hand-to-hand fight as the *zouaves* materialized from the musket smoke pointing their bayonets.

Harper spurred Santee to catch up with Porter after he lost sight of the *zouaves* in the wood. Monroe now rode in front of the color guard, still visible to the men but out of their line of fire. The Iowa men stood in their tight formation without the chance to return fire while the number of dead and wounded mounted. Harper's face flushed with anger at the waste of men. The friendly skirmishers in front of the battalion prevented the men in the main line from using their rifles.

"Sir, let's pull the skirmishers to the right to let the men in line open fire." Harper yelled to be heard above the din of thousands of muskets and carbines.

"I'm going to pull them back into their companies," Monroe replied over his shoulder. He turned in the saddle to face Harper, his brow in furrows and his mouth a frown of annoyance.

"Sir." Harper hesitated. He didn't want to start an argument with Monroe in the middle of a battle. "But with all due respect, won't that leave a gap between us and McKinsey's company on the hill? The Rebs will fill the gap and shoot down our flank as we go forward."

Monroe scowled at Harper, but Porter signaled his agreement with a discreet nod of the head. Monroe made his decision quickly.

"Go ahead, Mister Harper," Monroe ordered. "Move the skirmishers to the right."

At first, Harper did not respond. The colonel surprised him by wanting *him* to move the skirmishers.

"Yes, sir." Here was an opportunity for Harper to lead the skirmishers, but he must get them out of the way fast.

He looked to the far left of the line where Corporal Heisey led the skirmishers from Company E. Harper decided to leave them in place to help Streeper cover the left flank. Harper drove Santee into a gap between the color guard and Company D and galloped away. Taking his hat in his hand, he waved in order to attract the attention of the corporals leading the three remaining contingents of skirmishers.

"Skirmishers move to the right!" he yelled while he rode between the skirmishers and the the main body of Iowans. "Move right! Move right!" His shouts would not carry above the battle-noise. He tapped Corporal Wilhafen on the head to gain his attention. "Run!" Harper pointed with his hat to indicate the direction. "Get out of the way!"

Bullets zipped past. Harper hoped by keeping on the move he could avoid being hit, even though he was mounted and a prominent target.

Moving the first group of skirmishers took less than a minute, but it was too long. Harper spurred Santee in front of the skirmish line so they all could see him. This attracted more unwanted attention from the Rebels. When he stopped in front of the next contingent of skirmishers, Santee reared up as Harper yelled again, "Skirmishers move to the right! Skirmishers move to the right!" He waved his hat to show them the urgency. "Double-time!" Harper flinched when a bullet buzzed past his ear, leaving it burning.

Like most men, Harper believed *he* would not be the one injured. Until now, he had ignored the gnawing churn in his stomach caused by the thought of being shot. Even though he had been wounded in other battles, *this* bullet came within a half inch of blowing his head off. When he rode toward the last group of skirmishers, he forced himself to concentrate on the job at hand, pushing the pain and fear back into a deep corner of his mind.

Corporal Bilgar, in charge of the final group of skirmishers, saw Harper signaling. He ordered his men out of their firing positions, running to the right of the battalion's line. Harper raced ahead of the mass of skirmishers. "Follow me," he yelled. "Run!" Gauging where the new center of the skirmish line should be, he stopped when he reached a point fifty paces beyond the right flank of Company A.

"Here. Set up here." He returned his hat to its place and pointed to the ground in front of Santee. "Hurry." The first of the skirmishers reached him. "Set up here. Open fire." Ten pairs of skirmishers knelt down in front of Santee.

"Spread out!" Harper yelled to them. "Don't group up."

"Aye, Cap'n," Corporal Wilhafen answered in his riverman's slang.

More Rebel bullets passed close to Harper and Santee. He dismounted, but was surprised to see his hand shaking when he released the hair in Santee's mane. Leaving it to Wilhafen to spread his teams to their proper distances, Harper waited on foot with Santee for the next corporal to arrive. "Bilgar, post your men to the other side of Wilhafen."

Corporal Bilgar hustled his Company C men behind and past Wilhafen.

"Straub, deploy your men between Wilhafen and the battalion."

Harper was ready. He waved to signal Monroe and Porter. When he did so, more bullets zipped and buzzed past him and Santee, one passing inches from his face and causing him to flinch away. He looked at his men. Did any see the involuntary movement?

He could see through the scattered trees that the Iowa line now lagged behind the main attack, leaving Cruft's brigade open to flanking fire from the Rebels in front of the battalion. More men lay in the snow in the trail of his battalion, some moving and moaning, some still. Men killed without having fired their own weapons, the detritus of battle.

The skirmishers had their instructions, so Harper let the corporals do their jobs while he hurried Santee to a safe position. He tied the horse's reins to a tree branch but the mare became skittish at being restrained amid all of the noise and excitement. She pulled and danced against the reins.

Harper stroked her neck to soothe her. "You'll be all right here, girl. I'll come back for ya. Shh… Now, just stay calm. There's a good girl."

While the horse stopped fretting, Harper cursed himself because his hand still shook. He could feel Santee's tensed muscles and he guessed she sensed his own uncharacteristic fear. Harper had to get himself under control. "We've never been in a battle like this, have we Santee?"

Harper grabbed his rifle holster and closed his eyes. In his mind, he envisioned his fear, growing in the center of his brain. He imagined a force pushing against the fear from six sides at once, forcing it into a smaller and smaller package. When the fear was small enough to carry with one hand, he pictured shoving it into a closet where he would store it until the battle was over. He would deal with it then.

Harper released the rifle holster and opened his eyes. His hands no longer shook so he reached into a saddlebag and retrieved the canvas satchel with his ammunition and primers. After inspecting the contents, he hefted the strap over his head and across his body, letting his hip and sword handle take the weight of the ammunition. He slid his personal Sharps from its saddle holster and hung it from his shoulder by the sling. He left the delicate telescopic sight in its own saddle holster.

Giving Santee a final rub, he felt the easing in her shoulder and neck muscles. "I'll be back," he told her before he strode upright to the center of the skirmish line.

Harper watched his men continue to operate exactly as he trained them. He hoped Monroe saw and would learn from how he handled the skirmishers. But it was probably too much to expect from the man. If the battalion survived this battle, he needed to find a way to teach the company officers how to operate in open formation—whether Monroe liked it or not.

"First Iowa," Monroe shouted from the center of the formation. "Front rank! Kneel… Pre-sent!"

The surviving men in the formed companies brought their rifles to their shoulders and took aim.

"Fire!"

Smoke billowed from a hundred-and-seventy-five rifles discharged simultaneously. The powerful volley swept down the slope into the Confederates. Caught by surprise, a dozen or more Rebels fell to the ground and the survivors scrambled to better cover. Those who had been firing into Cruft's flank shifted targets to the First Iowa.

Harper looked to Corporal Heisey on the opposite side of the battalion. Heisey had already pulled his trained skirmishers to the left flank of the battalion, clearing the line of fire for the remainder of Company E. Together with their company-mates, they quickly overpowered the threat between the battalion and the main Federal attack.

"Prepare to advance," Monroe ordered. The kneeling men stood, loading their rifles. “At the walk, forward march! Fire at will!” The battalion stepped off into the acrid cloud of their own gunsmoke.

“Aim low,” Porter yelled. “Aim for their knees.”

In front of the skirmishers, Harper could see only shadows running through the fog created by the gunsmoke of both sides. He had to run to each corporal and shout instructions in order to be heard above the din of the muskets and rifles. “Straub, keep your men aligned on the battalion.” Harper moved to his right. “Bilgar, hold your men back to cover our flank.” He returned to the center of his men and waved both arms to move them forward.

Harper monitored his men while they continued to operate in pairs, so after one man fired, each team would stop and wait for him to reload before both would run ahead, one leap-frogging past the other, seeking cover from where they could find their next target. Even while performing the complex drill, they kept pace with the advancing double-line of the battalion.

The Confederates in this sector now concentrated all of their fire onto the advancing Iowans. Groups of Rebels opened fire, ranging from the valley bottom to the top of the opposing ridge. But they did not operate in pairs like Harper’s men. Each man required more time to find suitable targets and most fired with too much haste. Still, men of the battalion dropped—and the residue of prostrate men in blue uniforms, wounded or dead, extended down the slope as the battalion moved forward.

Looking past his own battalion, Harper saw Cruft’s regiments add their numbers to the fight for the wood. There, the Federal advance could only be marked by the gunsmoke in the trees rising to the crest of the ridge.

Harper saw a blue-clad rider pass behind him, then circle around and approach. It was Andy Reynolds, Company B Second Lieutenant

“Afternoon, Harper. Captain McKinsey’s respects and he wishes me to inform ya that Company B will maintain a position to protect the battalion’s flank. He intends for the company to remain mounted, against the possibility that the Rebels attempt to ride around ya.”

Harper looked toward the hill where he last saw McKinsey. Instead, he saw all of Company B on horseback in a double line-abreast.

McKinsey sat his horse in front of his men, fifty yards beyond Harper's right-most skirmishers. Harper waved to McKinsey to acknowledge the cooperation, relieved not to have the responsibility of the flank guard.

The Confederates facing the First Iowa began to back away and to retreat up the ridge on their side of the valley, imitating their countrymen in the center. Monroe urged the First Iowa forward, in spite of the volume of fire still coming at them from the valley.

Now, the men in the Iowa ranks took matters into their own hands. While they could fire and reload their breechloaders while walking, they could not do those things *and* maintain a tight formation. Harper watched with approval as the men of Company A began to imitate the skirmishers: advancing in bounds, firing, and using each tree, rock, or bush for cover when they knelt to reload.

"Form line! Form line!" Captain Compton and his lieutenants yelled, but the men continued to advance on their own. The sergeants tried pulling men from cover and into line, but as soon as they stepped off down the hill, the men broke ranks again to operate independently.

Harper saw Companies C and D follow suit in quick succession, and finally Company E at the far left end of the line. It seemed to Harper that the volume of fire from the battalion increased after the men dispersed. Now, they could load their breech-loading rifles faster when stopped and sheltered. The role of the officers and sergeants changed to keeping the men moving forward and not allowing them to stay in a sheltered spot or fall behind.

Looks like the men have their own ideas about how to use their rifles.

Harper looked for the command group near the colors. He wanted to see Monroe's response to the troops' reactions. The battalion commander's face was not clear through the distance and drifting smoke but the colonel's posture gave Harper the answer he wanted. Monroe sat passively, shoulders slumped with his hands on the pommel of his saddle, watching the actions of his soldiers and their officers' attempts to keep them moving forward. Monroe appeared to have given up the task to bring the battalion back under his control. Harper turned back to his own small command, satisfied at how the common sense of the Iowan infantryman won out over authoritative stupidity.

Gunsmoke from hundreds of weapons filled the bottom of the valley, obscuring the targets below, while protecting the Iowans from close-range shots. Without orders, the men shifted their fire to the Rebels on the opposite slope, firing over the obscuring smoke. Harper nodded his approval. With his skirmishers performing as expected, Harper, sat on the slope of the hill and aimed at a group of officers standing next to a regimental flag near the top of the opposite ridge. Because of the size of the group, he fired without selecting a specific target and grunted at his success when a man next to the flag-bearer fell over, clutching his hip.

In the center of the attack, Harper saw the signs of battle reach the top of the ridge, still obscured by the heavy wood.

Now, the Rebels in front of the First Iowa scrambled up and out of the valley, their men running a gauntlet of fire after they emerged from the cloud of gunsmoke. Monroe and Porter motioned the captains to keep the men moving forward. Harper knew they must also be yelling orders–he could see their mouths moving. But it was useless, even at this short distance. Harper's ears were ringing, and the gunfire smothered all other sound.

Harper ran through his skirmishers waving his rifle above his head. "Get up! Get moving! Let's go!" He brought the rifle down in the direction of the fleeing Rebels. "Follow me." He turned and ran into the sulfurous-smelling cloud of spent gunpowder without waiting to see if any of the men followed him. He assumed they would, and the cheering and yelling by the men when they charged confirmed it.

At the bottom of the valley, the air cleared enough beneath the haze of the smoke cloud to allow Harper to see the creek lying at the valley bottom. He saw shadows of the last of the surviving Rebels run up the slope opposite and disappear into the smoke cloud. He stopped to catch his breath and wait for his men. For now, he was alone. None of his men were with him. Did he imagine hearing them around him in the smoke cloud?

In the distance to his left, he could see other men of the battalion through the haze, running across the valley, jumping the creek, and moving up the ridge on the opposite side. But where were the skirmishers?

In spite of the din of the battle, Harper heard a distinct *click...click,* quite close. It was a sound he knew from his days as a lawman. He jumped sideways in the instant before the pistol discharged. A bullet singed the hair at the nape of his neck. In a clatter of rifle against sword scabbard, he rolled on the ground and came up searching frantically for the shooter. He heard a second *click... click* at the same time that he saw a fresh puff of gunsmoke floating into the cloud above.

Dropping his rifle, he darted behind a tree where the second shot impacted. He drew his hunting knife and charged in the direction of the second puff of smoke. Hatred boiled through him, burning his face and neck. Some son-of-a-bitch had tried to kill him! He saw a wounded Rebel officer on the ground ten feet away, using two hands to work the hammer of his pistol. Harper yelled a war-whoop when he leapt at the man.

Click... click.

Harper landed on the Rebel and the pistol discharged. Keeping the Rebel pinned to the ground, Harper drove his knife into the man's throat while using his body and free hand to control where the Rebel pointed the pistol. He pushed the knife in a second time and twisted. Blood welled out of the new wound, necklaced, and dripped into the mud. In less than a minute, the dying Rebel's strength ebbed away.

Harper raised himself and knocked the pistol out of the Rebel's hand before kneeling in the muddy snow next to the body. Smoke from the Reb's final shot lingered over the body. In addition to the wounds inflicted by Harper, the Rebel captain was gut-shot and must have been near to death by the time Harper arrived, because he lay in a pool of blood-tainted snowmelt. There was a burn mark across the man's left thigh from his final shot.

There was a matching powder burn on Harper's own thigh, and a bloodstain in the middle of his jacket. He pushed against the stain. There was lump there, but nothing hurt. The blood was not his.

He had to think for a moment to understand the lump on his chest before he reached into his jacket pocket for the pouch with his wife's and daughter's locks. He examined the outside of the pouch quickly. No blood stained the keepsake and he pushed it into his trousers pocket.

Harper whirled in place, knife ready, when he heard someone come up behind him. It was Corporal Wilhafen and his skirmishing partner carrying Harper's hat and rifle.

"That was damn brave. Eh, Lieutenant? I saw how ya jumped at him when he had the drop on ya."

Harper had not thought about what he was doing, only reacted. Now, when he stood up, his knee wobbled before giving out from under him. He grabbed Wilhafen to avoid falling.

"Are ya hurt, Lieutenant?"

"I'll be all right." He stretched the leg to be certain it wasn't injured. Back on his feet, he replaced his hat and retrieved his rifle. "Where are the men?" His hands started shaking again.

"They're coming through now, sir. We lost track of ya in the smoke cloud."

Harper took a moment to look around. He could see his men moving across the valley and up the slope on the other side.

"Did ya know you're bleeding, Lieutenant?"

"That's not mine, Corporal." He pointed at his jacket. "It's his blood."

"Sir." Wilhefen pointed to Harper's left ear. "It looks like the top part of your ear's been shot away. And your hair has a new crease on that side."

"Damn!" Harper touched the top of his ear then winced in pain. "I wonder when that happened." The ear began to throb.

"Must have been a while ago. Looks like it's dried once and started to scab over."

"Damn." Harper marveled at how he could be so involved in the battle he didn't notice getting shot. This must be the shot which made him so rattled today. He shook his head and refocused on the job at hand. "Let's get goin'." He gripped his rifle tightly to avoid exposing the shaking in his hands.

"Just one thing, sir. If I may."

"Go on."

"How come ya didn't use your pistol on that Reb?" Wilhafen pointed to the dead captain.

Harper was puzzled and he must have shown it because of the reaction from the two soldiers.

"Your pistol, sir." Wilhafen pointed to the unused holster on Harper's right hip. "Why didn't ya shoot him?"

Harper had no answer. "I don't know. I suppose I didn't think of it, Corporal." He hadn't. He had reacted out of pure, primitive survival instinct to the sound of the pistol hammer being drawn back. His actions became automatic after that.

"Can ya walk, sir?"

"Of course I can, Corporal. Now let's get moving."

"Yes, sir." Wilhafen saluted and smiled. He and his partner ran to catch up with the men of the Company D detachment.

Harper was thirsty from yelling most of the afternoon and from the taste of the gunsmoke. He stopped before crossing the creek and bent over to gulp from the flowing water. But he quickly spit it out. The pervasive, metallic taste and ferric smell from the blood surrounding him had fouled the water.

He stood up and felt his ear again, his fingers coming away tinged with blood.

"Damn."

****

The Iowa men swarmed up the slope unopposed. The skirmishers aligned on the battalion without additional command. Harper was the last of the skirmisher group to arrive.

At the crest of the ridge, Harper could see all the way to the Cumberland River, three-quarters of mile away, while the late-afternoon shadow of the ridge cast the valley on the opposite side into twilight. The entire battalion watched the last of the Confederate soldiers run back into their entrenchments.

The captured ridge branched into two parts on the far side. First Iowa found itself on the right-most, southern, part of the ridge which stretched almost to the Cumberland River before dropping into a pasture covered in undisturbed snow. Confederate entrenchments lay along the northern branch of the ridge. Their branch separated from the re-captured ridge only two hundred yards past where Wallace's main attack emerged from the wood. The far end of the Rebel branch ended at Dover, a town on high bluffs above the river. A muddy stream flowed down the valley separating the two heights and emptying into a backwater of the river, now filled with brown water stirred by the passge of hundreds of Rebel cavalrymen.

The size of the mob of Rebel mounted men making their way down the valley confirmed the fact that First Iowa fought against at least three or four times their number of dismounted cavalry. The Confederate horsemen followed the muddy stream onto a mud flat beside the backwater, obliterating the banks of the stream and leaving a trail of mud-mixed snow, more brown than white.

The head of the mob turned left onto a road leading back into Dover Town, inside the Rebel lines. But a few of the riders turned right at the road and waded across the backwater. Once across, they galloped away to the south. Not enough to be an organized group, Harper realized–probably deserters.

The First Iowa pivoted to the left to face the Rebel trenches. Here, tree stumps cut to within a few inches of the ground showed where cleared fields-of-fire extended from the Rebel lines across the shallow valley.

The retreating Rebels filled their trenches quickly, but were spread thin all along the line. Only an artillery battery posted in a bastion in front of Wallace's men opposed the Federal advance. The four cannon from that battery opened fire with a single volley which boomed down the valley and drove the *zouaves* and the other Federals back into the cover of the wood.

Although Harper was too far away to hear what they said, he watched Porter point out the battery to Monroe. It took a moment to realize Porter must want to suppress the battery using the range advantage of the Sharps rifles. Harper rested his rifle butt-first in the snow and let it balance against his hip while he studied the bastion. With enough men shooting, they should be able to place some rounds through those gun embrasures.

Monroe yelled the orders. "Captain Streeper, take that battery under fire with your company. Put as many rounds into them as you can. You don't need to hit them, but force them to keep their heads down."

Company E opened fire, fifty men firing five rounds a minute yielded a continuous roar and soon generated a smoke cloud which made it impossible for Harper to see the effect on the battery.

"Mister Harper, sir!" Harper looked to find who called him. Corporal Straub stood with his men, pointing across the valley. Looking to the Rebel positions, Harper saw a gray column of Confederate infantry trotting double-time from Dover Town, along the crest of the ridge, moving to reoccupy the empty trenches. Harper opted to act on his own initiative. The target presented by the column might not be there by the time he received orders from Monroe.

"Skirmishers, prepare to open fire," Harper yelled. At this range, the mass of marching Confederates made a perfect target. "Six hundred yards. Fire and adjust!" His men quickly ranged-in on the target.

His men–that sounded just about right to Harper. Why *couldn't* they be his men? Monroe could form an elite light company, the way the British and the French did. Even as a lieutenant, he could command the Light Company.

In quick order, the Federal bullets plucked at least a dozen Rebels off their feet. They fell into the other men in the column. Harper signaled to Porter, pointing to the Rebel column.

Captain Compton saw what was happening. "Open fire!"

In turn, Captains Pierson and Matthews ordered their companies to open fire.

Monroe rode over from watching Company E fire on the artillery bastion. Stopping next to the Company D commander, he shouted, "Who ordered you to fire, Matthews? What are you shooting at?"

Pierson pointed to the shattering Rebel column. Monroe raised his binoculars to look at the target.

Harper, eager to shoot at this lucrative target, sat in the wet snow and took aim himself. Across the valley, he could see the Confederate officers ordering their men to deploy into line, but more men fell when they attempted to do so, increasing the confusion. With bodies dropping all around, the column broke apart. The survivors ran to the rear, revealing a sheltered slope on the far side of the heights and out of sight of the First Iowa.

In time, the gunners in the battery targeted by Streeper's company gave up and filled their gun embrasures with portable gabions, shielding the crews from the rifle bullets. But the gabions also prevented the battery inside from firing in the direction of Wallace's men.

Harper sensed a rush of warm self-satisfaction, gratified because the rifles from his brother allowed the First Iowa to support Wallace's attack while keeping his own men out of danger. First, they suppressed the battery from almost half-a-mile away, then they routed an enemy regiment from a little over a quarter-mile.

"Cease fire, cease fire," Monroe commanded. "Captains, stand your men down, but remain in formation." He rode behind the line of soldiers. "Well done, First Iowa! Well done. That'll show them." Monroe must have spurred his horse in the excitement because it shifted to a prancing gait while its rider waved his hat to his men. The younger soldiers cheered their colonel. Veterans glanced at each other without a word and shook their heads.

Look at Monroe carry-on. Harper looked over to Porter, still mounted and standing behind Company E. Porter stared at Monroe for a few moments before he turned away and shook his head.

****

Katie stole glances over the heads of the soldiers playing cards at her table as Eagleton made his way to the bar and ordered a drink. Several of the other younger girls did, as well. Then they looked around the room to each other. Evilface always chose one of the young girls. Who would it be tonight?

Noah Kirchner served the major before calling into the office behind the bar. Franklin Bosley came out to give Eagleton a cordial greeting.

Eleanor taught her that word: cordial. Katie felt anything but 'cordial' toward Eagleton; and she was unhappy at how well Bosley treated the man. Was Evilface really so important? Katie turned her attention back to the card game where one of the four soldiers showed almost enough chips in front of him to take Katie upstairs. Maybe Evilface would ask for another girl tonight. Or maybe the private could win enough money in this hand that she wouldn't be here when Eagleton made his choice.

After two more hands of five-card stud, Loreena and Julia came to get Katie. "I'm sorry, gentlemen. I have another job for Baby Red right now." Loreena said.

Katie's spirit dissolved into despair. "That's not fair, Miss Loreena. We want Miss Katie." The winning private pointed to his stacks of chips.

Loreena pulled Katie's chair back from the table. "There's an officer who's asked that Katie join him."

Katie stood. A dagger in her heart at the thought of joining Major Evilface.

"But don't you worry, now. I've brought our Miss Julia to keep y'all company. And she's almost as pretty as Katie, isn't she?" Loreena cast a scolding glance at Katie. "Smile!" she hissed.

"Miss Julia is right pretty, missus, but we was playin' for Miss Katie. It ain't the same."

"Sorry boys, but y'all know that rank has its privileges." Loreena led Katie away while Julia took her place at the table.

****

A Federal rider emerged from the wood where the main Federal assault column sheltered. He galloped toward the First Iowa and Harper watched Porter ride up alongside Monroe as the messenger arrived. The messenger saluted and handed Monroe a copy of the orders.

Harper's normal duty was to receive the orders and record them. But, with no sergeant to manage the skirmishers, Harper convinced himself he could not leave the line.

"Mister Harper," Monroe called. "Release the skirmishers to their companies and join me."

Harper's lungs deflated. He had just commanded as many men as any of the company commanders and lost none of them. Did Monroe truly expect him to let them go so he could go back to being the battalion's chief *clerk*? So it seemed. He looked at the ground and shook his head.

The skirmishers began to wander off, so he called out before they dispersed. "Well done, skirmishers. The training paid off, didn't it? Put them boys to the run, eh?"

"Yes, sir, Mister Harper!"

"We sure did, sir!"

"Yes, sir!"

"All of ya did well today. But now it's time to go back into your companies." Harper looked at the men around him. "Skirmish detail–Atten-hut!" Those skirmishers in ear-shot stood straight and tall. Harper brought his hand to his hat in a salute. "Dismissed!" The men around him saluted and held it until Harper dropped his hand.

While the men of his ad-hoc command filed back to their parent companies, Harper walked over to where Monroe waited. He could hear the men around him talking excitedly about the battle. Several waved to him.

When Harper arrived, Monroe stared at him. "Are you hurt, Lieutenant?"

"No, sir. Not too bad, anyway." He touched his ear and felt the wound still oozing there.

Porter came closer and looked at the wound. "Best have that washed out before it goes septic."

"You look a proper mess, Harper." Monroe scolded. "You'll need a new uniform. Hell, even your sword is bent, and it appears you've been wallowing in a mud-hole." Monroe looked at Porter. "Can't have officers in this battalion looking like street-brawlers, can we Porter?"

"Is that *your* blood on your jacket, Jamie?" Porter pointed to Harper's stomach

"No, sir, it belongs to a Reb captain. I had some trouble when we crossed the valley."

"Must've become real personal for him to get so close."

"Yes, Major. It did."

Monroe opened his mouth but hesitated. "Well, certainly we're all happy you came away unharmed." Monroe's voice was a lackluster monotone. "Where is the Reb captain now?"

"He's dead, Colonel."

Monroe looked at Harper for a few moments. His gaze traveled over the blood stains and the scorch on his trousers. His face turned serious. Harper wondered if Monroe truly understood the nature of the fight with the Rebel officer.

Monroe handed Harper the written orders. "General Wallace wants us to remain here until Colonel Cruft's brigade arrives. Then, we are to move the battalion right to the end of this ridge and throw up breastworks facing both the enemy and protecting the flank. We will become the extreme right of the Federal line."

"Yes, sir," Harper replied. A thought troubled him with these orders. They were not complete, but he couldn't remember why.

"The battalion did well, McKinsey," Monroe continued, talking to the nearest company commander and ignoring Harper. "Wait until they hear about this back in Des Moines."

McKinsey smiled and nodded. "Yes, sir, they certainly did."

"Damn companies broke ranks against orders, but things still worked out for the best."

"Being able to load and fire from behind cover or kneeling down kept our own casualties down," Harper reminded the battalion commander. "And they kept moving forward, even in the loose formation. Like the *zouaves* did this afternoon."

"Maybe you're right, Harper."

Did Harper detect less disdain in Monroe's voice than normal?

"But next time, I want them to wait until *I* give the orders. Up until that point, the officers had them under good control."

"I can teach the officers how to command the loose line, sir."

Monroe frowned down at Harper. "Shouldn't you best be giving *my* new orders to the company commanders, Lieutenant?"

"Yes, sir." Monroe's rebuke registered in Harper's brain but he did not react. Instead, he saluted and left. Monroe might not welcome the idea of Harper training the officers, but Harper knew the officers and sergeants in the First Iowa would need to lead the men differently than they learned in training camp ten months ago. They needed to learn how Smith kept his *zouaves* moving forward after the soldiers took cover or went to ground. The skirmishers could do it by leap-frogging as they moved. But the officers would need training in the new tactics. Monroe didn't seem to understand that, and didn't seem inclined to have his adjutant explain it to him.

He could not find Corporal Powell who should record the orders and relay them to the company commanders, so Harper stuffed the orders into the breast pocket of his jacket, slung the rifle over his shoulder, and walked along the line of soldiers to inform the company commanders without Powell's assistance.

****

Loreena placed Katie's hand in the crook of her elbow and held it there with her other hand. With each step, weakness grew in Katie's stomach–the same weakness she used to feel when she waited for the school teacher's punishment when she was a child. The trepidation spread with each step she climbed. At the top of the stairs, they walked past Katie's room and up a second flight to the remote rooms on the third story over the restaurant where the servants and workers lived.

Katie's focus closed onto the carpet in the hallway while the weakness in her stomach spread and squeezed at her heart. She took such small, reluctant steps that Loreena pulled her along. They came to the door of the room the two mulatto girls and the negress shared–Katie's personal corner of Hell.

"Come along Katie. I know this hurts, but y'alls gettin' ten dollahs for doin' it, and you won't have to work for the rest of the night."

The room was the only one with a four-poster canopy besides the one in the Bosleys' own bedroom; Eagleton demanded the four-poster bed. Also, the room was far enough from both the saloon and restaurant so the other customers would not hear the goings-on.

Loreena directed Angel, the negress who cleaned rooms and sometimes entertained soldiers, to leave. "You know what to do," Loreena told Angel before she closed the door. Loreena turned to Katie. "Turn 'round, Katie."

The single lantern shed light that did not reach into the corners of the room. Loreena had to turn Katie's back toward the light in order to unbutton the dress. When Katie pulled her arms free, the top of her dress folded over the bottom, still riding on her single petticoat. Katie crossed her hands over her chest with a shiver. Before the dress could touch the floor, Loreena untied the knot used to hold Katie's petticoat around her waist and next the knot for the crinoline. The complete ensemble fell to the floor in a pile around Katie's ankles. She stood there in her corset, pantaloons, stockings, and slippers. Katie shivered against the chill in the air and against the despair in her mind.

"Step back." Loreena scooped the clothes from the floor and piled them behind the dressing screen without separating one piece from another.

"I want to separate them things to hang them up." Katie tried to move around Loreena, but the madam turned to push her away from the pile of clothes.

"No time for that now. Take off your girdle."

Katie frowned at the mistress and did not move. "Do I have to do this? Why me? Why is it always me?"

Loreena, who was a few inches shorter than Katie, grabbed the girl by the shoulders and forced her around. "Y'all know that you have to do this, Katie, so don't make such a fuss like last time." Loreena pushed Katie's long hair over her shoulder, out of the way.

Katie stomped her foot when Loreena began untying the string that squeezed the corset to Katie's torso. She wouldn't let them do this to her again. It *had* to be someone else's turn. She twisted so Loreena could not work the knot. "Why cain't it be someone else tonight?"

"Because he wants *you*."

Katie fidgeted enough that Loreena could not work the knot on the corset. Loreena slapped Katie's backside on top of a bruise that Katie still wore from her last evening with Evilface. "You have to do this, Katie. It's part of yo' job. And when it's ovah, you have the rest of the night off and still get a full night's pay."

The slap to her bottom surprised Katie. This was the first time Loreena had ever hit her. Normally, the men did the punishments in Bosley's businesses. But the sharp, short pain of the slap reminded her of other times with Evilface.

"Now, y'all be a good girl and this will all be ovah soon." Loreena untied the knot and pulled the corset and chemise over Katie's head. "Besides, I have somethin' for you. It might help."

After Loreena threw the corset and chemise on top of the pile of clothes, Katie let herself be led by the hand to one of the bedposts while covering her chest with her free hand. There was nothing she could do to escape what was about to happen. Loreena took a piece of cord from her pocket and tied a loop over each of her wrists. Katie didn't fight when Loreena pulled tight on the knot, forcing her wrists together. The madam tied the other end of the cord to the bedpost at the foot of the bed, making sure that Katie could wrap her fingers around it. Loreena looped the cord around the bedpost and tied it off, making sure the knot was beyond Katie's reach. Lastly, the madam wrapped two pieces of silk between the cord and Katie's skin.

The night's chill surrounded her entire body as she stood there with her breasts exposed. Although her legs were warmer, she knew she would lose that protection when Evilface arrived. The Bosleys did not allow the colored girls who lived in this room to have a stove, so the only warmth came through the walls and floor from other parts of the building. She stared at the bedpost while her body recalled the blows from the other times when she became Evilface's victim. Old bruises throbbed. The fear of pain was as much to blame for her shaking as was the cold. Katie sobbed and tears welled onto her lower eyelids.

"Stop cryin', girl. You know cryin' only makes him worse."

After checking the knot, Loreena looked around the room. She moved some breakables out of the way before satisfying herself that everything was ready. "I forgot somethin', Katie. I'll be right back."

Katie sobbed and pressed against the bedpost to cover her naked areas. She felt humiliated and Evilface had not yet arrived. But that was what Evilface wanted–her total humiliation. Was she so far below Major Eagleton for him to be allowed to do this?

But this night, she had a plan. A plan she worked out with the other girls after they learned how Evilface liked to be entertained.

Loreena returned with a small, dark-brown bottle. "I bought this for y'all to help with the pain." She produced a spoon from her dress pocket and poured the reddish-brown liquid. The room filled with the scent of licorice mixed with the type of tar used at the Marine Ways. "Take this." She offered the spoon to Katie.

"What is it?" Katie asked before Loreena dumped the liquid into her mouth. It tasted very bitter. Katie tried to spit it out, but Loreena held her mouth shut, forcing her to swallow.

"Laudanum," Loreena answered. "Now, maybe it won't hurt so much." Loreena watched for Katie's reaction to the drug. "That's a good girl, deah. I'll give the medicine a few minutes to take effect before I bring May-jah Eagleton. Do you remember the secret word?"

"Violets."

"Angel will be settin' right outside the doah. You use that word only if you have to. But remembah, if you don't let him finish, yo' won't get paid and all yo' suffering will be wasted." Loreena took a final, sympathetic look at Katie. "I'm sorry we have to do this, Katie, but the may-jah is the second-in-charge in the supply department at the fort. He can make things *ve'y* difficult for all of us if he wants to. We have to keep him happy."

The medicine burned in Katie's throat and stomach but just as quickly the burning passed and Katie felt her mind go fuzzy.

"How y'all feelin' now, Katie?"

Katie's gaze drifted around the room, trying to see the voice. She couldn't help but smile at the peaceful garden she found inside her head. There, her bruises no longer throbbed.

"Yo' ready," Loreena told her. She daubed away the residue of Katie's tears before she left the room.

****

Night brought quiet from the gunfire, a quiet broken only by the moans of injured men left behind on the battlefield. A full moon illuminated the valley and backwater where the Rebel cavalry had retreated earlier. Dark lines in the snow revealed the locations of roads and streams.

Seeing the road leading south from Dover brought Grant's final orders to Harper's mind and the problem with the orders Wallace gave the battalion at the end of this day's battle. Now with General Wallace visiting, he hurried to remind Monroe about Grant's last command to them: complete the encirclement. None of the Confederates should be allowed to escape.

After listening to Harper, Monroe addressed the general. "General Wallace, there's a road down there." Monroe pointed at the dark trace in the snow lying mid-way between the end of the ridge and the Cumberland River. "It goes straight from the fort, right past our flank." He swung his arm to demonstrate. "Shall I move my battalion to cover it?"

Wallace looked where Monroe pointed. After a minute, he gave them his decision. "No. I don't have enough troops left to cover my front if the Rebs come out again."

Harper had seen the regiments from Wallace's Division spread along the top of the re-captured ridge with the First Iowa on the extreme right. All of Wallace's regiments were in the line; there were no reserves. In each regiment, some of the Federals lined the forward slope of the ridge behind breastworks they had dug in the twilight of the setting sun. Their forms showed dark against the moonlight reflected from the snow cover.

The rest of the men, as well as all of the battalion's horses and mules, rested on the reverse slope preparing their evening meal and organizing their equipment for the battle in the morning.

"An attack ain't very likely, sir," Harper offered. "And General Grant specifically ordered us to cut off any escape attempts. What about using the cavalry to cover it?"

Wallace looked at Harper's face in the moonlight. He looked at Harper's epaulettes. He looked at the mess of a uniform Harper wore. His face turned stony. "Well, thank you for the recommendation, *Lieutenant.*"

The harshness in Wallace's voice surprised Harper. After watching Wallace organize the counterattack in the afternoon, Harper believed Wallace was a veteran officer. Veteran officers sought out the information available from all of their subordinates. Major Porter stepped in front of Harper, easing him into the back row of the group.

Wallace looked back at Monroe. "The cavalry are rounding up the stragglers and the slackers. They're scattered over twenty miles of back country."

Although Wallace seemed to know what to do earlier in the day, Harper began to suspect Wallace must be just another rich politician someone made into a general. How could he not be concerned about letting the Rebels escape? Or, did the possibility of being blamed if he lost a very improbable night attack carry more weight with the man?

"Besides, that road's flooded by the river." Wallace pointed to where the road crossed the backwater. "You couldn't get more than a few men through there. And, they would have to swim through freezing water."

Harper whispered to Porter, "Some of the Reb cavalry went through it this afternoon. I saw them." Wallace ought to know better than to gauge the enemy's actions by what he himself would do.

"What's that, Lieutenant?" Wallace addressed Harper. "Something more you want to say?"

Harper repeated what he saw during the Confederate retreat.

Wallace stood and said nothing. He looked down at the road and the backwater overflowing it.

"Those were General Grant's instructions, General," Monroe said.

"Thank you for reminding me, Monroe." After a final look at the backwater, he turned to face Monroe. "Set a *picquet* down there if you want to, Monroe. But it's more important you hold this ridge to protect our flank."

"Yes, General." Monroe nodded. In a darkness lit by the full moon, Harper could see well enough only to scribble the general's orders so they could be recorded later in the unit order book.

"I saw what your boys did to the Confederate column this afternoon. I'll expect you to do the same if they send any reinforcements from this direction tomorrow." Wallace paused to look at the group. "Any questions?"

"No, sir." Monroe and the other officers saluted as the general mounted.

Wallace looked across the valley to the Rebel fortifications, clearly visible in the light of the full moon and backlit now from the glow of hundreds of campfires behind their ridge. "Those fellows are probably as disorganized right now as we are, so I doubt they'll have time to sort themselves out for an attack tonight." He looked down at Monroe. "Still, be on watch, Colonel. Good luck tomorrow."

At last, the general made some sense. Harper also doubted the enemy could reorganize fast enough for a night attack. The glow from all of their campfires told Harper the Rebels were settling in for the night.

"Thank you, sir. Might I add that it was a pleasure to serve under you this afternoon? We won't let you down."

Wallace smiled at Monroe, ignoring the rest of the First Iowa officers. "It is a pity there aren't any of those newspapermen around to report on our successes today. The folks back home could use some good news."

"I'm sure the folks back in Iowa will hear about us, sir, first-hand."

"Some favorable publicity is always good, isn't it?"

"It never hurts, General."

"Good for the army, that is. That's what I meant."

"Yes, sir. Of course. For the good of the army. That's how I understood it. We don't want people's attentions turned only on McClellan's army. It isn't fair."

Harper knew who would write the "first-hand" account of the battle. He recalled the newspaper article which interested Monroe when they first met. Wallace's comments only reinforced Harper's opinion of the man as a rich politician made into a general.

After the general and his staff rode away, Harper made his way to the reverse slope of the hill and through the circles of men surrounding pillars of smoke rising from the wet wood in their campfires. He needed to find a lantern which he could use to record the general's orders. Still, he thought it remarkable the soldiers could scavenge enough wood for so many campfires in the neighborhood. He would have thought McClernand's men picked the area clean after the first three days of the siege. The smell of the wood smoke gave him a sense of normalcy after the day's fighting; the memory of the winter nights back in Sergeant's Bluff flashed into his head.

After he found the light he needed with the quartermaster's men and began transcribing his hasty notes, Monroe sought him out. Harper was preoccupied, thinking about how to execute the new orders; he assumed Monroe was, as well.

"Well, Mister Harper, thank you for your advice to the general about how to run his damn division."

Harper looked up from his notepad, his face in a frown, his simmering anger starting to rise. He fought the urge to answer back.

"Next time, wait until someone invites your opinion."

Harper started to respond, but saw Porter's warning look over Monroe's shoulder and let his gaze drop to his notepad. "Yes, sir," he replied. His pencil point broke against the notepad, but there was nothing to be gained by arguing any more.

"Good." Monroe saw Harper's pencil point break. "Now, go tell the company commanders to have their men ready to resume the attack tomorrow. Maintain a line behind the rifle pits, with patrols out front as far as the creek at the bottom of this hill, but no farther. I want at least a third of our men under arms at all times tonight."

Harper wrote it all down with the stub of his pencil.

****

Katie looked up from her place seated on the bed when the light increased in the room. She watched the door open.

"Remembah, May-jah. Yo' only allowed to whip her from the waist down. If there are any bruises on her back aftah, it will be an extra twenty dollahs." Loreena led the major into the room, being careful no one else could see inside. They crossed to where Katie sat waiting, her arms suspended from the bed post. Loreena lifted Katie's chin. "Are you ready, Katie?"

Katie heard the voice in a dream and nodded with a smile. Loreena helped her stand and positioned her at the foot of the bed. She wrapped Katie's fingers around the bedpost with Katie's back to the major.

Katie watched in silence while Evilface checked that the bindings on her hands were tight before he pulled his wallet from inside his uniform jacket. He handed Loreena sixty dollars which the madam folded into her cleavage. Loreena gave Katie a final kiss on the cheek, whispering, "Be brave, Katie. It will be ovah soon."

Katie smiled back at Loreena. She had a secret plan.

After Loreena left, the major strutted in front of Katie. "I hear that you've been a wicked little girl, haven't you Katie?" He looked into her eyes. "You've been whoring around with all of the boys, haven't you?" He traced a line across her shoulders with his fingertips. "You're such a whore that you couldn't wait for me on Wednesday and you ran off to fornicate with a common soldier."

Katie returned a blank stare through the cloud in her mind.

"Well, now it is time for your punishment." He removed his jacket and unwound the scarf covering the disfigured half of his face.

Self-control lost to the laudanum, Katie stared at the twisted scars and tissue reaching from his hairline to his chin. A troll in her garden of peace.

Evilface walked over to the bedpost and grabbed her by the hair at the back of her head. He twisted until her face was an inch from the damaged skin. "See it? See it? That's why you're going to be punished tonight, little girl. Because of this." He pulled her face into the mess of tissue.

Against her cheek, the tortured, twisted skin had the feel of stiff, thick leather and smelled of putrefaction. After a moment, he pulled her face away. Katie tried to spit the feel of the dead skin away from her lips. Frustration at his total control over her brought tears which almost escaped her eyelids.

Evilface stepped back to the bed and pulled the leather belt free from the loops of his trousers. With a smile, he laid it on the bed right in front of her–a two-inch wide pain-giver. She stared at the strap and remembered why it was there, the troll wanted to beat her away from her garden. Now, the troll sat on a chair to pull off his boots and stockings. Pushed out of her garden, the memory of the pain from last time the troll was there filled her mind. She pulled on the rope binding her to the bedpost but couldn't get free. She pulled again, harder. She dug her heels into the floor and tried to drag the bed with her.

The troll laughed. "You can pull all you want but you won't get free, you little whore. You're going to get the punishment you deserve."

Katie looked at the troll, hate boiling its way into her brain through the druggy cloud, her arms suddenly too heavy to pull against the rope binding her wrists.

"Remember dear, if you cry, or if you let out so much as a whimper, I will have to punish you for that, as well."

He stood in front of her and pulled off his suspenders letting his trousers fall to the floor in front of her. The troll stood there in soldier's long underwear, fondling himself. She saw his underwear bulge before he removed his hand and took the belt from the bed. The troll walked behind Katie, dragging the strap over her shoulder as he went past. Katie shivered at the touch of cold leather and twisted her shoulder away. She pulled again on the bindings at her wrists–her arms were too tired. The bed did not yield.

She felt him move up close behind her and reach in front to untie her underwear. Strangely, she could smell lye soap which dissipated when the troll backed away. As the pantaloons fell to the floor, he kneeled down and gently lifted her feet out of the clothing. A slipper fell onto the floor and the troll returned it to Katie's stocking-covered foot. He ran his hand up the back of her leg before massaging the globes of her bottom. Katie flinched when he nipped each one with his teeth; he grabbed her hips so she couldn't pull way. But her sensitivity in this area of welts and bruises sent a ticklish jolt between her legs; her muscles twitched under his teeth.

"You don't like that, Katie? Well, then, maybe it's time to begin your punishment."

****

The battalion settled into its nightly routine. Harper gave the orders to Corporal Powell who recorded them in the unit diary by the light of a single candle while he sat in the Company D area among his Burlington friends.

With Theo Guelich in the rear tending to the supply wagons, Harper sought out Sergeant Featherstone, whom he found at a campfire among the Company B sergeants. He invited himself to join the group. Conversation ended when Harper crouched down.

"Ev'nin, sir. Coffee's ready, but the beans are still cookin'." Featherstone dumped the contents of his own drinking cup onto the snow behind him. "Looks like you've had a hell of a day, eh."

The smell of the coffee was a treat for Harper's nose; he could taste it on his tongue. "Why do ya say that?"

"Just lookin' at your uniform, Lieutenant. Wilhafen's running around telling anyone who'll listen how ya wrassled a Reb officer and finally kilt him with your skinnin' knife."

"Not entirely true. The Reb was gut-shot and dying anyway. Still, the bastard tried to shoot me when I walked past."

"Well, I wouldn't tell anyone that part, Mister Harper." He wiped the lip of his empty cup on his sleeve before half-filling it from a pot sitting in the flames. "By this time tomorrow, the story will probably be that it was *ten* Rebs." He handed the cup to Harper. "Ya know how camp rumors go around."

"Thank ya." Harper sipped at the mixture in the cup, letting its warmth fill his insides. "Yeah, I know." He remembered how quickly the episode with Monroe's son had spread through the *Chancellor*. "How did your men do today?"

"Well as can be expected. Didn't lose anybody, sittin' up on that damn hill. Might've gotten a few Rebs at long range." The other sergeants nodded agreement while Featherstone poked at the pot of beans and stirred its contents with the same stick. "Sent two of the corporals with work details to help any nearby wounded and carry 'em back to Doc White." Featherstone looked at Harper's ear. "Ya might best do something about that ear, Lieutenant. It's still oozing."

"Damn. It doesn't seem to want to stop. It's been doing that all day."

"Why not let Doc White stitch it up?"

"Haven't found time yet. Do ya know where he is?" Stitching it would be painful as hell, but Harper knew it would be better than letting it turn septic.

"Corporals'll know. We could ask 'em when they get back from collectin' the wounded." Featherstone stared at the fire for a moment, then unsheathed his knife and laid it on a rock so that the blade poked into the campfire.

Harper looked around the area and for the first time paid close attention to the dark shapes lying nearby, unmoving in the snow.

"No one can help 'em," Featherstone said. "We've checked."

"Any papers on them?" Harper's duties included examining the possessions found on dead Rebels to see if they contained useful information about the enemy. He had set that responsibility aside until now to command the skirmishers.

"No. All of 'em are our'n. Rebs already got anything valuable."

Harper grunted and took another sip of coffee. He stared at the steam rising from the cup, allowing his mind to relax after the stress of the day's battle.

Someone called from behind him. "Mister Harper, a word please." It was Major Porter.

Harper stood up from the ring of men surrounding the low campfire and returned the half-full cup to Featherstone. He stepped out of the circle and walked over to Porter. While he walked away, he heard the sergeants resume their discussion about what they would do in Dover Town when they broke through the Rebel lines.

"Colonel Monroe had a chance to look around at the local terrain. He wants someone to go down to the road coming from the town to make sure the Confederates can't use it." Porter paused. "He wants you, specifically, to do it because he's counting on your scouting skills to be able to move down there, find out exactly how high the water is, and get back in the dark."

It was more of the same thing Monroe ordered him to do two days ago. If Monroe needed someone to find out how deep a body of freezing water was, that would be Harper's job. Or, so it seemed. "So, now he figures maybe I *do* know what the hell I'm talkin' about?"

"Jamie, he knows that. He knows how smart you are, and how valuable you are to the battalion." Porter turned so he couldn't be heard by the men around the campfire. "That's why you're still here. But it would help if ya learned when to keep your mouth shut and how to disagree with a senior officer without losing your temper or takin' it personal."

The two men walked away from the campfire. The way Monroe and Wallace had treated him tonight added to Harper's disdain for both men. Even though Wallace didn't care about closing the escape road, apparently Monroe still felt he needed to do something at least to *appear* to comply with Grant's direct order–just in case Grant was right. But, disdain for Monroe aside, Harper knew Porter wanted to be helpful, so he redirected his thoughts to the assignment. He didn't want to be the cause of more problems for Porter.

"All right." Harper replied. "Do I go by myself?"

"No, take some men with ya. If ya find the river *is* fordable, I want ya to set a *picquet* there for the night to give us a warning if they try to cross. Take them from McKinsey's company. If ya set the *picquet*, let McKinsey or Lieutenant Goodrell know they're out there so they can organize reliefs through the night."

"Yes, sir." Harper stood to attention and rendered a proper salute.

Major Porter raised skeptical eyebrows at this unexpected show of respect. He smiled at Harper and returned the salute.

Harper went back to the sergeants' campfire to gather up his belongings. "Off on a scout tonight." Given the chance for independent action, he felt a familiar twinge of excitement at the prospect of the up-coming patrol in the dark.

"Wait a minute, Lieutenant." Featherstone stood in front of Harper with the knife in his hand. "Let me treat that ear."

Harper touched his bloody ear and looked at the knife. He took a deep breath and nodded.

Featherstone brought the knife alongside Harper's head and lay the flat end of the heated blade on top of the open wound.

Harper flinched from the pain but stood still. The skin under the knife sizzled and popped and the smell of burning flesh filled the air.

After the count of ten, Featherstone pulled the knife away and looked at Harper's ear.

"Damn, that hurt."

Featherstone bent the top of Harper's ear to see the wound. "It should be all right, now, Lieutenant. Near as I can tell in this light."

****

Katie felt the troll stand and step back from her bottom. Nothing happened. She waited. Her bruises throbbed again. She turned to look over her shoulder at the troll.

Instead, Evilface stood behind her, waving the belt, waiting. A moment later, Katie heard the smack of the leather strap against the back of her thigh. Pain shot up, amplified by the older bruises. It flowed through her brain and flooded into the garden of peace. The leather smacked at her bottom twice more. The blows still hurt and caused her to grimace, but not as much as earlier times, because the garden pulled the pain into itself.

"You're not going to cry, are you Katie?" He looked at her face. She stared back at him in defiance and hatred.

"So, you're getting angry, are you? We'll soon see about that."

She suffered another blow on her bottom, this one harder than those before.

But she remembered–she had a plan. The tears were part of the plan, but what was the rest? If she could only think. Why was her head so foggy? Was the garden part of the plan?

She forced her mind to follow the trail of logic–if she cried, Evilface became enraged. Crying brought the strap down much harder. But the rage lasted for only a few strokes before the man was ready to couple. Once he coupled, it would be all over.

"Still think you can defy me?" Evilface called from behind her. Another slap fell across the back of her thigh.

Katie thought she could withstand this punishment for as long as Evilface could swing the strap if the garden kept helping her. But, that was not the plan. It was time to end the torture.

She closed her eyes and looked for the garden but couldn't find it. Her legs and bottom began to burn. The burning in the back of each thigh spread until it linked together across her most sensitive areas.

Katie forced tears out of her eyes. Even as she winced, she forced her thoughts to go back to her home and her time with mother. Mother always protected her. Mother wouldn't have sold her. Her mother's arms were a safe place to hide and get better.

Now, the tears flowed on their own. She saw her mother lying in the wooden box, face yellowed by the sickness. The men came and nailed a wooden cover to the box. They lowered the box into the ground and covered it with dirt. *Good-bye momma.*

The tears flowed down her face and splattered on the floor. A soft sob escaped.

Evilface came to look at her face. He smiled, triumphant at the sight of the tears.

"You are not allowed to cry, Katie. You must take your punishment without crying, remember?"

She nodded in feigned submission.

"So, now I shall have to work even harder, so I can make you stop." He moved back behind her.

The plan was working!

The next blow from the belt was the hardest yet. It fell across the back of her knees, causing her to collapse to the floor, her hands still tied high on the bedpost. A blow stung across her back. The tip wrapped around her chest and stung her breast. She yelped in pain before she could stop herself.

Evilface had his own surprise for her. She felt him grab her hair and pull her head back–hard enough that Katie felt a pop in her neck. Before she could react, Evilface pushed a handkerchief into her open mouth and pulled a cord tight around her head before she could spit out the handkerchief.

Her head spun from being pushed back and thrown forward. New pain in her neck made it hard to hold her head straight. What was happening?

The gag was a new part of Evilface's demands. No sound came when she tried to talk–the handkerchief prevented her from forming words. She leaned against the bedpost to steady herself and protect her breasts when the next blow of the belt came, followed by another–sooner, with increased force. All fell across her back. She would tell Loreena about how he is breaking her rules; maybe Loreena would make Evilface go away and not come back.

After half-a-dozen blows, Katie no longer thought about her mother. The tears she produced now came from pure pain. Through her tears, she tried to yell at him and twist the ropes from her wrists but he laughed at her struggles. She pushed her head against the bed post and let the tears flow.

The blows stopped. The room went still except for Evilface's panting for breath. She took several deep breaths. Her ordeal would soon be over. Her head was clear now, the fuzziness gone.

She had out-smarted him, causing him to stop sooner than in the past. But why gag her? A growing unease replaced the hatred she felt for this man. She pulled at the bindings again before staring at him.

Dropping the strap on the floor, Evilface untied Katie from the bedpost, grabbed her bound wrists and pulled her to the side of the bed. He pushed her face-down onto the quilt cover. Katie waited there with the gag still in her mouth breathing deep, cold draughts through her nose.

From their earlier sessions, she expected Evilface was unbuttoning his underwear. She made ready for him the way the animals did on the farm, back-to-front, bent over from the waist down, standing on her toes with her back arched to present him clear access to the target.

He kicked her legs farther apart and fell on her, grabbing her wrists to force them into the bedclothes. She was ready for him. The stinging from the blows against her bottom had triggered her wetness in spite of the pain. She spread her legs wider so she could end this fast. She grunted at the force he used.

But something was wrong. Tonight, Evilface didn't seem interested in doing it the right way; instead, he remained still, coupled to her. He bent over her back to bring his face beside her ear.

"How does that feel, Katie?" She smelled his whiskey breath, and her hatred flashed through her entire body. Someday, she would kill this man. She tried to rotate her hips but this movement angered Evilface. "Lay still, whore! I want to stay like this to savor the feeling. You're *my* little whore now, so do as I say."

Her drug-weakened stomach turned queasy; she convulsed against the gag in her mouth. What if she vomited with the gag in her mouth? Evilface continued to press against her, crushing his entire chest along her back.

She couldn't breathe now due to the man's weight. Nausea from the smell of him rose in her throat again and she began to struggle, fear for her life replacing the worry over his new demands. She screamed into the gag but only a soft squeak resulted. She tried to leverage him off of her, pushing up from her elbows. Evilface lifted her wrists off of the bed, her elbows went straight and her face fell full into the quilt. Even while both of his hands pulled at her wrists, he held his position inside her. Katie struggled as best as she could, trying to bounce Evilface off with her feet, or by rotating her hips violently.

"I told you to be still!" He rose from her back and in a quick move, grabbed her neck with one hand and slapped her in the head with the other. He forced her face deeper into the quilt.

The fabric sucked into her nostrils, cutting off the air flow. She screamed again, but with her lungs almost empty the result was so weak she was sure only she could hear. He slapped her again in the back of the head. She struggled harder now, trying to squirm out from under the man in her panic. He pushed her harder into the quilt while he forced her thighs against the mattress with his knees, lifting her feet from the floor.

Katie's consciousness flickered. The world closed in until it included her face and the piece of quilt under it and nothing more. Nothing else mattered. She needed to pull the quilt out of her nostrils. She brought two hands under the sides of her face and pushed with a force amplified by airless panic. Evilface slapped her in the head again. Then again. And again. The view of her small world flashed red lightning with each blow.

He was laughing at her! The slapping hand became a fist, punching her in the back and side of her head. She pushed the quilt away from her nose and filled her lungs with air. With her exhalation she screamed louder than she ever before, "VIOLETS! VIOLETS!" But only muffled squeals came through the gag. This aroused Evilface further.

He started pounding into her with his hips. She pulled the gag down but could not yell before he hit her again, and pushed her face back into the quilt with the strength of his finishing.

Both of Evilface's hands went to her neck and began to squeeze while he continued to thrust with his hips. She could not breathe at all now; she struggled in growing desperation as the world around her grayed over, narrowing to a single spot of white light.

****

The pain was gone. Her lower body did not burn. Her nausea was gone. Katie watched down through the bed's canopy while Major Evilface strangled an inert red-headed girl on the bed. The spot of light hovered above her where her mother stood. Katie-in-the-Air tried to move into the warmth and safety of the light, but Katie-on-the-Bed grasped her ankle in both hands with desperate strength. Katie-in-the-Air could not escape. She was stuck between the bed and the light. She looked to her mother, hoping for help. Her mother whispered something that she couldn't understand. Katie-in-the-Air stretched, trying to come closer. At last, she could hear her mother's words.

"Get out."

****

Harper found Captain McKinsey and Lieutenant Reynolds resting on their oilskins and leaning against their saddles while McKinsey's orderly cooked and tended their campfire. A fourth saddle closed the ring around the fire and Harper guessed it belonged to Harv Goodrell, McKinsey's first lieutenant. The orderly cooked the same fare as the enlisted men, dried beans and hardtack. But the smell of skunk onions and rosemary leaves rose from this cooking pot. Harper assumed these were the result of the orderly's initiative. A hip flask sat on the ground next to McKinsey.

"Captain, I've been ordered to go on a scout. I need three of your men plus a corporal in case we set a *picquet*."

"Who decided we needed a scouting party, Harper?"

"Colonel Monroe's orders, Captain."

"And when do ya need them? None of my men have eaten yet."

"Sorry, Captain. But we need to take a look down there right away." Harper looked in the direction of the river beyond their right flank. "We need to make sure the flank is secure and the road down there is closed. Ya should be able to send a relief for the first group in about an hour."

"Damn. Just when we were settling in." McKinsey's movements were stiff and slow, giving Harper the impression the man's old bones felt the decreasing temperatures.

"I'll meet your men over there." Harper pointed to a point where the Wynn's Ferry Road intersected the right flank of the battalion's rifle pits.

"All right, Harper." McKinsey needed assistance from Reynolds to stand. "We'll get ya some men."

Harper walked back to the battalion headquarters to find where Corporal Powell had staked Santee to prepare for the reconnaissance. In half an hour, the group was mounted and ready. Harper recognized Magnusson among the men McKinsey assigned and he nodded a greeting before they set off in column with Harper in the lead. After they passed through the breastworks, Magnusson caught up with Harper.

"Where're we headed, sir?" Magnusson asked Harper.

"There's a road down there that appears to be flooded. We're going to make sure the Rebs can't use it to escape."

"Think we'll be able to set a campfire?"

"Depends. We might not even have to set the *picquet*."

They rode alongside each other for a few more steps.

"With all due respect, Mister Harper, if one of these men gets hurt, I ain't leaving him."

Harper should have expected this kind of distrust, given the outcome of the last time they worked together and the reputation he gained from that battle. "You will obey my orders, Corporal."

"As long as they ain't orders to leave a wounded man behind, sir. Like at Belmont."

Harper could see Magnusson's face in the moonlight. His jaw was clenched tight while he stared straight ahead.

After a few steps, Magnusson spoke. "I'm sorry I couldn't obey your orders before."

Harper needed to shift Magnusson's mind off of the past battle, onto the present one.

"Well, things turned out for the best. The Monroe boy might not've have made it if ya weren't such a strong fellow."

"Yes, sir. Thank ya for saying so."

They arrived at the head of the trail, where Wynn's Ferry Road dropped over the lip of the ridge. Harper turned onto the farm trail in the hope that they could avoid being observed by the Rebels in their trenches along the more narrow path.

"Ya did well that day, Magnusson. I'm glad you're with me now." He meant it. Magnusson was the largest and strongest of the trained skirmishers–and one of the best.

"Yes, sir." Magnusson thought for a minute. "So far, we've had a good day, but I hope the water's too deep. We need some rest before the attack tomorrow. None of the boys have eaten anything since breakfast. I'd rather not have to keep 'em up all night."

When Harper guided Santee onto the trail, the moon was about an hour in front of its zenith. It reminded him, they would have to take care not to be seen against the snow. Even moving on the farm trail could give them away, although he doubted any Rebels watched this side of the ridge.

Magnusson followed Harper with the three privates falling into place behind. Under the full moon, Harper let Santee pick her way down the slope, while the other mustangs followed the lead mare in natural-bred silence. Once they intersected the road running from Dover Town, they would turn north until they came to the ford.

The forest around them, thin at the top the ridge, now became thicker with the leafless tress closing in from both sides. As the trees became more plentiful, visibility within in the woods dropped to only a few yards on either side of the road; although, someone looking down from the ridge could probably track their movements in the moonlight.

"Scouting mode," Harper ordered. He watched the four soldiers move so each surveyed a sector around the group, applying the lessons he trained into them during final week around Paducah. What was so hard to teach during the training the previous month now was a part of their natural behavior. In scouting mode, they would remain silent and use hand signals if they needed to communicate.

The farm track was easy to follow, a darker smudge in the earth set against the surrounding mud and snow churned by the tracks of the Rebel retreat. The night's chill made the mud in the trail stiffer, so the legs of the horses stayed clean. All of their horses came from Johnny's ranch, born in the wild and tamed, rather than broken. They moved by instinct though the dark, skeletal woodland.

Half-an-hour after they left the battalion, the trail leveled out and the horses found easier going. Ahead, Harper could see the spot where the trail widened, where he assumed the farm trail crossed the Charlotte Road. Shadows moved across the road in front of him. He reined-up and dismounted. Corporal Magnusson came up, dismounted next to him. Magnusson used hand signals to the others to halt but stay mounted in column.

"Do ya see that?" Harper whispered to Magnusson. "About fifty yards up the trail?"

Magnusson nodded but didn't speak.

"I'm going for a closer look. You and the others stay here and watch for any flank guards." Harper handed the reins of his horse to Magnusson.

Magnusson whispered. "Lieutenant, we've seen what we need to see. Let's git the hell out of here and report before something happens."

"I need to make sure who they are for my report," Harper said. "I want to make sure they aren't our own cavalry."

Magnusson looked back down the road at the passing horsemen. "Those are Rebs, Lieutenant. I can see that clear enough." He looked back at Harper. "Our cavalry ain't anywhere near here. They're rounding up deserters on the other side of the ridge."

Harper shook his head. "No. Not all of them are. Some should be over here protecting the flank."

"Sir, I can see pretty good." Magnusson's tone sounded more like a correction than an observation. "Those ain't our boys, Mister Harper."

"I'm goin', Corporal. You keep the men and horses under cover until I get back."

"You mean *if* you come back." Magnusson turned his back to Harper, looking at the other men in the *picquet*. "Shit."

"What did you say, Corporal."

"Nothin', sir." Magnusson returned to face Harper. "Just wonderin' what the hell we do if you *don't* get back."

"You'll have to use you own judgment, *Corporal*. You seem to be good at that."

Magnusson just stared straight into Harper's eyes. Harper could feel the angry heat coming from the corporal's face.

After a moment, Magnusson looked away and shook his head. "Yes, sir."

"Now, do it." Harper waited while Magnusson signaled the three soldiers to close up and move into the trees: one on the left of the trail, with him and Magnusson, and two on the right. When they were in place with their rifles ready, Harper crept along the tree line beside the trail moving so Magnusson could see him.

The old sensations returned, the excitement of stalking a killer in the night, staying hidden until the last minute. Except this time, he would have only the sight of the enemy to have a victory. How close could he get without being seen? He would take it real damn close.

About half the distance from where he started and twenty yards from the road, Harper watched the shadows solidify into mounted men moving south in a column three riders across. Harper knelt down, drew his pistol from under his overcoat, and pulled the hammer back. When he did so, he noticed his silhouette from the moonlight, dark on the smooth snow.

Crouching low, he shifted so his shadow blended with a nearby tree. From there, he ran in a crouch from tree-to-tree, pausing at each stop before jumping to the next. Still, Harper saw no sign of a flank guard. Finally, he found a holly bush not more than ten feet from the road, still in leaf and sheltered in the shadow of an old oak. From there, he could see the details of the riders. He had come this close and not encountered any flank guard for the column. The Rebels must be powerful tired to have forgotten to post a guard between themselves and the Federals on the ridge above.

****

From far away, Katie heard men yelling as her lungs filled with cool air. Warmth surrounded her naked body. Somewhere, a struggle went on, knocking against furniture and walls; it ended with a thud on the floor. Two sets of gentle hands rolled her over to raise her into a sitting position.

"Breathe, Katie. Breathe deep!" Loreena told her from somewhere to her right. Katie did so, opening her eyes.

"Hold your chin up high." Eleanor sat on her left with her arm across Katie's back. She cupped Katie's chin, trying to clear her airway.

Eleanor stroked Katie's hair. "There we are, *chéri*. It is all o-*vaire*." Eleanor's hand came away from Katie's head with blood on it. She showed the blood to Loreena, who held Eleanor's wrist high so Franklin Bosley could see.

"Get that sick son-of-a bitch out of here," Katie heard Bosley tell the men behind her. She turned to look but her head spun, causing the nausea to rise and she vomited onto the floor.

"Take him down to the river," Bosley told the others.

"Y'all can be just as sick as you want now, deah. It's all ovah."

Eleanor pulled the quilt more tightly around Katie's body and held her in both arms. Eyes filling with tears, Eleanor said, "I'm so sorry, Katie dear. We should have come sooner."

****

He set his hat on the snow next to him and crouched lower, closer to the holly bush, until the points of its leaves pricked at his face. He watched the road through its branches while he breathed into his overcoat so condensation would not expose his position. While he watched, he slowed his breathing though his heart still beat furiously.

The horses in the column carried a wide variety of saddles and tack, ranging from full bridles to simple ropes tied around the horse's muzzle or head. The riders allowed the horses to walk in the cold night but they covered ground swiftly. Some horses dripped water from their shaggy winter coats. Some carried two riders. A number of the ghostly riders rode mules. Harper could smell the wet, rangy animals.

He could not identify the riders' uniforms with certainty. Like the tack on their horses, they wore a mix of military and civilian coats, cloaks, or slickers, some of it from the Federal army. The riders carried a variety of carbines, shotguns, rifles, muskets, and pistols in holsters attached to their saddles. A few carried swords or sabers. Taken all together, these signs told Harper this was a sizable force of Rebel cavalry.

The riders moved along in near-total silence. They would have appeared to be a column of specters in the moonlight, except for the occasional jangle from a bridle or a squish from a horse's hoof in the mud. One rider wore the gold-braided "swallows nest" on his sleeve, the mark of a Confederate officer. Harper had his confirmation. These were Confederate cavalry moving south–out of the fortress, into the rear of the Federal lines. Harper allowed himself a brief moment of satisfaction at being right. Now, he needed to bring the information back to the battalion.

Pistol still in his right hand and his hat in the left, Harper inched back from the holly bush, watching to remain in the shadow of the oak tree beside it. Staying low to the ground, he edged around until the tree blocked the view from the road. He searched for the next bit of cover, saw a nearby tree which suited him, and crawled to it, using understory bushes for cover. Soft snow and mud oozed through the knees of his trousers.

He enjoyed this hide-and-seek. Like an Indian brave using a *coup*-stick, he touched the enemy by observing them and now would escape unscathed.

After ten yards or so, he came to a crouch while trying to determine if he was visible from the road. Too close. He crawled farther along the understory, deeper into the wood. If they saw him from the road, perhaps they would think they saw an animal. When he could not see the road anymore, Harper felt safe to stand in the shadow of the next tree. He looked around for any sign of a Rebel flank guard but saw nothing, so he walked to the next tree, using the slow caution he learned as a marshal.

Now, the night air carried the odor of unwashed humans. He turned to look deeper in the woods, his pistol ready. He sensed, more than saw, multiple dark shapes moving at him before stars exploded in his eyes. The blow to the back of his head drove him to the ground. Two bodies fell on top of him, pinning him in the snow. He jerked the trigger of his pistol, trying to send a warning shot. It fired into the ground, sending up a mound of muddy snow which covered the muzzle flash and smothered the discharge to a muffled *thump*. Another man yanked the weapon from his hand, leaving him helpless as the wetness of the snow began to seep into his overcoat.

"Lookee heah, boys. We got us a Yankee off-i-sah."

PART 4

NASHVILLE, TENNESSEE

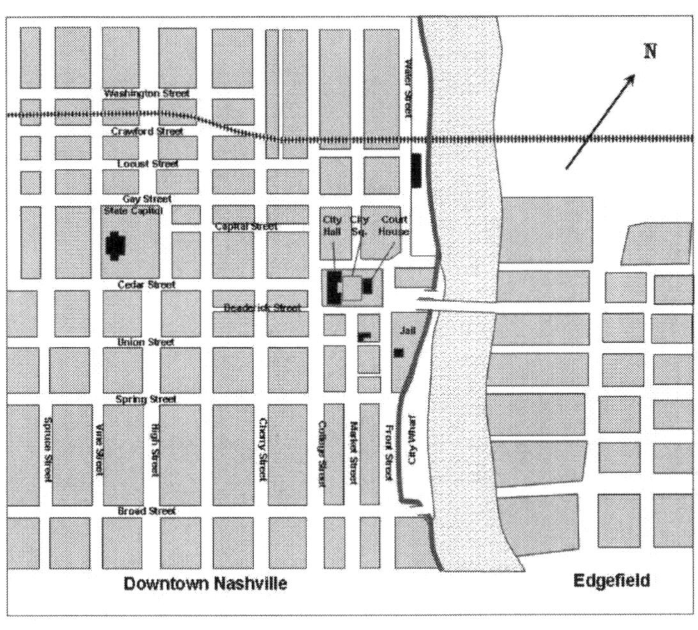

(Map prepared by Sean K. Gabhann)

Sunday, February 16th, 1862

All of the men in Harper's *picquet* were prisoners, taken by the Confederate flank guard before any of them could fire a warning shot. Now, the column of Confederate cavalry rode south and east throughout Saturday night and Sunday morning. Harper assumed they rode for Nashville or farther south, into Mississippi.

Harper had looked for ways to escape since sun-up, but there was little chance for that to happen. Once again, he tried to work against the knot in the leather straps holding his hands to the pommel of the saddle. If he did get his hands free, he might be able to pull Santee's reins loose from the guard's saddle in front of him.

During the escape, he could ignore the rope under Santee's belly which tied his legs together and made it impossible to dismount. If he succeeded in escaping, he could work that binding loose afterward. If he didn't succeed, it wouldn't matter–he'd be dead.

The knot at his hands stayed tightly in place in spite of his struggles.

At first, Santee balked at being led in this way–pulling back on the reins or trying to shake free of the bridle. But after ten hours, she followed her lead horse with only an occasional head nod or tug.

Even with some of the Confederates sleeping in their saddles, it would be impossible to cut all five horses loose. One man might be able to do it if any of them could get their hands free. It would require stealth and fast action to sneak away. Davis, riding at the end of the column, might be able to do it. But if all five of his men tried, the most likely outcome would be that at least one Rebel would see them and alert the others.

All of their weapons, including their hunting knives, Harper's binoculars, and his sword, were gone–distributed among the Rebel troopers. The men who now led the prisoners' horses had taken the Federals' overcoats. Harper and his men rode along, shivering, with their elbows clamped tight against their sides as if that would hold the warmth inside. Fortunately, the scarce warmth of the morning sun spread across their dark-blue uniforms, pushing against the night's chill. By mid-morning, the breaths of the horses and men were no longer visible, and the temperature had risen above freezing.

Blankets covered most of the Confederate troopers but the ice on their trouser legs began to melt from the places it had frozen after they forded the backwater. Some of the Confederates opted to expose their legs to the sunshine, trying to dry out their trousers, while others kept their legs covered with blankets, using body heat, instead. Each man's puffy eyelids and bloodshot eyes revealed their fatigue. Their frowns and furrowed brows showed the bitterness each felt from the defeat the previous day. The column moved in silence, the horses plodding forward, stepping into the hoof prints of the horse in front.

The prisoners rode in the last company of Confederate cavalry, the rearguard. Harper could not see the head of the column, but when they climbed a ridge ealier, he saw nearly a thousand cavalrymen ahead of him.

The frozen mud in the road had yielded to the late-morning sun by the time the Confederate column halted at a large village. By now, they must be forty or fifty miles south of Fort Donelson.

"Zeke." The guard leading Harper addressed the rider next to him. "Y'all's from these parts. Where ya reckon we are?"

"Don't know fer sure. We ain't got t' Charlotte yet, though." Zeke looked at the snow-covered countryside. "I got family there, if'n they ain't run off."

"All'a ya from Tennessee?" Maybe Harper could learn something useful for escape if he could get these Rebels talking.

Harper's guard looked over his shoulder at Harper. "Shut up, Yank! Don't make no never-mind to *you* where we's from. You ain't gonna be with us long 'nuff to git acquainted."

The company guarding the prisoners halted in front of the first house into the village, a white, two-story cube with a low, pyramidal roof made of sheet metal. A wooden porch extended across the front, white railings and posts with a gray deck. A gravel path, revealed under trampled snow, connected the porch to the road across a wide, snow-covered lawn.

Word moved down the column to dismount and take noon meal. "Untie the prisoners. Let them dismount," a lieutenant ordered. "Put them over there." He pointed at a picket fence protecting the front lawn of the house.

With cold-numbed legs, Harper dismounted. He pounded his feet on the ground, trying to improve the circulation in his legs and feet. The other prisoners shuffled over to the picket fence indicated by the Rebel lieutenant, where the three Federal privates sat together on tufts of dead grass which poked through the snow and used the white boards of the fence as a backrest. The corporal in charge of the guards assigned two men to watch the prisoners while he and the rest of the guards led the horses to an empty field across the street.

Harper joined Magnusson standing beside the seated men. "How are they doin'?" Harper used his chin to point to Bailey, Cooke, and Davis. Their faces were pale but they no longer shivered. Instead, they each carried the despondent look of over-tired men waiting for the next bad thing to happen.

"They'll be fine, sir." Unlike the privates, Magnusson's eyes were alert, looking from Harper to the guards and horses, then to the other Rebels nearby. But Magnusson betrayed his fatigue by leaning against the top of the picket fence.

Harper detected a hint of insolence in Magnusson's tone. He chose to ignore it. As a staff officer they only knew slightly, the enlisted men normally showed him an indifferent level of respect, anyway—noticeably less than they showed to their respective company officers. The incident at Belmont had exacerbated this, especially among the men of Company B.

Harper and Magnusson examined the Confederate troopers. Some removed their blankets and slickers when they dismounted and Harper saw none wore true uniforms, only mixed-up pieces of worn out gray uniforms, civilian clothes, and rags, interspersed with an occasional blue from a set of trousers or a jacket which once belonged to a Yankee soldier. These men had seen a lot of campaigning.

"Clear fields all around," Corporal Magnusson whispered. "We might make it to that house by the woods." He nodded toward a line of trees on the far side of an open pasture across the road.

Harper looked in the other direction away from the distant house, to avoid signaling to the guards that they were planning to escape. He whispered, "I don't think that will work." He looked for the two guards to see if they were within earshot. He found them across the road, sitting on a log supported by two tree stumps. The flat, undisturbed snow next to them and a similar arrangement of logs farther up the street, showed the preferred path leading into the open pasture. Both guards chatted while they held shotguns pointed in the general direction of the prisoners. The rest of the Rebel company spread onto the lawn of the white house with the porch and into an adjacent cornfield, now plowed-under, the rows detectable from the peaks of dirt poking above lines of melting snow lying in the furrows.

Harper used a soft voice. "Not with a whole regiment of Rebel cavalry around us. I don't think any of us could get half-way there. There's no cover."

The apparent owners of the white house, a man, a woman, two children, and three negro women, came out to walk among the soldiers, sharing the family's own dinner for as far as it went.

Out of habit, Harper counted the Rebels spread on the lawn and the cornfield. Forty-seven plus the three sentries in the road and the guards for the prisoners made fifty-five for this company. No telling how many companies like this were nearby–at least ten.

Several of the prisoners' guards began to pull items from the saddlebags of the Federal captives, scattering personal items in the muddy road. An officer and some sergeants watched without interrupting. The looters stuffed everything usable into their pockets or carried it over to their own saddlebags: blankets, rations, spare underwear, cooking pans, fresh coffee grounds, tobacco, tool kits for horse-care. The rifle ammunition went to the five men who took the Sharps rifles the previous night.

Magnusson's men stood to watch the looting. When Harper and

Magnusson pushed away from the fence to stand beside the three, the two guards on duty aimed their shotguns at the group. Harper and his men were helpless to do anything but watch.

The looters gave any foodstuffs to their messmates sitting at campfires made from dried cornstalks and the farmer's woodpile. Unused papers when into their pockets, while anything with writing on it was thrown into the street. One trooper unstrapped the saddle from a prisoner's horse and exchanged it with his own tattered one.

The youngest of the prisoners and the one who was losing his saddle, started to object. "Hold on there, Reb…"

"What'cha gonna do 'bout it, Yank?" The saddle thief turned to the smaller soldier, a grim, grimy, ugly face. "You ain't gonna need it no-way. Not where y'all's headed." He threw the worn-out saddle into the muddy street. His right hand unbuttoned the flap on his holster.

Harper walked over to stand facing the young soldier, his back to the guards and the looters. "There's nothin' we can do about it right now, soldier. Don't start somethin'."

Magnusson walked up to stand beside the soldier with his arms folded across his chest.

This was Harper's first opportunity to see each prisoner's face in daylight. "Your name's Bailey, isn't it?"

"Private Benjamin Bailey–sir." Bailey slouched against the fence while he watched the saddle-thief strap the newer, Army-issued saddle onto his own horse before leading it away to join a nearby group at their campfire. Bailey looked at Harper, his lip showing the briefest hint of a sneer.

Harper noted how Bailey seemed to be a smaller version of Magnusson, well built, blue-eyed, blond. Were they relatives? He already had enough troubles in the battalion from not knowing who was related to whom.

"Saddle your horse, Ben," Magnusson said. Harper gave the nearest guard a questioning look and the guard nodded his assent. Bailey did as he was ordered while Magnusson helped him. Magnusson addressed Cooke and Davis. "You other men pick up what's left of your gear."

Harper touched his jacket to feel the envelope with the locks of hair still in his breast pocket. It was still safe. When he went to collect his own scattered belongings, all he found was the Bible that his sister-in-law sent him and scraps of the letter of apology to Magnusson's father. He fetched the Bible before it sank into the mud. Although he had little regard for the Christian God, and no belief that that anyone's god would protect him personally on the battlefield, he was just superstitious enough not to tempt the fates. He left the pages of the apology to soak into the mud.

Based on the looks and attitudes of their captors, Harper had concluded that strict discipline did not work in this army of rebels. In fact, the appearance of some of the men and their lack of attention to personal details, like their uniforms or equipment, gave Harper a sense that if these men were not part of the army, they would be part of an outlaw gang. Harper had to consider the possibility that the Confederate officers would not control their men should they decide to harm the prisoners.

A negro appeared leading a mule on the road out of town, not yet a man–a teenager. A child rode bareback on the mule, another negro. The boy walked with his head bowed when he passed between the prisoners with their guards and the groups of Confederates cooking at their campfires. He walked the mule in silence, avoiding eye contact with the gray soldiers but the child stared with the full curiosity of a toddler.

Harper and the other prisoners stared back at the boy. These were the first negroes they had seen up close in Tennessee.

"Hold up there, buck." The sentries in the road halted the boy when he reached the end of the clusters of campfires. "Corporal of the Guard!"

The boy kept his head bowed but the hand holding the lead for the mule began shaking.

The Confederate corporal who was in charge of the Federal prisoners stood up from the campfire where the saddle-thief also sat. "What is it?"

"This here darkie wants to go past the sentry point. He's leaving town with the mule and the boy."

"What's your name, nigger?" The corporal didn't look at the boy, but at the mule instead. "Where are y'all goin'?"

The negro removed his hat and twisted it in his hands while he answered, head bowed. “My name is Paulus, massah. I’s Miss Rachel’s nigga, sah. We’s jes’ goin’ home now. Been workin’ in town dis mornin’ the way Miss Rachel said to, sah.” His hands fretted the brim of his hat.

Harper could hardly understand the boy’s words, the pronunciation so foreign to an Iowan.

“And where’d you git this mule, boy?” The corporal walked around the mule, examining it closely. “Is this Miss Rachel’s brand here?”

“No, massah. Dat’s Massah Robert’s mark. He done give dis mule to Miss Rachel after her husband got hisself kilt fightin’ the Yankees, massah.” Paulus looked up, shifting his glance between the corporal and the woods ahead.

“So, why do you have it?”

“Miss Rachel done tol’ me dis mornin’ to carry the firewood to Massah Robert’s store. The mule carried the wood. We’s jus’ goin’ home now, massah.” There was a note of pleading in the boy’s voice. “This nigga ain’t doin’ nothin’ wrong, sah. Honest. Jes’ doin’ what we been told by da white folks, massah.” The reins leading the mule shook. Harper traced the cause to Paulus’s hands.

“I’ll decide if y’all are doin’ somethin’ wrong boy.” The corporal finished his inspection of the mule. “That’s a right fine animal to be trustin’ to a nigger.”

“Sah, Paulus is a good nigga. Das why Miss Rachel trus’ him wiff d’mule. I been in they family since I’s born, massah. I ain’t goin’ to let nothin’ bad happen to dis mule. Miss Rachel needs dis mule, sah.”

“Is that so?”

On-lookers from the nearby campsites watched the corporal, some smiling, as if waiting for the climax of a play on a stage that they had seen before. Harper watched the scene, wondering what the soldiers were expecting. A sense of foreboding for the boy came to him.

“So where does Miss Rachel live, boy?”

“Jus’ ov’ dare, massah.” He pointed to the log cabin tucked between the fallow field and the edge of the forest. It was the same house Magnusson thought might cover their escape.

The Rebel corporal smiled. “All right then. Y’all move along, Paulus.” He pointed to the cabin. “You git yourself back to Miss

Rachel. And don't try to run away, on account of we'll be watchin'."

Paulus bowed to the corporal. "Yes, massah. Tankee, sah. Right 'way, sah." Paulus bowed to the corporal and smiled at the child on the back of the mule; he stepped past the corporal and the two sentries.

Harper watched the corporal draw his cavalry pistol and aim it at the back of Paulus's head.

What is he doing?

The boy was no threat. He hadn't shown any disrespect. Harper doubted that the boy was lying. The corporal could easily watch the boy walk the mule back to Miss Rachel's cabin. *These men are supposed to be protecting the Southerners.*

The gunshot startled several ravens gleaning the pasture. Smoke from the barrel clouded the scene. Everyone in the vicinity turned to look. When the smoke cleared, Paulus lay unmoving in a puddle of mud in the middle of the road, his brain exposed, blood oozing into the dirty water.

Harper stared in shock at the boy lying in the street. It took several moments before his brain would work. *Was this how everyone in the South treated their negroes? No wonder the Abolitionists were so hysterical.*

The child on the back of the mule screamed. He continued yowling as the corporal led the mule to join the prisoners' horses. The men around the campfires returned to finish their lunch, ignoring the body of the boy.

Magnusson joined Harper. "Did ya see that, sir? He killed that boy for no reason, except to steal the mule. They didn't need to kill the boy to take the mule."

The act confirmed Harper's sense that they rode among outlaws in uniforms. This could not be how the majority of Southerners treated their slaves–stealing from widows and murdering for pleasure.

"What do *you* think we should do, *Mister* Harper?"

Magnusson's tone had become comtemptous since their capture. Harper would have to deal with that later.

"We need to escape as soon as we can. The longer we stay with these men, the harder it will be—and the deeper we'll be in their country." There was no way to predict when their captors would turn their weapons against the prisoners. For the first time, Harper wondered why the Rebels kept them alive, even now.

Harper looked around, counting the numbers of campfires. "It'll be impossible for everyone to run past all of these men." He tried to keep an even tone so Magnusson would not hear his reaction to the earlier disrespect.

"One man might be able to do it, if the rest of us caused a distraction."

Harper considered this suggestion, trying to think through likely outcomes. "Maybe, but who would ya send?" He looked around for any nearby Confederates and continued in a whisper. "The privates would most likely get lost tryin' to get back to our army, and *I'm* not goin' to be the first one to escape." He twisted his head to look into Magnusson's eyes. "Are *you* willing to be the only one to get away?"

Before Magnusson could answer, a Confederate captain trotted up with an aide, coming from the center of the village. He stopped in front of the prisoners and looked down at Harper. "Colonel Forrest wants to see the Yankee officer we captured."

Harper stepped forward. "Here I am."

So this is Bedford Forrest's command.

Lieutenant Colonel Nathan Bedford Forrest had developed a fearsome reputation during the Rebel operations in Kentucky the previous summer and autumn. It explained the rough condition of the Rebel cavalry. They had been in the field for at least six months that Harper knew about. Now, Harper would get to meet the famous Confederate.

This captain seemed to be a tall man, but it was difficult to tell while he remained on the horse. His uniform was wrinkled but a degree cleaner when compared to his men. His shirt underneath the jacket showed through in several spots. Patches covered the knees. Harper could see the hint of a brown water stain extending completely up the captain's trouser legs, almost to his holster, probably the result of fording the backwater the previous night.

The captain looked at Harper. His gaze covered Harper from head to foot. "Damn, boy. You look a mess."

Harper said nothing. He tried to brush some of the dried mud from last night's struggle off of his jacket and trousers. He couldn't do anything about the blood stains or the scorch on his trousers.

The screaming of the child drew the Confederate officer's attention. He trotted over to the boy, now seated alone in the snow next to the mule, left there when the corporal returned to his meal. Harper watched while the captain and the corporal talked with each other. The corporal pointed to the dead boy in the road, then to the woods, but not the log cabin. The captain pulled his revolver from its holster and without dismounting fired twice, silencing the boy. The captain and the corporal laughed together at the bloody mess in the snow where the child lay.

Harper and Magnusson looked at each other. Harper spoke softly, slowly. "Don't let the men start anythin'. We'll figure this out later. They're keeping us alive for a reason, but these people might shoot any of ya for just for the hell of it."

"Yes, sir." Magnusson bobbed his head slightly acknowledging the order. His tone was more respectful than earlier.

"We still have a few days before we arrive where ever they're takin' us." He mounted Santee and waited in the road.

The Confederate captain walked his horse back to where Harper waited in the aim of a shotgun.

"If'n I have y'all's word as a *gentleman* not to try to escape, I'll let you ride with your hands free. Otherwise, I'll have to hog-tie you again."

Harper looked into the lined face of the captain trying to see what emotions revealed themselves. The Confederate looked back through tired, bloodshot eyes, but in spite of his obvious fatigue, he was smiling. It appeared he actually enjoyed shooting the toddler. Still he maintained the veneer of civility expected of officers in both armies.

"Ya have my word, Captain."

"Bell. Captain Anderson Bell." The captain wheeled his horse toward the center of town. "Good. Come with me."

Harper and Bell rode side-by-side with Bell's aide following. Bell rode a tall, bay-colored Morgan gelding. It stood a hand or two taller than Santee. Before he mounted, Harper had the impression of Bell being as tall, maybe taller than himself. Now, he could see that Bell was actually the shorter man. It was the horse which made Bell appear large.

If Bell was going to pretend to be a civilized person, perhaps Harper could extract some information from him. "Captain Bell, why did ya shoot the baby?"

Bell laughed. "Well, with the other nigger dead, I thought I'd put the little one out of his misery. He was cryin' so much. He must have really liked the big one."

"What did they do to deserve gettin' shot?"

"Corporal Stackpole told me they was tryin' to get to the Yankee lines."

"That's a lie. I saw what happened. That boy was goin' home after finishin' a chore for his mistress. He lived here. He wasn't a threat to anybody."

"That ain't what the *corporal* told me." Bell looked Harper in the eyes. The message was clear—Bell and his men lied in order to legitimatize their murders. Bell laughed again. "Besides, we can use the mule and it don't matter if a nigger or two gets killed. His owner can petition the government in Richmond to get his money back."

"The owner was the widow of a Confederate soldier."

Bell turned away and stared straight ahead.

Harper took the opportunity to examine Bell's uniform close-up. For the first time in the war, Harper was near to a Rebel officer who wasn't trying to kill him. Bell's uniform could only be described as ragged. While Harper's uniform was intact except for the blood smears on his jacket and the powder burn on his leg, Bell's gray jacket was rumpled and permanently stained. The formerly stiff collar now drooped over, covering most of the three stars signifying Bell's rank.

"What's your name, Yank?" Bell asked. "And your unit? I need to tell Colonel Forrest."

"James Harper, First Iowa Volunteers."

"How long y'all been fightin'?"

"Since the beginnin', about a year. We were in Missouri last summer."

While they rode, sections of the swallow's nest trim on Bell's forearm flapped where the threads holding it to the jacket sleeve were gone. And while Harper knew the insignia on his black Hardee showed tarnish, Bell wore a kepi with a split in its bill and the yellow cloth of the crown faded almost to white. Rusting base metal showed through the brass plating on the crossed sabers insignia on Bell's kepi.

"Was that your regiment we fought agin yesterday? They all wore black hats and rode horses, like you."

"Yeah. That was us."

"Well, that explains somethin'. All of your men carry them long rifles, didn't they?"

"Yeah, Bell. Ya saw them."

Bell's body stiffened at the answer. "You'll address me as *Captain* Bell, Lieutenant."

They rode past several houses, smaller than the one where Bell's men were camped. The lawn and yards of each were full of Rebel cavalrymen. Bell returned salutes from the sentries who, Harper assumed, marked the boundaries of each company's campsite.

"That'd be the reason y'all was able to keep us pinned down without us gettin' in a clean shot. Wouldn't it, Harper?"

"If ya say so."

"Don't hardly seem like a fair fight, does it? Does that seem like a fair fight to you, Harper?"

"Weren't tryin' to be fair, Bell. Ya know that." Harper steered Santee around a particularly large mudhole. "Those rifles kept ya back far enough so ya couldn't hit our men. That saved our men's lives and kept ya from comin' around our flank."

He wasn't sure how much more to tell Bell. So far, all Harper had revealed was information they had both seen during the battle.

Soldiers lay on their ground sheets in the lawns back from the road, using the sun to warm themselves, resting from the previous day's battle and the long overnight march. Townsfolk walked among them, offering food and drink, or helping to tend the wounded. Harper touched his own ear to find it scarred over and free of new blood.

"I lost half a dozen men. Don't seem right to me, them men dyin' when they ain't got a chance to fight back." Bell paused to return a salute from a group of soldiers walking in the other direction. "Now, y'all's the ones who cain't fight back." His face became a mask, emphasizing the words that followed. “Best be careful, Yank. We don’t usually take Yankee prisoners with us.”

Harper understood this comment to mean Forrest’s men shot their prisoners. The incident with the negro children convinced him this was the case. Were the men in Forrest’s other companies all murderers?

He could see a very large plantation manor ahead, with dozens of horses tied in front. More camps stretched alongside the road beyond the manor house.

“That horse of yours any good?” Bell asked. “What kind of horse is it?”

“Ya know about horses, Captain?” Harper rubbed his horse’s neck. “Santee here is a mustang from the Nebraska territory. She’s been with me for about eight years.”

They passed several soldiers on the side of the road, all dressed no better than the men in Bell’s company, lean, dirty, hard, and tattered.

“Course I do. Everyone in Tennessee knows about horses. Same as in the Ken-Tuck’.”

Most of the Confederates stopped to stare at him when Harper and Bell rode past. One spat a wad of tobacco directly in Santee’s path. Harper turned his head to feign indifference.

“How about your men? How long ya been fightin’, Bell? They’re some pretty rough-lookin’ fellows.” Harper wanted to learn more about Forrest’s command.

“*Captain Bell*. ’Bout the same as all y’all, Harper. Nearly a year. Royal’s my second horse. We’ve spent all winter in Ken-Tuck’ tryin’ to protect the citizens there. Runnin’ circles around your General Buell and his whole army. But Johnston ordered us to come back here to fight against Grant. My first horse was a thoroughbred, but she couldn’t stand up to campaignin’. Took her home at the end of last summer, then some Yankee son-of-bitch stole her.”

“How do ya know it was a Yankee?” Harper asked.

“Who else would it be? Bastards came down from the Ken-Tuck’ hill country and stole everythin’ they could take. They burnt my farm–everythin’ they couldn’t carry, the buildings *and* the fields.”

“Maybe outlaws? Same thing happened to me back in ’fifty-two, except it was outlaws. Anyone killed?”

"Weren't outlaws. It was a band of Yankee raiders comin' down from above Knoxville. My family weren't hurt. The bastards only wanted the livestock." Bell pulled up in front of the large plantation house. "That's why I hate all you Yankee bastards. Y'all took my entire livelihood. You left my wife and young-uns destitute. That's when I learned what kind of war this was goin' to be."

After they dismounted, Bell added, "You know, Harper. If'n it was up to me, you and all of your men would be dead now. 'Cept'n Colonel Forrest ordered us not to use our firearms last night less'n we had to. Shit, boy, we had the drop on y'all from the time y'all came down offa the ridge."

Harper's back went stiff when he heard this. He and his men never had a chance.

As they walked to the gate, Bell added, "And the fact is I'd just as soon shoot you right now, along with your men. Colonel Forrest says not to." Bell turned on Harper, their faces inches apart. "But you remember somethin', Harper, in case y'all are thinkin' to escape. Them who y'all killed were all good men—and neighbors, too. One was family. So if even one of your men escapes..." He raised the index finger of his gloved hand. "I'll kill the rest, the same as I did to that nigger baby. And none of my men will say anythin' different."

Rabid dog.

****

Harper followed Bell through the door of the manor. Orderlies in the entry hall directed them to a formal dining room which stretched the entire length of the south side of the house. Inside the room, a single dining table seated two dozen officers with room at the end for a half-dozen more. The smell of hot corn mash and bacon filled the room, sending Harper's stomach into a churn.

Captain Bell stepped to the head of the table and saluted while Harper waited behind. All conversation ended while the dining officers stared at Harper. A well-dressed civilian presided at the head of the table, most likely the owner of the house. Next to him sat a lieutenant colonel facing the large windows who was probably Bedford Forrest.

Forrest ate from a plate of mashed corn and bread, while reading a map spread in the center of the table. His gray overcoat, sword and holster belts hung over the post of his chair while the sabers of all the diners leaned along the wall behind him.

"We'll keep on t' Charlotte tonight, Thomas." Forrest addressed a major seated opposite him at the table. "Send a courier ahead to see if'n we cain't get an engine from there t' Nashville."

Forrest handed the map across the table to Major Thomas who nodded his understanding of the orders and folded the map. Turning his attention to Bell, Forrest returned the salute without standing, then turned his attention to Harper. "Well, heah's our guest."

"Lieutenant James Harper, Colonel," Bell announced while Forrest pushed his chair away from the table to face the prisoner. "From Ioway."

The noise of conversation returned. Forrest signaled Bell to sit down with the other officers. "Lieutenant Harper, take a seat." A servant brought a chair and placed it behind the row of men seated at the table. A captain at the middle of the table signaled one of the nearby orderlies to stand guard behind him.

Though both he and Forrest were seated, Harper could see Forrest was taller than most men. He appeared to be about ten years older than Harper but with the robust build characteristic to men who became natural-born leaders. His tanned face carried an overgrown Van Dyke beard with a few gray strands showing among the black hairs. Unshaved facial stubble showed on his cheeks. The set of his eyes, deep in their sockets, tired but brusque and impatient, intimidated Harper slightly and revealed no kindness for the Federal officer's predicament. Lieutenant-Colonel Nathan Bedford Forrest was a man not to be crossed or taken too lightly.

"Harper," Forrest asked, "is anyone followin' us?"

Harper was surprised that he had to gather his internal courage in the face of the larger man's harsh eyes. He quickly considered how he should answer the question. How would whatever he told Forrest affect his own men? He knew Grant planned to continue the attack today, but he did not know any details of that plan and there had been no sounds of a battle this morning.

"I don't know, Colonel." Harper decided to appear uninformed and insignificant. But, maybe Forrest would find it unlikely *any* officer would be totally uninformed. He would keep what he said to a minimum. "I heard some officers talkin' about General Grant attackin' again this morning, but I didn't hear any battle noises."

"No harm in telling you now, I suppose." Forrest looked to Major Thomas who shrugged his shoulders. Forrest turned back to Harper. "Grant won't need to attack. By now, Buckner's surrendered. That's why we 'uns lit out. I didn't raise this regiment for it to be captured because of the stupidity of our own god-damned generals."

"Buckner?" Harper asked. "I thought General Pillow commanded."

For the first time, Forrest looked at the details of Harper's uniform. "Are you injured, Lieutenant?" He pointed to the blood on Harper's collar and belly.

"Just here on my ear, Colonel. It's been cauterized."

Forrest glanced at the ear before he pointed again to Harper's belly. "What about that?"

"It's not mine. It's from..." Harper considered what to say. Several of the officers nearby stopped eating, waiting for Harper's answer. "Someone else."

Forrest must have understood Harper's discomfort. "One of my men?"

"Yes, sir." Harper looked at the other officers at the table, worried at their possible reaction. "I'm sorry." Maybe the apology would keep them from taking revenge. This was war, after all.

Forrest stared at the blood spot. "Well don't be. It looks like he died well."

"Yes, sir. That he did."

The officers nearby nodded. Of course, they would expect that their man died bravely. Harper would not tell them the blood came from a fellow officer, likely someone who would be in the room now if he hadn't fallen in battle.

Forrest resumed his story about the surrender of Fort Donelson. "Well, once he decided to surrender the fort, it seems *General* Floyd commandeered some riverboats and lit out with his Virginians after just bein' there two days; Pillow too–*by himself*."

Forrest directed his words to the men at the table. "They left

Buckner holding the bag, trusting Grant might be generous to him. Grant still owes Buckner money from their days in the army." Forrest's brow furrowed and blood rose into his cheeks. He pursed his lips and shook his head. "Damn gutless politicians." He pounded a fist onto the table. "Ten thousand good men–gone."

Forrest stared at his plate for a few moments. He took a deep breath. Eventually, he relaxed his fist.

Three negro servants carried covered plates of food from the cookhouse and placed them in front of late-arriving officers. A corpulent woman surpervised the servants, dressed in a simple gray day dress with her hair collected into side-rolls encircling her head. She had the manner of the lady of the house, directing both the servers and the kitchen staff.

Harper shifted his chair so he could capture more of the heat coming from one of the two iron stoves decorated with wrought-iron canthus leaves.

Noon-time sunlight flowed through the wide bank of windows extending across the other three walls. It filled the room with light and assisted the heaters to warm the room.

Forrest asked, "What were y'all doing sneaking 'round in them woods last night, then?"

"We were tryin' to set a *picquet* on the road where ya caught us."

Forrest chuckled. "Your bad luck we got there fust-est, eh, Lieutenant?"

A servant brought a plate of mashed corn for Anderson Bell. Harper saw the hostess look at the civilian at the head of the table then at Harper. Hoping she would bring a plate for him, Harper nodded but the woman left before she saw him.

The Confederate officers continued to eat, some using utensils, others dipping their bread into the mush. Unlike the dinner parties the room was designed for, very few of the men at the table spoke after the food arrived. The only sounds were the clatter of cutlery on dishes and the chinking of plates being taken away.

"This needs somethin'." Bell took a small glass bottle from his jacket pocket and sprinkled some of the reddish liquid into the mush; he offered the bottle to the officer seated next to him.

"They tell me y'all had special rifles when we captured you, Lieutenant. Is that true?" Forrest asked.

"Yeah, Colonel. That's true."

"What kind of rifles are they? What's their range?"

"They're Sharps rifles." With pride, Harper added, "Range is about a thousand yards."

The officers seated nearby looked up when they heard this. Harper knew the best range for most of the weapons Forrest's men carried was perhaps two hundred yards with anything like reasonable accuracy.

"A thousand yards! Ridiculous." A captain turned in his chair to face Harper. "Nothin' shoots so far and hits anything."

"I can," Harper answered in a matter-of-fact tone. "I did six hundred yards two days ago." Harper realized that his pride might get him into trouble, so he thought it best not to tell the group he shot four men on that occasion.

Forrest brought his hands together, steepling his fingers under his chin. "Were you a part of the dismounted unit we saw yesterday afternoon? On the right of the Yankee attack?" Forrest asked.

"Ya mean the attack which drove you Rebs back into the fort, Colonel?" Harper boasted with a smile, in spite of the circumstances. "Yes, sir. It was the First Iowa Mounted Rifles." Adding a little more braggadocio wouldn't hurt. "One battalion."

"Damn General Pillow won the battle for y'all, boy," Major Thomas replied. "The dumb son-of-a-bitch retreated at the *moment* we had y'all on the run; the very moment, by God. Claimed his men were exhausted and the victory was won. They needed to go git their lunch."

"Well, let's hope all of your generals are so capable."

Forrest's brow furrowed again in irritation. "So, it was your people." He looked into Harper's eyes and Harper pulled back from the stare. Harper's bragging might have gone too far.

"Well, son, they did right well forcin' my men to take to the ground. One of those fellows killed my flag-man while he stood right next to me." Forrest poked his finger through a hole in the skirt of his jacket. He sat back and his face relaxed into a joking smile. "Nearly got me, too, by God!" He laughed while he wiggled his finger in the bullet hole, showing it to those seated nearby.

Harper looked at the hole. He recalled his hasty second shot at the start of yesterday's battle. With two seconds more, he could have laid out the famous Bedford Forrest. Best be quiet about who fired the shot that made the hole.

"First Iowa Mounted Rifles. I'll have to remember that."

That made Harper uncomfortable. Having Bedford Forrest especially interested in the First Iowa might not be an honor to be sought out. Especially after what Bell's men had done to the slave children.

Forrest's attention shifted to the far end of the table. "Where are those rifles now, Bell?"

"I give them to the best shots in my company, Colonel. Harper's men each had a hundred rounds with them, too."

"That will keep us for a while," Forrest replied. "We'll get more from the Yankees later." He stated this as though robbing Federal supply trains was an easy thing to do. He smiled at Harper. "From the First Iowa Mounted Rifles, I suppose."

Shit.

The smell of the food caused Harper's stomach to rumble. Forrest glanced at Harper's stomach, but did nothing. Even though Harper hadn't eaten since the previous morning, his pride wouldn't let him reveal to these Rebels how much the hunger burned when he looked at the food on the plates. He used his Indian skills to push the hunger out of his mind, found the hunger sensation within his brain and imagined himself covering it with a blanket, bundling the blanket into a sack, shoving the sack into a closet. He would open the closet at a more propitious moment.

"So, as far as you know, no one is following us—correct?" Forrest relaxed against the back of his chair and stared at Harper. "Tell me, Mister Harper, why is someone from Iowa fighting to set Tennessee niggers free?"

"I ain't fightin' for negroes, Colonel. I'm fightin' to keep the union of the states together."

"Don't be naïve, Mister Harper. This war came about because the damned Yankee abolitionists tryin' to interfere with what we in the South want to do inside our own country. It ain't the role of the Federal government to be tellin' the states how to do their business. That's the way the founding fathers wrote the Constitution, son."

The officers nearby nodded at the comment while they continued to eat.

"Y'all ever read The Constitution, Mister Harper?" Major Thomas pointed a spoon at Harper.

Harper looked around the room. He doubted any argument would prevail in a philosophical discussion with these men in spite of all the oratory skills he learned at *Université de Notre Dame du Lac.* Nevertheless, he had to respond to Forrest–*keep it short*.

"Slavery isn't the issue, Colonel. I think we would have sorted out slavery peaceably given enough time–even with the Republicans in power. Instead, you Southerners decided to wreck the Union over it."

"Slavery made me a rich man, Mister Harper. And, it's the only way we can make a livin' in the South. Cotton won't harvest itself." Forrest leaned forward in his chair. "Damned Abolitionists." His gaze locked onto Harper's eyes. "Y'all's not an Abolitionist are you, Lieutenant Harper?"

"No, sir."

"By God, I'd hang every damn one of them if I could, including the women." Forrest's voice rose and the blood returned to his cheeks. "That's what I'll do if I ever catch one of the bastards." He brought his fist down onto the table. "The damn women are the worst. They don't listen to common sense."

This pronouncement from the senior officer brought silence to the hall. The diners stared at him, some stopped their meal in mid-chew.

"Women ought to know their place," Forrest continued. "And it ain't makin' politics.

"Besides, Harper, it ain't like the negrah is a human being." Major Thomas set his spoon aside. "Says so in the Bible. They're demons, the spawn of the fallen angels and human women. It's in Genesis. How about the Bible, Mister Harper? You ever read the Bible?"

"A little bit, Major." Harper recalled his father's plan for him to become a Catholic priest while at *Notre Dame*. "I couldn't care less what happens to the negroes, as long as we keep the United States together." Harper looked around the room. "How would it be if a state could secede every damned time the Federal government passed a law it didn't like? We'd soon be thirty some-odd separate countries; all fightin' against each other, even in the South. Is that what you want?"

"Mister Harper," the civilian host said, "the darkie ain't capable of bein' a free man. They cain't think the way a white man can."

Harper glanced at the negro servers, looking for a reaction. There was none that he could detect.

"They need a strong guiding hand. I have over three-hundred of them, so I know what they're capable of. Ain't that right Missus Laderly?" He looked to the lady of the house, still bustling about directing the servants.

"If you say so, Matthias," the lady said, not looking away from her hostess duties.

"Of course I say so!" Laderly said, smiling at his wife's response. Forrest and a few of the other soldiers chuckled.

"Well, you ain't won the war yet, Mister Harper, but you *are* an invader in my country." Forrest addressed Harper. "And, you are my prisoner until we arrive in Nashville. Then, I'll turn you over to Johnston." He looked down the table to Captain Bell. "When you've finished your lunch, Bell, take Lieutenant Harper back to the rest of the prisoners. But first take him to Doc Rutherford. Ask Rutherford to tend to Mister Harper's wounds. His men, too." He cast a warning look at Bell punctuated by a pointing finger. "Make certain you treat him as well as you would want our boys treated by the Yankees. There's gonna be a lot of our men in Yankee prisons for a while so we'll need Yankee prisoners to exchange for them."

"Yes, sir, Colonel." Bell looked up from his plate. Bell's smile gave Harper a chill. "Of course, sir."

Forrest, Thomas, and Laderly stood up from the table. The two officers fastened their sword and holster belts, then clipped their swords onto the belts and straps. "Thank you for hosting our lunch, Matthias." Forrest said. "We'll be leavin' in an hour. If I were you, I'd start doing what I could to protect my property. I expect the Yankees will be along in a few days. I don't know when our army will be comin' back."

"My pleasure, Nathan. Always glad to help out where I can." Laderly moved toward a set of French doors set into the wall of windows. "I expect I'll move the niggers and the other valuables south, except for the few we need to run this place until spring."

"Grant's been lettin' people keep their slaves in Kentucky," Thomas said. "He's issued orders for his soldiers not to molest the citizens."

"Let's hope he keeps the same policies toward the people of Tennessee. But I don't want any of my stock getting ideas to run off to the Yankee army."

Harper watched Forrest, Thomas, and Laderley walk out onto a side veranda, where Laderley opened an oaken casket and offered cigars to the two officers. With their commanding officer finished, the remaining officers ended their meals quickly and left for their units.

****

Harper and Bell rode side-by-side on the way back to Bell's company. The threatening rain near arrived and the cloud cover was breaking apart. The horses splashed through the little village on a road churned into mud by yesterday's rain and the hundreds of horses of Forrest's battalion.

"Do ya know what town is this, Bell?" Harper wanted to build a map in his head of the land they marched through. He felt slightly more comfortable knowing that Forrest wanted to keep him and his men alive. It was less likely that Bell and his men would find an excuse to leave them lying in a ditch.

"The locals call it Maysville. Ain't much of a town. Just Laderley's plantation and people who work for Laderley. Don't have a post office or nothin'. Don't know who Mays was."

So, Maysville was a day's march south of Donelson.

On both sides of the street, Harper saw soldiers inside the houses where smoke from the chimneys indicated large fires in every hearth. Some relaxed on the porches and verandas of the more prosperous homes, taking advantage of the new sun. Negroes scurried between the cookhouses and the main houses with platters heaped with food. Harper wondered how Bell intended to feed the prisoners.

"We was told to pull back, you know," Bell continued. "Y'all didn't whip us."

"I know. I saw them. But we did stop ya cold."

Interesting that Bell had his own version of yesterday's battle. Harper thought it might be interesting to compare with what he saw.

"It's all Pillow's fault. He pulled the center back after we had your boys whipped fair-and-square." Bell tipped his hat in response to a shopkeeper who waved from the open door of his store.

"I saw them." Harper remembered the men he saw marching away from the woods in the center of the Rebel lines before Colonel Taylor's attack. Those must have been Pillow's men. "But you only whupped McClernand's division. We still had two others."

"Stupid fool. There we was, tryin' to have an escape, and Pillow don't tell his men to pack any food. Now, how dumb is that?"

Harper grunted in agreement. "Seems like both armies have that problem." It must be the result of politicians choosing the generals.

"Now that we'uns is escaped, I 'spect things is gonna change." A smile appeared on Bell's face. "But 'course, you won't be seein' none o' that, will you?"

Bell must have meant that soon they would be in a prisoner-of-war camp.

When they returned to Bell's company, the Confederate cavalry were preparing to continue the march.

Harper looked to his men. Davis, Bailey, and Cooke were back sitting against the picket fence staring at the ground or looking ahead with a vacant, far-away look. Magnusson stood next to them, leaning against the fence and staring a challenge to the campfire where Corporal Stackpole finished lunch.

"Did you men get anything to eat, Corporal Magnusson?" Harper asked.

"No, sir."

"Water?"

"No, sir. Some of them fellows took our canteens, along with everything else."

Harper looked at the looted saddlebags. Overcome by anger and frustration, he yelled to Captain Bell, who stood in the road watching his company preparing to resume the march. "Captain Bell, where's the food for the prisoners?"

Bell turned slowly in the saddle and gave Harper a disapproving stare. He walked his horse to where the prisoners stood in a group by the picket fence. "Officers don't yell at each other in this army, Harper. 'Taint polite. To answer your question, they ain't no food for Yankee bastards in this whole regiment."

Harper did not know how far it was to their destination and he and his men hadn't eaten since breakfast the day before. Bell appeared to be willing to starve them indefinitely.

Harper stared at the captain. "Well? What about water?"

Bell smiled. "No, sir. 'Taint none of that available for you, neither."

"What about the horses?"

"The horses ain't your concern. They're now the property of the Army of the Confed'racy. We'll be in Kingston tomorrow. They'll have to manage until then."

"Ya know it ain't right to deprive prisoners of food and water." He stared at Bell in frustration before a thought came to him. "I'm sure the Rebels we captured at Fort Donelson have enough to eat." Maybe a reference back to Forrest's orders about the prisoners would work.

The smile left Bell's face. "Hell, Harper. If'n it was up to me, I'd've shot the lot of you back in those woods where we captured you. Now, get your men mounted, or I'll be obliged to do that now for tryin' to escape."

"Ya know men can't last for three days without water. What if one of these men or their horses fall out of line or collapse? What would Colonel Forrest say about that? Aren't a few buckets of water worth not havin' the whole column delayed because a prisoner fell out?"

Bell's face reddened in anger. He scowled, then spit to the side. Harper thought he might be winning this battle of wills.

"I'll decide when you git water. Hell, you'll soon have all the water you need when the rains starts up again." Bell looked around at his men standing nearby. Some stopped to watch the confrontation between their captain and the Yankee lieutenant.

A slight twitch appeared under Bell's right eye. Finally, he said, "All right, Harper. I don't give a damn about your worthless hides." Bell looked at his troopers then back at Harper. "I don't want to cause any delay for Colonel Forrest. Water your horses over at that trough."

He pointed across the street to a public hand pump with a trough next to it. It had already served most of the horses in Bell's company.

"Much obliged, Captain Bell." Reminding Bell of Forrest's orders worked this time. Harper hoped that it would continue to do so.

"After the horses are finished, your men can drink from what's left.

Harper said a prayer for the pump to still work.

Monday, February 17th 1862

Katie's bruises made it difficult to sit still, even after she added the pillow to her chair overlooking Market Street. Her head hurt, both on the inside and where the bandage over the cuts was too tight.

Loreena allowed Katie three days to rest. She had slept little during the two nights since Evilface's visit. Each day, she woke exhausted. Every noise she heard outside of her door made her jump. Her dreams filled with the sight and smell of Evilface's scars, the feel of his hands around her neck.

At breakfast, Loreena and Eleanor showed Katie a copy of the weekly newspaper opened to page four. Katie tried to read the small column but she had difficulty focusing her eyes on the paper. Eleanor read it aloud over her shoulder:

> The body of Major Ezra Eagleton of Chicago, Illinois, was discovered Sunday morning floating among the pilings under the dock at Fort Anderson. It is believed the major drowned after suffering a blow to the head. The military coroner reports the major fell from the dock sometime early Thursday morning and became unconscious when he hit his head on the stand-off logs below. Military officials gave no explanation for Major Eagleton's late-night visit to the dock.
>
> The nation has suffered a tragic loss.

> Sadly, the major did not die on the field of glory in our struggle against the great rebellion as he might have wished. The Reaper took him before his time. Major Eagleton gave creditable service to the Union as the assistant chief of logistics at Fort Anderson. The body is to be returned to his family in Chicago following preparation for the transportation.

"May-jah Eagleton will not be returnin' any more, Katie. Y'all are safe now."

"Yes, ma'am." Katie could put no energy into her response. He might be dead, but what if there were more men out there who liked to beat up girls? What would the Bosleys do then? She wondered if her nightmares would ever be free of Major Evilface.

And her heart wept at not being allowed to go with her mother.

Tuesday, February 18th, 1862

It took an additional day before the column arrived at Kingston, Tennessee. The rain ended during their second night march. As happened in Maysville, the companies of Rebels spread onto the lawns of the fine houses while the townsfolk filled the afternoon air with the smells of the food brought out to the soldiers. Harper watched from the end of the porch where he waited with the other prisoners and their guards.

Harper experienced a few episodes of dizziness during the march brought on by the lack of food. Hunger seemed to be affecting the men, too. Except for Magnusson, they looked listless and tired while they gathered together.

"What's goin' on Cap'n?" Bell's leading sergeant, the only one with stripes on his sleeves, asked after the captain returned from a meeting of Forrest's officers.

Bell dismounted and tied his horse to the rail at the front of the house where his company rested. He waved with both arms to signal his lieutenants and sergeants to gather on the porch. Harper sidled closer to learn if Forrest had a plan for him and his men.

While Bell's men gathered, Harper found it difficult to understand each man's role in the company. They dragged themselves up the stairs to the porch, heads down, shoulders slumped. Most dressed in the same hardscrabble mix of civilian, Federal, and Confederate trousers and jackets worn by all of Bell's men. Insignia were rare, showing only on the uniforms of the first sergeant and one man wearing a lieutenant's epaulettes. He might be Bell's only other officer. None of the men in the group had a sword or sabre, but everyone except Bell and the lieutenant carried large, hand-made Bowie-style knives.

"There ain't no engines here," Bell said after half-a-dozen men arrived. "So we're gonna have to march t' Nashville."

"Damn." Bell's men cursed and shook their heads in disappointment.

"The horses are done in, Capt'n. It's been three days since anyone's had any real sleep." The speaker carried a moustache which reached below his chin and wore a black Hardee hat like Harper's.

Bell looked out onto the lawn of the house where many of their horses stood tethered to pegs in the wet ground. The rain had melted the snow to reveal a wide lawn of dead grass which the horses muzzled.

Bell collected his leaders in a stare that covered the group. "The railroad men told us General Sydney Johnston's called all of the locomotives and rolling stock into Nashville." He paused to let the bad news sink in. "They need to move the men comin' down from the Kentuck' afore they git cut off."

"So, what are we gonna do, Cap'n?"

Harper stepped closer to hear Bell's answer. A guard moved between Harper and the group of officers. Harper ignored the man, but stayed where he was.

"Our orders are to stay here and rest until tomorrow mornin'. We march after breakfast."

The group nodded to each other in agreement.

"Good."

"Need it."

The sun sent a shaft of light through the clouds warming Harper's back. He looked to his men. Magnusson had them on their feet with their jackets open, trying to use the sunlight to dry their clothing.

"Is that who we're workin' for now–General Johnston?"

"I don't know," Bell said. "I 'spect we'll find out when we git to Nashville."

One of the men spat a wad of tobacco onto the lawn. He caught sight of Harper and continued to watch the Union officer while he said, "How far is it to Nashville, Cap'n?" He turned his attention back to Bell to hear the answer.

"Only twenty miles or so, and it's a good road. We should be there near-abouts noon time, I'd say."

Harper knew they were marching to Nashville since the meeting with Forrest. Now, he knew that they were less than a day's ride away

The man with the lieutenant's collar devices gave a report. "Cap'n, I spoke with Mrs. Stoner, the lady who owns this house. She reckons she can fit the entire company inside the house if we want. I told her it would be maybe sixty men, but she says they should all fit, as long as they don't mind sleeping on the floor."

Would that include the prisoners?

"Ain't that obligin' of her."

"Yes, sir. And she told me she has two empty bedrooms upstairs for the officers." He paused a moment before he went on. "Also, sir, Missus Stoner's husband was in General Buckner's division. I told her I thought he would be safe even though he might be a prisoner. I told her I was sure the Yankees would treat her husband as well as we're treating our prisoners."

"You told her that, did you?" Bell glanced at Harper and the other Federal soldiers. "Well, I hope it's true. Anythin' else, Lieutenant? She don't maybe have any obligin' *daughters*, does she?"

A couple of the sergeants snickered.

" 'Fraid not, sir. All of her children are young. They're all gonna stay in her bedroom tonight. She's only got but one family of slaves workin' for her and they stay in the shack in the back."

"Well, Joe, express my gratitude to the lady." Bell addressed the others in the group. "We're still the rear company, so we'll post the sentries for this part of town. Other than that, git your men some warm food and some rest. See to your horses and be ready to move out at sun-up." The group started to leave. "Tell your men to let Mrs. Stoner's property alone. I don't want no thievin' from the wife of one of our own."

"What about the prisoners, sir?" The lieutenant pointed to Harper.

Bell looked around the yard. "Put them in the corn crib. That should suit them." Bell looked at Harper standing at the end of the porch. "How about that Mister Harper, you think your boys will be happy locked up in a corn crib?"

"Wouldn't be the worst place I've ever slept, Bell."

"*Captain* Bell, Lieutenant."

Harper felt a blow in the center of his back which knocked him onto his hands and knees on the porch. The group of Rebel officers laughed. Before he stood up, he watched the guard, barely out of his teens, grinning through decayed and missing teeth, with the muzzle of his carbine pointed at Harper.

Harper must show strength in front of these Rebs. He stood up slowly. Equally slowly, he brought his hand up to a salute. "Captain Bell."

"And don't you forget it, Harper."

Harper turned to rejoin the prisoners, but he stopped before he stepped from the porch. The guard, still standing on the ground, tried to push him from the porch by using the butt of his rifle like a broom against Harper's hindquarters. Harper caught the weapon in mid-swing right at the trigger grip. The guard tried to pull it away but Harper twisted with such violence that the guard lost his grip. Harper had possession of the loaded weapon, now pointed at the guard. The man froze in place, staring at the muzzle of his own carbine.

Several of the men in the officers' group drew their pistols; Harper heard the hammers click. Keeping his hand away from the half-cocked hammer of the carbine, Harper faced the group of officers and smiled.

Several seconds passed with no one moving before Bell started laughing. "Impressive, Harper." None of the others on the porch laughed, although several eased the grip on their pistols or holstered them. "We'll have to be sure our guards are more careful." Bell gave the guard a glance full of disapproval.

Harper never intended to try to escape in the bright of the day while surrounded by a Rebel cavalry regiment. He did want to teach the guard to show greater respect. Having done so, Harper smiled back at Bell. "I suppose you'd better do that *Captain* Bell." Avoiding any quick movements, Harper eased the hammer of the carbine down, turned the weapon with one hand, and held it out to the guard, butt first. "Colonel Forrest would hate it if he didn't have any prisoners to exchange."

He stepped down from the porch, ignoring the guard, and walked back to where the other prisoners waited. The guard followed five paces behind with the carbine cocked and its muzzle pointed at the center of Harper's back.

"Lieutenant Saint Philamon, I suppose the corn crib might not be the best place for the prisoners. See if we can find more secure accommodations for them."

****

The sunlight scattered the morning curtain of rain clouds and warmed the front of Katie's dress while she sat alone in her room, watching the traffic on Market Square. It was a high-necked dress which Loreena gave her to wear while she worked in the saloon sitting with the soldiers. The madam of *Lafitte's Hideout* did not allow her to entertain any customers upstairs until the bruises on her neck healed. "Bad for business if they see you've been hurt," Loreena told her, and Eleanor agreed.

When the doctor came to attend to Katie's injuries, Loreena told her not to worry; the cost for the doctor would be added to Katie's debt, along with the usual cost for food. It wasn't fair. She got hurt doing what they told her to do. Why should she have to pay for the doctor herself, too? Her bill to the Bosleys went up and there was no cash left for herself this week–all because of Evilface. May he rot in Hell *forever*.

Still, a small part of Katie was also a little grateful for the break in the routine. Evilface was dead, but Katie still secretly dreaded the day when she would next take a customer up to her room. Could she ever trust another customer not to hurt her? What could she do about it if they did?

****

Corporal Gustav Magnusson sat in the dim light of the cell watching the shadows of his men sleeping on the floor. They huddled together on top of one of the blankets in the cell. Magnusson knew the ground could sap a man's heat faster than the cold from the air. So he insisted the men use one of the two blankets as a ground cloth.

Magnusson was warmer now that he was indoors, even if he was in the town jail. He had ordered the men to strip down to their underwear so their clothes might dry out after the rain of the last two days. The musty smell from the clothes reminded Magnusson of Sarah Featherstone back at the Paducah camp. She would never let "her boys" get into such bad condition.

Those jackets and trousers covered half of the floor of the cell, laid out in a group away from the cell door. Hopefully, they would be full dry by morning. It would be a miracle if none of them came down with some disease. He sounded like his mother. That was his job now–mothering these men, making sure that they stayed alive and healthy. It was hard to tell if Harper cared about them, or not.

Through the bars, he could see Lieutenant Harper lying on the cot in the adjacent cell, face up, staring at the ceiling. A single lantern glowed on the table next to the door of the small jail house.

Magnusson recalled the events which brought him to this point. He had considered himself fortunate to be visiting Mount Pleasant on the very day the recruiting office opened last April. That office filled its quota of volunteers in the first day, with the late-comers being disappointed. There were far too many volunteers for the quota from that city.

The regiment went off to fight in Missouri. On foot, they had chased Rebel groups away from the towns of northern Missouri for most of the summer, but they only had time to be in one great battle before their ninety-day enlistment ended. It was a frightening thing to stand in the firing line, face-to-face with the Rebs who were just as tough as he was, and who had the same weapons. But in their first battle he learned how poorly the smoothbore muskets used by both armies performed. They were heavy, and they kicked like a mule.

Rebels hit very few of the Iowa men in that battle, even when the battle lines stood only a few score yards apart. It seemed a random thing as to who got hit in the battle line. Magnusson also learned the Rebs could fight like devils. Still, the regiment had stood up to the Rebs good until General Lyon got killed. Without a general, the army retreated after that battle.

When they returned to Saint Louis, there were only two days before their enlistment was up. He agreed with most of the boys in his company that they were not going to go home with a defeat being the only record of the regiment. So, he re-enlisted for three more years.

His Quaker father tried to have him released from his enlistment based on religious beliefs, even going to the governor to get a discharge. But the war gave Magnusson the chance to live a life different from what his father planned. There were other things a man could do with his life besides become a deacon in a Quaker church in Salem, Iowa. When the opportunity came to leave, he volunteered without hesitation, and he was grateful to Major Porter for convincing his father to let him stay.

But now, it looked like he would spend the rest of the war as a prisoner. Magnusson wondered how long would it be. Lieutenant Harper said this afternoon that Colonel Forrest wanted to keep the prisoners safe so they could be horse-traded for some Rebel prisoners. Magnusson had never heard of any prisoner exchanges.

He looked across at Harper and wondered what was the point of having The Great U.S. Marshal from Iowa in the regiment if he got them all captured on his first assignment. He was supposed to know what he was doing. Magnusson had watched Harper lead the skirmishers from the hill where Company B had been posted. He did that well, letting them deploy so they wouldn't make a good target. At least, until Magnusson had lost track of the battle in the cloud of gunsmoke. But it was hard to know what Harper would do next.

Magnusson's stomach burned. It churned and twisted inside his gut. It growled at him. The Rebels hadn't given them any of the food from what the local people offered. He hadn't eaten since…when? Saturday morning, before the battle. What day was it now? The Rebs captured them on Saturday night before supper. They spent that night and the next sleeping in the saddle. Tonight was the third night, so that made it Tuesday night. Three days, nine meals missed—eleven, if he counted the missed meals from the day of the battle.

He had no idea how long could a man go without food. Three days? Four days? Bailey and Cooke might last longer, because they were smaller, but how long could men as big as him or Davis last?

They had to get away. Harper was right about that. The Rebel captain looked like a right mean bastard. He'd already said he would've killed them, except he had orders. Maybe now he wanted to starve them to death? No chance of escaping from the jailhouse tonight. Walls were made from cement, and it looked like there was a second cement wall around the two cells. No tools, either; only a single bucket for all four of soldiers to do their business. No wonder this jailhouse smelled so bad.

Would Harper be any use if we tried to escape?

If Harper hadn't taken the guard's musket, they might still be in the corn crib next to the farmer's field and close to the woods. It would've been easier to break down the corn crib than to get out of this jail. Harper didn't seem very interested when they talked about escaping on the first day.

Might have to leave him behind. It'd serve him right, after wanting to leave poor Billy Monroe behind.

Magnusson stood up from the cot. He spread the only other blanket, the one which his men had offered to him, over the three sleepers on the floor. He leaned his elbows on a horizontal stiffener for the cell bars and looked through the door into the front room of the jail. The two guards sat taking turns sleeping at the desk. Past them, he could see the town of Kingston through the large windows at the front of the building. Even now, they might escape; no one was moving in the town at this time of night. The Rebs had only two guards and one of them was asleep; if they could only get out of this cell.

Magnusson shook at the bars but they remained indifferent to his strength. He turned to look at the moon though a small window at the back of the cell. Was his mother looking at the same moon? His sisters? What did the army tell them about him disappearing? Did they even know? Tears filled his eyes.

Damn Harper. I joined the army to fight, not to get locked up.

Wednesday, February 19th 1862

Harper and the other prisoners now rode in the center of the column, still guarded by Bell's men. That morning, the jail-keeper at Kingston gave them a cold mush of congealed hominy grits. After three days without food the men ate the concoction without complaint. Now at noontime, Harper was not yet hungry. His digestion must have slowed because of the starvation imposed by Captain Bell.

Riding through intermittent rain, Forrest's column of cavalry rode into Nashville on the fourth day following their escape from the Fort Donelson encirclement. The city was in chaos despite the rain. Advancing along the Charlotte Pike and then along Cedar Avenue, Forrest's advanced guard drew their weapons several times to force open a passage through the mobs gathered in the streets.

Crowds had collected in front of warehouses with locked doors and guarded by Confederate soldiers. Unguarded warehouses went unmolested. Some of the shops adjacent to the guarded warehouses had their doors broken apart or windows smashed. Goods lay scattered around on the floors and onto the streets.

"Is the army comin' back into town, Captain?" A middle-aged civilian wearing a shopkeeper's apron fell in alongside Anderson Bell.

"We're here, mister, but we ain't the whole army." Bell pointed to the mob ahead of the column. "What're they doin'?"

"The mayor's promised the people of the town can collect all of the goods and supplies that the army leaves behind. They're bidin' their time until the guards leave." The man looked across the street to a leather goods store which still remained intact. "But some of 'em are breakin' into regular businesses. Is someone from the army goin' to come to help me protect my store?"

Bell looked down at the man. "I don't know nothin' about that."

Harper watched Bell's face play out an emotional conflict, first pursing in anger then becoming composed through forced self-control. He understood Bell's anger. Forrest's men risked their lives every day for the Southern cause and to this peddler they were only good for protecting his shop. But Bell did well to cover his anger. If Forrest wanted to use his men as raiders, he would need to keep the sympathy of the local civilians. Bell wouldn't aggravate this man without good reason.

Finally, Bell looked straight ahead. "We're here to fight Yankees. We ain't here to guard peddlers. What did you mean 'Is the army comin' back?' "

"Johnston and his army went south two, maybe three days ago. Right after we heard about Fort Donelson bein' captured. There's only a few soldiers left, tryin' to haul away the army's supplies."

Bell spurred his horse and trotted away from the man, splashing him when Royal's hoof plopped into a puddle. Harper stared back at the leather maker when the prisoners went past. The peddler spat in the trail of the last prisoner.

Harper flexed his wet fingers in the February cold trying to force blood to flow past the cord holding his wrists to the pommel of his saddle. As they did before, a guard led Santee by tying a rope to her bridle and attaching it to the pommel of his own saddle. Santee, who had fought against the lead during the first day of the march, now followed without reaction, head hung low.

Harper's concern now was the cold. After having the chance to dry their clothes in the Kingston jail last night, the rain came again during the morning march. All of the prisoners rode without protection against the weather or the cold. Their slickers and overcoats were now in the hands of Bell's men. Although most of the rain had passed, a chill west wind against their backs left Harper shivering and helpless to protect himself.

Beyond the area of shops and warehouses, the column passed the new, three-story state capitol building on its prominent hill. Harper could see the white limestone side portico, replete with Ionic columns and a paved avenue leading down to the street. A large force of Rebel infantry camped on the terraces surrounding the building.

Three blocks past the capitol hill, the column turned in front of two tall buildings with a covered marketplace stretched between them. The column circled past the building on the right were the Stars and Bars denoted a command post in the Nashville City Hall, until they came to the open, grassy town square between the city hall and market complex and the county court house. The government sector was relatively quiet when the cavalry spread out from its marching formation. Harper watched while the Confederate troopers dismounted and tethered their horses, ignoring the five prisoners. It was the first time during the morning march from Kingstown that the guards holstered their carbines.

If the city was in chaos, there might be a better chance to escape. But the rain seemed to have kept civilians away from the civic area, so there were no crowds where the prisoners could disappear. For now, with each of their horses tethered to the saddles of a lead rider, and with their legs tied together under their horses' bellies, they were helpless even to dismount.

Anderson Bell returned from receiving instructions from Forrest's staff and spent a few minutes giving orders to his officers; they were to establish a camp somewhere in the town square adjacent to City Hall. Instructions given, he strode to where the prisoners waited.

"Get them down."

The eight-man guard detail hurried to untie Harper and his men. Before any of them could dismount, the guards tried to push each man to the ground by lifting one leg and heaving it over the back of their horses. Harper and two of the others fell with a splash onto the soggy lawn. Their hats flew off and now were several yards down the square, blown by the wind. Magnusson and Davis were too large to leverage from their horses, so the Confederates left them to dismount on their own.

Harper, Bailey, and Cooke struggled to their feet. Harper stood in front of Corporal Stackpole. "Was that really necessary, Corporal? Or do ya just *like* bein' a bastard?" He shook his head and turned his back before Stackpole could answer.

Harper's legs felt wobbly, and he was certain the other prisoners' legs acted the same way. While each man flexed their fingers and hands and stretched the stiffness from their legs, Harper walked down the line, being careful to step slowly until the blood flow in his legs improved. He checked each man for injuries. Like him, all were shivering.

"How ya doin', there? Let me see ya move your hands and fingers." The prisoners followed Harper's demonstration, although it took Bailey and Cooke several attempts to open their hands against the stiffness brought on by the cold and the reduced blood circulation. Harper's greatest concern was the blue tint that he saw in Bailey's and Cooke's lips and fingernails.

The guard detail surrounded the Federals and herded them into a tight group.

"Mind if I get my hat, Bell?" Harper used a polite smile.

"*Captain* Bell, god-damn it! Go ahead, Harper. Git your damn hats."

Harper gave a mock salute. "I'm sorry, *Captain* Bell."

The three men chased after their covers while the guards stood and laughed. They gathered up their hats, brushed off the mud and returned them to their heads.

"Y'all look like my wife when she's out tryin' to catch a chicken for the pot." Corporal Stackpole looked at Corporal Magnusson. "Git your men into a column."

The four enlisted prisoners formed into a square with Bailey alongside Magnusson, Davis and Cooke behind.

"Git movin'." The guard detail pushed the prisoners along when Bell led the group past the court house toward an iron bridge over the river. They turned onto the last street before reaching the bridge and continued in a direction that Harper guessed to be southward. A street sign announced that the building was on Front Street. After a hundred yards, they approached a small brick building on the river side of the street. After a few more steps, Harper could read the sign above the porch of the building, "Davidson County Jail." Behind the building, the ground dropped off and Harper guessed beyond it lay the Cumberland

River–the same river which flowed past Fort Donelson where Grant's army waited.

"Got five Yankees prisoners who we want y'all to keep for us," Bell told the jail-keeper when they arrived.

The jail-keeper looked down at Bell from the front porch. He wore a full-length coat made from a single buffalo hide, with deep pockets sewn on the outside. He opened the coat enough to show his badge pinned to the shirt underneath. "I thought all of the Yankee prisoners were gone by now. Besides, we're only keeping civilians here. Yankee prisoners are over at the work house."

"No, those're gone. Sent south, already. All that're left is these 'uns. I want to put them here where I can watch them until I git orders from the colonel for what to do with them."

"Well, we're pretty full right now on account of the riots, Captain. Not sure we got room for any more."

"Listen, mister." Bell unbuttoned the leather cover of his holster. "I'm gonna leave these men here right now, and they had better still be here when I call back to git them."

Stackpole swiveled the barrel of his carbine in the general direction of the porch.

"Whoa, Captain!" The jailer held his hands up in front of him. "We'll find some space for them. It ain't no problem." He smiled. "Anything to help out the army."

"Why thankee, Deputy—" Bell smiled back as he re-fastened the cover of his holster.

"Shepperton. Deputy Sheriff Julius Shepperton."

"Take 'em in!" Bell yelled to the guards behind him.

The jail cells were in the back room of the two-room building, five cells separated by iron bars running from floor to ceiling. Each cell might hold three or four men, although there were only two cots in each. The cells formed a U-shaped pattern, with two cells along each side wall and a larger cell between them against the back wall. A single, pot-bellied stove tried to heat the entire room from its place along the center of the front wall. Its heat didn't penetrate Harper's rain-soaked uniform.

Deputy Shepperton opened two cell doors and moved the civilians there into adjacent cells. He assigned Harper to a cell along the right-hand wall, next to the doorway, and the enlisted men to the middle cell along the back wall.

Bell watched while the guard detail shoved the prisoners into the cells. "Enjoy your stay, Harper. I'll be back in a few days." He tipped his hat and laughed before he left.

At least we're safe from your *men, Bell.*

Shepperton took a final look around the cell room before returning to the front office, leaving the door open between the two rooms.

After Shepperton left, Harper assessed his situation, relieved at the warmth when he unbuttoned his uniform jacket.

Four civilians occupied the cell next to his with nine men in the cells across the room, all whites. Harper assumed he was in the cell by himself in deference to his rank, while the four enlisted soldiers shared the center cell along the back wall. The configuration did not allow him to talk with Magnusson without being overheard by the other prisoners, or by a deputy in the front room.

The civilian prisoners stared at the soldiers. Most dressed in common laborers' clothes. Two wore overalls. The men in the cell next to him were probably shopkeepers or other indoor workers, based on their dress. Probably wasn't a good idea for any of them to know he was a former lawman.

From his cell, Harper could see into the front office through the doorway connecting the two rooms. He saw only Shepperton, but he assumed at least one more deputy or helper would be nearby somewhere. The five soldiers might be able to overpower two deputies if they could open their cells and if the civilian prisoners did not interfere. He tested the lock, but he could not recognize the design. Besides, he had no tools to work it.

A window in each cell was higher than a tall man's head so from inside the cell, the prisoners could see only the sky through the dirty, barred windows. Harper pushed one of the cots underneath his window and climbed up. He worked the latch on the frame until it swung up and in, like an awning. After he propped the window open with a stick lying against the bars in the window box, he saw that the bars were built into the brick frame of the window box. These did not budge when he tested them. Still, the mortar holding them in place appeared old and cracked. He might be able to work the bars loose, but it would take a long time—if he could find a tool. He guessed he might be able to squeeze through the window if the bars were gone, but a large man, like Magnusson or Davis, would never fit. He needed to think of a different route for any escape attempt.

"See anything' interestin', Yank?" Harper heard one of the men in the cell next to his call.

"Why, yeah. Indeed I do, don't ya know?" He turned to look at the man. "Looks like a whole lot of people don't want to be here when our armies arrive." Harper turned to his men. "They're runnin' barge loads of soldiers and civilians across the river. People runnin' away from our armies. That must mean the either Grant or Buell is comin' closer–or maybe both of them. Maybe they'll be here in time to release us." Harper turned back to the window, hoping that his men would believe him.

A draft of cold, fresh air flowed in from the window, mixing with the stale air of the cell room. From this vantage point, Harper could see down the bluff to the Cumberland River and the city landing. The noon-time position of the sun's glow behind the clouds confirmed that he faced generally south. Below him, the river flowed out of the south, alongside of the bluff and behind the jail. If help came using the river, they would come from the opposite side of the jail or from across the river.

On the river, Confederate stragglers and various civilians crowded aboard the few barges available. Across the river, he could see civilians giving rolls of bills to the barge masters to carry them into Nashville, while armed soldiers on the far shore and on the barges kept order and ensured any stray soldiers boarded each barge before allowing any civilians.

After watching a while, Harper saw that the guards for one of the barges allowed civilians to board first, even when there were soldiers at the loading point. The guards on those barges must receive a portion of the fees collected by the barge captains. The barge crews hurried their passengers ashore after landing on the Nashville side before hurrying back across the river.

"Looks like the whole Reb army is pullin' back, Lieutenant," Magnusson commented from the window in his cell.

"That's because General Grant is comin', boys!" Stepping down from the cot, Harper could see the thought of Grant coming to rescue them from a prisoner-of-war camp caught the men's attention. Bailey smiled while the rest relaxed the frowns of discomfort on their faces.

"Once Fort Donelson fell, the Navy took control of the river all the way to here and beyond. The Rebs have to move all of their armies in Kentucky back across this river before they're cut off."

"You think so, Yank?" One of the prisoners across the room from Harper stepped up to the bars of his cell. "How long before you figure Grant's army will git here?" The speaker was a tall, thin man with large hands and a mustache which drooped past his chin.

"Couple of days," Harper answered. "Can't say for sure. But I don't think it'll take long. Grant doesn't like to waste time." He hoped it was true.

"What about us?" Private Bailey asked.

Harper knew he had to give his men some hope they would return to their unit and not be sent deeper into the Confederacy. "We need to work on a plan to escape."

"Won't be no soldiers here by the time Grant gits here." A man in the adjacent cell walked up to the bars separating his cell from Harper's. "Johnston's lit out already, with the rest of the army. All that's left is Floyd's men, and I 'spect they'll probably skedaddle at the first sight of any Yankees, like they did at Fort Donelson." This man wore linen trousers and the white shirt of an office worker. Harper guessed he was some sort of clerk from his pasty complexion and his uncalloused hands.

"With Forrest's men here now, that may change." Harper turned back to his own men. "If we aren't able to escape, we'll probably be exchanged for some of the Rebs who Grant just captured, but it might take a few months."

"Why ya here in jail?" Davis asked the man in the cell across the room.

"Thievin'," the man said. "We was tryin' to take home some of the food that the army is fixin' to leave behind. The mayor said we could have it, but I guess we picked the wrong warehouse. Turns out the one we tried to break into was owned by the sheriff's cousin. So we ended up here."

"Are ya sure we'll be exchanged, Mister Harper?" Private Cooke asked.

"To be honest, no. Not entirely." Harper glanced into the front office but could not see Shepperton. "That's why we need to figure out our own escape plan." He paused to collect his thoughts.

"When I passed through Saint Louis last month, General Halleck's staff was still workin' out the details with the Rebels for exchangin' the prisoners we lost last fall, includin' the men taken at Belmont." Harper looked toward the front office and lowered his voice. "I don't know how far along those plans are; that's why we need to make our own plans." He unbuttoned his white shirt to let the heat reach his long-johns. "Best get out of those wet clothes and try to dry off."

There was no telling how long the army would take to make exchanges, and Harper didn't want to sit in a prison waiting for that to happen. The four soldiers nodded in understanding. A few of the civilian prisoners laughed.

"You'll need a whole heap of good luck for that to happen, mister," the mustached man across the room said. "I been in and out of this jail more times than y'all could count, even if you took off your shoes. 'Taint no one never got away from here in all that time. I can't recall Sherriff Edmondson ever losin' a prisoner." He looked at the other men in his cell. "Any o' y'all ever heered of a prisoner have-in' a ex-cape when Edmondson was in charge?"

All of the civilians in the room shook their heads.

" 'Specially not with 'lection comin' up in a coupla weeks."

The man in the cell next to Harper added, "He ain't never had a prisoner escape, nor has he had to kill any for tryin'."

Harper looked at his men. They looked back at him.

"Don't worry boys, we're gonna get out of this." Harper wished it was true. Magnusson nodded, frowned, and turned away to open his jacket.

Thursday, February 20th 1862

Katie spent the entire morning in her room on the fifth day after Evilface, staring out the window, talking with no one. Loreena allowed Katie an extra day to recover but four nights had passed, and tonight Loreena expected Katie to return to work in the saloon. She did not go to the second-floor sunroom for breakfast. She was not hungry. Nevertheless, after breakfast ended, someone knocked on her door. Katie sat in silence and ignored it.

"Katie, *ma chéri*, are you all right?"

Leave me alone.

"Katie, may I come in?"

Go away.

Eleanor opened the door slowly. "May I come in, *chéri*?"

Katie did not answer. She was curious to know what her best friend would say, but she wanted to remain in her foul mood. Eleanor stepped into the room, crossed to where Katie sat by the window, and leaned against the window frame where Katie could see her. "What is wrong, *chéri*? You look so pale and sad."

Katie looked up at Eleanor. "I ain't made hardly no money this week. I just git more into debt."

"Of course, *ma petite*. You could not work. But you were paid extra for taking Major Eagleton."

"Most of that went to pay Loreena's doctor."

"But you will be back tonight, no? Let me see your neck." Eleanor tilted Katie's chin gently. "Ah. See? The bruises, they are almost gone."

"But I did what they told me to do. They let that man beat me so bad." Tears welled under her eyelids. "I nearly died." She turned away from Eleanor. Below her, a soldier waved to her from across the street. She shivered.

"*Chéri*, that is the nature of this job. It's not only about helping the sold-*aires* from being lonely. Sometimes, we must let the men do things they cannot do with their wives; but we make them pay much money to do it."

"I don't like that part."

"I know, *ma petite*." Eleanor stroked Katie's hair. "No one likes that part. So we position Angel there to listen, and keep Virgil and Thomas nearby."

"That made it even worse! Havin' someone there listenin' while he cursed and beat me. It was shameful. I cain't even look at Angel no more without feelin' that she knows everything about my private parts." She shifted in the chair and brought a handkerchief to her face. "And I don't like bein' beholdin' to Virgil. He's a nasty man."

"Angel doesn't care about your *con-con, chéri*. She told me she was so ''appy to 'elp you in time'. 'Av you spoken to her since that night?"

"No. I'm too embarrassed."

"Well, you should. She's *ve'y* concerned that she called us in time. She wants to know you will be all right. She thinks you stay in here because you are injured."

Katie stared out of the window, watching four wagons full of army supplies pass on Court Street moving toward the causeway. She could not see the drivers' faces under the kepi caps, but their blue uniforms brought another shiver.

"What happens if another crazy man wants me to go with him? This could happen all over again, couldn't it? Even tonight. What if he acted like a normal customer until he got in here? No one would know."

Eleanor took some time to answer. "*Oui*. That could happen, *chéri*, but it is not likely. There are not many men who act like Major Eagleton." She glanced through the window to the street below before she faced Katie. "Besides, tonight you will have no customers upstairs. I have demanded that from Loreena. You wear your high-neck dress and talk with the customers, but no bumba-bumba."

Katie continued to stare out at Market Square. Finally, Eleanor told her, "Get dressed. I will take you shopping."

****

When Davidson County Sheriff John Edmondson arrived for work on Thursday, he came to talk with the prisoners. "You boys comfortable?"

"Not very," Harper answered. His clothes were dry again, thanks to the heat from the stove. Like the other soldiers, Harper had spread them on the floor of his cell during the night and slept in his long underwear. Now, he stood in his trousers and stocking feet, looking at the Davidson County sheriff.

Edmondson walked around the room looking at the men in each cell. "Well I've been over to talk with the military provost about y'all. I'm supposed to keep you here until they come to collect you. They didn't say when that would be."

"Are there any other prisoners-of-war in town?" Harper came forward to the door of his cell.

"Not any more. The last batch left on Monday. Up to now, they kept them over at the work-house before movin' them down to Alabama. Don't really know why y'all ended up here, instead." Edmondson stopped in front of Harper's cell.

From the earlier conversation among the prisoners, Harper knew Edmondson held an elected office, the way most county sheriffs did. Elected officials liked to talk about themselves. Maybe he could learn something useful for their escape. "So what's happenin' in the town? Do the people know General Grant is bringin' his army here?"

"They know it. General Johnston left on Monday and put Floyd in charge. Burned down all of the bridges over the river before he left. Looks like Floyd is fixin' to leave, too, because *he* put Bedford Forrest in charge." Edmondson shook his head. "Turned the whole damned city over to Bedford Forrest." He chuckled and shook his head.

If the sheriff knew Forrest, he might have other information that might help in an escape. The other prisoners moved to the bars at the front of their cell, listening. Several of the civilian prisoners eavesdropped, as well.

"We saw the suspension bridge go down this mornin'." Harper pointed across to Magnusson. "At least, they did." Harper hoped to keep Edmondson engaged in order to learn more about the happenings outside of the cell room. "Forrest thinks Floyd doesn't know what he's doin'. Based on what he told me about Floyd, I probably agree with him. So what's Forrest doin' now?"

Edmondson looked into the front office. "I guess there's no harm to be done in telling you, since there's nothing you can do about it." He turned back to Harper. "The Army's still has a lot of supplies to move. The mayor told the people they could have what the army leaves behind, so there're mobs in the streets trying to slow the army from moving the supplies. If they start arresting people, we won't have enough room for everyone who is trying to git at the army's goods." Edmondson looked to the cell across from Harper. "At least the mobs aren't trying to break into any private warehouses, yet."

The man with the long mustache looked up from his seat on the floor of the cell and snarled at the sheriff. Edmondson looked at him and chuckled. "Not like the people who wanted to jump the gun, eh, Leroy?"

"Aagh!" Leroy, the mustached man, turned his back to the sheriff.

Edmondson returned his attention to Harper. "I was at headquarters to ask what I'm supposed to do with you five. I seemed to me Forrest forgot about y'all, at least from the way he reacted. 'Keep them there for now,' he said. 'I'll send some instructions later.' But I'm supposed to feed y'all, so they paid me in Confederate script. A hell of a lot of good that'll be when Yankees arrive."

"Did anyone at headquarters know how far away the Federal army is?"

"The river men say some of Grant's men are at Clarksville already. They could be here anytime they want to come upriver." The enlisted men looked at each other, Davis nodded to Magnusson.

Edmondson scratched his nose. "Buell's army is still marching down from Kentucky but the army men say Buell moves too slow, so there's no telling how long he'll take. At least two more days, they say."

Harper thought he could keep Edmondson talking if he asked him something about the local gossip. "So, ya know Colonel Forrest?"

"Hell, son, everyone 'tween Louisville and New Orleans knows Bedford Forrest. He's one of the richest men in Tennessee. The story is that he enlisted as a private. When he saw the state of the equipment they gave him, he went out and bought a whole regiment's worth of gear. Then he put himself in command of that regiment." Edmondson turned to leave.

"A rich man's son, I'll bet."

Edmondson turned back to Harper. "Don't you believe that. Not hardly. Born in the backwoods to a blacksmith with a whole passel of young-uns. Nope, everything he's made, he did on his own. Have to give that to him. A real smart son-of-a-bitch, but mean, too. You don't want to be on the wrong side of him."

It made sense to Harper. Forrest would have an easier time operating as a raider if everyone in the river country had this much respect for him.

"He hasn't let me or my men have any food after they captured us on Sunday night. Thank you for changin' that," Harper said.

"Least I can do for a prisoner."

"I met Forrest a few days ago. Cruel eyes. I nearly shot him at Donelson. Got his flag bearer, though."

Magnusson stared at Harper, a question on his face.

"He's killed a bunch of men in duels and knife fights; all legal you understand. Least, that's what the lawyers say. I heard him say he wanted to move some of the machinery out of the armory and send it south. No doubt he's already made arrangements with his business partners in Mississippi to get that equipment."

"Ya know, I was a lawman before the war. Up in the Dakota Territory."

"That so?" Edmondson sniffed at the air. He pointed to the partially-filled honeybucket in Harper's cell. "We'll take care of those." He called into the front office. "Shepperton, organize a work crew to get these buckets emptied and cleaned. Smells like an outhouse in here."

"Forrest's men seem like a rough bunch. If they weren't in uniform, I don't expect they'd be workin' on your side of the law."

"Most of them are good boys. But there's a few who I'd sooner see in here than y'all." Edmondson paused. "Here's something that'll tell you all you need to know about Bedford Forrest. Today, he decided to round up any niggers he finds on the street who ain't with their owners; even the freedmen. There's nothing I can do about it except warn the citizens. If I were to hazard a guess, I would say he's planning on selling them later if the army doesn't need them. That used to be one of his businesses, slave-tradin'. I can't do anything about it, 'cause he's declared martial law."

Martial law would make it easier for Forrest to control the city if he really did use the cover of war to make himself rich. It didn't seem likely, based on Harper's impressions from the lunch at Maysville. Forrest seemed to be more dedicated to the war effort than that.

The sheriff turned to walk back into his office. "Hope he leaves enough soldiers here to give me some help with looters."

"Had any problems yet?"

"Not too much yet, but I expect it'll start once the last of the soldiers leave." Edmondson stopped in the doorway to the front office. "You know, I had to let half of my deputies go when the state went with the Confederacy because they favored the Union. We had to combine the city and the county law enforcement when the army took over my offices and the work-house. I guess when the Yankees arrive, I'll have to hire back all the Northern men and let the others go."

"Sheriff, thank you again for the food and water." Harper looked at the enlisted men and nodded. It took a while for them to understand.

"Thank you, Sheriff," Magnusson said.

Edmondson nodded before he left. He gave Harper a lot of information about the town, but not much about the Federal armies coming to Nashville. No telling how accurate any of it was. But if Forrest thought Buell will be here in two days, they needed to be ready.

"So, y'all's a lawman, are you?" It was Leroy calling from the floor of the cell opposite Harper's. "Well, ain't that intristin'?" He saw the civilian prisoners staring at him.

Harper looked across to Magnusson and the others. They heard the entire exchange between Harper and the sheriff. He glanced at Magnusson. "We'll talk later." He gave his men a slight nod before returning to sit on the cot. He didn't want to make escape plans within earshot of the civilians or the deputies.

****

An hour after Eleanor's visit, the two women made their way up Court Street to avoid going through the town market, escorted this time by Toby, Bosley's negro muscleman. They walked facing the afternoon sun, wearing their overcoats over their simple day dresses, with bonnets tied under their chins against the chill. Eleanor turned onto Oak Street and stopped on the sidewalk in front of a shop across Broadway Street. The gilded lettering on the plate glass window read, "F. Hummel". Below it, "Gunsmith."

Katie looked at the weapons displayed in the window. Was this why Eleanor came out shopping? Katie tried to look into the store over a short curtain behind the display but could not see past her own reflection.

" 'Ave you ev-*aire* used a *pistolette*, Katie?"

"I don't know what that is."

"A *pistolette.* You know." She gestured with her hand. "Bang! Bang!"

"Oh." Katie saw the motion but it took her a moment to remember if she had. "I once tried to shoot one of Papa's pistols but I was too little and the gun was too heavy. I almost shot my foot. Papa took the gun away and I've been afraid to try shooting ever since."

Did Eleanor want her to buy a pistol? Katie was not sure how she would afford that. She wondered where she would keep it when she had customers. Still, the idea of having her own pistol was exciting. She imagined holding an ivory-handled six-shooter.

Eleanor led the way into the store; Katie followed, and Toby stayed just inside after he closed the door.

The eyes of the apprentice gunsmith, Lancelot Clark, widened in recognition when then women entered the shop. He called the proprietor from the workroom. Ferd Hummel came from Switzerland. He appeared in be in his mid-thirties but with a slight hump in his back and the start of a paunch showing in front. A devout man, he never went to Bosley's saloon, and he did not seem to recognize the two women.

"Yes, madam, how may I help you?" Hummel addressed Eleanor while Katie stood back from the sales counter. He still carried some of his native German into his daily speech.

Katie untied the scarf holding her bonnet in place before she looked around the shop at the handguns on display on a shelf under the counter and at the rifles in a rack along the wall behind the apprentice. While Eleanor and the gunsmith talked, Katie looked around the store. It was the first time she had been in a big-city gun shop. When she looked at Lancelot, he smiled back, looking more confident here in his native environment than he had on the landing two weeks earlier. In the shadows of the shop, Lancelot appeared older than when she saw him at the riverfront bazaar and he did not seem to be put off because of where she worked. He was thin, but handsome. Even so, she guessed he couldn't be much older than herself, perhaps seventeen or eighteen.

"I am looking for a 'Ladies Companion' for my young friend." Then, more softly so only Hummel and Katie could hear, "It needs to be small enough to strap around the leg."

Hummel's eyebrows arched and he looked at Katie for a moment before he glanced at Lancelot. "Please to come into the office vare we can haff privacy." He led the way through a side door. "Lancelot, you stay here und vatch the store."

"Yes, boss."

Katie gave Lancelot a glance and a demure smile as she walked past him. The boy blushed, but returned a shy smile. Katie could feel his stare on her back until Hummel shut the door to the office.

****

"Can't see none of our army, sir." Private Bailey stepped down from the cot under the window in his cell. "Just some more civilian fellas and a few Reb soldiers."

Harper spent Thursday afternoon trying to devise a plan for escape while watching the barge traffic at the river boat landing. He could overhear Edmondson's deputies report that the Confederate cavalry drove the mobs away from various warehouses. From listening to the reports that came into the front office, Harper got the sense Forrest's men were systematically going through the city loading military supplies onto wagons and railroad cars for the trip south.

Since the men learned Grant's or Buell's armies could arrive sometime during the next few days, Bailey and the others spent their time watching for signs of the Federal armies.

Deputy Sheriff Shepperton and two other deputies entered the cell room an hour before sunset, carrying shotguns and brooms. "Cleaning day, gentlemen."

Shepperton opened Harper's cell door and that of the enlisted men. "You soldiers git your coats on and go with Deputy Dodge." He pointed to the first of the deputies. "Don't git no ideas about tryin' to ex-cape. Dodge and Howard are crack shots, even with a shotgun, *and* they hate Yankees about as much as I do."

The deputy named Howard led them into the front office. "Put these on." He handed sets of leg-irons to Bailey, Cooke, and Davis. After each man fitted a ring around his own leg, Howard said, "Now put the other end around the next men's leg." The result was that the four enlisted men chained themselves to each other. Deputy Howard checked the locks on each set of leg irons before Dodge motioned them outside with the shotgun.

While Harper listened to the chains drag across the porch and down the stairs to the street, he surveyed the front office of the jail. Aside from the single desk in front of the rear wall, several chairs lined the side walls. Pegs for a coat rack projected from the rear wall behind the desk, with the large ring for the cell doors hanging from one. In the corner, on the side of the room away from the door to the cell room, behind the desk, he saw what he sought–an oak cabinet with a built-in lock. It had to be their gun locker.

Howard led the enlisted men into the street. Dodge motioned for Harper to follow. "You next, but don't git any ideas." The deputy cocked both hammers of the weapon.

"No leg irons?"

"I ain't worried about you, mister." Dodge smiled and leveled the shotgun at Harper's belly.

Dodge seemed eager to use the weapon. For a brief moment, Harper had the idea Dodge might shoot him on the spot. Instead, the deputy used the barrels of the shotgun to motion Harper through the front door.

The air was crisp and clear. They walked over soft soggy ground, empty of the snow of the previous week. Howard led the men between the jail and the feed store next to it, out to the edge of the bluff. He ordered them to sit and wait while the other prisoners cleaned out the cells.

Wet from the ground seeped into his trousers, but Harper was glad to breathe clean air again and he guessed the men were, too. The stain of the wet ground against his trousers would only add to the blood, dirt, and powder burn which already ruined his uniform.

The group fell silent and watched the river flowing below them where the barges ferried soldiers and civilians. The ruins of the suspension bridge still smoldered from its destruction earlier in the day.

"Where will the barges and boats go to hide before the army gets here?" Davis asked.

"Upriver, most likely, trying to git away from y'all's gunboats," Howard said. "Or, they'll wait until the army's gone and sell themselves to the Yankees."

Harper could see that these civilian deputies were a lot more forthcoming with information. They didn't keep secrets the way soldiers do. Maybe he could learn something more from them.

"Is that part of Nashville?" Magnusson pointed to the town across the river.

"No. That's Edgefield." Howard laughed. "They call it that because it's on the edge of fallin' into the river. Mostly white-trash workermen and free niggers live over there, except for the warehouses." In spite of Howard's information, Harper could see several large houses on the far side of the town.

The bluff at Edgefield sat farther back from the river and was not as tall as on the Nashville side, leaving better space for the riverboat landing and warehouses. Beyond the town, the land rose slowly, with a mix of farms and woodlands similar to the countryside they passed through during the march from Kingsville into Nashville.

Harper stood up. "You men see that road climbin' the hill out of the town?" He pointed across the river. "Well, that's where General Buell will be comin' from, unless General Grant gets here first usin' the river." He wasn't giving the deputies any more information than what they already knew, and it might cheer the men to see some concrete version of what he had been telling them about a possible rescue.

"How soon do ya think it will be, Mister Harper?" Bailey asked.

"Shouldn't be too long. After what we've seen, my guess is there's no more Rebs on that side of the river. Buell only needs to march on down here from Kentucky."

"How far is it to Kentucky?" Bailey asked.

Harper looked at Dodge to make sure he said it right. "About two days' march, I'd expect."

"Less than that." Dodge waved the barrels of the shotgun in the direction of Edgefield. "That's a lot of brave talk for a prisoner, Yank. You'll be lucky if you still here by then."

They watched the land on the opposite side, now empty, quiet, still–abandoned by the Rebels, not yet controlled by the Federal army. Harper walked to the bluff to look over the edge until he could see the mudflat at the bottom separating the bluff from the river. The river itself was perhaps two hundred yards wide, no doubt swollen from the winter rains. There was a causeway to Harper's right, beyond the ironworks neighboring the jailhouse. The causeway led from Front Street down to the riverboat landing. Two sets of burned timbers outlined the remains of fair-sized boats in the mud beyond the causeway. It looked to Harper as if both burned before they were complete.

"Thinkin' about jumpin', Lieutenant?"

Harper turned to look behind him to see the muzzles of Dodge's shotgun ten feet away, leveled at his chest. For a moment, he tensed, ready to leap at the deputy and wrestle the gun away and escape. The distance was about the same as when the Confederate captain tried to shoot him. But the deputy was ready and uninjured. He almost certainly would fire at the first sign of an attack.

"Not right now, Deputy. Maybe later, when you're not payin' attention." Harper gave Dodge a smile and turned to face his men. When he did, he saw Dodge lower the muzzle of the shotgun.

Harper dashed at the man. Dodge was too slow. Harper pushed the muzzle down and slammed his body into Dodge's chest, driving them both to the ground.

B-bamm! Both barrels discharged into the soggy ground.

Before the deputy could react, Harper used his left hand to pull the pistol from the holster at the deputy's hip. Dodge released the now-useless shotgun and punched Harper in the side of the head. He grabbed Harper's wrist, forcing the pistol away from the both their bodies.

Harper tried to roll to his right while he grasped the pistol in his left hand. He could not use it yet–it was backward in his hand.

Bamm!

Somewhere in the distance, Harper heard a single shotgun blast.

Are the others trying to fight?

Dodge held tight to Harper's wrist when Harper went into the roll. Now, Harper was under Dodge, still clutching the pistol, his free hand squeezing the deputy's throat. The feel of Dodge's windpipe and the guttural breathing sounds brought Harper's animal hatred alive. Heat surged through his veins and he squeezed harder–working Dodge's throat like a vise.

Harper withstood Dodge's continued punches against his head, each blow causing a blinding flash in Harper's eyes. But he lost focus each time his head hit the ground. He felt Dodge try to pull a knee up to pin him to the ground. Harper released his grip on Dodge's throat to push against the ground with his elbow and foot. This leverage set the pair into a second roll, during which Harper brought his own feet underneath him.

Harper heard the men behind him yelling but he could not understand the words. Only he and Dodge existed now, locked in a brawl which might cost either one of them their life.

He straddled Dodge and brought his knee up to pin Dodge's left arm. With a final tug, Harper pulled the pistol free. Dodge's eyes opened wider.

A shadow darkened the deputy's face and the ground around it. Harper shifted the pistol to his right hand before turning to see the source of the shadow. Blinded by the sun, what he saw was the butt-end of a shotgun before it slammed into his face. Pain exploded across his forehead while a hand grabbed the wrist holding the pistol, twisting its barrel skyward.

There were two men standing over him. Harper thumbed the hammer back before Dodge pounded a fist into his face.

A blow on the top of his head stunned Harper long enough for Dodge to take away the pistol while the second standing man held Harper's twisted wrist. When the gun was gone, the second man kicked Harper's ribs, doubling him over and pushing him off of Dodge.

Harper struggled to breathe. Before he could stand, the boot kicked him in the small of his back. Another to the side of his head blinded him.

He heard Dodge stand. A kick in the gut had little effect against the tight muscles there.

Dazed, Harper tried to stand but the boot kicked his knee from under him. He fell on his side and rolled onto his back in time to feel the butt of the shotgun pound his forehead again, sending stars shooting across his blackened vision. He pulled his elbows in to protect his ribs and used his hands to cover his head. The kicks now seemed to come from every direction. He drew his knees into his belly in a fetal curl.

The butt of the shotgun landed again, and Harper's world went black.

****

"Please to be seated," Hummel said to the women before he sat behind his desk. He leaned forward, resting his elbows on the desk with his hands folded in front of him. Katie followed Eleanor's example and removed her overcoat, which Eleanor carried to a coat tree standing next to the door before she and Katie took their seats.

"Unfortunately, missus, I do not haff any derringers at all. Nor can I get a new one from any manufacturer. They haff all shifted their production to firearms for the military. I could write to my agents in New York or Chicago to see if they haff any at their exchange stores, but I t'ink maybe dat would take longer than you are willing to vait, yes?"

"I am afraid so, *Monsieur* Hummel."

"This girl works in the barroom, yes?"

Eleanor held her chin high and stared past Hummel without answering. Katie stayed silent, following Eleanor's example.

"I see." Hummel looked at Katie. "Has this girl ever fired a gun before?"

"No?" Eleanor answered but looked to Katie, eyebrows raised. Katie shook her head.

"So, I t'ink maybe she cannot shoot, anyway. Und if she vas to try to load it herself, she might make mistake, yes?"

"That is certainly possible."

"Just so. But, I t'ink you are right. She needs self-protection. So maybe is best if we give to her a knife, instead." Addressing Katie, he asked, "Haff you ever use a knife for to kill somet'ing, miss? Mice, chickens, rabbits, perhaps?"

Katie did not understand the question. Her mind stuck on the fact that she would not get a pistol. She didn't use a knife in the bedroom. She stared back at Hummel without answering.

"*Chéri*, did you not tell me you worked on a farm before you came to Paducah?"

"Oh! Yes, that's true. Did you mean if I ever had to butcher one of our animals?"

"Yes, yes, dat vould be goot. Haff you?"

"When I got big enough, I had the job of killin' the chickens we ate and the extra piglets. Then I had to gut them and clean them."

Hummel sat back in his chair, fingers held in a steeple under his chin. He looked at Katie with renewed interest. After a few moments, he leaned forward again with his elbows on the desk.

"Good. So I t'ink maybe you can use what you know about a knife to protect yourself, yes?"

"I t'ink so." Katie heard herself mimicking Hummel's accent. It was not intentional, it slipped out. She glanced at Eleanor who smiled back.

Hummel did not seem to notice. He turned to Eleanor. "She carries it in the usual place, yes?"

"*Oui*."

"Stand up, girl. Please excuse, but I must make some measurements." He took a tape measure from the top drawer and he moved around the desk to kneel in front of Katie.

"You will now please lift your dress so I can see your leg from here to here." He touched her leg above the knee and at a point just above mid-thigh.

Katie looked at Eleanor. While she had no issue with showing her body as part of her job, she was not sure of the rules outside of *Lafitte's Hideout*. At least her pantaloons would still cover her.

"Do not be *timide*, *Chéri*. He needs to measure. "

Katie did as Hummel asked.

"Right leg or left?"

"Right, I think; is that so, Katie?"

"I suppose so."

"Which hand do you use when you haff to use the knife?"

"Right."

Hummel finished his measurements quickly over her pantaloons. "I t'ink she is tall enough for a three-inch blade." Unlike most of her customers, Hummel's touch against her leg was soft and professional while he worked, almost delicate–not what she had come to expect from a man. Hummel did a final appraisal of Katie's thigh. "Yes…very nice."

Katie blushed at the last comment. She lowered her skirt when Hummel stood. Furrows of thought showed on the gunsmith's forehead. He went into the front of the shop.

"So, not a *pistolette* but a dagger. Much more romantic, no?"

"I suppose so." Katie could not understand how the knife would change things, or even if she could use it on a customer.

****

The kicking had stopped. Harper heard the voices shouting at him while his consciousness pushed through the blackness inside his head. He pulled himself to his knees to catch his breath. The blows to his ribs made it painful to breathe.

"Let him up." It was Shepperton's voice. Harper turned to look at the voice. Shepperton stood next to Dodge who carried both shotguns. The civilian prisoners made a semicircle behind the two. Grinding his teeth and gasping with pain, Harper pulled his feet under him. Straining with determination not to show weakness, Harper stood up.

"So, you're ready for more, Yank?"

Shepperton approached. Before Harper could react, the deputy punched him in the stomach, doubling him over. Two of the former civilian prisoners grabbed his arms, keeping him from falling to the ground. Shepperton pummeled both fists into his body again and again, with the speed and force of a prizefighter. Harper kept the muscles of his body clenched, trying to protect the bones and organs underneath. It was all he could do.

Harper tried to pull away from the grips on his arms. Reaching into the depth of his inner core for strength, he twisted to push the man holding his right arm into Shepperton's fists. The deputy landed a blow onto this captor, causing the man to release his grip. Harper punched at the face of the man holding his left arm but that fellow held firm and soon the other man returned to grab his right arm.

Shepperton resumed his blows, this time aimed at Harper's face. Harper turned his face with each blow, preventing them from reaching his nose. Instead, the punches impacted both sides of his skull, each one causing stars to flash in Harper's eyes. His vision slowly closed to a pinpoint of light which faded and blinked out.

****

Hummel returned carrying a leather sheath with two short straps. He pulled out a dagger and presented it to Eleanor with both hands. All Katie could see was the handle, which was made from some sort of animal horn, and the shiny steel of the blade. Eleanor examined the weapon, while Hummel returned his attention to Katie's legs.

"Dress up again, please. Please spread apart, Miss Katie." He tapped between her knees with the sheath. Katie shifted her feet so Hummel could strap the sheath over the right leg of her drawers.

"Beautiful steel, *Monsieur* Hummel."

"Yes, yes. From Essen. Goot German steel. Very strong." He finished with the detailed fitting of the straps, trimming away the excess length.

"Is this some sort of deer horn in the handle?"

Katie looked across to Eleanor. She could see brown accents and many small, raised lumps on the bone-colored handle.

"No, missus. Elk. Very strong. Never split." He gave the leather on the outside of her leg a final shake to gauge how tightly it gripped. "*Sehr gut.*" He reached his hand toward Eleanor who gave him the dagger. Hummel sheathed the weapon, buttoning hold-down straps over the hand guards before he sat back on his heels to inspect his work. "Ya, dat vill vork. How does dat feel, miss?"

"A little strange."

"You will become used to it, *Chéri*. Soon you will begin to feel much safe-*aire*."

"Put your dress down please, miss. I want to see how it looks."

Katie did as she asked.

"Goot," Hummel said. "I t'ink goot, yes, missus?" The fullness of the dress and single petticoat easily hid the outline of the dagger and its sheath. It would be undetectable when she worn the crinoline.

"*Oui. Tres bon, monsieur.*" Eleanor stood and walked around Katie, inspecting. "Fine work, *Monsieur* Hummel. Turn sideways, *chéri*. Let's see if it shows when you move." Katie twisted from side to side to allow the skirt to flare out. Eleanor nodded with satisfaction.

"Now, you sit, please."

Katie sat.

"Does it feel too tight, now?"

"No, it feels fine." It was no tighter than the garters holding Katie's stockings.

"Goot. Das is very goot." Hummel returned to sit at his desk. "Miss Katie, please now give me back the knife."

Katie looked to Eleanor for guidance.

"Please, I want to show you how to use the knife."

Eleanor nodded, so Katie reached under her skirt to retrieve the weapon from its sheath. She passed it to Hummel handle-first while she held it close to the hand-guards.

"You will show her how to reach the knife through the pocket, yes?"

"I think Katie knows already. This is not '*aire* regul*aire* dress."

Katie blushed again. "I forgot that this dress had an open pocket." She was still a little rattled with letting a man work under her dress.

****

Harper woke with his face pressed against the soft, wet grass. He blinked his eyes open and watched a beetle crawl from one dead blade of grass to the next.

"Damn. The son-of-a-bitch is awake again."

If these bastards are trying to kill him, Harper was determined to take at least one of them with him. He pushed himself up from the dead grass and pulled his knees under him.

"That's enough, Julius," Dodge said. "We don't want to kill him."

"This won't kill him. He's a tough one."

Harper saw Shepperton's shadow approaching. The man's boots came into view. Harper saw the foot rear back. Then, he saw his escape.

Harper rolled in the last moment before Shepperton's boot landed against his side. The roll reduced the impact of the blow. Now, he was on his back. He did another roll while Shepperton tried to position himself for a second kick. One more roll. The last thing Harper saw before dropping over the edge of the bluff was Shepperton reaching to grab him.

****

"So, Miss Katie. This is not like your knife in the kitchen, yes? You see dat it is sharp on both edges und it comes together in a very sharp point, yes?" Katie nodded. "So, all three parts can be used when you need them."

Hummel continued his lesson in the use of the knife for self-protection, taking special care to show Katie which parts to use and where to cut in order to hurt an attacker without causing fatal injuries that might get her arrested. Then he showed her how to use the knife to kill, if necessary.

Katie gave her full attention to Hummel's lesson. When Hummel finished, he handed the knife back to Katie. He forced her to go through the motions of the lessons, using himself as the target. Katie had fun with this part of the lesson. Not only did she follow Hummel's guidance, but she added some of the tricks she learned while growing up. Hummel laughed when Katie showed him her own fighting skills and he showed her how to use the knife as part of those moves.

"Where did you learn to fight that way, *ma chéri*?" The surprised expression on Eleanor's face made Katie laugh.

"Tryin' to git away from the bullies in my school back home."

Following the lesson, Eleanor paid three dollars for the weapon. Katie knew she would have to repay Eleanor, and it troubled her that she could not guess when she would have enough money to do that.

****

"Maybe this is God's punishment on me."

Magnusson's voice pierced into Harper's consciousness. He opened his eyes to lantern light flickering on the ceiling of the cell room. The stench of the cell room signaled where he lay.

"What do ya mean, Gus?" Davis asked.

Harper tried to sit up. He made it half-way there before the pounding and dizziness in his head overcame him and he fell back.

"Corporal! It looks like the lieutenant's awake." Harper heard Bailey's voice through the storm of pain in his head. He took a deep breath–cut short by the stabbing pains in his ribs and back.

"Mister Harper, are ya all right?" It was Magnusson's voice.

Harper turned his head to look across the cell room. A fuzzy shape large enough to be Corporal Magnusson stood at the edge of the other cell, face pressed against the bars. The blond hair of the shape next to Magnusson told Harper that Bailey was up, too.

"What did ya mean when ya said all of this was because God wanted to punish you?" Harper ran his hands over his ribs. He pressed against tender areas to gauge the pain. He wanted time to find all of the injured parts of his body.

Magnusson looked surprised by the question. "Aren't you hurt, sir?"

"A bit." Harper winced at the pain in his ribs when he tried to sit up.

Magnusson watched Harper.

With the fuzziness clearing, Harper saw what he took to be genuine concern in Magnusson's large rounded eyes.

Magnusson continued his story, all the time watching Harper's movements on the cot. "Well, think on it. I ran away from my father and rejected his church-ways to join the army. Maybe bein' a prisoner is my punishment for not obeyin' my father."

Harper forced a laugh. "Do ya really believe some god is doin' this to you, Corporal?" Besides his back and sides, the only other pains were on his face and his head, both inside and out. He rubbed the sore spots on his face and the sides of his head. "I mean, in this big, whole war, with so many people sufferin', do ya really think your god has the time to give out a personal punishment to one corporal?"

He did not feel any pains from broken bones in his arms or legs, only soreness from multiple bruises. Shepperton and his friends were at least smart enough to make sure the prisoners they beat could still walk.

Bailey, Cooke, and Davis looked at each other. Their features were still blurry, but Harper could guess what they were thinking. Harper needed to keep them from feeling sorry for themselves.

"Besides, didn't ya tell your father ya truly believed in fightin' to save the Union?"

Magnusson nodded. His hands were on the bars of his cell and Harper could sense the large man's concern. Whether for Magnusson's transgressions against his father or for Harper's condition, Harper could not tell.

Prepared for the rush of dizziness, Harper sat up slowly and put his feet on the floor. He waited until the room stopped spinning.

"Do ya think God–if He is truly a just god the way the preachers say He is–would punish ya for doin' what ya sincerely believed was the right thing to do?" Now, Harper drew on his own religious training as a child and at the university.

Magnusson gave no answer for a few moments. One side of his mouth curled upward. "Ya know, that's what I told my father. But the real reason I joined the army is I wanted to go away from the farm and see what life was like outside of Salem. At least, partly."

"What's wrong with that?" Harper brought both hands to his head and ran his fingers through his hair, trying to massage the pain away. "Did ya know I did the same thing?"

Through his fuzzy vision, Harper could see all four of them

watching him. He couldn't sense any of the civilian prisoners. Harper gripped the edges of the cot and tried to force the dizziness to go away. "After we came home from the Mexican War, my father pulled strings so I could go to a new Catholic college in Indiana." The nausea came. He was able to find the honey bucket before the gushing started.

The dizziness subsided. The faces of the enlisted men came into focus. He must be hurt in the head, though, to be philosophizing with them about God's punishments on sinners.

He touched the bruise on his face which hurt the most. There was a welt the size of the silver dollar square in the middle of his forehead at the hairline. It hurt when he pushed on it. "How are you men? Was anyone else hurt durin' the fight?"

"We tried to take the gun away from the other deputy, but couldn't." Magnusson looked at the floor. "When ya charged the guard, the one coverin' us fired his shotgun into the air, then he just backed away with it still pointed at us. He said, 'Don't move. I'll git one of y'all with the shotgun and you'll have to drag him along while I use my pistol to finish the rest.' We started to run away, but he ran in front of us. By this time, he had his pistol out, too. He told us, 'That shot in the air could have just as easily been into one of y'all.' "

Magnusson looked at the door to the front office before he whispered loud enough for Harper to hear. "Sir, them deputies had it planned that way. I heard them talkin' about it after Davis and I carried ya in here. They had it all planned out. As soon as one of us tried to do somethin', one of them was to fire his gun into the air as a signal. Then the one who stayed behind would come runnin' out with a bunch of the civilian prisoners. It was the fella who stayed behind who hit ya over the head. I think they jes' wanted to beat up a Yankee."

Cooke and Davis nodded.

"Their plan almost back-fired," Davis said. "I don't think they expected Mister Harper to take the deputy's gun away."

Did he get a gun and not use it? Harper couldn't remember.

"Where are all of the other prisoners?" With his head clearing, Harper now saw the other cells were empty.

"The deputies let them go so's they could help beat you." Magnusson continued his loud whisper. "After the fight they all just walked off."

Harper stared down at the floor. He heard someone come through the door to the front office. A pair of boots stopped in front of his cell.

"You're lucky you ain't dead, Yank." It was Shepperton. "Got what you deserved, attacking a deputy sheriff and tryin' to ex-cape."

"That was a gutless trick, Shepperton. Ain't ya man enough to face me one-on-one?"

"We was jes' havin' some fun with you, Yank. 'Sides, it serves you right for invading my country."

"Wait until Grant comes. He'll show ya how much we care about your piss-ant *country*."

"You'll be in Alabama by the time Grant gits here." A grin lit up Shepperton's face. "Or dead."

"When I'm free, I'm goin' to even the score, Shepperton."

"I'll be waitin', Yank. *If* that ever happens."

"It'll happen. Count on it."

Rabid dog.

****

The February sun had gone behind the houses to the west when Katie and Eleanor left the store. They needed to hurry so they could prepare for the night's work.

"I cain't say when I'll be able to repay you, Eleanor."

"It is a gift, *chéri*. We are too long without seeing you 'appy."

"Does Loreena know?"

"Oui. We talked about it after din-*naire*. Most of the girls own a personal weapon."

"I didn't know that."

"Now, maybe you need not be so…so…*appréhender*."

It was true. While Katie walked down Court Street, her mood began to change. Feeling the heft of the knife against her thigh gave a sense of strength which led to courage–as if she would be able to take charge, no matter what happened. She reached into her pocket to feel the handle of the knife and imagined the lumps in the elk horn locking the knife to her palm, making it an extension of her hand.

"Katie, I am to go on a trip tomorrow with *Monsieur* Franklin and some of the oth-*aire* girls. We're going upriver to visit with the army officers. Do you promise not to be afraid while I am gone? I should be back in two days."

"Maybe I ain't afraid no more, Eleanor. Evilface is dead. I'll be all right so long as there are no more customers like him. The soldiers are usually nice, especially the younger ones. They usually follow what I say." And she now had her own dagger.

"I spoke with Franklin and Loreena about Major Eagleton. We decided we will not let anyone do that sort of thing anymore–to anyone. It is too frightening for us all."

"It makes me feel a little better." If she ever had another customer like Evilface, she would geld the man.

"Maybe when I come back, I can start to teach you how to become a *courtesan*."

This cheered Katie. Not only would she stop having to take so many men upstairs each night, but she would be making more money. She touched the comforting knife through her skirt and smiled for the first time in a week.

Things were going to get better.

Friday, February 21st 1862

The day after the beating, Harper lay still on his cot all morning, trying to avoid further pain by moving as little as possible. He had tested each injured part of his body throughout the morning and decided he might have a cracked or broken rib, maybe two, from where Shepperton kicked him,. The dizziness he experienced the night before was gone, leaving behind a pounding, throbbing ache inside his skull. Each time he used the honey bucket this morning, blood appeared in the flow. At least, there was a good fire going in the iron stove, keeping him warm.

The men kept to themselves throughout the morning and when they spoke, they used low voices.

"I keep watchin', Gus, but I don't see anythin' movin' over across the river." Harper heard Bailey call from the window in his cell. "Just some dogs wanderin' around and a few loose chickens."

Harper watched his men through half-closed eyes.

"Nothin' on the river, either." Cooke and Davis had taken turns watching from their cell window through the morning. "Only a rowboat and a couple of darkies on the riverbank fishin'."

With the other prisoners gone, Dodge and Howard had moved Cooke and Davis to the cell opposite Harper. Its window gave a view of the river and the city north from the jail.

"They're not comin', Gus. Wouldn't there be some scouts out there if they were only two days away?"

"Don't talk like that, Ben," Magnusson said. "Besides, they might be out there but ya can't see them because they're hidin' while they're scoutin' what's goin' on." Magnusson looked into Harper's cell then back at the other prisoners. “Now, be quiet and let the lieutenant rest. We still don’t know how bad he’s hurt.”

Good man, that Magnusson. He has control of the men, and he knows how it feels after a beating.

All of Harper’s muscles ached, both from the exertions of yesterday’s beating and from the bruises on his chest, belly, sides, and face. He also now knew for certain there were sixty-seven blisters in the plaster of the ceiling in his cell and seventeen courses of brick between the level of his cot and the bottom of the cell window.

****

When the sun neared its mid-day summit, Harper heard two men enter the front office. He tried to look through the open doorway to see who they were.

“Well, look-it who’s back. Yankee-lovers.” Deputy Dodge pulled his feet from the desktop and sat up straight in the chair behind the desk. “I guess y’all are back because the Yanks are comin’.”

“Look. Don’t start anythin’, Dodge.” The speaker was one of the new arrivals. “The sheriff hired us back because y’all are short-handed.” The man walked into Harper’s view when he hung his coat on one of the pegs on the wall behind the desk.

“Why not? I’m not the one who spawned a traitor, Morris.”

“My son is *not* a traitor. He joined the army because he thought it was the right thing to do.”

Harper could see the back of a large man with collar-length brown hair. He was about the size of Magnusson with some gray hairs in his mutton-chop sideboards.

“Well, that makes him a *dumb* traitor, doesn’t it? He joined the wrong army.” Dodge turned to Deputy Howard whom Harper could see sitting against the side wall by the window. “Ain’t that right, Zeke?”

“Hard to know how he got mixed up, Morris. What with all the other boys in town joinin’ the Confederacy regiments.”

Harper saw the contempt in Howard’s face, nose flared as if Morris emitted a foul odor.

“Hiram knew what he was doin’. He made the right choice.”

Harper heard another man enter the office from the street, but could not see him.

"The hell he did. He's a traitor to Tennessee and to all of his neighbors." Dodge was on his feet. "Jes' wait until he comes home. We'll teach him."

"At least he ain't in the army what's runnin' away, Dodge. Like Shepperton's son and your boy. I heard they're skedaddlin' all the way down to Franklin."

This remark brought Howard to his feet to approach Morris. Dodge came at Morris from the other side.

"Y'all just cool off, now!" Sheriff Edmondson stepped into view with his hands up to stop Dodge and Howard. Edmondson waited until the men halted. Morris backed away, out of sight from Harper. "Y'all need to work together. This city is on the verge of a riot and I need all y'all. I don't need y'all fighting with each other."

After a long pause, Dodge said, "I ain't workin' with no blue-bellied shithead, Sheriff."

"You bastard." Morris pushed Dodge backward; he fell into the chair behind the desk. Edmondson grabbed Morris by the arm and pulled him away from the confrontation, outside of Harper's field of sight. The new man came into view when he blocked a punch from Howard.

"Stop it, god-damn it!" Edmondson stared at Howard until the deputy backed away a step. "I'm making Morris and Holiday into a third shift. You and Howard will stay on second shift. Shepperton and Werts will be the first."

So the two pro-Union deputies would be in the same shift. That might be helpful for an escape.

"I don't like it Sheriff." Dodge took his coat from a peg on the wall behind the office desk. "I don't like it at all. Let's go, Zeke." Dodge walked to the door and waited for Howard. "Morris is a traitor to his country and so is his god-damn son. Wait until Shepperton hears about this."

"I'm in charge here, Dodge, not Shepperton."

"Until the next election, Sheriff. Meantimes, we'll see what he has to say about it.

After Dodge and Howard left, Edmondson sat in the chair behind the desk. Morris took a seat along the opposite wall from Harper while the other man stepped out of view onto the porch.

Edmondson asked Morris, “How is your son, Jonathan?”

“I don’t know, Sheriff. I ain’t heard from him since right after Christmas. I think he’s still in Buell’s army, though.”

“If that’s true, I guess we’ll get to see him in a few more days.”

“Maybe.” Morris looked out of the window. “I hope so, Sheriff.”

If the son favored the cause for the Union, Harper thought, maybe the father did, as well. Harper needed to talk with these new deputies.

****

After their lunch of corn-mash gruel with a few kernels floating in it, Harper called to Deputy Morris who came into the cell room. Edmondson had left the jail by the time the prisoners finished eating.

“I’m gettin’ stomach cramps somethin’ terrible from eatin’ nothin’ but mash and water.” Although Harper actually did feel the need, here was an opportunity to talk with one of the supposed pro-Union deputies. “I’d like to go to the outhouse, if that’s alright?”

“That’s what the bucket’s for.” Morris pointed to the honey bucket. His eyes sat deep into their sockets and the skin around them was the color of charcoal.

Harper grabbed a cell bar with one hand and doubled over, bending his leg and gripping his stomach with his free hand. He signaled Morris to come closer.

“Please, deputy.” Harper dropped his voice to a whisper. “Shepperton and his boys messed up my insides yesterday. I’ve been pissin’ blood all mornin’. I don’t know what will happen if I try to use the bucket.” Harper looked across the room at the enlisted men. “If there’s a problem, I don’t want them to know how bad it is. I need some privacy.”

Morris put one hand on the bars of the cell and stared at the floor.

“It’s not like we’re real criminals.” Harper acted out another cramp and stayed bent over a little longer than before, gasping for breath. “Please. Ya have my word. I won’t try to escape.” He gasped for air as if recovering from the fake cramp. “Hell, I can barely walk after the beatin’ they gave yesterday.”

Morris watched Harper act out the cramps. "I heard they worked y'all over pretty bad."

Harper looked up from his cramp. "Please."

Morris stepped back from the wall of bars. "Okay. Let me tell Holiday what's goin' on. Can y'all walk?"

"I can manage by myself." Harper, still bent over, changed his expression to a smile of gratitude. He nodded his head and winked at Magnusson.

****

"Would ya mind if I could sit out here on the porch for a while?" Harper asked as the two men walked back to the jail. It was an outrageous request for a prisoner to make, but Harper wanted the chance to talk with this man. "My head's still hurtin' from yesterday, and the smells inside make me dizzy. I get sick to my stomach."

"Why would I do that?"

"Maybe because I ain't a real criminal, and because I'm sick.

Morris seemed unsure what to do. His brow furrowed in thought. He looked into the office but Deputy Holiday did not look up from his paperwork. "Y'all won't try to escape, will you?"

"I give ya my word of honor." The fresh air helped relieve some of the pain in his head.

" 'Cause I need to keep this job real bad."

"I swear it. I know how hard times are."

The deputy hesitated. He looked up and down the street and at the cavalry camp. "Oh, what the hell. It ain't like you're some kind of criminal. But if y'all take one step off of the porch, I'll use this shotgun, mister, even if you are a Yankee. And I want to handcuff y'all to the chair. If anyone asks, I'll tell them that you're sick. And it'll show Shepperton and Dodge I'm not afraid to do as I damn well please."

Shortly after, Harper sat cuffed by one hand to a rocking chair on the front porch of the Davidson County Jail enjoying the feel of the sunshine of an unusually warm February afternoon and clearing his lungs with the rich scent of fresh wet earth. He overheard several passers-by repeat the rumor the Confederates would abandon the town the next day. A number of persons greeted the Yankee officer openly despite the blood and dirt on his uniform and the handcuffs holding him to the rocking chair. Some tipped their hats when they walked past. Others reached over the porch rail to shake Harper's free hand. One offered a cigar which Harper broke in half and shared with Morris.

"What's your name, deputy?" Harper let Morris light their cigars. He already knew Morris's name, but this question would open the conversation.

"Jonathan Morris." He shook the match stick to make it go out. "Yours?"

"Jamie Harper." Harper tried to shake the man's hand but the handcuffs prevented it. "Pleased to meet a Union man in Nashville." He took a puff from the cigar. "Ya know, I was a lawman myself before the war started."

"I ain't really a Union man. I don't own any niggers and there ain't much Federal government goin' on around here. Tennessee can stay or go, it doesn't matter to me. Nothin' would change." He looked across the street. "All I want is for this damned war to be over and for my son and his friends back home."

Up close, Harper saw a tired man with worry-lines around his mouth and eyes, around forty years old. But where earlier he thought he saw a robust, large man from the back, now he could see Morris's skin sagging from the line of his chin with very pronounced cheekbones and dark, sunken eyelids. Harper looked away, convinced the man must be suffering from some disease or, more likely, a lack of good food. Besides, he wanted to examine the yard across the street which had become a corral behind a large building with a sign on the roof announcing it was the Saint Charles Hotel. Morris's dilemma wasn't his concern. He set the rocker into motion.

"Whereabouts were y'all a lawman, Lieutenant?"

"Hunh? Oh, up in the Nebraska Territory, along the Missouri River." He blew a smoke ring.

Bell's company must have imposed themselves onto the hotel for billets. Their horses were secured under a shed roof behind the hotel. Piles of dried dung around the horses reflected the company's attitude toward their animals. Harper tried to find Santee among the horses.

Near the middle of the Tennesseans' herd, he saw a gray horse with three dark stockings, a dark mane, and a white nose like Santee's.

"Now, it's called the Dakota Territory, since they made Nebraska a state."

The battle flag for Bell's company fluttered beside the rear doorway to the hotel, a red square with the figure of an armed mountain man hand-drawn in the center,

"How'd y'all git along with the Indians?"

Harper rocked back and forth. "Quite well, actually. My brother trades with the Yanktons and the Poncas, so I knew many of 'em before I started. Some even helped me to track the wanted men." An idea came to Harper. "We used to use Indian calls when we got close to an outlaw. Ya want to hear one?"

Morris looked left and right. There was no one nearby. "Sure, go ahead."

Harper leaned forward in his chair, halting the rocker. He cupped his hands in front of his mouth. "Kye-yip-yip-yahh." He watched the horses at the hitch. The gray horse looked up and stared at the jail.

"That was a coyote sound. We would use it when we were spread out to signal when one of us found a trail or some sign of the men we were trackin'."

And Santee remembers. Good girl.

"Wouldn't be too useful here, Harper."

"Why not?"

"Because there ain't no coyotes in Nashville!" Morris laughed.

Harper laughed with the deputy but watched the horses. Santee nodded her head and pawed at the ground. After watching for a several moments, he resumed rocking.

"Morris, I overheard ya arguin' with Shepperton when ya arrived this morning. Your son's in Buell's army?"

"It's true. Him and some of his friends went north and joined a Kentucky regiment."

Santee pawed at the ground, then shook her head and let out an angry "Bur-r-r-r-…" She stared at the porch.

"Did it bother ya?" Harper shifted his gaze between Santee and Morris.

“A little. It’s hard to git letters through to him.”

Harper sat back in the chair and let the afternoon sun warm him. Thinking too much made his headache worse. He closed his eyes so the scene from the street didn’t add to the chaos in his head. “I’d guess that’ll change once Buell or Grant take control of the city.” Harper didn’t open his eyes.

“ ’Spect so.”

Harper heard Morris’s chair squeak. Then silence. He opened his eyes to see Morris sitting forward and looking closely at his face.

“Y’all feelin’ all right?”

“My head still hurts from yesterday.”

“Shepperton said y’all attacked Israel Dodge. Is that true?”

“Partly. I walked into a trap set by Shepperton. I thought I could get me and my men out of here.” Harper closed his eyes again. “Sheriff Edmondson told us he would need to hire his Union men back when the Yankees arrive. Are ya one of those?”

“I reckon so. That’s the reason he told us when he fired us a year ago. Been out of real work ever since.” He sat back in his chair. “Been livin’ off of what I can make as a night watchman for the sheriff’s cousin and what the wife can make cooking for the Union prisoners at the work house. Now, that’s over.”

Morris needed this job. It wasn’t likely he would risk it to let the prisoners go free.

“Here they come.” Morris used his chin to point south on Front Street in the direction of the causeway to the riverboat landing.

Harper stopped rocking and followed Morris’s stare to see a most unlikely group to be inside a city caught in the path of a war.

A dozen attractive women walked toward him. They walked one behind the other on the wooden sidewalk, led by a well-dressed businessman. The man might be their father, but Harper sensed he wasn’t. Behind the women were two large white men, dressed well, but obviously bodyguards.

The ladies wore bright-colored evening dresses with hoops wide enough to cover the width of the boards of the sidewalk. The hoops required they walk one behind the other in a colorful parade. Other people on the street stopped to stare. Their prosperous appearance was wildly out of place in a city panicked from being abandoned to the enemy.

"Ain't that interestin'." Harper always enjoyed the sight of beautiful women, even if they were ignoring him, so he sat back to enjoy the view as the ladies passed. But as they walked past, each shifted her parasol at the sight of the blue uniform. Harper never saw their faces but he did enjoy the airs of perfume as each woman passed.

He did recognize one face in the group–Bosley, the saloon-keeper and whorehouse owner from Paducah, led the parade. It was five weeks since Harper last saw the man, but he was certain it was the same whore-monger.

The jailer chuckled at Harper's undisguised interest. "There they go again."

"You've seen them before?"

" 'Bout once a month or so. There's a party at the commander's house. They go back to their boat in the mornin'."

Harper turned in his chair to watch the group as they continued up Front Street and turned onto the street neighboring the Town Square where they entered the house on the corner, Bedford Forrest's personal quarters. The lights came up along first floor windows of the house, followed shortly by the sounds of a string quartet.

"So the ladies stay overnight?" Harper asked.

"Not sure I would call them *ladies.*" Morris nodded his head.

Harper sat back in his chair, smiling. Rank had its privileges. He chuckled. Even in an army of rebels.

****

Later that night, Harper lay on the cot in his cell looking out at the clouds and stars through the dirty glass of the window. *Morris wasn't likely to help them escape.*

What was Bosley doing here? Obviously, he was making money off of his women. They must have used a riverboat so they would have a means to transport the women's fine clothes and to give them a place to dress. Somehow, they sneaked past Fort Donelson–probably a bribe. *But why Bosley?* There must be other proprietors on the Confederate side of the river who could provide their army the same services, especially in a city as big as Nashville.

He fell asleep thinking about Bosley, and that triggered a dream about the red-headed girl on his last night of Christmas leave, Baby Red. Reliving that pleasant night, he snapped awake.

The girl asked a lot of questions afterward. It sounded like casual conversation. What if all of the girls at Bosley's asked similar questions of all of the customers and told Bosley what they learned? Some smart person working at Bosley's could learn a lot about the army's plans from the soldiers who passed through the bar and the upstairs rooms. Morris said Bosley and his women passed by the jail once a month. Often enough that he could recognize them.

Harper's head clouded when he closed his eyes. In the darkness, he allowed himself to float down into the sea of dreams. Events of the past days drifted at random in his head–passed each other until two collided with an explosion which jolted Harper awake.

Is Bosley a spy?

Saturday, February 22nd, 1862

By Saturday morning, the mobs were gone and the Confederate troopers went about their work unmolested. Harper had watched the riverboat landing from his cell window. An hour past sunrise, he saw Bosley lead the procession of women and bodyguards aboard a small, single-deck paddle steamer. Shortly afterward, the boat backed away from the landing and turned down river, out of sight, toward Paducah.

Now, Harper's jacket lay on the cot, while he felt along the line of the black and violet bruises. The dull pain radiating from the bruises exploded across his chest each time he pushed in the right spots. But he forced himself not to show the pain while the enlisted men watched.

Sheriff Edmondson arrived in the front office. "It looks like we'll have a quiet day today. The army's finished clearing out the warehouses. There's nothing left for people to steal."

Harper buttoned the top of his long johns and his white shirt before he moved closer to the door, trying to hear as best he could. Unlike yesterday, he didn't feel dizzy from the quick movement, although his head still ached.

If Forrest had finished his assignment, Harper needed to learn what he could about the Rebels' plan for the prisoners. There wasn't much time left before they were on their way deeper into Dixie.

Edmondson took the seat at the desk, beyond Harper's field-of-view.

Harper heard Holiday ask from the chairs along the side wall, "Did they say how long it would be before the Yankees get here?"

"Forrest thinks they're about a day away. We might see some of their scouts this afternoon."

"What are we supposed to do with the prisoners?"

"I don't know. Hell, maybe they might even have forgotten about them in the confusion."

Harper called from his cell. "I doubt that's true, Sheriff. Captain Bell will certainly remember."

"You're probably right, Lieutenant." Remaining in his chair, Edmondson poked his head around the corner of the doorframe. "You'd best gather yourselves together. I expect y'all'll be movin' today. Tomorrow, at the latest."

"With our army comin' back to Nashville, Sheriff, maybe you could just let us go? After all, we're not *your* prisoners." Harper looked into Edmondson's eyes. "I'll make sure General Grant knows about it."

Edmondson looked at the floor, appearing to think about the proposition.

"Ya would be savin' us from years in a prison camp. And you'd be doin' something that the new military governor would consider an act of loyalty."

Edmondson shook his head and looked back at Harper. "Sorry, Lieutenant. The town's under martial law, and what happens to you is a military matter. It ain't my concern." He stood up and walked into the doorway. "Besides, I don't favor the idea of gettin' shot in the back by one of Forrest's bushwhackers." He looked at the other prisoners. "You men get ready to move. If you're still here tomorrow, I'll see if I can work a special breakfast for y'all."

He turned away and closed the door separating the cell room from the front office.

****

At mid-morning, a Confederate officer came to the jail. Harper could hear enough of their conversation through the closed door to know that it concerned the prisoners. Deputy Morris entered the cell room and released Harper, directing him into the front office, closing the door to the officer afterward.

The officer stood in the rectangle of light coming through the window in the side wall. He wore the black slouch with one side pinned up next to the crown and a white star in front. A brassard adorned the sleeve of his precise uniform. Harper assumed he was some sort of duty officer for the day. Maybe there was hope yet if their fates were to be placed in the hands of someone besides Bell. At least, this officer looked a cut above the criminals who made up Bell's company.

"Morning, Lieutenant. My name is Frank Dupree, Eighth Texas Cavalry. Let's sit down." Harper saw a man slightly taller than himself, with light-brown hair. Dupree carried himself with the easy confidence of a man used to holding authority. Like Harper, the Rebel officer appeared to be about thirty.

"James Harper, First Iowa Infantry."

Dupree signaled Morris and Holiday to leave them alone. Morris looked at Harper and nodded before picking up the shotgun lying on the desktop. He waved for Holiday to follow him onto the porch. Morris sat near the door, within easy earshot of their conversation.

Harper took the opportunity offered by the interchange between Dupree and the deputies to look around the front office for easy access to any weapons. The oak rifle cabinet in the corner appeared to be locked.

Dupree closed the door to the cell room before he took the seat behind the desk. "Have a seat, Lieutenant."

Harper brought a chair from along the wall of the office and sat facing Dupree across the desk. The Rebel captain wore an immaculate gray uniform showing all of the requisite insignia and gold braid appropriate to his rank in the Confederate army, with wear spots at the elbows and knees. Harper felt like a common street urchin in his plainer blue uniform with blood and grass stains, dirt, and powder burns from the battle seven days earlier.

Dupree dropped his cavalry gloves on the desk, laid his large black hat over them, then pushed these to the side. There was an eagle's feather sewn into the band behind the pinned-up brim, apparently the only departure from the regulation uniform Dupree allowed himself.

"I have a parole order from the city's military commander for you, with further orders to send you back down the river on your own." Dupree spoke with an accent Harper did not recognize. "Here is your parole, Lieutenant." Dupree took a paper from the inside pocket of his jacket and pushed it across the table.

Harper reached for the paper, but stopped short when pain shot through his right side and back. He used his left hand to take the paper and unfold it. While he did so, Dupree took a scented handkerchief from the sleeve of his jacket and held it in front of his nose. The smell of lavender wafting across the desk caused Harper to look up from the papers.

"I need you to sign a receipt for the parole and you're on your way. You're to take no active role in the war until you've been exchanged for one of our officers of equal rank."

Harper watched Dupree's expressions, trying to detect any duplicity in the man's brown eyes. There was none to be found. Dupree maintained the stiff features of a man ordered to carry out an unpleasant task. "This doesn't say anythin' about the enlisted men. Do ya have paroles for them, Captain Dupree?"

"We don't parole enlisted men, Harper." Harper saw Dupree's head shake ever so slightly and one side of his mouth dip, as if in disappointment. "Sorry."

Dupree's handkerchief reminded Harper he and his men still wore the same clothes from their capture a week earlier. He was accustomed to the smell, but now, he realized the dried blood would have gone to corruption, adding the smell of death to the reek from his own body. There was nothing he could do about it until he had a chance to bathe and to wash the clothing.

Harper returned his attention to the parole certificate in his hand. "So, I'm supposed to simply walk away and leave them here?" This wouldn't do. He needed to persuade Dupree to break the rule.

"They'll get marched south when we leave and then come home when they're exchanged or the war is over. They'll be all right."

"Everyone says that it's gonna to be a short war. Do you believe that, Dupree?"

"That's what people say."

"What do *you* think?"

"I don't know." Dupree broke eye contact and looked away.

That said it all. If his men went south as prisoners, they would be there for years. The South was just too large and the hatred over the politics was too strong. Every single southern city would need to be subdued. It would take years for Federal armies to occupy all of them, and it would take hundreds of thousands of Federal soldiers to control the entire southern population. Soldiers who did not now exist. And the National government was unlikely to win the war if it did anything less than occupy all of the Southern states.

"What happens to your men is going to happen whether you stay or not. If you don't accept the parole, you'll be sent to an officers-only prison in Atlanta once we evacuate Nashville."

Harper had only one more day to find a way to escape. He did not want to spend years in a Rebel prison. But if he left these men behind, he'd have a tough time living with that decision. Added to the mistake at Belmont, no one would ever trust him again.

They had tried for six days to find an escape. There had been no opportunity during the march and as long as they stayed locked in the cells it was hopeless. On the other hand, he needed to get word back to Grant's headquarters that Bosley was a spy. With the parole, he could travel down the river unmolested until he reached Clarksburg or Fort Donelson. Maybe that would be enough justification for leaving the men. He could never join another Iowa regiment, but maybe Grant could find some useful role for him.

"What would y'all do, Captain Dupree? Just leave your men here?" Harper heard himself unconsciously slip into southern usage after a week among the Rebels. It was a slip of the tongue. He wouldn't let it happen again.

"Fortunately for me, Lieutenant, I don't have to make that choice. *You do.*"

Harper paused to think. He heard voices from his men still in their cells, although he couldn't understand what they said.

"Captain, I can't make a decision like this in such a short time."

"How much time do you think you would need, Harper?"

"A few hours, I think."

"In that case, I'll be back this afternoon." Dupree collected his gloves and hat. "Jailer!"

Harper stood when Dupree did, forcing himself upright through the pain in his back. He handed the parole back to Dupree.

Dupree rose from his chair when Morris and Holiday entered. "I've finished with Mister Harper. You can put him back into his cell."

****

Deputy Morris locked the door to Harper's cell. "Looks like you're goin' to be here for another day, Lieutenant." His smile was friendly enough, although Harper noticed how he was watchful against any sudden motions Harper made.

Harper stared back through the cell bars at Morris. "I need to get out of here, Morris. Myself and all of the men. We need to get back to the army." Once more, Harper tried to play on Morris's loyalty; the man's son was in the Federal army, after all.

The smile left Morris's face. "There's nothin' I can do to help you. Sorry." He looked away from Harper.

"The man we saw last night with the whores goin' into Forrest's headquarters is a spy. I need to get that information back to General Grant." Maybe Morris could be persuaded if he thought he was part of a counterspy scheme.

Morris turned toward the door. "There's nothin' I can do. No one's escaped from this jail in the twenty years that I've worked here and I'm not gonna be a part of letting someone out."

"But we're not criminals!" Harper took a breath. "We are the army of the legitimate government of this country."

Morris took a step toward the office. Harper reached through the cell bars to grab his sleeve. "Ya wouldn't be lettin' criminals escape, you'd be doin' a loyal service for your true country."

"I can't do it Harper." Morris pulled loose. "Not now. I'm sorry."

****

Exactly one week after her encounter with Evilface, Katie found herself following Eleanor into the main entry of the newly built McCracken County Courthouse on Walnut Street. Word had come to *Lafitte's Hideout* on Wednesday that many of the wounded soldiers from nearby battles had arrived in Paducah for treatment before being sent to hospitals closer to their hometowns. General Sherman's garrison troops had converted the large four-story courthouse into an army hospital along with several of the churches and other public buildings.

Katie knew that Eleanor had come to the hospital each day since then, but this was the first time that Eleanor had asked anyone else to come with her. Normally, they would all be preparing for a busy Saturday night crowd.

"Why have you brought us here, Eleanor?" Maggie, tall and mature, the newest of the women working at *Lafitte's*, walked alongside Eleanor in the lead. Katie walked behind with Julia, a former assistant postmaster from Hopkinsville, Kentucky.

"I need your assist-*ance* to carry these baskets and there is something that I want all of you to see."

Each of the four carried a wicker basket on her arm, under their cloaks to protect the contents from the dust and chill of the February afternoon. These were filled with various breads, jerky, and sweetmeats for the wounded men and covered by large napkins. The women wore sunbonnets with their hair tucked up underneath. The bonnets included stiff side panels to hide their faces from passers-by. Eleanor had ordered Toby and Thomas to stay with the buggy, parked a discrete distance away on Clark Street at the side of the building.

"Eleanor, did you ever learn if Miss Loreena's brother was one of the men captured?" Katie asked as they approached the stairway leading to the hospital entrance.

"*Mais, oui*. The men have told me that his regiment was not at the Fort *Henri*."

The four-story building was a massive cube with the main entrance on the second floor above a partially sunken cellar. When she looked up into the windows which covered the front façade of the building, Katie could see soldiers seated behind most of the windows, now closed against the February chill.

A blue-coated soldier held the front door open for the women before continuing on his way. After she passed through the door, Eleanor crossed a large lobby with the other three following. Walls made of half-wood, half-clouded windows, lined the sides of the lobby with four sets of matching doors on each side, each aligned to a counterpart across the lobby.

Eleanor stopped at a large counter which blocked access to a wide stairway at the rear of the lobby. There sat a sergeant with two women, one on either side. The soldier and the lady on Katie's left had watched them since their arrival. The other woman, dressed in a plain gray frock with a folded white kerchief covering her hair, continued writing on a stack of papers.

"Good morning, *Serg-ant* Wortman, I've brought some friends today. We have special treats for the soldiers."

Katie, Julia, and Maggie stayed behind Eleanor.

Wortman smiled back. "Afternoon, Miss Eleanor." He looked at each of the other three women. "I reckon they'll be glad to see you."

"Do you think you're going to give them to *my* boys?" The eyebrows of the woman next to Wortmann were arched and her lips seemed set in a permanent frown.

Katie was surprised by the harshness of the woman's voice. It seemed out of place for a hospital, especially since they are there to offer help.

"We all do what we can to help, Missus Little." Eleanor bowed slightly to the woman. "We would be *'appy* to share with the men on the second floor, if *you* would allow us."

"Those good boys don't need your kind tendin' to them." The woman looked at each of the women from *Lafitte's Hideout* before turning her glare back at Eleanor. "They have plenty of decent volunteers from town who are proper ladies. They do just fine seein' to the patients' comfort and to help them keep in the Lord."

The woman wearing the nurse's uniform stopped writing and looked up at the four visitors, examining each one, assessing.

"And I am *certainement* that the sold-*aires* are immensely grateful to your ladies, *madam*."

Eleanor must have known that there would be problems, because she had directed all of them to wear their plainest house dresses and no make-up. Eleanor's face was blocked from Katie's view, but she heard something in Eleanor's tone that sounded less than friendly, in spite of the words being said.

"For helping them to stay on the path of *virtue*–especially since they are barely able to escape their beds." Eleanor turned to face Wortmann and Katie could see that her expression remained pleasant. "I wouldn't wish for *our* presence to make them ov-*aire*, uh…*stim-u-*

lated, non?"

A chuckle forced its way past Wortman's lips before he could stifle it with a stern expression. The nurse hid the tiniest of smiles by looking down at her papers.

Little scowled at Wortman before looking back at Eleanor. Blood rose into her face. "I- I-I should say n-not."

"*Bon*. Then, we agree. I'm cer-*tain* the blue sold-*aires* prefer the company of your ladies–with their Bibles, of course."

Wortman's gaze caught Eleanor's partial smile and he had to bring a hand over his mouth, twisting his lips to avoid the threatening grin. Recovering quickly, he produced a thin steel spike from the top drawer of the desk. "I'll have to examine each of the baskets, Miss Eleanor."

"Certainly, *Serg-ant*." Eleanor placed her basket onto the counter and Wortman used the spike as a probe.

"I wouldn't want any of you to get into trouble for bringing any weapons into the prisoners."

"*Serg-ant*," Eleanor turned to the three women before she gave Wortman a coquette's smile and a small curtsey. "*We* would nev-*aire* do such a thing."

Katie wondered why the sergeant thought they were taking the treats to prisoners. Were the wounded soldiers also prisoners while they were in the hospital?

After Wortman finished with Eleanor, he moved around the counter and in turn probed each woman's basket.

"Do any of you have any level of medical training?" The nurse spoke for the first time.

Katie looked at Eleanor to see if she would answer the question. Julia and Maggie did also. But Eleanor remained silent.

After a brief silence, Maggie spoke first. "No, Sister. But I did raise three young-uns on a farm before the war took them. I'm the one who treated them when there were accidents. The farm hands too, plus some of the animals."

"Our young Katie used to be a farm girl, as well." Eleanor turned to address Katie. "*Chéri*, did you not tell me that you sometimes helped *sa maman* when people became ill?"

Katie looked up from Wortmann's poking in her basket and

nodded. "Yes, ma'am."

Wortman moved to examine Julia's basket.

"Nurse Cathcart, are you asking *them* to help nurse the soldiers?" Little stood up, fists on her hips.

Cathcart ignored her. "What about you?" She pointed the end of her quill pen at Julia. "Are you afraid of the sight of blood?"

"No, miss. I've seen blood and accidents. But I used to be a school teacher, not a nurse."

"Do you think you could wash out a serious wound?"

Julia's gaze shifted to Eleanor then back to Nurse Cathcart. "I suppose so."

"You can read, *non*?"

"Of course. I was a teacher."

"You're *not* going to let them work on *my* boys." Little's cheeks showed bright red.

"Missus Little." The nurse frowned at the indignant woman. "Remember, Missus Little, you are a *volunteer* in this hospital." She tapped a stack of papers on the desk. "*I* am the Director of Nursing, and I'll decide who can work here."

Little's face went to crimson. She emitted a *pfft* from her lips before she turned away in a grand swirl of her skirt and sat back down. Wortman returned to his place at the counter and stood between the two women.

Cathcart turned to address Eleanor. "Before the war, we were staffed by the government to treat as many as three hundred patients. Now, we have five times that number. I don't have enough nurses to do right by these poor men. Missus Little and her ladies do excellent work helping." She glanced over at Little and nodded with a slight smile. "But still there are not enough."

Eleanor looked away, tucking her basket under her cloak.

Cathcart nodded in the direction of the three women behind Eleanor. "I know that you have a number of women working for you who might have the skills that we need right now."

Little threw a stone paperweight onto her work area. Papers scattered and a *carte-de-visite* fell over revealing a Federal soldier and a piece of black ribbon pinned to it. Little snatched the *carte* and stood it properly on her desk.

Eleanor turned to the side and backed away a step. She glanced at each of her three companions, then back at the nurse. Katie could not understand the expression on her face: a smile on the lips but her brows were low and furrowed. "These women have their own work to do. They need to support themselves."

Katie looked at Julia and Maggie but their sideboards blocked her view of their reactions. As for herself, she was trying to think of how she would work at *Lafitte's* if she did volunteer.

"We would only need three or four at a time, and then only at the busiest times, an hour or so before and after meals."

"My *ladies* won't work beside *whores*." Little folded her arms under her large bosom, somehow making herself look larger and taller in her chair.

There was that word again, *whore*. Why was this woman so angry at them for earning a living entertaining the soldiers?

"We will go work at another hospital. There's plenty of them in the city, now that the war has really started."

Cathcart turned back to Little. "Ruth, dear," she smiled, her face calm with a sweet smile but cold eyes. "You know how short-handed we are. If these women are willing to help out, I'm sure we can keep them separate from your lovely volunteers, can't we?"

"I haven't said we could spare any of them, Sister."

At the same time as Eleanor spoke, Little demanded, "Now, how would you do *that*?"

The nurse continued. "We are the most short-handed in the prisoners' ward. So, Ruth," she nodded to Little, "If they come to work with us, I would put them in with the Rebels. Your women don't really care to go in there, anyway. They often leave poor Nurse Wells by herself most of the day."

Katie was confused. Who were the prisoners? It seemed that the 'nice' ladies would work with the good soldiers while the women from the saloon would work with the criminal soldiers. Katie had worries about just how bad these soldiers might be and for the first time hoped that Eleanor might say '*non*'.

Cathcart turned to Eleanor. "And you, Eleanor. I've seen that you usually visit in that ward anyway. Could it be true that you have some special feelings for these men, being from the South yourself? And not just you, but at least two of you others, eh?" Cathcart focused on Maggie and Julia.

The prisoners were from the South; maybe they were Rebel soldiers. Katie wondered how they would behave. They might also be evil soldiers or they might be here only because they, too, were wounded.

Katie followed Cathcart's glance and saw Julia and Maggie nod. Julia had once told Katie that she was from somewhere north of Nashville and her accent proved it. But Maggie's accent was nearly the same as Katie's, so Katie had assumed that Maggie came from the river country like her. Katie wondered how Cathcart decided that Maggie came from farther south.

"So, they would work only with the prisoners?" Little's brow relaxed, but not entirely; the pursing in her lips became less pronounced. "And we would not have to work with—" she flipped the back of her hand at the four visitors. "Those?"

Cathcart nodded and opened her mouth to speak.

"Just keep your whores away from my volunteers and from my patients." Little pointed to the staircase. "I don't want them using the main staircase, even if they do have to climb up to the fourth floor."

The nurse paused. "Miss Eleanor's women could use the stairs at the ends of the wing."

Katie could see that furrows and a pout were now on Eleanor's face. "We volunteer to help the poor sold-*aires*, and we are not to be treated with respect? We must use the servants' stairs?"

"No, no, no. You misunderstand. The side stairs are not for negroes. The nurses use those stairs so they can treat the patients and not have to go through the public areas around the staircase."

"I must think about this, Sister."

"Please do, Eleanor. May I call you 'Eleanor'? You've *seen* there are so many of them and they have no one here. It would help *so* much. Many suffer quietly. I think they're afraid to show how badly they are hurt because they think we will abandon them. Maybe if they hear a Southern woman's voice, it would help them to heal."

"*Humpffft*!" Little gathered the papers in front of her into a pile. Wortman took his seat.

Eleanor looked at Little. Katie saw the tiniest of smiles hint at the corners of Eleanor's mouth. With a sudden turn, Eleanor faced Cathcart. "Yes, Sister. We shall do it."

The nurse smiled. "Excellent. That will be such a great help."

"May we go up now?"

"Yes, of course. We can talk about the details for your volunteers later." Cathcart rose from her chair and offered her hand. "Missus Little, please log Miss Eleanor and her friends into the volunteers' record book."

"I'm doing it now." Little pulled a ledger book from a shelf under the counter. She read out loud as she wrote. "Start time, one-thirty. Four whores."

****

Gustav Magnusson waited until Morris passed into the front office and onto the porch. "What did the officer want to talk about, sir?"

Harper did not answer immediately. Magnusson watched him stand on his cot and open the window above, breathing the cool, fresh air.

"Sir?" Magnusson asked a second time.

Harper's actions seemed suspicious. He waited for Harper to step into the corner of the cell closest to Magnusson's. The officer spoke in a low voice, so the words would not carry to the front office. Bailey moved next to Magnusson in the corner of their cell, while Cooke and Davis cupped their palms around their ears to hear.

"He was the duty officer for the city garrison," Harper said. "He wanted to talk about givin' us paroles."

Magnusson had heard about paroles but didn't really understand how they worked.

"What's a parole, Mister Harper?" Bailey asked.

"It's an official document where a prisoner agrees not to fight anymore, and the captors agree to let him go."

"They can do that?"

"Sometimes they do, Bailey. But if they catch you fightin', then you'd be executed dead on the spot."

Davis laughed. "Kind of like callin' 'time-out' when we was kids fightin'."

"In a way." Harper looked at Davis and Cooke in the cell across the room.

"Ya mean that they give us a piece of paper," Cooke said, "And if we promise not to fight we can go home?" Cooke looked at Davis. "I'd like that!"

"Almost correct." Harper addressed Cooke. "Since y'all are still under your enlistment, you'd still have to follow orders, as long as it didn't involve gettin' into a battle. And it would end if the two armies did an exchange; if our army let some of their men go in exchange for our men."

Magnusson looked at Cooke. "That sounds too easy." He shook his head when his gaze shifted to Bailey before he looked back at Harper. "How come they didn't do it up to now? Why haven't we seen Yankee prisoners comin' back from the Rebs with paroles?"

Harper took a few seconds to answer.

Magnusson tried to read Harper's eyes. Harper glanced away, eyebrows lowered.

"What are you not telling us, Lieutenant?"

Harper stared straight at Magnusson. "Because up until now, they only gave paroles to officers."

Davis slapped a bar on the cell wall. "Of course." He turned his back on Harper and walked back to his cot.

Cooke said, "Officers always git treated special while the enlisted men do all of the work and suffer the most." He rattled the door of his cell.

Bailey fidgeted at Magnusson's side.

Harper stayed silent. But Magnusson didn't see any deception on Harper's face. Harper's frown and fixed gaze at Cooke and Davis seemed to Magnusson a sign of genuine disappointment.

"So, Mister Harper," Magnusson said, "does that mean you're gonna get out of here while we stay locked up?" As the senior enlisted man, Magnusson had to ask the question so they would all know for certain.

Harper pursed his lips before turning to face Magnusson. But he didn't meet Magnusson's eye. "No. I don't think so." He paused. "The Reb captain didn't have a parole for me. We talked about the possibilities. He's gone back to ask his commanding officer."

"Oh." Cooke folded his arms and leaned against the bars of the cell with one shoulder.

It didn't make sense to Magnusson that, if the Reb officer was ready to let Harper go on a parole, that they didn't have it prepared when he came to the jail. "So maybe we'll all get paroles, even though the Rebs haven't ever given any to enlisted men?"

"I hope so, Corporal."

Magnusson turned away. This was useless. They were all headed for a prisoners' camp. He would have to find some way for them to escape without Harper. "Ben, git back up on the cot. You too, Cooke." He turned to look at Harper. "See if you can *scout* any of our cavalry."

****

"Four visitors for the Rebs, Corporal Rose." Sergeant Wortmann led the way onto the fourth-floor landing.

Katie climbed the last few steps behind Julia and Maggie. On this floor, the landing was confined by new-built walls which closed off access to one wing of the hospital. A porcine corporal sat behind a desk in the spot where the nurses' station stood on the second and third floors and a single armed sentry stood guard in front of the double doors on Katie's right.

The rest of the area was filled with cots crowding the space where six or seven Federal soldiers lounged in the dim light. Most wore only their trousers over their long-john underwear. Weapons, mostly muskets but a few pistols and knives, leaned against the wall or hung from pegs within easy reach of each cot. At the sight of the women, several soldiers sat up, while others remained supine and leered at the unusal sight of known saloon girls inside the hospital.

"Howdy, Miss Eleanor." The corporal at the desk stood when he recognized the leader of the visitors. "I have to search your baskets before I can let you in."

"I've already taken care of that." Wortmann addressed Eleanor,

"I'll get back downstairs. I am so glad that you'll be working with us. These men need help."

"Thank you, *Serg-ant*, and for your help with *Madame* Little."

Wortmann addressed Rose. "Today is the first day that these women will be working with Nurse Wells. They'll be in and out, but they need to keep to the stairwells at the ends of the wing. Let all your men know."

"All right." Rose looked at the women again.

Katie was glad she had left off her make-up and worn her plainest day dress. The men around her stared but not in the way the soldiers did in the saloon. Katie stepped aside to allow Wortmann to descend the stairs.

"Here to see anyone in particular, Miss Eleanor?" With Wortmann gone, the corporal sat back in his chair and folded his hands over the bulge of his belly.

"No corporal, just to try to tend to the injured men. They get so few visitors."

Katie could feel sweat pooling at the base of her neck and soaking into the chemise under her dress. The heat from the rest of the building must collect at this landing because of the stairway. The two small windows were both closed, so no breeze moved the stale air.

"Hey, Baby Red, why are you wasting those goodies on the Rebs?" One of the lounging soldiers stood and walked over to Katie, the odor from the dirty top of his long-johns arriving ahead of him. He lifted her cloak and grabbed the basket underneath. Katie bent her arm so the basket handle locked into the crook at her elbow; she used her free hand to help hold the arm with the basket against her side.

Eleanor reached back and slapped the soldier's hand; she laughed when he let go. "They are all God's children, *Private–non*?" A scolding look accompanied Eleanor's emphasis on the man's apparent rank.

Addressing the corporal, she said, "I have a pass signed by *Cap-i-tain Jean-cock*. May I pass?" She carefully pronounced each syllable of Johncock's full rank and name, all the time maintaining her coquette smile despite the implied demand in her voice.

"Of course, ma'am." Corporal Rose fished a key-ring from a side drawer of the desk and stood up. "Get out of the way, Potter."

The smelly soldier backed away from Katie, clearing the way to the guarded doors. "Jes' havin' a little fun with Baby Red, here."

Katie scowled at her saloon name and looked away from the man, blocking him from her view with the sideboard of her sunbonnet.

Rose crossed to the double doors. "Open it. "

The guard on duty lifted a cross-beam out of the way so the corporal could work the doorlock.

"All clear, inside?"

A voice behind the door answered, "All clear, Corporal."

Rose unlocked the door and opened it. A uniformed private stood in the doorway who carried no weapons. When he saw the visitors, he stepped back to let them pass. "Afternoon, Miss Eleanor."

"*Bonjour.*" Eleanor entered the ward with Katie and the others following behind.

The smell of the place made Katie cough. It seemed as if she had walked into a wall of foul odors: sweat, urine, rot, vomit. She drew a scented handkerchief from her sleeve to place over her nose, but Eleanor stopped her.

"You must not, *chéri.*" Eleanor pulled Katie's hand away from her face. "These men know how *'orrible* it smells in here but there is nothing they can do to correct that. You will embarrass the wounded men instead of helping them."

Katie coughed to clear her throat of the smell and almost gagged. After a moment, she nodded her understanding to Eleanor who released her hand. Katie bowed slightly to smell the handkerchief a final time while she returned it to her sleeve.

The door slammed behind them, causing Katie to jump. This seemed an awful place, and she was no longer sure that she wanted to be here with its foul odors and scores of staring soldiers. *Enemy* soldiers. The cross-brace scraped the outside of the door before the guards dropped it into place with a thud. She was locked inside.

At least this room was cooler than the landing.

In front of the four women from *Lafitte's*, Katie could see hundreds of men lying on beds to her left and right. The beds were set with their headboards lining the walls, or in two rows of cots arranged along the center of the ward. There were dogs curled on pallets between both the beds and the cots. Odd that they would allow dogs in a hospital. When Katie looked more closely, she saw that these were not dogs but more men laid out on pallets.

"Let's go to work." Eleanor led the group to the side wall where they removed their cloaks and sunbonnets and hung them on pegs. Julia's long brown hair fell from the bonnet half-way down her back. Although Julia was twenty and once married, Loreena had required her to wear her hair long, the way an unmarried teen would.

There were three other women in the ward. Each sat with a soldier, but none wore a nurse's uniform.

"Maggie, you and Julia go that way." Eleanor pointed to the portion of the ward on the right. "You know what to do, *oui*?"

Maggie nodded.

"Katie and I will tend to this side." Eleanor pointed to the left side of the room.

The four women separated and approached the first groups of beds. Katie automatically stepped to avoid burning herself against a large, square, cast-iron stove placed between the junction of the rows of beds and the door to the rest of the hospital. The stove was matched by an identical unit at either end of the ward. To her surprise, the stove was cold, despite the time of year. Perhaps the hospital felt it unnecessary to heat the rooms in the early afternoon, but there was no pile of logs near the stove, either.

She followed Eleanor over to the first group of beds. Here, a window separated two beds and two soldiers lay between the beds where there should have been open floor space. For the first time, Katie saw that there was at least one crutch alongside each bed or cot.

Katie stood to one side, listened, and watched while Eleanor sat on one of the beds and spoke softly with each soldier in turn. Letting them know that she was from Louisiana, and that beginning today, she would be bringing more help for the nurses, asking where they came from, and how badly their wounds hurt. Most were from Tennessee, with a few from deeper south in Mississippi and Alabama. It occurred to Katie that she had never before met anyone from Mississippi or Alabama.

When she moved from group to group, Eleanor asked if the men had written home yet and if they needed help to write or to post any letters. She offered to post any letters for them. At each group, she held the hands of the man with the worst injuries. Then she let each man who was able take one or two treats from the baskets before moving to the next group.

Katie also watched along the ward at how Maggie treated the men. She looked so kind. On their side, both Maggie and Julia sat on the soldiers' beds while they visited. It surprised Katie how the two of them, as well as Eleanor, could act so light-hearted in this place. The men looked so miserable.

"Why aren't the nurses working?" Katie asked, referring to the other three women. She and Eleanor were a third of the way down the aisle, making their way to the next set of beds.

"They are not nurses, *chéri*. The only time the nurse comes here is an hour past meal times to help the sold-*aires* relieve themselves and to inspect their injuries. The women 'e-ah now are relatives of the wounded men." She nodded to the nearest woman. "The nurses count on them to change the bandages and to clean out the wounds each day. Also to clean up after those who cannot be moved."

Eleanor continued the story between visits with each group. "They are the only ones here who will help, except for what the men can do for each oth-*aire*–but that is not much."

They came up to one of the visiting ladies. She was close enough to have heard Eleanor's explanation. The woman added detail to Eleanor's story. "The soldiers are here because they're hurt so bad, they ain't nev-ah doin' any soldierin' again. Most have lost a leg or an arm. Others have worse damage inside."

Eleanor and Katie moved to join the men in the next two beds and one who lay on the floor between them.

"Is everyone all right this afternoon?" Eleanor asked.

"Is it true that saloon girls will be helping us here?" The woman watched Eleanor chatting with the men while talking with Katie.

"I think so. That's what Eleanor told the nurse downstairs." Katie looked at the woman's face to see tired, puffy, bloodshot eyes, surrounded by worry lines. Crow's feet and wrinkles along her frown line were set deep. But no gray showed in her hair. That made it difficult for Katie to guess her age.

"I suppose it's better than having no one here." The woman watched Eleanor in silence. The lines on her face gave her the appearance of a stern woman. "I'm Amanda Marstair." Amanda offered her hand to Katie, palm down.

Katie had seen ladies greet each other this way and knew what to do. She grasped Amanda's fingers and performed a short curtsey. "I'm Katie."

They both turned to watch Eleanor. Katie watched carefully to see the effect Eleanor had on the men. The faces of most lit up at the chance to talk with the beauty. Their color improved, and each seemed to have more energy. But some did not engage in Eleanor's conversations. They only stared at the ceiling or out of the window.

"The men don't seem to mind having saloon-girls tend to them."

Katie nodded. She wasn't sure what to say to the woman.

"What about you? Can you do anything except stare?"

"I do what Eleanor tells me, ma'am." Actually, Katie had not thought to do anything except follow Eleanor.

"Well, let's hope that the rest of your women can do better." Amanda reached for a bucket filled with bloody rags and red-tinted water. "Can you carry water, Katie? That would be a great help and doesn't require any nursing."

Katie looked at the noisome bucket. "I don't mind doing nursing, ma'am. So long as Eleanor says it's all right." She glanced back at Amanda's face. "And I know *some* things already."

Amanda looked skeptical. She turned to address Eleanor. "We need water, Eleanor. Shall we have young Miss Katie here fetch it?"

Eleanor looked up from her conversation with a soldier with an eye-patch and most of his left arm missing below the shoulder. "Yes. That's a very good idea. Katie, leave your basket 'ere. Get the wat-*aire* and then see what you can do to 'elp the men on the cots. Watch what Amanda does."

****

"Don't be stubborn, Harper. The parole is already drawn up. All you need to do is sign it. Then go back to Saint Louis or Iowa and sit out the war for a while." Brightly lit by the setting sun coming through the front windows, Dupree lay the parole certificate on the desk in front of Harper.

Dupree had reapplied the lavender scent after their earlier meeting and this odor mixed with the stench from Harper and his clothes. The sun lit the entire office, warming the air, increasing the effect of Dupree's lavender. Deputies Dodge and Howard, on duty since noon, waited on the porch.

"No, Dupree. I won't do it. I'll stay with the men." Harper pushed the parole back across the table to Dupree. There might still be chances for escape on the road after they left Nashville.

"You know that I had to work hard to get that parole, Lieutenant."

"I appreciate it must have been difficult, Dupree, but I won't go without the others."

Dupree frowned and shook his head before he snatched up the paper and held it out for Harper to reconsider.

Harper shook his head.

"Then, you'll have to share their fate."

Harper sat back in his chair, hands folded in his lap. "So be it." He hoped events would prove it was the right choice.

Dupree stared at Harper. He started to say something more, but stopped. He folded the paper and returned it to the breast pocket in his jacket. "So be it." He frowned. "I respect your decision, Harper, but I hope you don't come to regret it." He stood to leave and held out his hand.

Harper, too, doubted the decision was the right one, but there were no good choices. He stood and shook the offered hand, disguising the pain. "Thank ya, Captain Dupree."

Dupree went to the door but stopped before going through. He looked across the street at Bell's camp. "Jailer!" He looked back at Harper. "Mister Harper and I are going to take a stroll." He addressed Harper. "Come with me." Dupree walked past Dodge and Howard, not allowing them the opportunity to object. Puzzled, Harper hastened after Dupree into the chill air outside the jail.

Dupree did not respond except to allow Harper to catch up. They walked north along Front Street, paralleling the bluff above the river. Dodge and Howard remained behind, standing in front of the jail. The low sun stretched their shadows over the edge of the bluff. A four-horse wagon passed by, overloaded with furniture and other household items, moving south out of town. The gravel in the road crunched under its weight.

"What did you do before the war Harper?"

What did Dupree want? "I was a Deputy Marshal in the Nebraska Territory. What about you, Dupree?"

"My family are brokers. We export whatever Texas has to offer the world, mostly cotton. And we import manufactured goods from the North and from Europe."

Dupree carried himself like a man who was conflicted about something. Why else would he have brought Harper out of the jail, beyond the hearing of the deputies? If so, that could offer an advantage. He tried to keep the Texan talking, hoping to draw out the information held by the Rebel captain. "How'd ya come to be in the cavalry?"

They passed a causeway leading down to the boat landing next to the ruined bridge.

"Being in the right spot at the wrong time, I think. I was working in Paris when South Carolina left the Union. I came home when it became clear there would be troubles. But they didn't need me in Houston for the family business. So, when Colonel Terry sent out his call for volunteers, I joined him. Our families are very close." Dupree looked around. Satisfied, he stopped on the sidewalk under an elm tree.

Americanized French was the accent Harper heard in Dupree's voice. He had heard that accent among some of the trappers in his marshaling days. "So, your people are Cajun?"

"That's right. My family came to Houston from New Orleans right after Texas independence."

A company of three dozen riders passed, turning from Front Street into the city square. Dupree answered a wave from the lieutenant commanding the detachment.

"Your boys?" Harper asked.

"No. That's what's left of Company E. I'm on Colonel Wharton's staff." Dupree watched the troop ride past. "I'm Colonel Wharton's adjutant."

The troopers dismounted in front of the command tent. After being dismissed, they tied their horses' reins to the company hitch, a taut rope strung between two stakes driven into the ground. They undid the cinches on their saddles and began to tend to their animals.

Harper waited, wondering if Dupree was ready to discuss the matter which brought them out of the jail house. But Dupree remained silent and stared at the ground. Whatever he wanted to say must have him very troubled. Harper examined the cavalry camp surrounding the court house. Forrest's battalion filled the closer, southern half of the square. The mess of a camp recalled the hodge-podge of uniform parts Harper had seen during the march. Their tents scattered wherever the troopers decided to pitch them. The Tennesseans set their company taut lines on the edge of the square, facing Front Street.

There was a second unit camped in the northern portion of the square. Unlike the Tennesseans, this unit's tents lay in neat rows, all aligned with the long side facing south. Harper thought that was an interesting idea. Laid out that way, the tents would catch as much warmth from the winter sun as possible.

This unit's horses also faced Front Street in line with those of Forrest's battalion. The flag for this unit flew in front of the tent where the lieutenant had disappeared. There was a gap of ten yards or so between the Tennessee and Texas encampments.

"Dupree, do ya know what unit that is?" Harper pointed to the camp at the north end of the square.

"That is the Eighth Texas Cavalry. We call ourselves Terry's Rangers, even though Colonel Terry died in our first battle."

For the most part, the men in the Texas unit all wore the same gray jacket, red shirts, and brown trousers. It was a sharp contrast to the motley mixture of clothing Harper believed all of the Confederate cavalry wore. Oddly, the trimming on their gray jackets was bright red, the color normally reserved for the artillery. The fact they were Texans explained the white star most of the men worn on their wide-brimmed slouch hats, black like those of the First Iowa, but with a soft, creased crown perhaps half the height of the Hardee hat.

Their unit flag was different from that of Forrest's battalion. Both had dark blue fields inside wide white borders and white circles in the center. The new unit's flag was a rectangle, compared to Forrest's square, and in the center of the white circle it displayed a red cross with some insignia inside which Harper could not distinguish.

"Who is Colonel Wharton?"

"Colonel Terry was killed almost as soon as we arrived in Kentucky. Wharton took his place."

Each man in the Texan patrol brushed his horse after the lieutenant went inside the command tent. Harper nodded approval. "They know how to take care of their animals."

"Well, they've had enough practice for the last few months. Hell, we've seen most all of central Kentucky since November." Dupree nodded toward the Texas cavalry with a partial smile. "Besides, most men in Texas know how to take care of horses. It's born in them."

Without thinking, Harper began to count the company horse hitches for both units: twelve for the Tennesseans and ten for the Texans; that would give him a close estimate of the number of men. Twelve lines in Forrest's battalion, so twelve companies. He wasn't sure if he would ever be in a position to use the information, but force of habit drove him to calculate: nine or ten hundred in Forrest's battalion and six to eight hundred of the Texans.

Dupree turned to face Harper, suddenly earnest. "Tomorrow, Harper, look after your men."

****

Katie brought the bucket of clean water to the cot where Amanda sat talking with a captured soldier. She placed it next to the cot and handed Amanda the bundle of rags she had washed before she turned to walk back to Eleanor.

Amanda stopped her. "Watch me, Katie. Eleanor wants you to learn how to treat the wounded men. Stay here."

Katie looked to Eleanor for confirmation, but Eleanor was engaged with another soldier and was too far away to ask without raising her voice. She turned back and nodded to Amanda.

After they finished treating the soldier, they moved to the next cot. Here lay a teenager barely older than Katie, with chin-whiskers struggling to form into a stringy, thin beard. The boy tossed from side to side on the cot in tattered underwear soiled with dirt, sweat, and urine. Both arms showed above the blanket but Katie could see that the blanket was flat where his right leg would normally be. Instead, she saw a wet spot on the blanket, stiff and hard, below his hip. The smell of rotting meat was stronger around this cot than in most of the ward.

"Poor Esau." Amanda shook her head when she came next to Katie. "There isn't much we can do for him."

The boy's face was flushed, so Katie placed her hand on his forehead. It felt much warmer than a normal person, but without sweat. Katie had seen fever at home, and by the way the boy tossed back and forth on his cot, Katie knew that his time of suffering was coming to its end.

Esau kicked from side-to-side and his blanket slid to the floor. When Katie bent to retrieve it, she came face-to-face with the source of the boy's torments, inches from her nose: the open wound festered purple, black, and white with fresh blood and greenish-white fluid making a puddle on the cot. A crude tourniquet made from a stick and a twisted lether strap, probably someone's belt, kept the boy's life-blood from flowing completely away. An inch of the splintered bone projected from the messy flesh.

"Oh!" Katie recoiled from the violent smell of the corrupted flesh and bone, falling backward before she could catch herself.

Everyone nearby turned to look at her sitting on the floor, while the boy in the cot started to shout.

"I ain't a'feared of no damn Yankee, Jacob." The boy's entire body flinched. "C'mon, let's get at 'em!"

"Are you alright, *chéri*?" Eleanor stood from the bed where she had been joking with a flirty soldier. She placed the soldier's hand on his chest and came over to Katie.

Katie felt her face warm in a blush. "Yes, ma'am. I'll be all right." She brought her feet under her and Amanda helped her to stand.

"She'll be alright, Miss Eleanor. She jes' got a little too close to young Esau's spoilt leg." The soldier in the cot next to the boy's pointed to the rotting stump. "Jes' let her catch her composure." He smiled at Katie. She returned the smile then dipped her head to hide her blush.

Eleanor whispered, "*Chéri*, it is so sad. But there is nothing left to do for that boy." In a low, calm voice she said, "There is no doctor, *chéri.* Not for the pris-o-*naires*." She placed her hand on the side of Katie's shoulder. "And only one nurse. That is their fate."

Amanda looked at the floor when Eleanor said this.

"Where is the doctor, Eleanor?" Katie looked at the other women in the room, then at the guards. "How could they let him get into this condition?"

"He came to us that way, Katie." Amanda stared at the boy on the cot.

The soldier next to Esau spoke again. "He got shot early-on when the Yankees first got to Fort Donelson. A sharpshooter hit 'im. He would have died if'n the sergeant hadn't carried him back to cover. But because of the sharpshooters, they had to wait all day until dark before they could carry him to a doctor."

"How can that be?" The notion that no doctor would come to tend to these men confused Katie. It did not make sense that there would be no doctors in a hospital.

"All of the doctors have gone to *l'armée* or else they are working in other *l'ôpitals*."

Amanda continued. "There are only four doctors here and they spend all day working with the Federal soldiers. They only come up here if they have time to spare, and they almost never have time to spare. There is a nurse, but she is assigned both here and downstairs."

"Eleanor, that ain't right, somebody needs to do something."

"That is why I brought you, *chéri*. To help. All of these men are too badly hurt to go to a prisoner camp. The army has sent out the word that they will be released because they cannot fight any more. So, they wait here for the two armies to agree on how to send them 'ome."

"How long will that take?"

"No one can say. In the meantime, *l'ôpital* and the *l'armée* do not take responsibility for them."

Katie looked at Esau fussing on the cot and remembered that she still held his blanket. She spread it over the boy. Steeling herself against the signs and smells, she knelt down next to him and tried to calm him by stroking his head. Amanda gave her one of the cleaned rags. Katie dipped it in the bucket, wrung out the excess water, and folded it across Esau's forhead.

At her touch, Esau froze in place and after a few strokes, a small smile grew from hot dry lips and his face lost the contours of his delirium. "Mama?"

"We will need a lot of clean water." Amanda rolled back Esau's blanket and began washing the torn flesh. Someone had already cut away the trouser leg to expose the wound. Amanda shook her head. "Not even a badage large enough to wrap around his leg. There is never enough."

Katie was still unable to believe that a hospital would treat these men worse than she had treated the sick animals when she lived on the farm. "We must do something, Eleanor."

"We will, *ma petite soeur*." Eleanor stroked Katie's hair while Katie continued to soothe Esau's torment.

Katie felt a wet drop on her head. She looked up at Eleanor's water-filled eyes.

"We will."

Katie felt a flush of warmth surround her heart and she leaned her head against Eleanor's skirt. It was the first time anyone had called her 'sister'.

****

"Forrest's headquarters is a mess: men running around, issuing orders, sending messengers everywhere, trying to move what's left in town down the road south." Dupree looked around the street. "I'm sure they've forgotten about you prisoners entirely. I know no one over there is thinking about how to move your men tomorrow."

Harper took a step back and looked at the trunk of the elm. Was this the reason for Dupree's conflict? He must have seen busy headquarters before. There must be more.

"I-I'm afraid that those Tennesseans are planning something else before they leave." Dupree nodded toward Forrest's camp.

Harper had to lean forward again.

"Every one of them on Forrest's staff seems to hate Yankees like they hate the devil. They've caught it from Forrest."

Harper looked across at the Forrest's flag lying limp on its flagpole.

He recalled Captain Bell's willingness to let them starve during the trip from Donelson and the discussion about how Bell's company dealt with prisoners.

"I'm concerned they may decide to leave you here…but not alive. That's why Colonel Wharton was willing to sign a parole. Since he's not in charge here in Nashville, he really doesn't have the authority, even if he is senior to Lieutenant Colonel Forrest."

Harper looked into Dupree's eyes. He could see the Confederate officer honestly considered murder a possibility. Dupree was taking one hell of a risk.

Already, Harper had seen Bell murder without a second thought. But, did what Dupree said change things? If he took the parole, he would live to go back to Iowa. The men under his command would all be dead. He would have to live with that for the rest of his life.

The information about Bosley probably wasn't worth the lives of his men. Someone else would discover Bosley's duplicity, eventually. But to delay reporting might lead to more Federal soldiers being killed in the next battle. Harper looked up at a leafless branch, traced its arch with his eyes. Those were theoretical soldiers. His men were here, now. He turned to face Dupree. "I'm grateful for your kindness, Dupree, but I need a parole for all of us."

Dupree drew back and stared at Harper.

After a few moments, the frown returned to Dupree's face. He shook his head. "If you're resolved to do this, you need to know that I go off provost duty tomorrow morning at roll call. If they plan to do anything, it will happen afterward. You're obviously a brave man. I won't insult you by asking again if you'll reconsider taking the parole."

"Ya already know my answer. I wouldn't respect myself if I was coward enough to leave them behind to die." Maybe there was something he could do before Bell came looking for them.

Nearby, bells from a church tower sounded: *Bong. Bong. Bong. Bong. Bong.*

Dupree looked in the direction of the sound, then back at Harper. "Your men will need you in the morning, I fear." The Rebel captain turned and walked back toward the jail. Harper fell in alongside him. At the jailhouse, Dupree nodded. He offered his hand. "Good luck,

Harper. I'll stop by tomorrow, if I can."

Harper would stay with his men, but he had no idea how he could change what was coming.

****

Katie waited for Maggie and Julia to climb down from the buggy while the sun still hovered above the houses across Market Street. They had returned early from the hospital so they could prepare for the Saturday evening crowd. Loreena had insisted that they return early so that there were enough girls available. Eleanor stayed behind to make arrangements with Nurse Cathcart.

"We should use the door to Loreena's office," Maggie said. "That way, we don't have to go through the saloon or the dining room. It wouldn't do for the customers to see us in our regular clothes."

"Why not?" Katie asked.

"It might destroy the mystery, dear. The men come here to live out their sex dreams. Deep down, every man who comes here thinks that he is so manly that he can have a beautiful women whenever he wants. They want their conquests to be beautiful."

"You're beautiful already, Maggie. You and Eleanor and Julia."

"It isn't the same thing, Katie. If we were to look less fancy, like their wives or their sweethearts or their sisters, it would ruin their make-believe." Maggie looked up at the door to Loreena's office.

Loreena held the door open for a man dressed in a business suit. The man tipped his hat to them as he passed on his way to the gate that opened onto Court Street.

Loreena welcomed the three women into the office. "It's so exciting, ladies. So exciting."

"What is?" Maggie asked.

Katie closed the door against the February chill and stood next to the small office stove while she undid her bonnet.

"Well, it won't be official until Frankilin and Eleanor can sign the papers, but I've just agreed to buy the Patterson house down the street."

Katie wondered which one was the Patterson house. The buildings on Court Street were all businesses in both directions, and the public market filled Market Street on one side, so Loreena must be talking about one of the two large houses in the other direction on Market Street.

"Are you and Franklin planning to move, Loreena?" Julia unbuttoned the throat clasp on her cloak and folded it over her arm before untying the ribbons of her sunbonnet.

"That would be nice, wouldn't it?" Loreena took the seat behind her desk and lean back looking with a distant stare. In a moment, she refocused. "No. Not that."

Loreena leaned forward and picked up a pile of papers which she held out to Maggie. "We are going to buy the Patternson house and turn it into a gentlemen's club."

This news interested Katie. She could guess what the difference was between a saloon and a gentlemen's club. Her head filled with images of large men sitting in overstuffed chairs smoking pipes and reading large books, the way she had seen on the posters in the market which advertised pipe tobacco and cigars.

"Eleanor will be in charge over there, and she wants you," Loreena pointed to Maggie, "and Julia, Amelia, and the two Annas to shift over there when they're ready."

Loreena hadn't mentioned Katie's name as one of the women to transfer to the new place. Katie wondered if there was a mistake. "What about me, Loreena? Why cain't I go over there?"

"Just a minute Katie." Loreena faced Maggie. "We're going to call it *The Officer's Club*. The army officers will go there now instead of having to use the card room in the saloon. We'll make it more refined and the girls will be assigned to entertain one officer each night. You know, quiet conversation, music, book readings, poetry, maybe dancing. They'll pay a flat fee each night, whether they want to stay for the night or not. It'll even have darkies working as house servants."

To Katie, this sounded like Eleanor's plan to create a place that was more high-class than the saloon–a place where Eleanor would have *courtesans* working for her. But Eleanor had promised to teach Katie how to be a *courtesan*. This was happening too fast. Katie hadn't started her training yet the way Eleanor had promised. Katie was going to be left behind.

"Well, that sounds very nice." Maggie said. "I know Julia and

Anna. They'll be good for the new place. But Amelia and the other Anna just started working here. Are you sure they're suitable?"

"They both worked with me and Eleanor in Memphis. They'll do nicely." Loreena looked at Katie. "Don't pout so, Katie."

Katie didn't realize she was pouting. She tried to recover her composure. "I-It's just that Eleanor sometimes told me that she would teach me to be a *courtesan* so I could entertain the richer customers and make more money."

"She hasn't forgotten, Katie." Loreena's face was kind. "There's good news for you, too."

Katie pushed the news about the new business to the side of her thoughts. Good news for her? "What is it, Loreena?"

"We are going to hire more girls to work here. More and more soldiers are going to be coming into town this spring, and we want to be ready. So we needed to shift you and Julia into a smaller room."

This didn't sound like good news to Katie.

"So this afternoon while y'all were at the hospital, I had Virgil and his men move your things."

She was the one who was moving? That wasn't fair. She had been here longer than most of the other girls. The smaller rooms were at the back for the house and were the first to see the morning sun each day, making it more difficult to rest each morning.

"Why do I have to move? Why cain't it be Ruth or Nancy or other of the other girls? And you let Virgil and his men go through my things? How could you do that?"

Loreena held her hand up to cut Katie off. "Katie, just calm down." She lowered her hand in a patting motion as if trying to soothe a child. "I made sure that William watched them so that nothing went missing or got broken."

William was the upstairs manager. It was his job to protect the girls and to ensure that the customers followed the rules. If he kept watch over Virgil and his men, then things might not be as bad as Katie imagined. Even so, she would have to check to make sure that none of her jewelry, clothes, or other things were missing or damaged. It was a good thing that she had her money purse and her dagger with her.

Loreena folded her hands on the desk. "Eleanor hasn't forgotten you. She wants you to work at *The Officers' Club*, too."

Katie took a step back, surprised. Her curiosity quickly overcame her anger at having those vile men handling her clothes and belongings. "What do you mean? How can I do that? You just said who was going to work there."

"We want Julia to teach you some of the refinements that you need to entertain officers."

What refinements? Katie knew that she was just an uneducated farm girl, but she had been learning how to be a lady every day since she started working at *LaFitte's*. "What sort of refinements? Why cain't I just go to work there right away?

Loreena cast a frustrated glance at Maggie, then paused before answering. "Katie, you've been learning everything we've taught you quite well. But there's more to learn."

"Like what?"

"Well, how to hide your true feelings better no matter what you hear and to always speak softly, even when you're upset."

"Are you saying that I cain't do that now?"

"Well can you? It doesn't look like it to me."

Loreena had trapped Katie. The way she was behaving was exactly what Loreena said wouldn't be right.

"And you'll need to change that farm-girl language–'can't' instead of 'cain't', for instance." Loreena looked up at Maggie again.

Maggie walked over and put her arm around Katie's waist. "Come on, dear. We all want what's best for you. I'll help, too."

Loreena said, "Eleanor and I both think that you need more training. I'm sorry, Katie."

Katie's disappointment and anger melted. If everyone was going to help, maybe it wouldn't be so bad. "How long do you think it will be before I can work for Eleanor?"

Loreena looked at the stack of papers she had waved earlier. "If Franklin and Eleanor sign these tomorrow, we'll own the house by Monday night. Eleanor has some changes she wants to make to the way that the rooms are laid out both on the first floor and the second. There's even a servants' area below the first floor and extra sleeping areas in the attic."

Katie realized that changing so much in the house might take a long time. Maybe long enough for her to prove to Eleanor that she could be a *courtesan*, too. "How long will all that take, do y'all think."

"I'm not sure, dear." Loreena looked at Maggie. "Any idea?"

"I would expect at least a month. Maybe more."

Loreena addressed Katie again. "So, Katie. Maybe in a month you'll be ready?"

"Yes, I will." Katie nodded her head.

"Now, y'all go and get ready for work."

The noise coming from the saloon had risen during the few minutes of their conversation.

Loreena nodded in the direction of the saloon. "Sounds like they're ready for you."

Maggie used her arm to guide Katie toward the door to the hallway.

"Oh, Katie." Katie stopped face Loreena. "Eleanor told me that she wants both you and Julia to come to *The Officers' Club* at the same time. So that means that Julia will stay here teaching you until Eleanor thinks that you're ready. I think she has a special evening planned for when that happens."

That made Katie smile. It meant that Eleanor was certain Katie would learn fast and was planning a special party for her.

Life was getting better.

Sunday, February 23rd, 1862

Harper lay on his cot, listening to the Sunday church bells call their congregations to worship, fingering the pouch in his tunic pocket containing his wife's hair. On impulse, he pulled the pouch from the pocket and opened it. He laid both locks of hair on his chest and stared at them, remembering the days they had all spent together. The ribbons faded long ago, but still kept the locks gathered together.

How different his life would have been if they had lived. He would probably not be here in the cell this morning. Instead, he would be living with Emily in a ranch house on a bluff above the Missouri River, tending stock in a partnership with his brother and selling them to the emmigrants moving west. Ten-year-old Magda would be starting to grow into a young lady as beautiful as her mother—probably with a passle of younger brothers and sisters to look after.

But he had not been there when they needed him. Now, his men needed him and he had run out of ideas.

Harper's reality had become lying awake most of the night considering Dupree's warning. The morning light seemed to give greater clarity for the course he must choose. There *had* to be a way to escape. He couldn't let these men down. And Bosley had to be called to account.

On the riverboat landing, someone yelled commands. Harper rose and stood on his cot to learn what was happening. Below, the two remaining steam-powered tugs operated in the river abreast of the landing. Deckhands aboard the tugs and aboard the last of the beached barges worked with urgency, but not panic, to pass tow lines between the vessels. Harper watched the action for a time, but couldn't think of any way the action on the landing could be used in an escape attempt while he remained in the jail cell. It required most of the morning to organize the tows. When all was ready, the last river craft in Nashville steamed upriver.

The Federal army must be getting close. Confirmation that the Confederates had finished their assignment to evacuate the military stores and war-production equipment from Nashville came when the wife of Deputy Sheriff Morris brought a late breakfast for the prisoners, accompanied by her husband. She carried a steaming pot which hung from her arm by its large handle. But she hesitated before she came into the cell room, waving her hand in front of her face as if to push away the bad odors.

The thin woman, dressed in a modest but stylish navy-blue dress, shook her head and shoulders to gather her strength, then straightened her back and set her face in a forced smile before she stepped into the room. "Special treat for y'all today." She began to scoop scrambled eggs onto a metal plate held by Deputy Morris. "Bacon and eggs–because it's Sunday."

"The town seems quieter this mornin'." Harper watched the lady's sunken eyes while she completed the plate by adding three scraps of bacon. Maybe the wife would be more talkative than her husband.

"Ready Sarah?" Deputy Morris placed the wicker basket he carried onto the cell room floor before he drew his pistol.

She wiped her hands on the apron which protected the embroidered white trim on the bodice of her dress and spread across the front of her skirt. Harper saw a woman who was once a beauty. Her face now showed both the graying of age and creases of worry, while her cheek bones protruded from loose skin.

Instead of taking the plate she offered, Harper pointed to the cell holding Davis and Cooke. "Them first."

Morris and his wife moved across the room to the cell where the two enlisted men waited.

"Looks like the army's gittin' ready to leave." Sarah Morris continued preparing plates of food for Davis, Cooke, Bailey and Magnusson.

"Thank ya, missus." In turn, each man expressed his gratitude when he took his plate through the opening in the bars designed for this purpose.

After each of the enlisted men had a plate of eggs and bacon, Sarah Morris retrieved the wicker basket from the floor and removed the napkin covering a dozen warm biscuits. Each man politely reached through the bars of his cell to take one. The smell of warm eggs, pepper, bacon, and biscuits filled the cell room. Harper's mouth watered and his stomach let loose a growl.

"This is the best food we've had since we've been here, Missus Morris," Private Cooke said. His mouth made a crackling sound as he bit into a piece of crispy, hot bacon.

"Thank you, son," she answered. "It's the Lord's Day, and that's special. 'Sides, Jonathan tells me that y'all are goin' with the army today, so I thought to make y'all an extra special meal."

"Maybe the Rebs will forget about us, and leave us behind," Private Davis said between bites while he sat on his cot.

"Wouldn't that be nice?" She moved to Harper's cell.

Harper shook his head. "It's not likely. We're too valuable because they can exchange us for five of their own men."

"I suppose that's true." She prepared a plate for Harper. "I don't really understand about military things." She set the pot holding the leftover eggs in front of the cell bars where the men could ladle up second helpings. She and her husband shared breakfast in the front office with Dodge and Howard.

Each of the enlisted men took a second helping of the eggs. But the scraping noises from the pot when Bailey ladled up more eggs told Harper there was no second helping for him. Afterward, Sarah Morris collected the plates, bowls and spoons through the cell bars and left.

"Thank ya for your kindness, Missus Morris." Harper watched the lady leave. He sensed that the gray streaks in her hair told the story of the couple's struggles brought on by the war.

****

Following breakfast, Corporal Gustav Magnusson rested on a cot. His skirmishing partner, Ben Bailey, stood on the other cot looking out their cell window. For the first time in nearly a week, their bellies were full with solid food and not the watery gruel which caused cramps in his gut. Now he lay on the cot, thinking about what might happen to them next.

"Looks like the Reb cavalry are breaking camp." Lieutenant Harper relayed what he saw to the other prisoners shortly after the Morris woman left.

We have to do something soon.

Magnusson doubted that Harper would be much use in an escape. The deputies had hurt him pretty bad. The short, nasty one might have killed him if Harper hadn't rolled down the bluff. Harper must be a tough one to stand up to those men for so long. He was unconscious when they went to get him, and he didn't wake up until several hours after sunset. Was Harper even thinking about escape now? After all, the Texan would have a parole for Harper, alone—if he had asked for it. Magnusson was certain of that.

Magnusson could see the pain in Harper's eyes each time he moved, even though Harper tried to hide it. Someone would have to teach those deputies a lesson one day. It wasn't right for them to beat up prisoners, especially since they weren't even supposed to be in a civilian jail.

The rest of the morning passed quietly with very little activity on the portion of the landing that Bailey and Magnusson could see from their cell window. Magnusson could trust Bailey's sharp eyes to let them know if there were any Federal soldiers on the opposite side of the river. Nothing yet.

Church bells sounded the noon hour, when Shepperton and a young deputy came on duty. "You." Using his shotgun, Shepperton pointed to Cooke. "Bring out your bucket."

Shepperton was an arrogant son-of-a-bitch. Would the short deputy be so brave if he didn't have that shotgun?

Magnusson watched Cooke carry the honey bucket to the cell door.

"Go ahead, Werts. Open the cell." Shepperton moved aside, keeping Deputy Werts out of the line-of-fire.

Werts opened the door to the center cell only wide enough to allow the bucket through. Magnusson passed the bucket to Cooke who transferred the contents into a single bucket before moving to Harper's cell. Once Cooke collected all of the wastes, Werts directed Cooke through the door to the front office, heading down to the river.

"Well, how're y'all doin' this mornin'?" Both hammers cocked, Shepperton walked past each of the cells tapping the barrels of the gun against the iron bars. "All comfy-cozy I 'spect."

Magnusson stood his ground at the bars when Shepperton approached. His scorn for Shepperton held him in place.

"You back away, boy." Shepperton poked Magnusson's shoulder through the bars with the barrels of the gun.

Magnusson stayed silent, staring at the ceiling. He towered over the deputy by nearly a head and did not budge, even when Shepperton pushed the muzzle of the gun into his belly. He knew Shepperton wouldn't fire the shotgun. There would be too much to explain, and there were too many witnesses.

"Corporal, no!" Harper was at the bars to his cell. "Not now."

Magnusson stayed in position, staring down into Shepperton's eyes.

"Best back away, boy. I've kilt men bigger 'n you."

"This isn't the time, Corporal," Harper said. "Don't give him an excuse to shoot."

There wouldn't be a better time. Only one deputy now, within easy reach, with a gun and the keys to the cells.

Davis was on his feet and in the corner of his cell closest to Magnusson's. He tried to grab Shepperton but the deputy avoided the hand. Seeing Davis's actions, Bailey moved up to the cell bars next to Magnusson.

Magnusson looked across to Harper who shook his head.

"Humph." Magnusson took a step back.

The tension left Shepperton's face. "Scared, big boy? You'd best git back." He rattled the barrels of the shotgun against the bars.

In an instant, Magnusson grabbed the weapon and pushed the barrels toward the ceiling.

B-bam!

Both barrels discharged together, their sound amplified by the brick and plaster walls of the cell room. Inside the cloud of gunsmoke, Magnusson's ears rang. Pieces of the ceiling plaster fell around both himself and Sheppperton. With his free hand, Magnusson grabbed the deputy's shirt and pulled him against the cell bars. Bailey stretched through the bars for Shepperton's pistol. Davis tried, but could not reach far enough to help.

Shepperton released the shotgun and reached for his pistol. His hand collided with Bailey's. Both men fought for the gun. The deputy tried to back away but couldn't escape Magnusson's grip. The large corporal watched Shepperton's expression shift from surprise, to anger, to fear.

With his free hand, Magnusson lifted the shotgun by the warm barrels. He pounded the stock down onto Shepperton's nose. The deputy staggered backward, knocking into the stove. Dodge and Howard came through the door from the front office, pistols drawn. They aimed at Magnusson.

"No!" Harper yelled and reached through the bars to push Howard's gun hand down.

Dodge walked to the cell bars and pointed the pistol at Magnusson's forehead. He clicked back the hammer. "Back away, son. I don't much care to shoot a prisoner in his cell, but I will if I have to."

Magnusson threw the unloaded shotgun to the floor in front of Shepperton. With a spit in Shepperton's general direction, Magnusson turned his back, walked to the cot and lay down. He had done all he could–for now.

The deputies stayed alert, watching the other prisoners but keeping their pistols pointed at Magnusson.

"It's all over, deputies," Harper said. "No one is makin' trouble here except Shepperton."

Dodge and Howard swung their pistols from cell to cell watching the movements of the prisoners. Shepperton used both hands to cover his face, fingers pushing against his bleeding nose.

"Git back, god-damn it!" Dodge waved his pistol at Davis and Bailey. "Back against the walls." Howard tested the locks on each cell door while keeping his pistol aimed at the prisoners.

Werts and Cooke arrived, both breathing heavily. Werts pushed Cooke toward his cell before taking a place alongside Shepperton. Cooke moved to the cell, his brows arched into a question. Dodge opened the door and pushed Cooke inside.

"You son-of-a-bitch Yankee-bastard!" Shepperton moved to the bars of Magnusson's cell. "You broke my god-damn nose."

Magnusson did not react. Shepperton was lucky his nose was all Magnusson could reach. Instead, Magnusson fixed his gaze at the ceiling where the smoke from the shotgun spread across the plaster ceiling.

"Ya deserved it," Harper said.

"Shut up, you." Shepperton yelled, but did not turn away from Magnusson.

Magnusson watched the smoke drift across the ceiling, its sulfurous smell of spoiled eggs replacing that of the scambled eggs. "You're lucky I didn't break your neck. I've had to deal with your kind before. You're nothin' but a bully with a badge–a gutless little shit with a badge." He rolled on the cot and sneered at Shepperton.

Shepperton reached for his pistol.

"Hold it, Shepperton," Harper said. "What do ya think will happen to you when our army gets here and learns that ya murdered a Yankee prisoner who was locked in his cell?"

Dodge grabbed Shepperton's arm. "Don't do it, Julius. This ain't like the other day."

Shepperton stayed frozen for a moment. Pistol half out of its holster.

"Not now." Dodge kept his hand on Shepperton's arm. "Not here."

"Go ahead." Magnusson swung his feet to the floor and stood up, arms opened wide. "Let the little shit coward shoot a locked-up, unarmed man."

A glob of blood leaked from Shepperton's nose. Magnusson watched it drop to the floor.

"Don't think I wouldn't do it Yank." Shepperton pushed the pistol into its holster. "But y'all git yours Yankee-boy…Soon!" He turned and walked to the door, wiping the blood from his nose on his sleeve. At the threshold, he yelled back. "Y'all's gonna git what you deserve, and right soon, now."

One-by-one, Werts, Howard, and Dodge backed out of the room. Dodge was last to leave. Through the haze of the gunsmoke, Magnusson heard: "Thank god we'll be rid of them this afternoon."

****

"Mister Harper," Cooke whispered across the cell room. Harper stood and went to the cell bars. Magnusson came to the front of his cell to listen, but signaled Bailey to stay back, so as not to draw the attention of the deputies in the front room.

"Sir," Cooke continued, "just now when I was I down by the river, I saw one of our cavalry boys on the other side. He saw me too–I made certain of that. He drew a bead on the deputy, but I stood between 'em and broke up the shot. I held up five fingers so he could see there were more of us."

Here was probably their best opportunity to escape. The Confederates might not have the chance to transport them south. Buell might attack while they were still in the jail.

"There they go," Dodge called out from the front office. "Packin' up their tents and gittin' ready to skedaddle." Harper could see Dodge through the door to the front office, standing at the front door of the jail, watching the soldiers tear down the cavalry camp in the town square. "Damn army's jes' gonna leave the city to the Yankees." Dodge spat a wad of tobacco into the street.

Harper thought fast. At any moment, Forrest's troopers could be coming to put them onto the road south. There were now four deputies in the jail because Dodge and Howard did not leave when Shepperton and Werts came to work. These were the same deputies who attacked him. There wasn't much chance of them looking the other way while the five soldiers escaped.

Cooke whispered across the room. "Maybe 'em cavalry will come across the river and get us? Do ya think, Mister Harper?"

"Maybe." Harper glanced toward the front office. "How many did ya see?"

"Just the one."

Magnusson climbed onto the cot and looked through the window of his cell. "There's a few more out there, Mister Harper," he said. "But not more than a patrol. I don't see any others." He stepped back from the window and took off his blue tunic.

"What ya doin'?" Harper asked.

"Ben, open that window." Magnusson turned to Harper. "I'm goin' to hang my coat out and wave it around, so's the fellows over there know where we are. I figure if they see the uniform, they'll try to help us." The rusty hinges on the window squealed in protest when Bailey propped the window open.

Magnusson's idea made sense to Harper and it would give them something to do while Harper tried to think of an escape plan.

"Y'all fixin' a jail break?" Deputy Howard asked, either expectation or hope in his voice. He carried a double-barreled shotgun in addition to the pistol at his hip.

"Can't. There's still the bars over the window," Magnusson answered.

"The boys are fixin' to wave hello to our cavalrymen on the other side of the river." Harper smiled. "If ya let us go, I'll put in a good word for ya with General Grant."

"You go to hell, Yank." Howard swung the barrels of the shotgun toward Harper. "You *and* your General Grant!" He turned and walked back into the front office.

"They'll be here tonight!" Harper yelled at Howard's back.

"Maybe. But you all won't be. Here's Captain Bell comin' right now to git y'all."

****

"What happened to him?" Bell pointed to the corner of the office beyond Harper's line-of-sight.

"Had some trouble with a shotgun." Howard laughed.

"Go to hell." Shepperton's voice sounded like a honking goose.

Dodge and Werts brought the prisoners out two at a time, leaving Harper for last. When each prisoner entered the front room, one of Bell's men tied their hands behind their back and led them out to the porch.

When it was Harper's turn, he looked at Shepperton as he went through the office. A swollen, flattened, black-and-violet nose covered Shepperton's face with two wads of reddened cotton stuffed into his nostrils. Dried blood covered the front of his shirt. Shepperton stared back, full of hatred. Harper chuckled at the deputy.

Once outside, Harper took his place at the end of the column of the prisoners. Bell had brought eight troopers with him, including Corporal Stackpole, who Harper already knew to be another murderer. Harper and his men were surrounded by rabid dogs.

Stackpole's appearance as part of the group concerned Harper; he was the man who shot the slave boy in order to steal the mule. A man without a conscience. Harper was certain Bell's corporal would do whatever criminality Bell ordered, and do it without asking any questions.

"All right, let's show these Yankees how we feel about bein' in their god-damn nigger-lovin' Union." Bell pointed down the street in the direction of the ramp to the riverboat landing.

Harper looked across to the cavalry camps. "Where ya takin' us, Bell?"

"*Captain* Bell, you son-of-a-bitch." Bell stopped. Harper watched him regain control of his temper. Bell smiled. "We have somethin' special planned for y'all."

The column set off, Davis first, Bailey next, followed by Cooke and Magnusson. Harper marched next to Bell in the rear of the group. A Confederate trooper escorted each prisoner, with his carbine ready. Stackpole and a private led the way while two more troopers followed Harper.

Many wagons with furniture and other household items piled high moved along Front Street, all headed south. These formed a long column out of the city. A few carriages of the well-to-do and some single riders mingled with the loaded wagons. Some of the people cast disdainful glances at the group, but Harper could not decide if these were intended for the prisoners or the Confederates who were abandoning the city.

The street was dry, the mud evaporated by the sunshine of the past three days. Harper looked overhead at the clear blue sky and small scattered clouds. Today was a beautiful day.

"You shouldda taken the Texan's parole," Bell told Harper.

Magnusson looked over his shoulder at Harper, a question in his eyes. Harper met the gaze, then quickly looked away.

"I wasn't going to leave them behind."

Harper felt helpless to prevent the killing he was now certain would happen. He twisted his wrists, testing, trying to loosen the bindings. He looked on the ground for something to use as a weapon.

"Maybe you shouldda *stayed* in Iowa and left us to live the way we want."

The lead troopers turned off of Front Street and headed down the causeway to the vacant riverboat landing. The column picked their way through the scattered crates and boxes left at the bottom of the ramp by the retreating army. On the upriver side of the causeway, the scorched timber ribs of burnt boats projected upward out of the mud.

Bell ran to the head of the column and directed it back along the mudflat until they reached a point beside the sand-colored bluffs directly under the jail house, out of view from Front Street. Here, perhaps ten yards of fishy-smelling mudflat separated the river's edge from the bluffs.

"You five sit there." He pointed to the foot of the bluff and the guards pushed their prisoners to the ground. "You Yankees may have won a few battles but I'm gonna even-up the score a little bit."

Harper looked behind himself, hoping to find some sharp edge that might be strong enough to slice into his bindings. He tried scraping the leather against an angular protrusion in the cliff, but the soft loess crumbled under the effort.

"I want four of you men to form a firin' line right here, goin' that way." Bell pointed north, downriver, along the mudflat. Four of Bell's men stood abreast across the mudflat, led by Stackpole.

The mudflat stretched alongside the river for at least four hundred yards, probably more. Harper looked across the river for the Federal cavalry patrol, but could not see anyone. If he was alone, he could probably swim across the river even with his hands behind his back. Cooke and Bailey might make it across, as well. But the two farm boys, Magnusson and Davis, couldn't swim when they were on the training ride in January, and it was unlikely they had learned since then. He continued to work the leather cords holding his hands. By stretching the soft leather, he might be able to force them loose enough to pull his hands free.

Bell pointed to Private Davis, after Magnusson, the largest of the prisoners. "Com'ere, boy."

Davis's guard pulled him to his feet and pushed him up to Bell. "We're goin' to have a little bit of fun today." He untied Davis's hands. Davis rubbed them together. He looked to Magnusson, then to Harper.

"Bell, this is murder," Harper shouted. He tried to stand, but a guard hit him in the shoulder with the butt of the carbine.

Magnusson tried to stand, but his guard pushed the butt of his weapon into the corporal's chest and Magnusson fell back into place.

Bell laughed when he saw Harper fall back against the bluff. "You two git to go last, so's you can watch what happens to these men first." He paused. "And it ain't murder, Harper, 'cause we're gonna let you boys escape right now." He turned to look at the prisoners. "You boys all want to escape, now don't you?"

No one answered.

"Well, here's your chance. All's you need to do is run down the beach to where that rock sticks out from the bluff, and you're free. You have my word for it."

Harper could see the rock at least two hundred yards away. "This is *murder*, Bell, and you'll pay for it." Scolding Bell and his men seemed the only possibility left. Harper stood up in his place under the bluff. His guard raised the butt of his carbine and held it ready to use if Harper moved forward.

"Shootin' blue-bellied Yankee-bastard prisoners who are tryin' to escape ain't murder." He turned back to Davis. "So, what's it gonna be, Yankee boy? You want to escape—or not?"

Davis looked back at Magnusson, who also stood up, but didn't say anything. Davis looked at Harper who shook his head.

Harper felt the leather give a tiny bit. He twisted his wrists. "Don't do it, Davis," Harper shouted. He addressed Bell. "Does Colonel Forrest know you're doin' this?"

"Colonel Forrest told me to take care of the prisoners. He wants me to protect you sons-of-bitches." Bell's face reddened. "It don't matter what Forrest wants now. He's thinkin' y'all been sent south already."

"How about your men?" He looked at the men in the firing line but avoided Stackpole. "Do they know they'll be hung when they're caught?"

The guards chuckled. One laughed out loud and said, "Killin' Yankees ain't murder. It's like killin' varmints, 'cept easier."

Harper now knew for certain this was not their first time killing prisoners.

"What will Forrest do when he learns you've disobeyed his orders? Sooner or later, you're going to pay for this." He watched for a reaction from Bell's men. The threat of Forrest's punishment pushed the smiles from their faces.

"Shut up, Yank." Harper's guard used his carbine butt to hit Harper in the plexus. Harper fell to his knees gasping for air.

"Look-it, son," Bell told Davis. "You only git two choices." He pulled out his pistol and pointed it at Davis's head. "Run, and maybe escape, or git shot right here." The smile returned to Bell's face. "It don't make no difference to me."

From his place in the mud, Harper watched fear spread across Davis's face when the man realized there was no other way out. Again, Davis looked to Magnusson, then to Harper. His eyes were wide and he took short, fast breaths.

"Don't run, Davis. He can't kill you unless you give him a reason," Harper said.

"Move!" Bell pushed Davis toward the rock. "We'll give you to the count of ten before we shoot." He pushed Davis again.

With his feet moving, Davis kept going. He started running downriver but his booted feet sank to the ankles in the mud of the riverbank. After he went ten yards, Bell started counting, "One…two…"

Harper watched the scene unfold, not wanting to believe he was helpless to do *anything*. Time slowed, increasing Harper's agony.

Davis was running as fast as he could, but appeared to be in slow-motion. With each step he took, he sank deeper into the muddy riverbank. The mud grabbed at his boots. When he pulled his foot out of the track, the mud clung, adding weight to Davis's flight. Davis's guard joined the firing line.

"…three…four."

Davis turned toward the bluff. Standing up, Harper could see there was less mud there because of the sandy erosion from the cliff face.

Davis was forty yards from Bell's line when the Rebels took aim. The remaining prisoners stood up to watch Davis.

"Run, Joe!"

"Keep goin'!"

"You'll make it!"

"...five...six..."

Davis reaced the firmer ground at the foot of the bluff and began to open the distance.

"...seven...eight..."

On the firmer ground, Davis was making good progress toward the point where the mudflat narrowed to pass the rock. Harper guessed that by the time Bell reached ten, Davis could be as much as a hundred yards away. With luck, he just might make it. A hundred yards was about the effective range of the carbines Bell's men used.

Bell must have noted the opening distance as well. Harper heard the count move faster.

"...nine...ten."

From where Harper stood, it appeared Davis only had to make it a few dozen yards farther to reach the rock. By God, he might make it. Bell's men would have a tough shot at this range.

"Fire!"

Davis appeared to be stuck in a mud hole. Harper's face and arms burned with impotent rage at Bell's actions. He ran at the line of shooters, trying to push them into each other.

The five carbines erupted nearly at the same time. Harper's guard caught up and swung the butt of his weapon into the back of Harper's head, knocking him to the ground. Looking up, Harper watched Davis pitch forward. Davis tried to rise onto his hands before collapsing with a splash. He lay still at the edge of the mud-hole.

****

Katie struggled to lift the water-filled bucket onto the landing. It surprised her how heavy the bucket seemed when compared to the times that she hauled water from the family well on the farm.

She and Julia had arrived just past noon. Saturday was the busiest night at *LaFitte's Hideout,* and Eleanor had had to force them out of bed this morning in time for breakfast at ten, then ordered Thomas to drive them to the hospital. Katie was to help care for the wounded soldiers while Julia wrote letters home for each of the men. Thomas delivered a box of Eleanor's personal stationery from the buggy before he returned to *Lafitte's*.

Muscles in Katie's legs, chest, and arms now burned. She had stopped using her 'farm' muscles when she came to work at *Lafitte's*. Hauling the water from the well in the courthouse yard and up four flights of stairs now tried her strength.

The soldier standing guard outside of the prisoners' ward rested his musket against the door and climbed down the six stairs to the mid-floor landing. "Let me get that." He lifted the bucket from her hands.

Katie gave the soldier a tired smile as she rested to catch her breath before following him.

"Are you feelin' all right, Miss Katie?" The soldier placed the bucket of water next to the door and lifted the wooden cross-beam away before he turned to watch her.

Does every soldier in the army know who I am?

On her first trip for water, the previous guard had tried to force her to reach between his legs. He, too, knew that she worked at *Lafitte's Hideout* and had threatened to take for free what he would have cost him three-and-a- half dollars at the saloon. She controlled the man with a slap and a shout for help.

On the next two trips, she had asked Cordelia Clyburne, one of the visiting relatives, to come with her as far as the landing and the guard had behaved better. This new guard seemed more polite.

"I'm all right. Just gittin' a bit tired."

Katie steeled herself for the foul odors in the ward while the guard unlocked the door and held it open for her. She stepped through and had to blink at the afternoon sunlight slanting into the room. The unarmed guard inside the door on this end of the ward looked inside the bucket before letting her pass.

While she shielded her eyes, Katie took in the squalid scene of nearly two hundred injured men left on their own to suffer. The number kept growing each day. She noted how almost none moaned or complained. Katie had seen how severe their injuries were. Many, like the boy Esau, would die here. Others, those who could not lift themselves out of their beds or cots or pallets, lay on sheets or even mattress ticking, soiled with sweat or blood, or filth.

"Over here, Katie."

Katie found Nurse Harriet Wells waving at her from a bed mid-way along the aisle to her left. She hurried along, past the stares of the men. She set the bucket between Cordelia, who stood at the foot of the next bed to be treated, and the nurse, who sat beside the next patient. Katie knelt down at the head of the bed next to Wells.

"Let's see what we have here." Wells reached for the bandage wrapped around the chest of the wounded man. "What's your name, soldier?"

"Jimmy Lee, ma'am. Jimmy Lee McGuckin."

Amanda Marstair and Kitty Reynolds came to stand beside Cordelia and watch the nurse. With the three of them standing next to each other, Katie noted for the first time how each had bloodstains on the canvas aprons protecting their skirts. She would need to get an apron, too.

Julia, sat with a group of soldiers in the far corner of the ward.

"I'd like to take a look at where you got shot, Jimmy Lee."

"I think it might be getting better all by itself, ma'am. I cain't feel it no more."

"All right, son." Wells felt the outside of the bandage wrapping. "I think you might be right, Jimmy Lee. I don't feel any oozing yet." She turned to Kitty Reynolds, a petite blonde with short hair and a friendly face. "Kitty, help him to sit up so we can see what's underneath."

Reynolds moved to the head of the bed. With Katie's help, she pulled Jimmy Lee into a sitting position and slid behind him. She let the man lean back against her chest.

"Your turn, Katie. I'd like you to help treat this patient." Wells stood up. "Come sit here."

Katie glanced at the other three women who were nurses' helpers. She saw only kindness in their eyes as she sat down and Wells stood beside the chair.

"First, I want you to unwrap the bandage. You see where we've attached the end with that hat pin? Well, pull the pin free and hand it to me. Then reach behind the patient and unwrap the bandage."

Katie found the pin and pulled it free. She had to sit on the bed next to Jimmy Lee in order to reach behind him. When she brought her other hand around to take the bandage on the other side, the result was that their bodies touched. Jimmy Lee put his hands along both of Katie's sides and gave her a hug. Katie started in surprise and pulled away.

"We'll have none of that, Jimmy Lee." Wells slapped his hand and pulled it away. "Katie, normally the nurses don't sit on the beds when giving treatment. You should be able to work the bandage around the body if you stand up and reach over. That way, we don't get the patient over-excited."

"Ain't no harm done ma'am. I mean Katie's not like a regular nurse, now is she? I'm not the first man to give her a sweet hug. We all know where she comes from."

Katie grabbed the end of the bandage and stood next to the bed. Her face burned with embarrassment. She couldn't meet the soldier's eyes.

"You're talking about the woman who is nursing you, soldier. Remember that. And if she wasn't here, you'd still be lying in your own filth."

Wells spoke loud enough for the entire room to hear. "From now on, when you address this woman—" Wells took Katie's hand, "you will call her *Miss Katie*. She is learning to be a nurse and you will treat her with the same respect that I've heard Southerners have for all womanhood."

Katie could only look at the floor. Her face burned. In the corner of her eye, she could see Amanda Marsted and Cordelia Clyburne look away and shuffle their feet. They must have been the ones who told the patients that Katie was a saloon-girl. Or it might have been the guards. It really didn't matter. She only wanted to disappear completely; merge into the nearby wall, or jump through a window.

"You Rebs should be grateful the Katie and her friends are here. Remember what this place was like last week?" Wells scanned left and right. "So, unless you want things to go back to that, all of you start behaving." She paused and looked over the entire ward. "Does evryone here understand?"

There was silence. Katie didn't move.

"Good." Wells turned back to Jimmy Lee. "Are you going to

behave yourself, soldier? Otherwise, we'll move on to the next man."

"Yes'm. I won't try nothin' else."

"Katie, let's finish removing the bandage." She patted Katie's hand. "Katie? Back to the bandage."

The touch from Wells brought Katie's attention back to the patient. This time, she remained standing while she unwrapped the bandage. When it was free, Wells handed it to Cordelia, who folded it and placed it on the bed.

Wells addressed the patient. "What did the doctor tell you when you saw him, Jimmy Lee?"

"That were four days ago when they loaded us onto the boat to come here. He said that the bullet went straight through." The soldier leaned back but stayed upright, supported by Kitty Reynolds. "In the front and out the back."

"Did he tell you what the damage was on the inside?"

"He thought that I broke a rib in the front but not in the back."

"Katie, if his rib is broken, you'll have to be very careful whenever you have to move him."

"Yes, ma'am."

"Did he say if your lung was hit?"

"No, ma'am. He didn't say nothin' 'bout that." His face lit up. "But I don't feel any pain on the inside, anymore."

"Let me see you take a deep breath."

Jimmy Lee inhaled a shallow breath before gasping and grabbing a spot at his left rib cage.

"Hmmm...Katie, gently prod around that area where he's holding. Use your two fingers."

Katie waited until Jimmy Lee moved his hand. The area did not appear to be badly injured, but there was some swelling. Suddenly, the patient winced.

"That must be your broken rib, Jimmy Lee." She looked at Katie. "You can stop prodding, Katie." She turned to the other three helpers. "Ladies, do you see that swelling and redness? That's where there is damage is under the skin. Because it hurts too much for him to take a deep breath, that's how the doctor knew it was broken and not just bruised or cracked."

Wells looked back at Jimmy Lee. “And the doctor never said anything to you about any damage to your lung?”

Katie watched how Wells, herself, was behaving. The nurse appeared to examine Jimmy Lee’s face, judging his reactions.

“No, ma’am.”

Katie shifted her attention to the patient’s face while she listened to Wells’s questions.

“I don’t think he would have put you in with these men unless he thought that your lung was damaged. But I can’t tell, for sure. The broken rib won’t let you take a full breath so I can test your lungs.”

“I don’t think so ma’am. I can’t feel anything inside my chest on that side. There ain’t no pain.”

Katie tried to image what damage the bullet had caused. She could see the bruising and the oozing at the spot where that bullet went in. But the wound was in the front and the broken rib was in his side. The rib must have flexed when the bullet hit it until it couldn’t flex enough. Then, the rib must have broken like a stick when you try to bend it from the end.

“There wouldn’t be any pain.” Wells paused. “Except around the wounds. But, my guess would be that there are broken pieces of that bullet buried inside your lung. No one will know for sure until the rib heals.”

If the bullet had broken apart inside his chest, Katie realized it might have hit anything. She had seen the insides of an animal’s chest and knew there were not just the lungs and heart, but also a lot of blood carriers and the white nerves.

“Good. Let’s get those wounds cleaned up. Jimmy Lee, can you roll onto your right side?”

Kitty and Katie helped Jimmy Lee roll and held him in place.

“Katie, do you see where those stiches keep the wound closed?”

Katie followed Wells’s pointing finger to a large, sore area on his back, nearly opposite the wound on his chest. There, three stitches closed the exit wound and were surrounded by bright pinkish skin.

Wells dipped a cloth from her bag into the bucket of water and handed the cloth to Katie. “Wash around the wound and clean away any dried blood and pus.

"That feels nice, ma'am."

"Do you see how the skin around the wound is all pinkish in color? Not red?" Wells waited until Katie, Cordelia, Amanda, and Kitty nodded. "That's a good sign."

"Katie, give that area a pinch on either side of the stiches. Not too hard." The bruises turned white under the pinching fingers but nowhere else. "It means that there isn't any corruption here. It's healing well."

"Now, hold the back of your hand about a half-inch away from the wound and tell me what you feel?" Wells watched the man's chest rise and fall as he breathed. After a half-dozen breaths, she smiled. "Do you feel anything, Katie?"

"No, ma'am."

"No wind coming in or out of the wound"

"No."

"Excellent. That means it's closed completely."

Wells took a cloth and a metal flask from her bag and handed it to Katie. "I want you to wipe this over the two wounds."

Katie could smell cheap whiskey on the cloth. A second look at the grime on the cloth confirmed that it had already been used many times.

"Now, count out five drops from the flask onto the cloth. Try to find the cleanest spot left. Then wipe it directly onto the wound and the area around it.

Katie did as ordered. She had heard people talk about pouring whiskey onto a bullet wound, but she had never seen anyone do it before.

"You got some corn squeezin's there, Nurse Wells?" The man in the cot across the aisle from Jimmy Lee had gotten a whiff of the alcohol.

"You don't want to drink this, son. It's so bad even the town drunks can't swallow it."

Katie dabbed away a drop that threatened to run onto the sheet from Jimmy Lee's back. When she finished, she pulled the cloth and flask into her lap.

Wells signaled Kitty to let the man roll onto his back.

"Are y'all sure 'bout that, ma'am." The man on the cot smiled at the nurse. "Man get's a powerful hankerin' just layin' in bed."

Wells smiled back. “Whiskey won’t help you heal none, and I want to get you boys out of here just as soon as possible.” Then she turned her attention to the wound in Jimmy Lee’s chest.

This wound appeared to be in the same condition as the one in the back. Katie asked, “Why do you rub whiskey on the wound?”

“That’s just something my mother taught me. It seems to help keep the wound from getting septic. Go ahead and wipe it onto the other wound.”

“Septic?” Katie set five more drops onto the cloth and rubbed the front wound.

“You know, corrupted? Poisoned?” Wells took the cloth bandage from the foot of the bed. “Help lift him up.”

“Oh. Now, I know what you mean.” Katie found the lid to the flask and screwed it shut while Kitty pushed the man into a sitting position and held him there.

“Go ahead Katie, wrap him up.”

Katie took the bandage and wrapped it back into its original position, this time being very careful to avoid making contact with any part of her body but her hands.

“Whiskey ain’t all a man gets a powerful hankerin’ for.” Jimmy Lee smiled up at Kitty Reynolds before settling his head between her breasts.

Kitty blushed. She struggled to get out from under the man, but couldn’t. Jimmy Lee trapped her between himself and the headboard. All she could do was turn her face away.

Wells pursed her lips and shook her head before she reached into Jimmy Lee’s bed clothes. She grabbed a handful of organs below his waist and twisted. Then she pulled the handful up from the bed. Jimmy Lee howled in pain and doubled up, letting Kitty Reynolds escape.

“I’ve already warned you about that. Maybe the doctor will have to cut this part off too, Jimmy Lee, if y’all’re going to be such a nuisance. I’ll give you a permanent reminder why the nurses are here.”

She released his private parts and the man collapsed onto the bed, cupping his hands around the injured organs.

“What do you think, ladies? Do you think Jimmy Lee’s going to need that leg in the middle?” Wells looked over her shoulder at the women standing at the foot of the bed.

All of them, including Katie, covered their giggles with their hands. Kitty Reynolds turned away, blushing.

Wells winked at Katie who couldn't help but laugh.

Wouldn't it be nice if I could do that at Lafitte's sometimes?

Jimmy Lee tried to protect the appendage from the imagined surgery by covering it with his hands.

"You rest now, Jimmy Lee McGuckin." Wells checked the bandage Katie had wrapped. She nodded approval. "You need to be strong for your trip home."

Jimmy Lee was still covering his private area. "Yes, ma'am."

The nurse returned the flask and the wiping cloth into her bag.

Jimmy Lee looked up at Wells. "Do you know when that will be, Nurse Wells?"

"I'm sorry, no. I haven't heard anything." Wells took a last look around before she picked up her bag. "And don't go making any more trouble for Katie or the other girls while you're here. Otherwise…" She formed her fingers into an imaginary scissors and made a snipping motion.

"Yes, ma'am." He shook his head and watched Wells's fingers. "No, ma'am."

Nurse Wells moved to the cot across the aisle from Jimmy Lee's bed. The soldier there smiled when the women circled around him. Katie set the chair and the bucket beside the cot.

"Ladies, let's take a small break." Wells looked down at the soldier before taking a deep breath. "Can you wait a few minutes soldier? I need to get a drink of water." She motioned to Katie. "Come with me."

"Yes, ma'am." The man on the cot was polite but Katie saw the new light in his eyes dim as Wells walked toward the side door.

"We'll be back soon." Katie picked up the water bucket and followed Wells. As she did so, the soreness in her muscles returned. They went past the guards and the barricaded door, down the stairwell and out to the outhouse in the back yard.

Nurse Wells waited for Katie to finish before walking to the hand-pump covering the well. She poured water from a can hanging on the spout into the top of the pump to prime it. Then Wells operated the handle by herself. When water finally spilled from the spout, Katie worked the handle while Wells washed her hands using soap from her bag and tried to clean the wiping cloths as best she could.

"I've read where a doctor in England is teaching his hospital staff that they must wash their hands regularly when they work with the patients. That's why I had you fetch so many buckets of water. Thank you for doing that. I know that the buckets are heavy."

Finished with washing the blood and stains out of the wiping cloths, Wells took hold of the pump handle. "Now, you."

Afterward, Wells pointed to a nearby bench. "Let's have a little rest before we go back up."

When they were both seated, Katie realized that the bench was located in the ideal spot to catch the afternoon sun which now warmed her. But she felt a little awkward outdoors without her cloak or sunbonnet. Eleanor always told her to cover her face, and especially her long red hair, as much as possible when they went into the town. But if Nurse Wells wanted to stay here for a while, Katie didn't mind. A warm breeze blowing from the farms to the west of the city carried the familiar smells from her childhood and scattered the strands of her hair across her face. She gathered them between her fingers and held them back so she could enjoy the view.

"So you work for Eleanor Saint Croix, do you? Tell me how that happened. You seem very young to be working in a saloon. How old are you, Katie."

"Fifteen, ma'am. Fifteen-and-a-half."

Katie saw Wells's head snap backward and her eyes open wider.

"Fifteen. That can't be right. You *are* too young to be working in a saloon."

"Mister Bosley bought me from my pa for three hundred dollars."

"And your mother just let him do that?"

"My mother died last spring."

"They can't buy and sell you. You're not some negro field hand." Wells sat back and looked at Katie. The shock on her face melted until Katie only saw kindness. "How long have you worked there?"

"Since before Christmas." Katie looked away from Wells. She stared at the toes of her boots poking out from under her skirt and petticoat. She did not like the way this conversation was going. No wonder Eleanor did not let her meet any of the local women during their daytime walks.

"Katie, have you ever been to a church? Have you ever heard of the Whores of Babylon?"

"When I was little. I don't remember many of the stories, only that the preacher would talk for too long and yell too much. We would hitch up the wagon and go to the church on Sundays, and then to the picnic afterward." The memory brought a tightness, constricting Katie's throat. She could feel tears under her eyelids, ready to leak out. "We stopped going just after Mama got sick and Papa started drinking the corn liquor instead of sellin' it." Tears balanced on her lower eyelids.

Wells moved closer and put her hand on Katie's forearm. "It's all right, dear. I know it's not your fault."

Katie pulled the scented handkerchief from the cuff of her sleeve and dabbed at her eyes.

"Your papa should never have sent you away." Wells's hand patted Katie's forearm. "Especially not with a saloon owner. Your mama, bless her soul, would never have let him do such a thing. She would have protected you if she had been living."

My mama still protects me when I need her the most.

Katie's gaze remained on her boots. "Why do you say that? I don't do anything wrong at the saloon. I do what they tell me and it makes the soldiers happy. And that makes me happy." She turned to face Wells. "That's not so wrong." Katie wasn't as certain about this as she had been before this week. "Is it?" She felt her insecurity attach itself to the last two words.

"I'm sorry I upset you so." Wells took hold of both Katie's hands.

Katie looked away.

"But Katie, I like the way that you treat the patients. You're very gentle with them. Plus, you're strong enough to help move them when we have to do that." Wells paused until Katie looked at her. "I would like it very much if you could come to visit the patients as much as you can." Wells eyes alternated looking into each of Katie's. "Would you like that?"

Katie sat up straight and tall, blinking the wetness out of her eyes.

“Katie, would you like that?”

“Yes, ma’am, I surely would.”

Wells smiled back at the girl. “Then it’s done. I’ll ask Miss Eleanor to send you over as often as possible. I’ll tell her that you have a special way with the men.” She looked away, down at the ground. “Of course, it will probably last only until the Rebels are gone.” She looked at Katie, who smiled back.

“I heard the nurse on the first floor tell Eleanor that she didn’t know how long that would be. That’s one of the reasons why Eleanor told Julia to come: to help the soldiers write home so their folks could come and git them.”

Wells looked at the sun, now dropping close to the roofs of the buildings across the street. “It’s time for us to be getting back inside. I think that your buggy will be here soon to take the two of you, uh–home.”

****

“Good shootin’, men!” Bell turned to face Harper. “*That’s* for stealin’ my stock.”

The prisoners stared at Davis’s body in silence.

“Reload,” Bell ordered. Pointing to Harper, he said, “Get him up out of the mud.”

Turning to the prisoners, he pointed to Ben Bailey, the youngest and smallest. “You! You’ll be a harder target.”

“We need to do somethin’, Mister Harper,” Magnusson whispered when the guard shoved Harper against the bluff. “That captain’s brainsick.”

Bailey’s guard pushed him forward. While he approached the starting point, Bailey surveyed the opposite riverbank. His guard untied his hands. Bailey eyed the men in the firing line pouring powder and shot down the barrel of their carbines.

“He might try to swim for it.” Magnusson whispered to Harper. “He’s a good swimmer.”

But when Bailey took an extra step toward the river, his guard poked him in the back with the barrel of his carbine. Bailey didn’t stop. His guard raised the carbine and clubbed it into the middle of Bailey’s shoulders, inches below his neck, forcing Bailey down into the mud.

"Ya ain't supposed to kill prisoners, god-damn it!"

Harper looked to Magnusson, surprised at the anger he heard from the usually stoic soldier.

The firing line finished reloading. The shadow of a man grew from the shadows of the bluff on the riverbank. Harper looked up and saw Shepperton wave to Bell. The jailer sat down to watch, recognizable by the bloody white cotton in his nostrils.

"This is how we need to treat all Yankee prisoners, ain't it boys?" Bell was laughing. Turning to Bailey, "Ready, Yank?"

Bailey looked at Magnusson. "Gus, do something."

Harper became frantic. What could he do? He stepped toward Bell and Bailey before the guards could react.

Magnusson pushed against his own guard. He tripped the smaller man to the ground, but Magnusson could not work free from the cords holding his hands.

Bell fired his pistol into the air before leveling it at Magnusson. "The next one is for you, big man. Now, be still."

Magnusson took another step forward, and Bell pulled the hammer of the pistol back.

Harper also walked forward until Stackpole stepped out of line and swung the stock of his carbine at Harper's head. Harper ducked and the blow went wide. On the back-swing, though, Stackpole drove the butt against Harper's arm. On the up-swing Stackpole connected with Harper's chin. At the same time, a guard kicked the back of Harper's knee. The two blows forced Harper to his knees.

Harper looked up. His gaze followed the barrel of Bell's pistol to where Magnusson still glared back at the Rebel captain. Magnusson's guard stood and drove the butt of his carbine into the corporal's belly. The large man took the blow without reacting. The guard brought the barrel of the carbine across Magnusson's shoulders. Magnusson stood strong.

"Stop this now, Bell." Harper pulled himself to his knees. "You're insane."

"Ain't insane, Harper. I jes' want you people out of my land so's you'll stop burnin' and stealin', like you did on my farm." Bell's smile turned maniacal, lips curling back, eyes bulging, flushed in the face, while he yelled the last words. His twitch was back. "This is the fastest way I know to do that."

Harper felt his hands loosen in their bindings. He kept twisting and pulling. Somehow, he was going to kill Bell with his bare hands.

"Hold on there!" A rider shouted from the causeway. Harper turned his attention to the rider and his companion, who spurred their horses to a trot and rode up to the group. "What the hell is going on here?" It was Captain Dupree, riding a spotless gray gelding. Deputy Morris was with him, atop a bay-colored nag.

"Ain't nothin' here for you, Texas." Bell stepped up to Dupree's horse, pistol pointing vaguely in the Texan's direction. "Jes' exercisin' some prisoners."

"I heard shooting."

"Well, one of 'em boys jes' tried to escape." He pointed up the beach. "We got him, though."

Dupree looked up the beach at Davis's body now surrounded by a trio of ravens. "Pretty careless, Captain, letting him get so far."

Harper yelled. "This bastard is tryin' to kill us all." Harper positioned himself between Dupree and the warehouses across the river. "He set Private Davis free, so he could make it look like an escape attempt."

"That's a pretty serious charge, Lieutenant." Dupree addressed Bell. "What do you have to say?"

"Don't make no god-damn difference what I've got to say. This ain't no business of yours, Texas. Now, git the hell outta here afore I arrest you for interferin' with the prisoners."

Harper couldn't let Bell win this argument with Dupree. "This crazy son-of-a-bitch made a sport out of it." Harper pointed with his chin to where Davis's body lay in the mud. "There's the proof ya need."

Is Dupree here to stop these murders or not?

Dupree looked down at Harper and shook his head. "Be careful what you say about a commissioned officer of the Confederate Army, Mister Harper." He turned to address Bell. "Actually, Captain, you can turn the prisoners over to me now. I have a parole for all of them."

Dupree opened a button on his jacket and took a cluster of folded papers from the pocket inside. He handed the papers to Bell, who slowly read each one.

"These ain't no good. Who the hell signed 'em?" Bell handed the papers back to Dupree. "Besides, except for the officer, they ain't got no names on them."

"There's four papers there, one for each of the enlisted men. That's Colonel Wharton's signature."

"Well, Wharton ain't in charge here. Bedford Forrest is, and I'm followin' *his* orders. You can take your *paroles* and use them to clean your ass for all I care."

Dupree recovered the papers and returned them to his pocket.

The small hope Harper felt when the Texan arrived began to fade. "Captain Bell, don't ya think you should check with Colonel Forrest before you kill any more prisoners?"

Maybe, with Dupree and Morris as witnesses, Bell would have to wait until a later time to continue his game.

"Shut up, Yank! I'll do as I damn well please. Prisoners don't git a say in it."

But Bell hesitated. Harper knew that with Dupree here, Bell was in a predicament. If he reported to Forrest for clarification about the paroles, Forrest would want an explanation justifying why the prisoners were still in Nashville, and maybe why he killed Davis. Harper felt certain that Forrest did not order their execution. The colonel was too smart for that.

"These men burned out my family," Bell told Dupree.

The comment appeared to startle Dupree. He looked down at Harper.

Thump! Zzzzz! Zzzzz, zzzzz! Thump! Thump!

Two of Bell's men in the firing line fell over before anyone realized they were being fired upon. Now came the sounds of the hidden weapons' discharges, and everyone turned to see puffs of smoke drift from the warehouses across the river. Dupree's horse reared up in fright and turned away from the direction of the shooting. Blood trailed down the animal's shoulder.

As Harper had hoped, the noise from killing Private Davis attracted the Federal scouts on the other side of the river. Six puffs of gun smoke revealed where the shooters hid on the opposite bank.

Bell looked to his men. Harper, with his hands still tied behind his back, pushed his shoulder into the nearest guard, driving the man backward until he tripped over one of his dead companions. The guard assigned to Magnusson drew bead on Harper but Magnusson shouldered him from the side, throwing off the trooper's aim as the carbine fired. Harper felt the rush of air on his neck when the bullet buzzed past.

Dupree pulled the reins of his horse down and back to force its head down. As the beast limped to a halt, Dupree stroked her neck. "It's alright, Thunder Cloud. Shhh. Shhh." Dupree bent over the horse's right shoulder to examine the wound.

Bell yelled for his men to take cover. Seeing this, Harper yelled to his men. "Get moving! Go! Go!" Harper heard Shepperton, up on the bluff, fire once across the river before he ran for the cover of the bench behind the jail.

The guard next to Cooke tried to grab his prisoner, but Cooke spun out of his grasp. Each man broke into a run, the Rebel back toward the causeway, and Cooke in the opposite direction along the foot of the bluffs toward Davis's body.

Bailey's guard stood his ground, blocking Bailey's attempt to run away. With his hands free, Bailey wrestled the Confederate soldier for possession of the carbine. Holding the weapon, Bailey drove his knee into the guard's groin and yanked it away. He turned the weapon and pulled the trigger with the muzzle three inches from the victim's face. The guard's head exploded across the mud. Bailey fell to the ground–shot in the back by Bell.

Seeing Cooke moving down the riverbank and Bailey on the ground, Harper yelled at Magnusson. "Follow me!"

Harper ran toward Dupree's and Morris's horses, watching Bell over his shoulder while he did. Magnusson yelled for Cooke to join them. Bell fired three wild shots at the running prisoners before clicking on an empty chamber.

Now came the turn of Bell's men to run a gauntlet, caught in the open on the mudflat. Corporal Stackpole fired his single shot across the river while he ran.

Bell drew his sword and chased Harper, who twisted away from the blade and ran to shelter behind Morris's horse.

Two more of Bell's men fell before they reached the hulks.

Dupree pointed his pistol at Bell's face. He cocked the weapon before flicking it to signal Bell to move away and join his men.

With Bell and his surviving men running toward the hulks, Deputy Morris pointed his horse in the opposite direction, north along the riverbank. Bending low over the animal's neck, Morris shielded the three prisoners.

"We'll go this way, Mister Harper." Dupree bent low over his horse and waved with his pistol toward where Davis lay.

"Not yet, Dupree." He looked up at Deputy Morris. "Cut me loose."

Morris looked across at Dupree. When Dupree did not react, the deputy drew his sheath knife and cut the straps holding Harper's hands before he gave the knife to Harper, who cut Magnusson free.

Sergeant Stackpole and the two men with him reached cover while Bell dodged bullets from the cavalry patrol before diving behind an empty packing crate.

"Gus, help me get up!" Bailey reached with his hand while he tried to sit up, but he fell back, blood pulsing from a belly wound. Harper heard the call and looked for Magnusson who was several steps away, ready to run to the fallen Bailey.

Harper stepped in front of the large man. "Stay here." He could see that Bell and his men were engaged with the scouts across the river–pinned down by the greater volume of fire coming from the Federal cavalry.

Magnusson glared at Harper. "I can get him."

"No. Undo Cooke." Harper paused to look directly into Magnusson eyes. "*I'll* get Bailey."

Magnusson stared back at Harper–holding the knife between their faces. When Magnusson leaned forward to move past, Harper blocked him. After a few seconds, Magnusson yielded. "Yes, sir." He took the knife and turned to cut Cooke's bindings.

Morris drew his pistol, looking for targets at the top of the bluff.

Harper ran from behind Morris's horse, sprinting the short distance to where Bailey lay. He fell to his knees beside the bleeding soldier and examined the man's injuries. A bullet zipped past his left shoulder, thudding into the mud. The bullet came from behind and above him, probably from the top of the bluff. Shepperton!

Dupree rode up with his pistol drawn. A second bullet zipped past Harper's right side and hit Bailey in the forearm, shattering the bones. Bailey howled in pain. Dupree fired two rounds toward the top of the bluff before he turned to Harper and Bailey. "Can you move him?"

"Don't know for sure. He's been shot in the back and it looks like it went clean through."

Bailey lay in a pool of blood. Blood no longer pulsed from the belly wound, but oozed up and out.

"Is it near the spine?"

"I can't tell."

Magnusson pounded up to the group. "Mister Harper, we need to get goin'. There's more Rebs up there by the jail house."

Harper looked up to see several troopers lining the bluff, shooting across the river. Soon the Federal cavalry would be overwhelmed. For now, the Rebels above ignored the small group around Bailey.

"Put him up here," Dupree said.

Harper and Magnusson looked at each other. Neither knew how far they could trust this Rebel officer.

"I've got him, sir," Magnusson replied as he rolled Bailey sideways. Bailey yelped in pain. This exposed the entry wound in Bailey's back where more blood dripped into the scarlet puddle.

Magnusson positioned himself facing away from the prostrate man.

"Wait." Harper opened his jacket and tore two squares from the tail of his shirt. He wadded one and forced it into the hole in Bailey's back. "Roll him back." He stuffed the second piece of his shirt into the larger wound in Baileys gut. He would treat it better when they were safe.

With Harper holding Bailey's ruined arm, Magnusson lifted Bailey onto his left shoulder. The younger soldier screamed, then passed out.

"Put his legs here." Magnusson patted his right shoulder and Harper slung Bailey's legs over. Dupree urged his wounded, limping horse around to act as a shield between the group and the men on the bluff.

Harper helped Magnusson to stand. The large man staggered in the mud for a few steps, but found the proper balance and moved quickly to where Morris and Cooke waited in the sandy area close by the bluff.

More Rebel troopers joined the fire fight. Behind Harper, the shooting from the Federal side increased as well. He ran to retrieve a carbine lying next to one of the dead Confederates from the firing line and pulled the man's cartridge box free. If he could, he would end Bell's career as a murderer.

He located Bell hidden among the wooden cargo boxes at the causeway, reloading his pistol. Harper knelt and fired. The wooden crate splintered next to Bell's face.

Bell aimed at Harper with his reloaded pistol, but doing so exposed him to the Federals across the river. Several bullets hit the crates and ground near Bell, and the shot went wide. With Bell and his surviving men pinned down, Harper ran to join his own people. "Let's get out of here."

Magnusson set the pace and the group moved down the riverbank, keeping close to the bluff to avoid being seen from above. Harper stayed behind, leaning against the bluff to reload the stolen carbine. Ready, Harper backed away from Bell's men, using whatever cover the contours of the eroded bluff provided.

When they reached the place where Davis lay, Harper and Cooke went to examine the body. The ravens were gone, scattered by the noise from the firefight. There were three neat entry holes in Davis's back and another in his shoulder, each opened wider by the birds.

"Turn him over."

Davis's face was frozen with his final determination to escape.

"Looks like he died straight out, sir."

"Thank God it was quick." Harper stared into Davis's sightless eyes. "I'm sorry, soldier." He covered Davis's eyes with his hands, and closed the lids using his thumb.

The group, Harper and Cooke on foot, Magnusson carrying Bailey, and Dupree and Morris on hoseback, turned behind the rock which Bell had set as the goal in his sick game. They picked their way through the debris of twisted iron beams and sliced wire cables from the destroyed bridge until they reached a causeway leading back up to the city.

Harper remained among the bridge debris, his battle lust rising. He fired at Bell and took a new cartridge from the ammunition box.

"That will be enough, Lieutenant Harper."

Harper turned around, poised to attack, only to see the black hole of Dupree's pistol barrel pointed at his face. Magnusson, Cooke, and Morris waited at the ramp, out of danger, watching.

"Put the carbine down and move over with the others."

Harper raised the carbine part way, before he remembered it was not loaded.

"Harper, I'm going to leave you now. You should be safe until your army gets here." Keeping his pistol aimed at Harper, Dupree awkwardly pulled the paroles from his jacket with his left hand and gave them to Harper. "Take these."

"Looks like I don't need them anymore, Dupree. But thanks all the same." Harper looked at his men. "It appears we have escaped."

"If that were true, Harper, I would be required to shoot you right now. Otherwise, I might be accused of abetting Yankee prisoners. But, if you are still a prisoner, the worst I can be accused of is protecting prisoners in my custody from being killed by Forrest's renegades. You see the difference, don't you?"

"I see." Harper answered although he was confused over the technicality. "So why did ya help us escape?"

"That's exactly the point. I didn't help you escape. You're still prisoners in my custody. This pistol says so."

"We'd better get your man to a doctor, Lieutenant," Deputy Morris said. Harper saw Bailey's pallid face and the fresh blood covering Magnusson's shoulders.

"We don't kill prisoners in Terry's Rangers. Remember that, and tell your generals when you get back. That's why I couldn't let Bell finish. I'm sorry I didn't arrive there soon enough to save your first man."

Harper rested the carbine against a large, burnt beam. "Well, Dupree, I am grateful for ya comin' at all."

"So, you'll accept the paroles?"

"Bailey's in a bad way, sir," Magnusson called to Harper.

"I suppose there isn't much choice." Harper reached up for the papers.

"Sign the receipt." Dupree holstered his pistol to take out a pencil. "And you'll need to make a list of the names for me to take back."

Harper found the receipt in the stack of papers, signed it, and wrote Gustav Magnusson's, Benjamin Bailey's, Johnny Cooke's, and Joseph Davis's names on the back before he returned it to Dupree. Having Davis's name on a parole might be useful if Captain Bell ever came to trial.

"Good luck, Dupree." They shook hands. "My respects and gratitude to Colonel Wharton."

"Is that true what Bell said about you burnin' him out?"

"It wasn't our men. First Iowa was in Missouri until Christmastime. After that, we were in Paducah until this campaign started."

"Good luck then, Harper. I must have my horse attended to." Dupree turned and rode up the ramp back to Front Street. The noise of the firefight increased behind them. More Rebels must have joined from the cavalry camp.

"I know a place where you can hide," Morris pointed away from the direction of the Confederate camps. "My house is only four blocks from here. After we get there, I'll see if I can find a doctor for your man."

Harper turned to Magnusson. "Y'all go with the deputy. Make sure Bailey is bein' tended properly. Make him comfortable." He looked back in the direction of the cavalry camps. "I'm goin' to get Santee back."

"Who's Santee, Lieutenant?" Cooke asked.

Magnusson shifted Bailey's position on his shoulders. Fresh blood ran down his neck.

"My horse."

Magnusson, Cooke, and Morris stared at Harper. Harper looked away.

"*Your horse*!" Magnusson shook his head. "After all we went through, you're goin' to risk it all for a horse!?"

"I am."

Morris holstered his pistol. "That will violate your parole, Lieutenant."

"We'll let the military authorities decide that. Not yourself,

Deputy."

"Is it true, Mister Harper?" Cooke looked confused. "Would that make the paroles no good?"

"Only mine, not yours." He addressed Magnusson. "Once you're in a safe place, stay hidden until ya see someone from our army. Buell or Grant should arrive in a day or two."

Magnusson appeared confused. He took a step backward. "Are ya sure, Lieutenant?"

Bailey did not move, nor did he make any sound. Harper looked closer at the wounded man to see a tinge of blue around his lips. The skin around his eyes was darker than before. Bailey started to shiver. Harper looked at his fingernails. They held a bluish cast around the edges.

"Yeah. Now go. Hurry. Bailey needs a lot of help."

"This way." Morris tugged the reins to point his horse downriver, away from the cavalry camps. "The ramp here comes up right in front of the Court House. It'll be safer if we move farther down. Wait until I look around."

He rode a quarter-mile along the mudflat until he passed the ruins of the railroad bridge. From atop his horse, he signaled to Magnusson and Cooke that the way was clear.

Harper handed their paroles to Cooke. "Keep these and add all of your names to them as soon as ya can, includin' Davis's. Keep out of sight until our army arrives. There is no way to know if any of the Reb cavalry will respect the paroles, so ya should stay out of their way."

He looked at the last parole in his hand, his own. If they captured him with this in his pocket, any Reb would hang him on the spot for what he was about to do–with justification.

"Hold this for me, Cooke." He handed the fifth parole to Cooke.

Cooke looked at the paper and added it to the others. "Are ya sure, sir?"

"Yeah." Harper smiled at the soldier. "I'll be back for it tonight."

The odds of him returning to collect the parole were not very good. Cooke's frown showed he believed the same thing.

"And whatever else you do, Cooke, don't come after me, or else the Rebs will hang you, too."

"Good luck, Mister Harper." Magnusson gave Harper a final glance, concern and confusion in his eyes. He turned and made his way along the mudflat with Bailey.

"Good luck, sir." Cooke paused. "I'll come look for ya after the Rebs are gone." He ran to catch up with Magnusson.

"Good luck, men."

****

There were no guards on the causeway. Harper made his way up the ramp, staying in the twilight shadow of the abutment of the destroyed bridge. He crouched for the final steps before stopping. Slowly, he rose from the crouch until he could peer over top of the ramp.

Rising enough to peer under the wagons lining Front Street, he saw the Confederate cavalry busy striking camp in the town square. The court house loomed to his right, three stories tall in the center of the block across Front Street. The taller twin buildings of city hall filled the block behind the court house. On the other side of the ramp leading to the bridge, the buildings facing the court house blocked the sun, now low in the south-western sky. Scattered civilians watched from the side streets surrounding the square.

When a cavalry patrol approached, Harper could not find a place to hide on the causeway. He ran down to the mudflat, reaching the bridge rubble before the first trooper appeared at the top of the ramp. Harper listened for the sound of hoof beats on the packed earth of the causeway, but none came. The run had caused the pain in his ribs to return, making breathing difficult. He watched the shadows of the riders move along across the ramp until they were gone. Staying low to the ground, he looked around the burned timber beam in time to see the last troopers in the patrol continue past.

Harper needed a plan to move close to the horses of Bell's company. This time he couldn't count on help from across the river. To get their support, he would have to shout, and that would draw too much attention. He removed his blue jacket. It was too conspicuous in a town already alert to the arrival of the Federal army.

While he waited for the pain in his ribs to subside, he chuckled to himself at the lack of common sense others would see in risking a hanging to rescue a horse.

Santee had been his favorite horse since the mid-fifties, and had seen him out of more life-threatening situations in the Sioux lands than he could remember. She was the only living thing that kept him sane through those first years after his wife's and daughter's murders. He would not leave her behind to die from abuse, neglect, or overwork by the Rebels. In this war, Harper and Santee would live or die together.

He removed the leather pouch with his family's locks of hair from the pocket in his jacket. If it was to be, so be it–he was ready to join them today. He pushed the pouch into his trousers pocket.

And there were scores to settle with a certain deputy sheriff and a couple of Reb cavalrymen.

His regulation blue trousers with the pale blue stripe along the seams might alert an intelligent sentry, but Harper decided not to find another set. Many of Forrest's men wore the same color trousers, with a variety of blue, red or yellow stripes, taken during raids or from stripping dead Federals.

Leaving his jacket behind, Harper climbed the causeway again, watching both ways for any other roaming Confederates. He saw none. He stood up straight and stepped into Front Street, crossing the court house lawn to join a crowd of civilians standing along Deaderick Street watching the soldiers break camp. He watched Forrest's men strike their tents and load these and the other accoutrements of camp life into wagons. He studied the way the men moved to and from each area of the camp.

A Confederate trooper looked at him with more than passing interest, so he moved back into the crowd before any of Bell's men could recognize him. He was the only spectator not wearing a coat or a jacket in the chill February air. His white shirt showed the grime from eight days of wear, but Harper doubted the soiling was enough to prevent the blouse from being conspicuous in the crowd.

Santee, of course, was not here with the rest of Forrest's men. She was with Bell's company in the yard across the street from the jailhouse. He looked at the jail a hundred or so yards down Front Street. There was where he could steal a civilian jacket. At the same time, he could also fulfill a personal promise. He made his way back to Front

Street and crossed into the side yard of the tack and feed store next to the jail.

Through the side window, he saw a general store lit only by the rays of the sun low in the sky. It was unoccupied on Sunday afternoon. Harper climbed into the shadows on the porch and tested the front door. Locked. He slid across the porch, keeping close to the plate glass of the store front. At the opposite side of the porch, a trellis and leafless vine provided a place to watch without being seen.

No one was on the porch of the jail. Harper tried to look into the front office through the side window. He could see a single shadow moving inside, but could not identify it as one of the deputies. Rather than risk drawing attention from the jail, he moved back to the opposite side of the porch and circled behind the building. He ran from there to the rear of the jail. The only windows covering the rear of the jail were the high ones he and his men had used to watch for rescue. He moved along the brick wall of the jail until he came to the side window of the front office.

****

The lawn lay in shadow from the large courthouse. On the street in front of the hospital, Katie stepped back to allow Julia to climb into the two-horse carriage with the top now in place. Thomas watched until Julia sat before he offered his hand to assist Katie.

Katie, concentrating on Nurse Wells's promise, took Thomas's offered hand without thinking. But when she was half-way into the coach, Thomas interrupted her thoughts when he grabbed her backside and squeezed, pretending to help her up the steps. Katie's cheeks flushed with anger and embarrassment. When she saw Thomas's leering face reveal his true intent, she shuddered and turned away when she sat next to Julia.

"Mind your manners, Thomas." Julia leaned forward, blocking Thomas's view of Katie. She pushed her face through the open window when he closed the carriage door. "Treat any white woman like that again and I'll have you whipped."

"Yes, missy." Thomas's face went blank. He stepped back from the carriage door.

"Wait, wait!"

Katie recognized one of the fourth-floor guards running toward them, though she couldn't recall his name. He hustled down the steps of the hospital and along the concrete walk across the water-logged lawn. He held an envelope in front of him. Thomas turned toward the man, blocking his path to the women.

The guard handed the envelope to Thomas. "It's for the whorehouse owner, from the nurse on the fourth floor."

"I'll git it to him." Thomas opened his coat and started to push the envelope into his inside pocket.

"The nurse told me to give the letter to one of the whores."

Katie winced at the word 'whores'. She had heard it too many times since coming to the hospital. No one ever used it in a kind way.

Thomas grunted at the soldier and jammed the letter into his pocket.

"Give it here, Thomas." Julia held out her hand through the open carriage door. "It's not for Franklin. I'll make sure Eleanor gets it."

Thomas curled half his lip and pulled his eyebrows low when he looked at Julia. He made no move to retrieve the letter.

"It wasn't supposed to go to some darkey." The soldier stood his ground in front of Thomas, in spite of the height and strength differences. "Now, hand it over, boy." His arrogance toward the mulatto was clear.

Julia closed and opened her extended hand.

Katie watched Thomas's face harden, his curled lip pursing, his fists moving to his waist while he looked down at the soldier. She could see the evil in Thomas's anger and looked away, pushing deeper into her seat.

Thomas slammed the carriage door shut, forcing Julia to pull back into the cab.

"Thomas, get control of yourself." Julia knelt at the carriage door with her head out of the window. "This man is only doing what he was told." She thrust her hand through the window. "Now, hand me that."

Thomas turned slowly to face her. "Yes, missy." His voice was flat, controlled. He pulled the letter from his pocket with deliberate movements and held it out to Julia. Thomas's hate-filled gaze never Julia's eyes. "He's yo' letta."

Julia tugged it from Thomas's outstretched hand. "That's better." She pulled herself back into the carraiage. "Now, let's get going back to *Lafitte's*."

"Damned right, boy." The soldier backed away from Thomas so he could look inside the carriage. "Nurse Wells said to give it to that Eleanor woman."

Thomas snorted down in the soldier's direction before he climbed into the driver's chair.

Julia looked back at the soldier. "I'll see that she gets it." She pushed the envelope into the side pocket of her dress.

Katie let out a breath of relief. That should be the letter from Nurse Wells. Katie wanted to read it to be certain but she would have to convince Julia to let her see it. She liked working as a nurse for Wells. She would work so hard if Loreena would let come back–both at the saloon and the hospital.

The soldier stood back from the carriage. "Yes, ma'am." He looked up at Thomas's back. "You need to teach your nigger better manners, if you don't mind me sayin' so."

"Yes." Julia glanced to where the top of the carriage blocked the sight of Thomas in the driver's chair. "You're right." Louder, she called, "Ready to go, Thomas."

No answer came down from the driver's chair. But the carriage jolted into motion. Once they were beyond earshot of the soldier, Katie heard Thomas talking. He spoke as if to himself but his voice was loud enough for both women to hear.

"Thomas don' need take no talk like dat fum two whores, jes cause dey be pretendin' to be nursies. Thomas'll git dem back fas' to Massa Bosley so's dey kin git back to bein' proper whores. Let the white soldiers fuck the hell out of 'em, so's I git my payday. I might be half-nigger but at least I ain't no whore."

Katie heard all of it. She was so tired from her day. Now, she had to hear Thomas's nasty words. Were whores truly lower than darkeys? She bowed her head as tears filled her eyes. It was just too much too take.

The whip cracked and Katie was pushed harder against her seat when the carriage lurched forward.

Maybe if she was a nurse, people wouldn't be so mean. She looked at Julia's dress pocket which held the letter and dabbed the tears away, moving from her own thoughts and fears back into their present situation. She looked to see if Julia heard Thomas's comments.

Julia's body was tense and her back was straight, not touching the cushions on the seat. She couldn't see Julia's face because of the sideboards of the sunbonnet. But, Julia's hands clenched and unclenched under her cloak.

Thomas turned the carriage onto Court Street. The extra speed pushed Katie hard against the side wall while Julia bounced sideways and fell across Katie's lap. The letters from the soldiers scattered all over the carriage.

"Thomas! Slow down! Miss Julia's gittin' bounced around somethin' awful."

The carriage continued to speed down the street, splashing mud to the sides.

Julia regained her seat. "Slow down this carriage, god-damn it!"

No change in speed. The only answer from the driver's chair another crack of the whip.

Julia shifted to the front bench of the carriage and slid open the small talking window. She pounded her fist into Thomas's back. "Slow down you worthless nigger!"

No response.

Julia pulled a derringer through the pocket of her skirt. She pushed the muzzle against Thomas's back. "You feel, that boy? If you don't slow down now, I'm going to pull the trigger. I'll tell Franklin you attacked me and Miss Katie."

Katie watched, frozen in her seat. She never suspected Julia could be so cruel or angry.

Julia pushed the barrel harder against Thomas's back and clicked the hammer back. "Now, boy!"

"Whoa-oa horses."

Katie felt the carriage slow and the bouncing ended. Julia smiled at her.

"That's better, Thomas." She pulled the derringer away. "Now, let's have a nice smooth ride for the rest of the trip."

"I'm sorry, missy. Sumpin' mussa scared the horses."

"Well, you'd best be takin' better care from now on, you hear?" She shifted back to her original seat and eased the hammer of the pistol back to the half-cock before she turned to face Katie. "You can't accept that kind of behavior, Katie. Not from a darkey."

Katie stared back at her roommate wondering where Julia learned to take control that way. "Yes, ma'am." She didn't even think to use the dagger on her leg to control Thomas or the nasty soldier in the stairway. She would from now on, though. With her hands on her lap, she felt for the weapon through her dress. It hadn't left its sheath in the whole time since Eleanor bought it for her.

"And he can damn-well pick up those." Julia pointed to the letters on the floor and the bench across from them. "I don't give a damn what happens to them."

They rode the next block in silence while Katie tried to think of a way that Julia would allow her to read the letter. But the soldiers walking along the side of the street drew her attention. So many soldiers. There were women there too; some strolling alongside the soldiers, but others by themselves, standing in front of the houses or leaning over fences and calling out to the men walking past. Once a woman grabbed a soldier by the arm, forcing him and his group to stop and talk. Another lifted the shawl around her shoulders to expose her breasts in the chill air.

"Look at that, Julia." Katie pointed to a group of four women on her side of the carriage. The women blocked the way for four soldiers.

Julia's view followed Katie pointing finger. "Those women are street-walkers, Katie. They gather on this street because the cavalry camp is right there." Julia pointed to three long buildings that appeared to Katie to be barns, but stretched out longer than any barn she had ever seen.

"They take the soldiers behind the houses and sex them in the back yards or in the sheds or stables most people seem to have in this part of town."

"But the houses in this part of town look so nice and big. The people who live here must be rich, yes?" Katie looked at another group farther along the street. "They wouldn't let their women do that, would they?"

"Oh, those women aren't from Paducah. They come from all over." Julia sat back in her seat. "Most came here looking for proper work." She turned her face away, looking out of the window on her own side of the carriage. "Like I did."

Katie tried to understand. Did Julia mean she came to Paducah to find proper work for a lady, or did she mean she used to be a street-walker?

The carriage crossed Oak Street. Katie watched the people on the left side while Julia stared out the right. After they crossed Locust Street, Julia pointed to a house on her side without turning to look at Katie. "There's where I lived when I first came here. It's a ladies' boarding house. That was last summer, after the men in my town killed Mister Snodgrass for trying to recruit men to fight for the Union."

"Oh, no! How could they do that?"

"My husband was the postmaster of our town." She lowered her head but kept it turned away. "When the call went out from Washington last July for more volunteers, he tried to raise a company from the boys of the town."

Julia's back was stiff and straight again. Katie couldn't see her face.

"Four days later, on a Saturday night, a band of secessionists bought liquor for every man in the saloon. After they were well-on drunk they marched up the street to the post office. They smashed the windows and broke up all of the furniture and office equipment. When they found the National flag folded on the counter, they threw that out into the street."

Katie saw Julia's thumb stroking the handle of the derringer in her lap. "So what happened next?"

"We lived in the same building, behind the main office." Julia's head stayed low. "Hiram went into the office to try to stop them, but they beat him. I don't know how many there were but they beat him until he couldn't walk. I tried to help him but they pulled me away. Two men held me while the others put a rope around my husband's neck. They dragged poor Hiram behind a horse. Up and down the street, two, maybe three times, back and forth, with the flag tied around his neck."

Katie saw tears drop onto Julia's hands. She put her arms around Julia and hugged the smaller woman the same way Eleanor and Loreena had held her after Major Evilface almost killed her. The carriage approached the market. Here, there were many fewer soldiers on the street.

"Later that night three of them came back for me after leaving Hiram's body layin' in the post office." Julia tightened her grip on the derringer. "I was ready for them. I used Hiram's pistol to kill one in our parlor. I put a bullet into the leg of another one when they ran away."

The carriage turned onto Market Street. They were a block from *Lafitte's*.

"Did the sherriff come to help you?" Katie didn't know if Julia had finshed telling the story, but she wanted to know how it ended.

"The sheriff came, all right. He hadn't been there to face down the drunken mob, but he was sure ready to arrest one small woman for killing a drunk in her own parlor." Julia raised her head. She didn't look at Katie, but stared out of the window instead. "But I knew I needed to get away. I stole the money from the post office. I packed that with our family savings and some clothes.

"I was saddlin' a horse when he arrived. I told the son-of-a-bitch I was leaving and pointed Hiram's pistol at his chest. He didn't do anything to stop me. I rode away. He had been Hiram's friend. I expect he let me escape."

The carriage halted at the gate to *Lafitte's* rear yard. Thomas climbed down from the driver's seat and opened the gate. Katie opened the door of the carriage herself by reaching over the window ledge. She climbed down and stepped away from Thomas to wait for Julia.

Julia pointed the pistol at Thomas before she let Katie help her down. When she was on the ground, she ordered, "Thomas, you collect up those damn Rebel letters. Give them to Miss Eleanor." The scattered letters were visible as white squares in the dark interior of the carriage.

"Yes, missy." Thomas kept his neutral expression and bent into the carriage. As he scooped up the letters, Katie realized the blank expression was almost the same one she used when she was with a customer she didn't like. She used it like a mask to hide her unhappiness. Thomas must be hiding something too; probably the hatred felt for her and Julia.

Julia backed into the yard, watching Thomas as she went and keeping the pistol under her cloak pointed in the mulatto's direction. Once they were well away, she turned and Katie followed her past the rear door of the saloon. They used the door to Loreena's office and made their way to the room they shared.

After Katie locked the door, both women sat on their beds. "I'm so tired." Katie untied the bow of the sunbonnet, tossing it onto the bed. "I hope that Miss Loreena don't make us work tonight." She stood up and undid the clasp of her cloak.

"Eleanor said we would have tonight off." Julia had already hung her cloak and bonnet on the rack behind her personal dressing screen. She turned her back to Katie to have her dress unbuttoned.

"I'm glad that she did." After Katie hung her cloak and bonnet on her own rack, she came over and worked the buttons on the back of Julia's dress. "So, how do you know about the women being street walkers? What happened when you came to Paducah?"

Julia pulled the top of her dress down so it fell across the skirt before turning around to unbutton Katie's dress. "Well, I lived in the house I showed you. The lady who owns it was nice to me as long as I still had money to pay the room and board.

"I tried to find work with the Army but they didn't believe I was the assistant postmaster for my husband, and there weren't any positions for a school teacher here. Nearly everyone here has moved their children out of the city."

"Come to think of it, I don't recall seeing any young-uns since I've been here. The people must think that if there are soldiers here, there will probably be some fightin'."

After finishing with Katie's buttons, they took it in turns to pull the dresses over each other's heads.

Julia continued talking while they hung the dresses. "So, when my money ran out last December, the lady would have set me out into the street." Julia pulled the letter from her dress pocket and laid it on the bed. "She told me she would let me share her tool shed with two other girls, but I would have to pay her two dollars a week for rent. She told me what I should do to make the money. The other two girls were both street walkers already."

"Is the letter sealed, Julia? I want to see if Nurse Wells talks about me in it."

"No, it's just tucked into the envelope."

"Well, what does it say? Does it talk about me going to work at the hosipital?"

Julia opened the letter and read it. "It thanks Eleanor for letting us work today and that she wants you to come back as often as you can. She promises to teach you nursing skills if you do come back."

Katie's heart flew to the ceiling. She crossed to Julia and looked at the writing. It was hard to understand the handwriting, but there were the words that Katie wanted. Without thinking, Katie grabbed Julia in a hug for joy.

"You'll get it wrinkled." Julia folded the letter and returned it to the envelope.

"Sorry." Katie skipped to her side of the room and sat on the bed, hugging herself.

Katie watched while Julia stepped over her petticoat lying crumpled on the floor, picked it up, and tied it to a hanger. Julia gave a sigh. Her story must have made her melancholy.

"So, tell me the rest of the story. About you and the boarding house lady."

Julia untied the string on her girdle. "Well, the day before I would have to leave, Miss Loreena came to the house. The owner sent for her. Loreena looked me over before she explained that she wanted me to come and work here. She paid the boarding-house lady twenty-five dollars, and I came back with her."

Katie stood and spun her petticoat around so she could untie it. She let it fall to the floor. "But you were a proper lady. You didn't mind bein' a saloon girl?" Katie poured water into the basin and washed her face. It was easier tonight because she wasn't wearing rice powder or eye make-up.

"I minded it, all right. But, Katie, I'd been in Paducah six months by that time. Loreena came and I had already resigned myself to becoming a street walker so I wouldn't starve. Winter had come and I'd be out in the cold. I didn't have any more money to try in another city.

The truth is, I had already had a soldier up to my room for money. So, when I went with Loreena, I wasn't happy about it, but I decided it was better than any other choices."

Katie tried to sort it out. In the city, street walkers were lower than saloon girls. That made sense. Saloon girls lived safer and got paid better. And being a courtesan, like Eleanor, must be better even than being a saloon girl. And every kind of white woman, even a whore, was better than any kind of colored, including mulattos like Thomas.

Katie sat on her bed. "I'm so tired. I could just fall asleep right now." She felt a happy kind of tired from all the work at the hospital. Surely, Eleanor would let her work there sometimes. She *had* to.

Katie looked across at Julia loosening the strings on her girdle. "Can I see your pistol?" Katie pointed to the holster strapped over Julia's pantaloons.

Julia glanced at the knife on Katie's right thigh. "All right." She drew the weapon and popped the primer cap off before tossing it across the room. "Besides, Katie. You know we make very good money working here, don't you?"

"Umm, uh-hunh." The pistol fascinated Katie. She pulled back the hammer to full-cock and pointed the barrel at the dressing screen.

Julia went to the wash basin, dumped the used water into the chamber pot, and poured fresh water.

"Bang." Katie raised the pistol in her hand, imitating the recoil as if she had fired it. "I still owe Mister Bosley too much. I ain't makin' as much as the rest of you." She walked across and handed the pistol back to Julia, who reset the primer and eased the hammer to half-cock before she returned the gun to the holster. Julia hung the holster by its straps on the bedpost next to her pillow before both women sat to pull down their stockings, balling them into their shoes.

Katie undid the knife sheath from her thigh and placed it under her own pillow. She yawned aloud. She could feel her 'farm' muscles going stiff and sore as she crawled under the covers.

Below them, they could hear the noises from the saloon rising with the usual Sunday busness. But Eleanor had excused them for tonight, and Katie was grateful for that. Eleanor was so smart; she knew they would be tired. Eleanor took good care of them.

The people outside *Lafitte's* called Eleanor a whore, too. But Eleanor wasn't evil the way Nurse Wells said whores were supposed to be. The street walkers looked like the evil type of whore. Katie took her three Cypressville dollies from their shelf beside the bed and held them close while she closed her eyes.

The room grew darker as the final twilight faded. Katie was looking forward to a long night's sleep. She heard Julia's voice in the darkness.

"You know, Katie, people call us whores now, and being called that hurts a lot. But I think there are going to be many, many women like us before the war is over."

"What do you mean?"

"You know. Women who are being soiled by the war." Julia paused. "I think there will be so many of us. The men coming home when the war is over won't mind it as much as people did before the war. The rules will be different."

"Uh-hunh." In her mind, Katie slipped into a dark room where she knew there was no danger, only comfort. She would become a nurse; that was hard work but she loved doing it. And it was a nice thing to do for the injured men. Eleanor was nice. If Eleanor could be nice and not evil, but still be a whore, maybe Katie could be a nice whore, too. After she learned to talk like Julia, Eleanor would teach her to be a *courtesan.* And a nurse. With a broad white apron. Nurses were better than any kind of whore.

"At least we're in a safe place for now, with a roof over our heads and food to eat." Julia's voice floated through the darkness.

Katie smiled to herself for being safe, and warm, and not hungry; and for being tired from the hospital work. Maybe a little bit hungry, but it could wait until morning.

"Not like the soldiers, camping out in the winter weather."

"Ummm…" What did Julia just say?

A single musket went off somewhere in the distance.

"And no one's trying to kill *us*."

****

Deputy Shepperton sat alone at the main desk in the office, watching the activity on the town square through the front windows, his face puffed blue and black from the blow which broke his nose. Cotton stuffed his nostrils. The other two pro-Confederate deputies would have gone off-duty by now. Harper did not see Shepperton's assistant, Deputy Werts.

There would be guns he could use in the cabinet, but he needed to get past Shepperton. Harper's head and ribs still ached from the beating three days earlier. Getting past that man was a necessity, which would also be a pleasure.

It would take too long to deal with Shepperton using his bare hands, especially if Werts showed up. He moved to the yard behind the jail. Close to the edge of the bluff, he found what he wanted–a rock the size of a fist, rounded by the action of some long-ago river. A second rock, about the same size, lay near it. Harper gathered both and made his way back to the front of the jail.

The jailhouse blocked the sunlight; Harper needed to hurry. He returned to the side window and saw Shepperton still seated behind the desk. He crouched below the side window. Keeping his face down so Shepperton wouldn't identify him, he stepped onto the porch, walked past the front window, and through the door with a rock ready to throw.

The muzzle of Shepperton's pistol pointed straight at Harper's face.

"I saw you sneaking around outside." Shepperton stayed in his seat and cocked the pistol. "I was hoping I'd see you again, and here you come, right to me."

Harper threw the rock at Shepperton's bloody face and dodged for the door to the cell room.

Click.

There was no gunshot.

Harper's rock connected with Shepperton's face, slightly above the bridge of his broken nose. Shepperton fell back into the chair.

Harper jumped on top of the deputy, toppling the chair backward. "I told you I'd be back." Harper pounded the second rock into Shepperton's cheek with as much strength as he could while lying atop the man. It tore at the flesh, opening a new wound.

Harper shifted to sit on Shepperton's chest. Shepperton pushed against Harper's knee, trying to wriggle out before he was pinned to the floor. His eyes went wide with fear when Harper gained his seat. Using both hands, Harper brought the rock down again, landing in the center of the face and forcing the cartilage from the broken nose through the solid bones behind. The rogue deputy yelped at the pain and grabbed for Harper's arm with both hands while blood flowed into his eyes.

Harper pushed Shepperton's outstretched arms aside. He captured them between his own arm and his body. With all of the force of adrenaline, frustration, and hatred, he brought the rock down again, impacting squarely between Shepperton's eyes.

Shepperton's forehead seemed to collapse into the sink-hole of his nose, expanding the size of the depression. His eyes went blank and he lay still.

Harper brought the rock down again with all of his strength onto the same spot and was rewarded with a final, satisfying crunch.

Harper could feel the energy drain from Shepperton's body under him. It slumped, face frozen. Blood ran onto the floor. The left eye dangled past the edge of Shepperton's eyesocket – staring over Harper's shoulder. The lifeless right eye watched Harper's face.

The rabid dog lay on the floor. Not blinking. Not moving. Not drawing his pistol. Not cursing Yankees. Not abusing prisoners. Still breathing. Blood gurgling at the back of his throat.

The ache in Harper's head returned and he had to lean against the desk while the dizziness passed. While he waited, he checked the windows and saw no one.

He retrieved the cell room keys from a peg on the wall and slid the large ring onto his forearm. Returning to Shepperton, Harper hefted the inert deputy over his shoulder and deposited him on a cot in the shadows of the side cell farthest from the doorway. He unbuckled Shepperton's gun belt before he rolled the body onto its side facing the wall.

"Oh-h-h-h." A groan came from Shepperton when his head drooped sideways onto the cot last used by Private Davis.

Damn. The bastard is still alive.

Harper looked around the cell for a way to restrain Shepperton should he regain consciousness. Nothing. He returned to his plan, yanked on Shepperton's holster and pulled the gun belt from under the body. A jangling noise drew his attention to a set of handcuffs hanging from the belt next to a sheathed hunting knife. He found the key in Shepperton's pocket and cuffed the inert man to the frame of the cot, making it impossible for him to roll over.

Harper buckled the gun belt around his own waist. After taking a final look around, he locked Shepperton's cell door and threw the handcuff keys into the fire box of the stove.

In the front office, he moved to the gun locker in the corner and tried using the keys on the large ring. None worked. He looked in the drawers of the desk without success.

This was taking too long. Not only would Deputy Werts return, but he saw more of Bell's men bridling and saddling their horses across the street. They were almost finished breaking camp. He returned to the gun locker and started working on the hasp with Shepperton's hunting knife.

A tread on the steps to the porch alerted him. He spun around and hid behind the sheriff's desk. Shepperton's pistol lay at his feet.

"Shepperton, I'm back."

Harper waited until Werts was well inside the office before he stood with Shepperton's misfired pistol.

"Stop, Deputy."

Werts halted short of the desk. Slowly, he raised his hands, his eyes taking in the room.

"Where's Shepperton?"

"You'll see. Slowly hand me the shotgun–stock first."

Werts did as Harper ordered. Harper grabbed at the weapon and turned it on Werts. He put the misfiring pistol on the desk.

"Now, with your left hand, unbuckle your gun belt and place it on the desk."

"Take it easy, Lieutenant. I'm not gonna make a fuss." Werts placed his gun belt next to the pistol. "I wasn't part of the plan to beat you. That's why Shepperton ordered me to supervise the men cleaning the cells that day. I'm sorry they did it."

"Good. In that case, we can do this the easy way. Go!" Harper pointed to the cell room.

Werts stared at Shepperton's body while Harper pushed him into the cell adjacent to Shepperton's and locked the door. "Now, be quiet until I leave." He looked at Werts's pockets. "Where is the key to the gun locker?"

"It's on a chain Shepperton keeps around his neck."

"Damn."

Harper reentered Shepperton's cell. Blood had formed a pool on the floor under the injured man's head and there was no reaction when Harper pulled the leather from his neck. Harper dropped Shepperton's head onto a pillow, now soggy with blood, its ferric smell filling the cell. Shepperton's breathing no longer gurgled in his throat.

"Is he dead?"

Harper locked Shepperton's cell. "I don't know. His skull's been caved in." He crossed to the door. "I'll be gone in a few minutes. If ya start yellin', I'll come back here and make sure ya can't yell anymore."

Werts looked across at Shepperton. "I'll be quiet."

"Good." Harper closed the door to the front office. It would muffle Werts's shouts after Harper left.

Harper strapped Werts's gun belt around his waist, over Shepperton's, with the holster backward on his left hip. He checked the load in Werts's gun; six full chambers, but percussion caps on just five.

Inside the gun locker he found four shotguns and two long rifles. Above these, six Navy Colts lay in their holsters on a shelf. Harper set these on the desk along with a box of paper cartridges and a box of percussion caps from the top shelf in the gun locker.

After he determined that the six pistols were fully loaded, he added the missing caps to all of the pistols except the chambers under the hammer. He examined Shepperton's pistol to see if he could clear the misfire quickly. The gun hadn't misfired at all. All of the chambers were empty. Shepperton must have forgotten to reload after shooting down at Harper and his men during the escape. He took six paper cartridges and five caps from their boxes and reloaded Shepperton's gun.

He pulled a large buffalo-skin overcoat from its peg and tugged it on. This would hide his white military-issue blouse. The long brown coat covered him to his boot tops. He pushed the boxes with the remaining cartridges and caps into the deep pockets of the coat before he dropped two pistols into each pocket. The two remaining pistols went under the coat, into his waistband. He drew Shepperton's and Werts's hunting knives from their sheaths and placed them beside the pistols in the overcoat before working the buttons up his chest.

Taking Shepperton's brown slouch hat from the pegs on the wall behind the sheriff's desk, Harper left the jail. Across the street, Santee and the four other stolen horses still stood tethered to a taut line set by Bell's men. From this perspective, she looked thinner, perhaps hungrier, and she fidgeted against the tether to the taut-line.

Harper stepped onto the porch. He kept the hat brim low over his face while he watched. On the court house lawn, most of Forrest's battalion had finished striking camp and men were already mounting, moving to the assembly points at the opposite end of the lawn. Others carried the paraphernalia of camp life to be loaded into the regiment's supply wagons. The horses in Bell's company stood without their saddles or bridles while the men lounged around the back yard of the hotel. Four bodies lay on the side of the road next to the yard where Bell's men waited–probably the men killed by the Federal scouts earlier that morning.

Bell's men had moved their horses out of the stable serving the hotel and into Front Street. They waited there, secured to a taut line along the side of the road. There was no sign of Bell or Corporal Stackpole. Lieutenant Saint Philemon gave direction to the men of the company.

Harper made his way to the court house lawn. Harper entered the supply area, where teamsters supervised groups of negroes who loaded the wagons along Front Street. Hopefully, none among them would recognize the battalion's former prisoner. Even though this put him farther away from Bell's horses, approaching from this direction would draw less attention than moving straight to the horses from the jail.

Taking a deep breath, Harper stepped out of the confused bustle within the supply area and made his way back toward Santee and the other Indian ponies. Ready to react if anyone recognized him, he made it safely the half-block to the yard where Bell's men waited. Ignoring the Confederate soldiers, Harper approached Santee.

"There, there, girl. I'm here now." Santee sniffed the air before she turned to look at Harper. She snorted and nodded in recognition.

"What in the hell do you think you're doin' there, boy?'

Harper turned to face the speaker, a typical trooper from Bell's command. This fellow was part of a group of men lounging closest to the horses, perhaps farriers or the guards responsible for protecting the mounts.

"Orders, mister." By now, after a week in custody, Harper's voice had taken on some of the accent of a west Tennessean. He put a hand into the pocket of the buffalo coat and found the knife in his right pocket before walking toward the man. "The quartermaster sent me to git three of y'all's spare horses to help pull a wagon."

Harper wasn't sure he could handle more than three horses in an escape attempt. With Davis dead and Bailey crippled, that's all he would need. When the trooper came closer, Harper wrapped his fingers around the hidden knife.

"No one told me about that. I'm supposed to be watching to make sure no one steals any of them horses." The horse guard pointed to Santee. "Well, you cain't have that gray one. That's Cap'n Bell's personal horse."

"It's got a Yankee brand on it. How can it be the captain's personal horse?"

"I'm jes' followin' my orders. You cain't have that one. Take the three next to it." He pointed to the left of Santee.

"These three?" Harper looked past the soldier. The men from his group watched but did not bother to stand up.

"Yup. You can take those. They're too small to be much good as cavalry horses."

"Yes, sir." Harper touched his fingers to the brim of his hat. "Much obliged." He pointed to the three horses next to Santee with the unique brand of the First Iowa, the letters US surrounded by the outline of the state of Iowa. "I'll jes' take those three instead."

The guard walked back to his friends without answering. Harper ducked under the taut-line and faced the designated horses.

Instead of a halter, each of the former Iowan horses was secured using a simple rope looped around its neck and tied to the taut line. Through the corner of his eyes, Harper continued to watch the guards while he untied the first two horses. He led them sideways against the third, the one next to Santee. None of the men in the group seemed to be paying attention. Deftly, he undid the knot of Santee's rope and tied a slip-knot around the taut line without being seen. Before untying the third horse, he stroked Santee's face above her white nose.

"Shhh… It'll be all right."

He saw the First Iowa's brand on the horse on the opposite side from Santee, the only gelding in the group of five. Harper rigged his tether, too. After he untied the third horse, he pushed the three designated horses backward, out of line and walked them past the guards. "Thanks, soldier."

None of the guards looked up. Harper led the horses up the street in the general direction of the supply wagons. He turned onto Deaderick Street where the teamsters assembled and harnessed the four-horse teams needed for each wagon. Harper could not decide if the teamsters were civilians or Confederate soldiers. He kept his head down and continued walking until he emerged at the end of the row of wagons, close to the spectators.

"Y'all fixin' to steal them horses, mister?" A uniformed man approached Harper. The three straight stripes connecting the tips of three yellow chevrons, signified he was one of the regiments' quartermaster sergeants.

"No sergeant. I'm jes' gonna bring 'em under these trees out of the way until the driver is ready for them."

"Which driver is that?"

Harper cast a quick glance at the nearest wagons to see which looked like it would need the extra horses. "I don't know his name, sergeant, but he has a black beard and long black hair."

"How come y'all don't know his name? Don't you know everyone here? How long y'all been in this battalion, boy?"

"Sergeant, sir, I only jes' joined on when y'all came through…" Harper struggled to recall the names of the villages they passed through during the escape from Fort Donelson, "…er, Maysville, sergeant." Harper watched to see if his hesitation raised the sergeant's suspicions.

"Well, y'all sure ain't one of my men. What company you in?"

"Cap'n Bell's company, Sergeant."

"Well, then, git the hell out of here and go back to your company.

Y'all can tie the horses to that tree."

"Yes, Sergeant." Harper walked toward the selected tree, an oak, under the suspicious gaze of the sergeant.

"Well, ain't we lucky. Here's Captain Bell comin' now." The sergeant looked at two men walking from the headquarters in City Hall. "He can vouch for your thievin' hide."

Harper unbuttoned the front of the buffalo overcoat while Bell and Stackpole approached. They turned to avoid the busy quartermaster's area.

"Captain Bell." The sergeant waved. "Captain Bell, would all y'all come over here, sir?"

Harper tilted his head so the brim of his hat hid his face. Bell knew about the paroles. If they captured him now, then Bell would have full justification to hang him on the spot, maybe from the very tree which now shaded him. Harper put his right hand into the pocket of the buffalo coat and wrapped his fingers around the handle of one of the pistols. His mind prepared for the coming fight.

Bell stopped and turned to face the sergeant. "What is it, Madrigal?"

"Over here, sir. It'll jes' take a minute."

Bell's voice carried on the rising evening breeze when he and Stackpole walked toward the sergeant. "Damn, that was near-run, Stackpole. I don't think the colonel really believed we took them prisoners down to the river to clean them up." A scowl contorted Bell's flushed face.

"Well, done is done, Cap'n." Stackpole spit a wad of tobacco juice at the ground. "I guess the colonel's got more important things to worry about. At least you're still in command of the company and we'll be headin' for home once we git to Shelbyville."

"Guess Forrest knows if'n I leave, most of the company will come with me."

Bell must be returning from explaining the escape of the prisoners and the cross-river firefight afterward. His company must be waiting for their captain to return before saddling their horses and riding away.

"What do you want, Madrigal?" Bell and Stackpole stopped in front of the sergeant, about ten paces away from where Harper held the tethers for the three horses.

"Captain Bell. I caught this man stealin' some of our horses." Madrigal pointed to Harper. "He says he is one of y'all's men. Is that true?"

"Let me see him."

"Right over here, sir. Is he one of y'all's men?"

"I can't see his face clear." Bell approached Harper, followed by Stackpole and Madrigal.

Harper took position in front of the horses. Keeping the tether lines in his left hand, he pulled back the hammer of the pistol, felt it click into place.

"What's your name, son?"

Harper tilted his head back to reveal his face.

Stackpole's eyebrows were the first to rise in surprise and recognition.

Bam.

Stackpole, the overseer of the violence against Harper's men, was only able to unbutton the flap of his holster before Harper put a bullet into his chest, somewhere near the heart. An acrid cloud of gunsmoke blew past Harper.

Madrigal reached for Harper.

"Harper, you son-of-a-bitch." Bell had his pistol out but Madrigal was in the line-of-fire.

Harper dodged to the right to avoid Madrigal's grab and fired at the sergeant.

Bam. Missed.

The horses followed the pull on their tethers, stamping their feet and trying to pull away from the gunshots. Harper circled behind the horses, putting them between himself and Bell. He took hold of the mane of the nearest, a bay mare, and pulled himself onto her back. He gasped at the pain in his ribs.

Bam. A bullet zipped between Harper and the horse's neck.

Madrigal was still on his feet and grabbed the tether of the nearest horse.

Bam. Harper's shot missed when the sergeant ducked under the horse's neck. Harper looked for Bell through the cloud of gunsmoke.

He saw the Rebel captain taking careful aim.

B-bam. Harper and Bell fired at nearly the same instant.

The haunch of the outside horse erupted with a bloody pop from Bell's bullet. The sorrel roan reared up at the injury, knocking Madrigal to the ground. Harper strengthened his grip on the rope tethers and fired a second shot at Bell before all three animals galloped away together, heading for the river.

Bending low over the neck of his horse, Harper saw groups of soldiers getting to their feet and looking around. He aimed at the nearest and pulled the trigger.

Bam, click.

Empty. He threw the useless weapon away and used both hands to steer the horses down Front Street. Two men wrapped in blankets separated themselves from the crowd of civilians on the court house lawn and moved to intercept Harper. He drew a pistol from the left coat pocket, cocked the weapon, aimed at the larger of the two men and squeezed the trigger.

The larger man threw off his blanket and Harper saw Magnusson's all-blue uniform immediately before the pistol discharged.

Bam.

He rode past the smoke cloud from the discharge.

Thank God that *one missed.*

Both of the men continued running to intercept the horses. The group spilled across the street and onto the bridge ramp opposite before they could bring the small herd to a halt.

"I told ya to stay out of sight!"

"Yes, sir." Magnusson grinned at Harper. "And I told *you*, sir, I wasn't goin' to leave anyone behind." Magnusson took the tether for the outside horse from Harper.

"Let Cooke have that one. It's been shot and he's smaller than you."

Magnusson put his hands into a cup and hoisted Cooke atop the sorrel roan.

Harper tossed the tether for the center horse, the true sorrel, to Magnusson. While the large corporal struggled to mount the bareback horse, Harper looked at the Rebel camp, pistol ready. Most of the remaining soldiers were on their feet, watching–trying to sort out what was happening. Bell himself ran toward him yelling and pushing men to get their weapons.

"I'm ready."

"Here." Harper passed the pistols from his waist band to Cooke and Magnusson. All three fired at the Rebels who started chasing them. Their pursuers dropped to the ground.

Warm gratitude swelled in Harper's chest for these men who would risk their lives to rescue him. Now, he needed to get all of them out of the current chaos so they wouldn't all be hanged.

"This way!" Instead of riding across the court house lawn, Harper led downstream, away from the camps. The crossing-shot would make them more difficult targets for anyone shooting from the camp. A few Confederates fired but missed. The civilian by-standers ducked under cover.

Harper bent low and put his head alongside the horse's neck on the side away from the shooters. His men followed his example, holding tight to the tethers and manes. Cooke's horse limped and fell behind.

At Charlotte Street, Harper waited until Cooke caught up before he pointed ahead, down-river. Magnusson and Cooke galloped away with the Rebel wagons shielding them from fire by the remaining soldiers in the main camp. Cooke's horse did its best to keep up. Harper spun to face in the opposite direction. He needed to find Santee.

"Kye-yip-yip-yahh!" Harper looked down Front Street to the taut line for Bell's horses. As he expected, there was a disturbance there among the horses, although he could not be certain Santee was free.

"Kye-yip-yip-yahh!" Harper watched the confusion among Bell's horses.

Bell's men showed activity now–some moving to control the horses, others running in his direction. Behind Bell's men, Harper saw mounted Confederates turning onto Front Street. They would block his escape to the south.

A bullet carried his hat away, reminding Harper he had to keep moving.

Harper fired at his nearest pursuers again before he spurred the horse farther up Front Street, toward Bell's milling horses. His animal bolted forward, and Harper almost slid off. Gripping with his knees and holding tightly to the tether, he halted halfway to Bell's taut line. He looked at the jail to see if anyone emerged. No one did.

"Kye-yip-yip-yahh!" He watched the stir among the mob of horses.

"Kye-yip-yip-yahh!" He waited.

Now, he saw Santee's gray face with the dark spots and white nose, kicking her way toward him. When she was clear, her three black stockings confirmed it was Santee.

"Kye-yip-yip-yahh!" Santee galloped toward him, followed by the black gelding, the last of the horses from First Iowa. The other horses stayed near the company area, with Bell's troopers busy rounding them up.

Harper turned to follow Magnusson and Cooke. Instead, he saw a loose line of Rebels blocking the street.

Damn.

Several of the men ahead of him shot quickly, the bullets zipping past his head. Behind him came the group of mounted cavalry. These halted when the men on foot fired. Bell's men ducked for cover to avoid the bullets coming from the line in front of Harper.

To his left lay a solid row of buildings. To his right, buildings overlooked the river; he knew some of these had fences which extended all the way to the edge of the bluff. These would block an escape along the bluff through the rear yards.

He was cut off.

Harper pulled the tether tight around his horse's neck and wrapped it around his right wrist. It would tend to pull the horse to the right, away from the main Rebel camps. He drew the last of the pistols from the pockets of the buffalo coat, one in each hand.

"Kye-yip-yip-yahh!" Santee was alongside now. Harper spurred his mount at the line of Rebels blocking the street. He aimed for the men on the extreme end of the line, closest to the river. Bent over the horse's neck and firing, he emptied both pistols. Several of the men in the street fell. Still more men crowded in against him, forcing Harper and the free horses against the front wall of O'Neill's Stables.

Halted by the crowd of Rebels, he tried to break through by swinging at the men pushing the horses against the building. There were more shots, in front of him, farther away–he was too busy with the Rebels around him to look for the source.

Two of the men in front of Harper fell over, shot in the back. Others turned to look behind them. Alone, one Rebel held the tether for Harper's horse, grinning and using his free hand to point a carbine at Harper's belly.

"Gotcha, Yank."

Harper swung at the weapon, pushing it to the side.

Bam.

The carbine discharged under the buffalo coat. Harper felt the burn of a new wound in his side when he swung at the man's face. The trooper backed away–out of reach, but still grasping the tether of Harper's horse.

The Confederates who had turned around now aimed at some distant target, but Harper concentrated on the man who blocked his way. Santee pushed into the Reb as she tried to force her way past. The gelding slipped past the man and his companions, cutting him off. The combined weight of Santee and the horse Harper rode forced the man backward, still holding the tether, still grinning.

Harper dropped the empty pistol in his right hand and retrieved the one from his right holster. He caught the grinning man by surprise when he brought the pistol across the horse's neck and squeezed off a hasty shot. It took off the man's hat and grazed the top of his skull. This shot, so close to her ear, terrified Harper's horse. She reared and kicked the Rebel holding the tether in the chest. He fell to the ground. Harper squeezed the horse's sides with his knees and feet to stay mounted.

Still, the Reb held tight to the tether. The horse's hooves landed on top of him

Crack. Crunch.

Harper heard and felt one of the mare's hooves stove in the man's chest. The horse stumbled but she did not fall. Harper threw the empty pistol in his left hand at the next closest Rebel. Once the horse regained her feet, Harper spurred her forward.

"Kye-yip-yip-yahh!" Together the three horses pushed past the surviving Rebels. The corpse underneath Harper's horse hung from the tether for several steps before it slipped from his hands.

They were through the roadblock, leaving half-a-dozen prostrate Rebels in the street, the rest, reloading.

Ahead, near the bridge approach ramp, he saw two riders in blue, Magnusson and Cooke. He galloped toward them. They had to be the ones firing at the road block. Looking over his shoulder, Harper saw the mounted Confederates on Front Street pass through the broken line of Rebels.

Then he saw the new threat. A second group of mounted cavalry appeared on the court house lawn, scattering the quartermaster's men.

Magnusson and Cooke waited for Harper. They must be out of ammunition. The group on the Court House lawn would reach them before he did. He would not let these men be captured as their reward for coming to rescue him.

Harper fired at the new group. At this range, across his body, from a moving horse, Harper knew there was no chance for a hit.

The Federal corporal took a full second before he understood the situation. He and Cooke turned and galloped away along Front Street. The group of Confederates to Harper's front split when they reached Front Street, some blocking Harper's escape down the causeway, others chasing Magnusson and Cooke.

Harper pulled his horse to a halt. Santee and the gelding halted at the same time. He heard the Confederates closing behind him, the ones in front of him leveled their carbines. There was only one way out.

Harper turned the mare toward the river. The horses made their way through a side yard of a carriage factory until they reached the edge of the bluff next to the bridge abutment. Harper kicked the sides of the mare and slapped her rear. She hesitated to go over the edge.

The Rebels behind him turned into the side yard and halted, weapons ready. On foot, Captain Bell pushed his way through the line of mounted men. Harper thought he saw a trace of blood staining the hip of Bell's trousers, partially hidden by the jacket.

"You're trapped, Harper." Bell's face was crimson red, lips pulled back to expose teeth clenched in hatred, the twitch under his right eye was back. Bell's rabid-dog face.

"No need to take you prisoner. You're in civilian clothes and that makes y'all a spy. So where's your *parole* now, Harper?" Twenty paces from Harper, Bell raised his pistol. "Time to die, you bastard." Bell took aim.

Harper placed the barrel of his pistol along the horse's rump, pointing at the ground behind her. "Not today, Bell." When he fired his last round, the horse's reflexes to the sting from the noise and heat of the muzzle blast drove her forward over the edge of the bluff. Harper grabbed the tether with both hands and leaned back.

"Kye-yip-yip-yahh!"

Santee jumped, and the gelding followed over the bluff.

Bell's bullet ploughed through the fur collar of the buffalo coat and burnt a trail along Harper's cheek. Shots from the other Rebels went high before Harper dropped out of view.

It was all up to the horses now. Would their wild-born instincts get them down this bluff? Could they negotiate the steep slope? Harper knew Santee could, but he did not know this horse. She slid on her rump while her front hooves tried to slow the drop. Harper leaned back until his torso lay on the horse's rump, his legs trying to find a grip along the horse's flanks.

Dust rose when the horse dragged her rump on the soft loess. The mare crashed downward, larger stones surrounding her hooves and cascading alongside her. Her forelegs pawed for any secure place to land. Once, Harper's legs lost their grip and he felt himself sliding forward when his horse reached for the ground at the steepest part of the slope. His knees and feet found purchase around the horse's neck and he stopped sliding. The gelding following Santee tumbled past, landing with a thump on the mudflat thirty feet below, covered by a slide of dirt and stones knocked loose during his fall.

By the time Bell's men reached the top of the bluff, Harper was nearly to the mudflat. The bay mare sprang forward from her hind legs, landing softly. Santee waited at the bottom; the gelding found his feet and stood beside Santee with bleeding knees. Several bullets from atop the bluff punctuated the soft mud around them with muffled thuds.

"Kye-yip-yip-yahh!" Harper used his heels on the mare's sides to gallop the small herd north, downriver. He guided the horse to remain as close to the bluff as possible. It was better going there, and it made them a more difficult target to men firing down from above.

He stopped in the shadow of the bridge abutment and pulled the pistol from the holster on his left hip, checked the number of loaded chambers in his final weapon: five rounds.

He looked behind and could not see the group with Bell. Harper doubted they would risk their animals in a descent over the bluffs. They would either use the causeway by the ferry landing or gallop along Front Street to get ahead of him. It would take them only moments to decide.

Harper made his own decision quickly. He holstered the pistol and dismounted to recover his blue uniform jacket in the gathering darkness, throwing Shepperton's buffalo coat into the Cumberland River. He started to remount the bay mare when Santee poked him in the back with her muzzle.

Harper laughed. "Okay girl. I missed ya too." He rubbed Santee's face spots. "Now, let's get out of here."

Before he mounted Santee, he gathered the three tethers together and tucked the leads on the bay and the gelding under his legs, one on each side. He wrapped Santee's lead around his right wrist. Last, he pulled his remaining weapon.

He allowed Santee to make her way through the bridge debris with the other two horses close on either side. When the group emerged from the debris field, Harper kicked Santee into a gallop. Coming clear of the bridge abutment, he saw the lead Confederate making his way down the causeway. He sent two bullets into the chest of the man's horse and watched it drop to its knees, then tumble over–blocking the causeway.

Harper and Santee raced along the mudflat. The tethers of the other horses pulled free from his legs. Still, the bay and the gelding followed Santee's lead in the race alongside the river. Gunfire sounded from behind him, wild shots. In response, puffs of gunsmoke blossomed from the buildings on his right, across the river, many more than earlier in the day.

After all he went through this week, would he now be shot by his own army? They should be able to see his blue uniform in the shadow of the bluff. Harper pointed Santee's nose at a copse where the trees overhung the mudflat and branches reached into the river.

The Federals in Edgefield concentrated on his pursuers. Harper sped away. Once past the copse, no more bullets came his way. A rock projecting from the bluff blocked their path, so he led the horses into the river to go around it. Once beyond the rock, he felt safe from his pursuers, and at least a mile away from the cavalry camps. He took a deep breath. It caught against the old pain in his ribs, much worse than when he first climbed the causeway.

Blood oozed down his left leg from the new wound in his side. He felt more blood running down his neck from the bullet's trail in his cheek. He would tend to these after he found a safe place to hide for the night.

He slowed Santee to a walk. The other two horses fell into a column behind Santee as the group faded into the moonless night.

****

After Forrest's column left Nashville, Mayor Cheatham crossed the Cumberland River in a row boat and surrendered the town to the Federal lieutenant of cavalry who was the senior officer among the scouts lining the eastern bank. General William Nelson, acting under Grant's orders, arrived by riverboat from Fort Donelson with five thousand men on Monday morning. General Don Carlos Buell, with the main part of the Army of the Ohio, did not arrive until Wednesday, February 26th.

PART 5

DOVER, TENNESSEE

The Dover Inn
(Historic American Buildings Survey)

Tuesday, March 4th, 1862

Harper sat waiting in the rays of the fading sun slanting into the parlor of the Dover Inn inside the Fort Donelson fortifications. He was grateful to be clean, with a new set of long-johns under his uniform. The wounds to his ear, chin, and side were clean and healed well enough that they would not turn septic.

He had no head cover, lost during Santee's rescue. The local quartermaster did not have Hardee-style hats in supply and Harper refused to wear a kepi scavenged from the dead of the battles in early February. When the wind blew cold or the sun was high in the sky, the lack of headgear still caused him occasional dizziness from the beating by the Nashville deputies.

The delay in returning to the First Iowa frustrated Harper. Monroe would probably replace him while he was gone. But the parole was the cost imposed by Dupree for release of all the prisoners–and thus, for their three lives.

After Harper and the others escaped the Confederates, Colonel Monroe sent orders from the camp at Crump's Landing, Tennessee, a few miles north of the border with Mississippi. Monroe directed them to wait at Fort Donelson for the arrival of Captain Brice McKinsey. McKinsey was the company commander for the four enlisted men in Harper's *picquet*. Monroe's orders stated that Harper must file a report describing the full outcome of the mission. Also, McKinsey would need more details about the deaths of Davis and Bailey in order to include the information in condolence letters to the men's next-of-kin. However, because McKinsey came himself, instead of his deputy commander, Harper suspected that this meeting would be more that a simple report. McKinsey, another politician, was the company commander who was closest to Monroe. McKinsey could be here to do Monroe's dirty work.

The hotel staff had set the dining room for evening meal before Sergeant Hopkins opened the door to the small office opposite Harper's chair. Corporal Magnusson appeared in the office doorway and walked past Hopkins. The corporal looked at Harper, and rolled his eyes. Harper nodded back in recognition, puzzled with Magnusson's reaction. Maybe Magnusson was too impressed by the formality of the process.

"You can go in now, sir." Hopkins worked for the army judge advocate's office and was in Fort Donelson to assist McKinsey with the inquiries.

"Just a minute, Sergeant Hopkins." McKinsey emerged behind Magnusson. "I want to take a personal break first, before we talk with Lieutenant Harper."

"Of course, sir."

Harper watched McKinsey's wide back while the captain made his way to the hotel's back door. McKinsey had ordered the three former prisoners to meet with him separately. Cooke's interview had taken place that morning. Harper arrived on time for his mid-afternoon meeting, but found he must wait until McKinsey finished with Magnusson.

McKinsey soon returned from the outhouse. He took a moment to look at the blood stains on Harper's uniform. "Come in, Mister Harper." McKinsey led the way into the office. Sergeant Hopkins followed Harper and closed the door. The fact that McKinsey did not use his first name gave Harper more reason to be suspicious following Magnusson's eye-roll.

Harper walked into a wall of hot air, fueled by a large fire in the brick hearth of the small hotel office. McKinsey took the chair behind a common, work-a-day desk, with several folders set to one side of the blotter. A silver tray holding a ceramic pitcher and six clear glasses occupied the other side of the desk. Sergeant Hopkins sat at a student's desk along the side wall next to the fireplace, facing inward toward McKinsey. Harper sat in the single chair in front of the desk, although two other chairs lined the front wall of the room.

"Well, Mister Harper. Looks like you all had some adventures durin' your capture." McKinsey set his hands on the desk, fingers spread. "Assumin' Magnusson and Cooke can be believed." He picked up two piles of handwritten papers as he named the men.

"We saw a lot. Did ya know the owner of the whorehouse in Paducah is probably a spy? I saw him with some of his women entertainin' Bedford Forrest's officers in Nashville."

"Truly? Well, you'll have to put that in your report. From the looks of ya, there must be quite a story to tell."

McKinsey glanced down at Harper's uniform jacket and trousers. They showed worn patches in the wool from the wear and tear of the campaign and his escape, though it was less than three months old. It was clean. However, the washerwomen could not remove the blood stains completely, neither his own nor the Rebel captain's. Neither could they remove the powder burn from his trousers.

"What's this about, Brice?"

"Captain McKinsey, please, Lieutenant." McKinsey's smile was pleasant but the smile did not reach his eyes. "Colonel Monroe has sent me here to conduct a court-of-inquiry about the circumstances of your capture and your subsequent actions, particularly since they resulted in the death of two of my men, Privates—" he picked up his notes, "Bailey and Davis."

Harper sat up in his chair. First McKinsey insisted on using his formal title, now there was a formal inquiry. "Is this a trial? Why? What does Monroe think happened?"

McKinsey shook his head. "This isn't a court-martial, Lieutenant. No one's on trial. I'm here to document what happened while you and the others were away from the battalion. That's all." He tapped the papers in his hand on the top of the table to align their edges. "We need to know for the record."

For the record–hell. McKinsey was here to get him drummed out of the army. That's why he had the sergeant from the judge advocate's office here. Harper knew he was not a favorite of the captain's. Not only was McKinsey one of Monroe's political allies, but Harper had had two recent run-ins with the man.

The first was aboard the *Chancellor* after the Belmont battle when they argued over the casualties and Harper's authority to order McKinsey's men to assist in rescuing General Grant. The second was on the day the battalion arrived at Fort Donelson when McKinsey went over Harper's head for approval to use that barn. And, Harper understood McKinsey shared the opinions of most of the battalion that Harper was careless of the well-being of the men. McKinsey was perfect man to prove Harper should be dismissed, or worse.

McKinsey addressed Hopkins. "Are ya ready, Sergeant?"

"Yes, sir." Hopkins picked up a pen from the desk and wrote a heading on the paper in front of him.

"Mister Harper, would ya tell us what happened after ya left the camp on the night of February fifteenth?"

"What have the others told ya, already?"

"I need your independent statement, Lieutenant. So, I can't divulge what they might have said. Please, begin."

Harper sat back in his chair. He fumbled with where to place his arms and hands, since the chair had no arm rests. Finally, he folded them in his lap.

"Let's see," Harper began. He described the events of the night the Rebels captured them. He would tell the story as it happened, without embellishment or deception. If this was to be an honest inquiry, let the chips fall where they would.

He related the events as completely as he could remember them. When he related Bell's information that the *picquet* was doomed from the beginning, he watched to ensure Hopkins recorded all that information. Again, he slowed the narrative to give the precise details of the final day when Bell tried to murder them all. Hopkins recorded Harper's statement as he spoke, raising his hand whenever the description outpaced the rate at which he could write. McKinsey jotted down a few notes.

"All right, Lieutenant, thank you," McKinsey said when Harper finished his narrative. “Did ya get everythin’, Hopkins?”

Harper glanced at the window behind McKinsey. The darkness outside surprised him. The testimony went longer than he realized.

“Mostly, sir.” Hopkins asked Harper to repeat certain sections of the testimony.

“All finished, Captain.”

“Now, I have some questions, Lieutenant Harper.” Harper nodded and Hopkins laid a new sheet of paper on his desk.

Now we’ll see what McKinsey’s really after.

“You’re certain ya fired a warnin’ shot before ya were disarmed? Because neither Magnusson nor Cooke mentioned it in their reports.”

“The Rebels had me on the ground. They forced the muzzle into the snow before it fired.”

“So. A pistol shot no one could hear.”

“I heard it.” Harper stared unblinking at McKinsey, lips set in a thin, straight line.

McKinsey wrote a note on the page in front of him. “What happened to your weapons, especially the five Sharps rifles?”

“Bell gave them to troopers in his company.”

“And the ammunition?”

“That too.”

“So you lost five excellent sharpshooter rifles to the Rebels.”

“That’s right.” Harper sat upright in the chair. “*And* my telescopic gunsight.” He leaned back and folded his arms across his chest. “Because we were out there alone with no support from the battalion.” He looked to see if Hopkins had recorded all of that.

McKinsey looked to Hopkins while his transcribed Harper’s remarks. When Hopkins looked up, McKinsey went to his next question.

“What information did ya give Forrest when ya talked with him?”

Harper needed to think for a moment to recall the conversation. “Not much. He was worried our boys might be chasin’ him. I said I thought General Grant would attack the fort that day, instead. I didn’t think that would be any news to Forrest. But we didn’t hear any noises from combat that day. Forrest told me it was because the Rebs planned to surrender on Sunday." The effort to remember the discussion with Forrest brought a pain under the large bruise at the center of his forehead.

"You're certain of that?"

"Of course I'm certain." Harper chuckled at one memory. "I did learn that I nearly shot him the day before. He showed me the bullet hole in his jacket." Harper used his finger to show on his own uniform where the hole in Forrest's jacket would have been.

McKinsey sat back in his chair, fingers templed together in front of his chin. He stared at Harper. "Why do ya suppose the Texan offered ya parole which didn't apply to the enlisted men?"

The first question about his conversation with Forrest seemed routine but this one about Dupree right after caused him to try to follow McKinsey's train-of-thought. "Captain Dupree said he wanted to avoid lettin' Bell murder the prisoners."

"But they gave ya preferential treatment in the jail, too, didn't they? Allowed your own cell? Allowed to sit on the front porch in the evenin'?"

"I had to work hard on that deputy to get him to let me do that. From the porch I could work out a plan for escapin'." The pain in Harper's head spread across the front of his skull. "What are ya implyin'? Do ya think I traded some secrets for the better treatment?"

McKinsey sat back and twisted into his chair. "You tell me, Lieutenant. I'm only tryin' to learn the facts."

"Well the facts are these: Captain Bell tried to starve us durin' the march to Nashville despite Forrest's orders. It's only because we survived long enough to reach the civilian jail that we got anythin' to eat or drink. Then, that bastard held his sick game of run-the-gauntlet."

Harper's voice was louder than he intended. "Why aren't ya askin' me about that? Or about why Bosley and his women went to the Rebel headquarters?"

"Because that is not the purpose of this court-of-inquiry." McKinsey leaned over the desk. His face flushed. "We're here to put *your* actions on the record." He thumped two fingers onto the papers holding Magnusson's and Cooke's testimonies.

Harper was now certain of the real purpose of the court-of-inquiry.

After a moment or two staring at Harper eye-to-eye, McKinsey regained his composure and looked down at his notes. “Why do ya suppose Captain Dupree came to your rescue?

“You’d have to ask him.” Harper looked away from McKinsey to a painting of a riverboat on the side wall. After a moment, he answered. “I suppose because that’s what an *honorable* man would do, McKinsey, even in a war.” He watched to see McKinsey’s reaction to the accusation. There was none. McKinsey was a cool one.

Harper fell against the back of the chair. He brought his hands to his forehead, trying to rub the headache away. “Even you should know that.” He rubbed his temples.

“I know the rules of war, Lieutenant. I was fightin’ Mexicans when you were still at your mama’s teats.”

“I was in Mexico, too, McKinsey. Except I stayed until the end of the war and didn’t hurry home at the end of my enlistment.”

“Damn you, sir! I came home from Mexico with pieces of a musketball in me. I was lucky not to lose my leg.” McKinsey stared back at Harper.

“Forgive me, Lieutenant. I forgot that your daddy took you along with him so you could keep his boots polished. How old were you? Thirteen, Fourteen? Not quite a real soldier, eh?”

Harper looked away. These insults weren’t going to help end this farce.

“The Texans I saw seemed to be very proficient. It seemed a matter of personal honor to Captain Dupree.”

He owed his life to the Rebel Dupree. Harper could have torn up the parole documents once he returned to Federal lines and no one would have been the wiser, unless the Rebels captured himself or one of the others later. But Dupree’s chivalry impressed Harper, and that chivalry now made the issue a matter of Harper’s own personal honor to adhere to the terms of the Texan’s parole.

“On the other hand, I’m certain now that the Tennesseans have been shootin’ prisoners. It was clear Captain Bell’s men have.”

“Do you have any proof, Mister Harper?” Sergeant Hopkins

interrupted the questioning for the first time. McKinsey's eyebrows arched at the interruption.

"No. Only they didn't show any doubts when it came time to shoot Davis. They just laughed when I said it was murder *and* that it was against Forrest's orders. It seemed like somethin' they did often." He paused. "When you find Private Davis's body, it'll have four musket balls in his back."

A mouse scurried across the floor between Harper and Hopkins, into a hole caused by a broken brick in the fireplace.

"I have another question for ya, Mister Harper."

Harper turned to face McKinsey. The movement brought on a spate of dizziness.

"Why did ya order the two remainin' men to assist in recoverin' the horses–in violation of their paroles?"

"That's a lie!" Harper jumped to his feet and bent over the desk, supporting his weight with his fists on the desktop, pain pounding inside his skull.

"Sit down, Lieutenant!" McKinsey stayed seated while he yelled. He pointed back to the chair.

Hopkins stood and moved around his desk to stand beside Harper.

In a more controlled voice, McKinsey said, "Please, sit down, Jamie. Explain it to me."

Harper backed to the chair and sat, massaging his head with both hands. The pain there caused his vision to blur. Hopkins resumed his place.

McKinsey bent forward in his chair to watch Harper. "Are ya unwell, Lieutenant Harper? Would ya like to stop now and start again in the mornin'?"

"How much longer do you think we'll be?"

"One more question after this."

"Let's get it over with." Harper let his hands fall into his lap.

"All right." McKinsey picked up the transcript of testimony from one of the enlisted men, found what he wanted and reread the statement before he addressed Harper. "If ya did not order them to help recover the horses, why do ya believe they came anyway?"

Harper winced from the pain in his head and looked at the ceiling before answering. “While we were prisoners, I came to believe that Magnusson is one of the most loyal soldiers in the battalion–more to his subordinates than to the officers–but loyal enough to both. You should be grateful to have him in your company. Also, he has a greater sense of responsibility for the welfare of his men than most of the corporals...” His stare returned to McKinsey. “And some of the officers.”

Harper bent forward on his armless chair and he watched McKinsey’s face for a reaction. There was none. He gazed passed McKinsey’s shoulder to the dark window. “Last, Magnusson told me two days ago that he knew I rejected Dupree’s offer for a separate parole in order to stay with them. I guess he felt he had a debt to pay.”

A sudden dizziness spun Harper’s vision. The headache approached a level he had last experienced the night of the attack, throbbing with each pulse. The heat in the room inflamed his face. “Can I have a drink of water?”

“Of course.” McKinsey set a glass in the center of the desk and tipped the ceramic pitcher, filling the glass. Harper retrieved the glass and sipped. He dipped two fingers into the glass and rubbed the water into his forehead.

“Just one more question, Lieutenant.” McKinsey watched Harper’s face.

Another one? I thought that was the last.

Harper composed himself despite the pain in his head; he grabbed the edge of his seat against the dizziness.

“Explain to me again what ya *think* was your justification for murderin’ the civilian deputy sheriff?”

Harper pulled himself straight in the chair. When he felt composed, he recited the response he had rehearsed. “It wasn’t murder, Captain.” Harper paused to look at Hopkins. He waited until the recorder looked up at Harper’s silence. Then he spoke slowly, with determination.

“Deputy Shepperton tried to interfere with me when I was performin’ military tasks. He had earlier led a gang who beat me durin’ a failed escape attempt. They used far more force than they needed and damn-near crippled me. On that last day, he fired at us from the top of the bluff durin' the shoot-out along the river. When I tried to retrieve the horses, he attempted to interfere, even though he knew I was on parole. He acted as if he was a part of the Reb army."

Shepperton was a bastard and got all he deserved.

"You mean military tasks that violated your parole, yes?"

Harper sat silent, staring at McKinsey but making no excuses.

After a full minute without a response from Harper, McKinsey addressed Hopkins. "Do ya have everythin' ya need, Sergeant?"

"Yes, sir. I think so."

"Good." McKinsey turned to Harper. "You and the men should return to the office late tomorrow mornin' to sign the transcribed copies of your testimony."

"Wait a minute, Brice." Harper was eager to leave the stuffy room, to walk outside in the cold, clean air but he needed to ask his own questions. "What are ya goin' to do about Captain Bell? And Bosley, the whorehouse owner?"

McKinsey pushed back from the desk and stood, collecting his papers. "That is not my concern, Harper. I'm not sure who ya should notify."

"Sir," Hopkins said from his desk. "Mister Harper. When you return to Paducah, you can report what you learned to Colonel Anderson's staff. There is an officer there who is in charge of catching spies. Come to see me when you arrive. I'll take you to him."

"There, that's settled then." McKinsey handed all of the paperwork to Hopkins, still seated at the smaller desk.

With the testimony over, the pain in Harper's head began to subside. He took another sip of water and closed his eyes. It helped.

When Harper and McKinsey entered the hotel lobby, they found the adjacent dining area bustling with the supper service, but Harper wanted to go outside first to try to relieve his headache. He pulled his new overcoat from a peg by the hotel door. The garment came straight from the box at the quartermaster's warehouse yesterday morning, without proper airing to remove the camphor smell. He had yet to find a set of lieutenant's epaulettes to sew to the shoulders.

"Dinner, Jamie?" McKinsey asked.

The invitation surprised Harper. He stopped working the stiff buttons of his new overcoat, thought about his headache and about the opportunity dinner with McKinsey would give him to learn more about the battalion. "I'd like that, Captain." He might even discover McKinsey's conclusions from the testimonies.

"Can ya leave the coat out here?" McKinsey said, pointing to the pegs on the wall next to the front door. "So it doesn't make me sick. There is an intensive odor about it."

"Yeah, there surely is." Maybe the headache would subside if he ate something. Harper returned the coat to its peg and the two men crossed into the dining room. If McKinsey invited him to dinner, perhaps Harper's suspicions about the court-of-inquiry were silly.

Wednesday, March 5th, 1862

"I need to go for a walk," Magnusson told Cooke after they signed their statements and left McKinsey's office.

Cooke followed Magnusson through the front door of the Dover Inn. "Mind if I come along? It's a while until noon meal, eh."

"Don't mind at all." Magnusson stepped out, looking for the road which led south out of the town. He wanted to see for himself the road the Rebel cavalry used for their escape. And he wanted some time to sort things out. The two men walked along the side of the street to avoid the mud caused by the rain of the previous three days.

"Glad to see that we finally got some sunshine." Cooke looked at the sky, now clear of any clouds. "Ya know, Gus, the last time we were here, this was all snow."

Magnusson shivered at the memory. "Looks like spring comes earlier in these parts than in Iowa."

With the thoughts of the cold came the image of the field behind the Rebel works and his first opportunity to lead the trained skirmishers. He recalled how surprised he was with the Sharps rifles the first time they used them against actual targets. Folks said that the rifles were Lieutenant Harper's idea. The training too.

The bravery of the Rebel sergeant had impressed him when the man carried his wounded private back into the trenches, and he laughed to himself when he thought of the last Rebel soldier running back-and-forth trying to get to safety and no one in the battalion being able to hit him.

He and Bailey had acted so well as a skirmish team during the real battle the next day. Now, Bailey was dead, and he missed the little guy.

Hopefully, that deputy in Nashville was keeping his promise to get Bailey a decent burial so his family could find him after the war.

"That was kind of a dirty trick, don't ya think, Gus?"

"What was?"

"Captain McKinsey changin' our words, eh, to make it look like Mister Harper ordered us to help him get the horses."

Both men had read their entire transcriptions before signing them. Toward the end Magnusson crossed out the statement that Harper ordered the men to help rescue the horses. He had shown the cross-out to Cooke. After a glance to McKinsey, Cooke crossed out the identical line in his transcript.

"Yah, it was." That single sentence was the reason Magnusson needed to walk. His brain seemed to work better when his feet were moving.

McKinsey had asked what they were changing, but before McKinsey could say anything, Sergeant Hopkins told them that it was all right to make minor changes, as long as they put their initials above the cross-out.

"I wonder if Captain McKinsey would have ordered us to change it back if the lawyer sergeant hadn't been there?" Magnusson turned onto the road leading to the ford.

Cooke stayed beside Magnusson. "What do ya mean?"

"Nothin'. Just a thought."

McKinsey had wanted that sentence in the testimonies. The captain had tried to trick Magnusson into saying it. He supposed that Cooke had had the same experience.

Their path led them along the road to the backwater where Bell's men captured them. They could see their former campground along the ridge on the opposite side of the backwater and the trail they rode to post the *picquet*. Magnusson decided he wanted to visit the fording spot before returning to camp. He still hadn't sorted out the reason for the court-of-inquiry. Cooke followed him.

"Mister Harper seemed to think it would be okay, eh. He was sure the report would be honest."

"I don't think he was sure of that at all."

"Why d'ya think that, Gus?"

"I 'spect he's just sayin' that to us. I think he's worried, too."

It always happened that way when two officers argued. If an enlisted man approached, they would stop the argument and pull a mask over their expressions. The enlisted men could never know that the officers couldn't work together. Magnusson knew Monroe didn't favor having Harper in the battalion and McKinsey was Monroe's man.

"Ah jees', I'll be glad when we get back to the battalion." Magnusson stopped walking. They were at the spot where the road began its drop to the ford below. "I don't like sittin' around here with nothin' to do and with people treatin' us like we did somethin' wrong because we got captured. Especially in a uniform that still has Bailey's blood all over it."

Ahead of them, a silvery fish leapt from the surface of the backwater speeding toward the river. Two more followed, chased by a larger fin and a surface wake.

Two covered carriages turned onto the road from the riverboat landing. Magnusson and Cooke watched the paired horses struggle to haul the loads up the steepest part of the ridge before they stepped aside to let them pass. The coach shades were up, and inside there were several women, dressed as if they were headed to a ball.

A girl with long red hair seated next to the window of the first coach caught Magnusson's eye. She smiled and waved at him before the woman seated across from her closed the window shade.

"That girl reminded me of Baby Red from back in Paducah, eh?" Cooke said as he watched the coaches disappear into Dover Town.

"Who's Baby Red?"

"Oh, that's the name they gave to one of the girls at Bosley's."

"That couldn't be her." Magnusson turned back toward the watercourse at the foot of the hill. "Those women must live here. How else would they be able to get a coach?"

"Still. It sure looked a lot like her. I've seen her often enough."

"You've been away from the sportin' ladies for too long." Magnusson laughed before he stepped off, down the hill. "Besides, she was way too pretty to be working in a saloon."

"You're right about the part of bein' away from it too long." Cooke hitched his pants, then hurried to catch up. He took a dozen paces before speaking again. "Did ya know that part about the Rebs hangin' us if we got caught?"

"A-yah. Harper warned us about it right before we split up." Magnusson didn't stop his steps down the hill. He admired the countryside with a farmer's eye for land. It seemed so much warmer and peaceful than three weeks ago. In some spots, the warmer days of the approaching spring enticed the hillsides to take on a blue-green under-tint amid the brown of the dead winter grass.

"I might not have gone if I had remembered that, eh."

"Not for a bunch of horses." Harper's gray must be one damned special horse. Magnusson picked up a cartridge box from the grass alongside the road. It was empty. "But I'd sure rather get killed fightin' than bein' hanged."

The two stopped to watch a hawk dive on its prey somewhere beyond the wood on the opposite side of the ford.

After watching the hawk for a few moments, Magnusson said, "I already knew that Mister Harper gave up a parole for himself to get ones for all of us. I overheard the insane Reb captain say so."

Cooke stood quietly for a few moments. "Wait. Mister Harper already had a parole for himself when we were in the jail?"

"A-yah."

"Okay. Then why did he lie to us?"

Since their parole, Magnusson had had time to ask himself the same question. "I figure he was tryin' to get paroles for all of us, not just himself." He threw the box into the dead grass. "Maybe he thought we wouldn't trust him if he told us the truth. He was right about that."

"What?"

"Us not trustin' him if'n he had his own parole."

They resumed their walk toward the ford, passing through the former Rebel fortifications. These already showed the signs of neglect from erosion and scavenging just three weeks after the surrender. The war had moved on. The land was healing itself.

On their left, high on the bluff where the city lay, they saw Federal soldiers at work on a new bastion whose cannons would dominate boat traffic coming down-river from Nashville and beyond.

"What do ya think will happen to Mister Harper now?"

The road dipped and they were at the level of the ford.

"That's up to the officers." Magnusson thought he knew. Colonel Monroe hated Harper and wanted him out of the battalion. Everyone knew that. All for the one mistake back at Belmont. McKinsey and the court-of-inquiry were probably part of Monroe's plan. That would explain why McKinsey asked the questions the way that he did and why he had added the part about being ordered to rescue the horses.

They stayed silent while they approached the ford and stopped to look across the expanse of water covering the road. The thrill of spying on the Rebel fort near the big river during the long training ride flashed into Magnusson's memory.

Harper said it was the Mississippi River. They covered a lot of territory and learned a lot of special skills during that ride. And they did it in the cold and wet of January with no one going sick.

"I won't be a part of any scheme to get Mister Harper sent home." Magnusson kicked a loose stone into the backwater. "Not after he gave up the chance to have his own parole. It's because of him that we ain't lyin' dead on that river bank."

After all that happened: at Belmont, at Donelson, and at Nashville, Magnusson knew Harper was a damned sight better officer to have around in a battle than most of the others–especially McKinsey, who was too old and didn't understand the new tactics.

"Me either. I'm with ya."

"Harper's damned good when it comes to a fight." Magnusson stared into the distance across the ford. "The men need to know they can trust him."

"We'll tell 'em, Gus."

"Yah, we will."

The two soldiers turned and climbed the hill, following their shadows back to Dover Town.

****

Monroe's plan for Harper was clear. Harper would be blamed for their capture and the loss of two men, even though the *picquet* stood no chance of success. The court-of-inquiry was a ruse to force him to resign. The outcome had been decided by Monroe even before

McKinsey left Crumps' Landing. That would fit the back-stabbing way the politician did things.

Harper saw McKinsey emerge from the office and into the front parlor after collecting Magnusson's and Cooke's signatures.

"What happens now, Captain?" Harper asked.

"Just routine, Jamie. I'll read the three sets of testimony and then write my report to Colonel Monroe this afternoon. I plan to ride over to Fort Henry tomorrow mornin' and board a boat back to the unit tomorrow night or the next day. Need to get all this finished. *I'm* gittin' back to fightin' Rebs, eh."

McKinsey was going back to the war and Harper was not.

"When can I see your report?"

"You'll be able to read it after Colonel Monroe has signed it. I'm sure Corporal Powell will keep a copy in the battalion files. You'll have to send him a letter requesting it."

McKinsey reached into the breast pocket of his uniform jacket. "In the meantime, Harper, here are your orders. All of you parolees are to report to the quartermaster at Fort Anderson for duty until the exchange."

"Quartermaster?"

"A-yah, the quartermaster. Colonel Monroe appointed Lieutenant Guelich as adjutant while ya been gone. He promoted Quartermaster Sergeant Howard to acting lieutenant and made him the unit's quartermaster, so you'll be takin' orders from Howard while you're workin' at Paducah."

Harper stared at McKinsey without moving. His brain refused to work. It was stuck on one fact. He would be working *for* the junior lieutenant in the battalion.

"So, if ya have no more questions, Lieutenant Harper, I'll get to writin' my report." Without waiting for an answer, McKinsey walked toward the office, but turned when he reached the door. "Oh. Did ya hear the rumor?"

Harper shook his head. The camps where always full of rumors. Harper had stopped giving them any attention.

"Your man Grant was relieved of command of the army yesterday by General Halleck." McKinsey gave Harper a smile as he closed the office door–not a friendly smile, more of a smirk.

Grant's gone? Is the army insane?

Harper stood alone in the middle of the hotel parlor in a smelly overcoat, bloody uniform, and no hat–wondering what the hell he would do next.

He could use his back-pay to buy a new set of civilian kit, take off his uniform and disappear into the western frontier, the way he had fled college. He would become a wanted man, one of the very outlaws he had hunted in the past.

Except, there would be no honor in abandoning his duty.

He had sworn an oath to Captain Dupree to abide by the provisions of the parole. Dupree was an honorable man and Harper would remain one, as well.

Accepting the orders to return to Paducah would keep him in good standing with the Army—and he had unfinished Army business. Somehow, he would show Monroe's damned court-martial for the farce that it was. There were enough new units being formed, and he could transfer, if necessary.

Some things remained that must be dealt with. Bosley's spying operation still needed to be handled. Once in Paducah, he could recruit the aid of Magnusson and Cooke to help him destroy whatever dangerous web Bosley had woven. That thought steadied him.

And, somewhere in Tennessee, Captain Anderson Bell still lived.

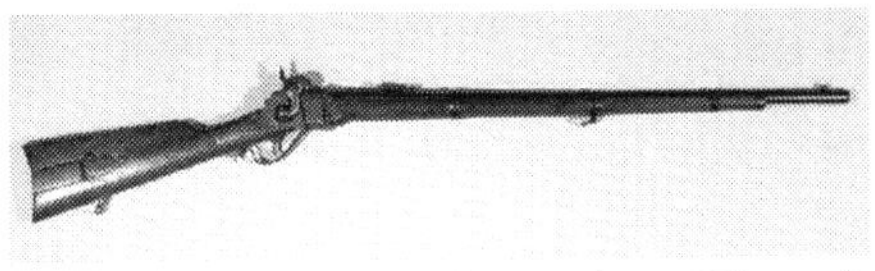

(National Museum of American History)

About the Author

Sean Kevin Gabhann first became interested in American Civil War history during the centennial celebration and he owns an extensive library of primary and secondary material related to Civil War. He especially wants to write about campaigns in the West because of a fascination with the careers of U.S Grant and W.T. Sherman. Gabhann lives in San Diego, California with his wife, four sons, two daughters-in-law, three grandsons, three dogs and a cat named Pepper who sometimes thinks she's a dog.

The story continues. While Grant's army pushes deeper into Tennessee and Katie Molloy struggles against the death of friends and betrayal by those she trusts the most, the men of First Iowa battle spies and saboteurs while on parole in Paducah, Kentucky in Harper's Rescue. The survivors rejoin their battalion during the army's build-up around a small country church in Harper's Shiloh.

26530685R00224

Made in the USA
San Bernardino, CA
30 November 2015